DOMINION

CE SHORLAND

CHAPTER 1

As the sun began its descent, casting an orange glow on the watery expanse, Beth pressed her forehead against the cool glass of her window, her eyes fixed beyond the glass pane, tracing the endless blue that stretched from the shores of Catalina Island to the horizon. The ocean was a canvas of tranquillity, yet for Beth it was an expanse of isolation, a barrier between her physical form and any semblance of hope. She searched for a speck, a silhouette, anything that might resemble the boat carrying Ben and Austin back to her. But the sea offered no such solace, only the relentless march of waves against the shore below. The salty scent mingled with the fading warmth of the day, a sensory reminder of the vastness that separated her from those she yearned for. Her heart pounded in rhythm with the lapping of waves, each beat echoing her growing anxiety. She had been scanning the horizon for months, and all she could see was an endless canvas of blue, a tranquil yet isolating barrier offering no sign of anyone, turning every passing moment into a quiet battle between hope and despair. Her intrusive thoughts had started to get the better of her as she gazed out into the seemingly endless ocean, her eyes dropping slightly to the concrete below. The act of her own death was a dark and heavy shadow that loomed over every thought, casting a grim aura around every decision. The image of her body plummeting to its end on the ground below was haunting and heartbreaking, yet she was overwhelmed with a sense of freedom every time it crossed her mind - a constant reminder of the endless agony she experienced, leading her to make such a final and irrevocable decision. It was a dark and all-consuming force, like a black hole in the depths of space, pulling her towards its ever-approaching event horizon. The heaviness of it weighed on her like a leaden cloak, suffocating and unrelenting. It was the ultimate act of despair, a final surrender to the endless void that seemed to stretch out before her, but its calling was a siren song leading to a treacherous and final fate. It was the ultimate act of isolation and the ultimate barrier between the living and the dead. A gentle breeze seeped through the gaps in the window, caressing Beth's cheeks. She closed her eyes and envisioned Ben's touch, his hand delicately resting on her skin, his thumb wiping away a solitary tear trickling down her face. She gently placed her hand on top of his, hoping that she could feel the warmth of his skin against hers, willing the barrier between her palm and her cheek to be real, and not a manifestation of her own making. The pain in her chest was raw and almost unbearable as she strained to feel every detail of his hand. In her mind, she could see his smiling face looking down at her and hear his soothing voice telling her to hold on. But they had spent more time apart than together, and she couldn't be sure if what she could see and hear and feel was a true representation of him, or just a creation in her own mind from fleeting moments and fragmented memories. Blissful moments that had been interrupted by snowstorms and starvation, by gunfire and rapists and murderers. Memories that had been taken away by cruel individuals who had no regard for the moments that had yet to come, a life that could have been cherished forever. The click of the door handle broke her pensive silence, and Sabrina sauntered in with the entitlement of one who had never known boundaries. Her hand rested possessively on the swell of her abdomen, a gesture not lost on Beth.

"Victor wants to see you." Sabrina announced, her tone laced with a satisfaction she didn't bother to hide.

"Couldn't knock, could you?" Beth retorted without turning, her voice steady despite the simmering anger that bubbled beneath the surface.

"Wouldn't want to interrupt your little daydreams about being rescued." Sabrina quipped mockingly, moving to stand beside Beth, her presence like an unwelcome shadow. Beth finally turned, meeting Sabrina's eyes.

"You seem pleased with yourself." Beth looked towards the floor, refusing to acknowledge Sabrina's growing stomach with any emotion she might mistake for happiness.

"Why shouldn't I be," Sabrina's lips curved into a smirk, "after all, I'm carrying Victor's child. That makes me untouchable."

"Untouchable or smug? It's hard to tell with you." Beth challenged, the words sharp as flint.

"Jealousy is unbecoming, Beth," Sabrina's voice dripped with condescension, "especially when it's because you're no longer the favourite." Beth clenched her jaw but kept her composure. She wouldn't give Sabrina the satisfaction of seeing her unravel.

"Favourites are fickle," Beth said, turning back to the window, "today's adoration is tomorrow's disdain. Enjoy it while it lasts." Sabrina's smile didn't falter, as if the very idea of falling out of Victor's favour was inconceivable to her.

"I'll be sure to tell Victor you said so," she said before sitting playfully on the end of the bed, refusing to leave Beth alone with the vast and silent sea, "once my baby is born, you'll be nothing but a ghost here, completely dead and forgotten." Sabrina said, the words flitting from her lips like an afterthought as she stroked her swollen belly. Beth didn't dignify the remark with a response. She knew that engaging with Sabrina only gave her more ammunition, more opportunities to twist the knife of psychological warfare that Victor so loved his minions to play. Beth approached her bedroom door, holding it open for Sabrina to leave.

"Get out." She spoke deliberately and authoritatively, as if each word had its own significant weight.

"Very well," Sabrina sighed mockingly as she rose from the bed, striding to the door, "I can tell when I am unwelcome."

"Could've fooled me." Beth's hand pressed firmly against Sabrina's back, ushering her out with an unspoken urgency that bordered on desperation. The door clicked shut behind them, sealing off the quiet sanctuary of Beth's room from the oppressive ambiance of the hallway. As Sabrina sauntered down the corridor, Beth waited until her light footsteps were out of earshot. Finally convinced she would be left alone, Beth opened the door and turned in the opposite direction, beginning her slow trek through the hotel's hallways to Victor's room. Her fingertips traced the rivets in the ornate walls, each cold indent marking the steps between hers and Victor's rooms. This path had become a ritual, one she could navigate blindfolded, counting her footsteps under her breath, the number creeping higher with each footfall. The almost daily summoning to Victor's room was not lost on her, she knew what to expect every time she entered the lion's den. Victor's repeated unending questions about where the others would have disappeared to on the mainland were tedious and futile, never mind the torture that came with the interrogation. The months she had spent in captivity had been a slow and calculated agony, like watching a leaf being burned slowly by a magnifying glass in the searing summer sun, or a slow and agonising dance with the devil, each step a fiery brand on her soul and each breath an icy grip on her heart. Her mind shifted to the first night he had summoned her to his room, his imposing figure casting a shadow over her trembling form. She remembered the way his eyes bore into hers, cold and calculating, as he demanded answers she didn't have. The room felt suffocatingly small as Victor paced back and forth, his questions growing more aggressive with each passing moment. He would be silent for minutes which seemed to tick on like hours, and then suddenly burst into a fit of rage which was accompanied by punches and kicks, slaps and beatings, which seemed to have no end. He would scream at her for answers that she didn't have. Her body had been marred by bruises and scratches, an improperly healed finger dislocation, and a fractured cheekbone which still caused pain months later when she chewed food on the right side of her mouth. Despite the fear coursing through her veins, Beth refused to give in to Victor's intimidation tactics. She held her ground, determined to protect her friends at all costs, even if it meant enduring Victor's relentless interrogation. Never mind the fact that she had no idea where they would have gone, she refused to provide him with an iota of information about where they had even been before that. The memory of that night still sent shivers down her spine, and every interrogation since, but it also fuelled her resolve to resist his tyranny. She was so engrossed in her silent counting and pensive thoughts that she almost collided with Tim as she rounded a corner. He stood there, still as a statue, his eye patch giving him the aura of a pirate displaced in time. It was a menacing look, but Beth saw beyond it to the wounded man beneath.

"Tim." She greeted, her voice a tentative whisper, trying to pierce the ice of his demeanour with a hint of warmth. He grunted in acknowledgment, his good eye fixed on some unseen point down the hall.

"*Beth*." He said coarsely with a mocking disdain.

"Sabrina's on a particularly high horse today," Beth ventured, hoping to find a sliver of the man who once aided their dreams of freedom, "she's especially narcissistic."

"Forgive me." Tim looked down at her, his expression unwavering. "For what?"

"For giving you any kind of impression that I care at all about the way Sabrina treats you." He pushed past her slowly, careful not to touch her.

"I wish you wouldn't be so unkind." Beth whispered, placing her hand gingerly on the wall to steady herself.

"Kindness died with Kevin." Tim replied curtly, his voice void of the camaraderie they once shared. The betrayal that had severed his captivity to Marcus had also severed his bond with Beth. The torment he endured was etched into the hard lines of his face, evident by his missing eye, a constant reminder of the price of disobedience. Kevin's body had been found in a corridor, along with Estelle and Maureen. It had seemed that he had been aiding in their escape before being gunned down. Beth's mind wandered to the night she tried desperately to forget, the night she and Chantelle had been left behind, the night so many casualties had been an expense she had not been prepared to yield. They had sat side by side against the wall at the top of the hill, watching as the guards came towards them with a fiery determination that seemed surreal. Beth had gripped Chantelle's hand tight as she sobbed, wondering if they would be executed on the spot, or taken away for questioning, or worse.

The latter seemed to be the way their life had been since then. Beth looked up at Tim and nodded, accepting the silence that followed as the conclusion of their conversation. She resumed her journey, leaving Tim to his solitary vigil. Each step felt heavier than the last, the distance to Victor's lair not just a measure of space but of the deepening despair that seemed to cling to the very air she breathed. Beth's knuckles rapped softly against the polished mahogany door of Victor's room, the sound muffled by the thick, salt-laden air of the coastal hotel. She hesitated for a mere second, steeling herself for what was on the other side, before the door swung open with an eerie silence. The opulence of Victor's quarters never ceased to suffocate her - the plush carpets, the elegant furniture, all tainted with the stench of corruption and cruelty. Her gaze, however, was immediately drawn to the figure sprawled across the massive bed. Chantelle lay there, the rise and fall of her chest the only indication that the night's torments hadn't stolen her away completely. The sheets failed to cover the marks that marred her skin, a testament to the brutality she had suffered through the night. Despite the violence etched into every bruise, Chantelle's breaths were even, the deep slumber a temporary reprieve from the relentless nightmare they endured. Beth swallowed a lump of sorrow, her heart aching for Chantelle, for all of them really, as she stepped further into the lion's den.

"Victor." She called out softly, almost afraid to wake Chantelle yet knowing he expected her presence.

"Outside." Came the callous reply from the balcony, a voice that always seemed to carry the chill of the ocean's deepest trenches. Moving past the bed with a lingering look at Chantelle, Beth stepped through the gauzy curtains onto the balcony where Victor stood, his silhouette dark against the morning light. The sea spread out before them, endless and indifferent.

"You wanted to see me?"

"Did you think about my question?" Victor asked without preamble, his back still turned to her as he gazed over the railing at the expanse below. Beth's throat tightened, but she managed to keep her voice steady.

"There was no time to discuss plans of escape, Victor. You all kept us apart." Her words felt hollow, recycled too many times, worn thin with each repetition.

"Yet, somehow, they found a way." He said, finally facing her, his eyes searching for a truth she did not possess. Beth met his gaze, willing her own to reveal nothing but the resolve to endure. Inside, a tempest of fear and hope clashed, hope for a rescue that seemed increasingly like a fool's dream, and fear of the man who could make her cease to exist with a simple word or small gesture.

"Believe me or not, I've told you everything." She murmured, her voice barely above the whisper of waves against the shore. She knew it was futile, Victor's trust was a fortress she'd never breach, his suspicion a sentinel ever watchful. But in her heart a defiant ember glowed, unwilling to be extinguished by his tyranny or her own despair.

"You've told me nothing." Victor studied her for a moment longer, the scrutiny of a lion stalking its prey. Then, with a flicker of disinterest, he turned back to the view, the conversation apparently concluded, at least for now. Beth took a quiet breath, taking solace in the brief reprieve, her spirit reaching towards the horizon where freedom lay just beyond grasp. His brow furrowed in contemplation as he studied Beth from the corner of his eye, his gaze darting across her face and body like a chess player analysing their next move. His expression was unreadable, a mask of disinterest that hinted at underlying indifference. The air was tinged with the faint scent of salt and sea, carried by the soft ocean breeze that swept across the balcony where they stood.

"I've told you everything I know." Beth whispered, letting herself relax for a small moment, taking in the ocean air and views from Victor's top-floor hotel room. He had taken the biggest one for himself, naturally - his leadership style since succeeding Marcus had been more of a tyrant than any of them could have imagined. Marcus had been cruel and challenging, but predictable once you could figure out his patterns. Victor was cruel in nature but unpredictable at times which set Beth on edge every second that she was around him, which was essentially all the time. Without warning, Victor's hand struck with the suddenness of a snake, his palm connecting with Beth's cheek in a sharp crack that echoed off the balcony walls. The sting radiated across her face, a brutal reminder of the power he wielded over her. She stumbled back against the railing, her hand instinctively flying to her cheek as she stared at him in shock and fear. She was confounded at her own surprise, and angry for allowing herself to momentarily let her guard down.

"How dare you lie to me." He snarled, his voice low and menacing. Beth tried to speak, but her words caught in her throat as she struggled to find another way to tell him that she knew nothing. But she knew there was no persuading him. He was convinced that she knew something and she would perpetually pay the price.

"I, I didn't—" She started, but Victor cut her off with another sharp strike across the face. This time, she fell to the ground, clutching her cheek as tears filled her eyes. She kept her hand pressed to the burning skin, not so much to soothe the pain but to shield her vulnerability from his predatory gaze.

"Don't make it worse by lying again." He spat, his tone cold and unyielding. He towered over her like a dark shadow, his presence suffocating and overwhelming. Beth cowered on the ground, trying to make herself smaller as she waited for another blow that never came. Instead, Victor turned on his heel and walked back to the railing without another word, bracing his arms tensely as he glared out over the ocean. Beth stayed where she was for several minutes, trembling with fear and anger. She hated him, hated how he could control every aspect of her life with just a look or a gesture. But more than anything, she hated herself for getting pulled into this world of deceit and danger.

"Yet they all escaped," Victor said, his voice as cold and cutting as the ocean breeze, his words hung between them like a guillotine's blade ready to sever the last tendril of hope that she clung to, "where did they go!?" Beth lay still for a moment, trying to catch her breath before standing and facing him. He turned from her, looking out over the ocean towards the mainland, as if he could see it from where he stood, studying it to figure out where the others might have escaped to. Staring at his back as he faced the ocean, one push could send him flying over the edge to his death but she knew she would have no strength to do so. She could, if her unwilling body would allow, hurl herself into him and the two would tumble down together, but despite all the daydreams she had of killing Victor her feeble frame wasn't strong enough to bring him over the edge with her. She knew any attempt would only bring upon her own death.

"I don't know." She turned slightly away, her eyes drawn to the vast expanse of the Pacific. She peered out at the endless blue, her vision blurring as she tried to steady her breathing. There was nothing there - no sign of salvation, no distant speck of a returning boat. As always, the sea held no answers, only the reflection of her dwindling resolve. Yet she couldn't stop searching. It was the last shred of hope she had, the thin thread tethering her to the life she once knew. In an instant, Victor's grip was on her nape, fingers digging into her flesh with unyielding force.

"Where were they planning to go!?" He pushed her forward, bending her over the railing until the hard edge pressed into her stomach, squeezing the breath from her lungs. Her feet dangled precariously, toes grazing the surface below in a futile search for purchase. She could feel it, only just, as he pushed her so far over the edge that her stomach and pelvis were crushed under the weight of her own body.

"Victor, please—"

"Tell me!" He hissed into her ear, his breath hot against her skin. But words were lost to her now, trapped behind the vice of fear tightening around her chest. Her thoughts raced, chaotic and desperate, yet amidst the turmoil a defiant spark ignited within her. She wouldn't give him the satisfaction of seeing her break. Not today, not ever.

"I," Beth struggled to speak as the force compressed her lungs, "I don't—" Victor's voice sliced through the air, a sharp threat that promised more pain.

"I have ways of tearing the truth from your pretty little lies." Growling, his fingers were like steel bands around the back of her neck.

"Vic—" her breath came in shallow gasps as the balcony's edge bit into her abdomen, "Victor—" She tried to speak, to protest, but the pressure stole the words before the sound could escape her lips. Her mind, once racing with plans and memories, stilled. She knew from the angle she was on that if he chose to let go she would fall to her demise. In this suspended moment between life and death, she found an eerie sense of peace. She thought it would be better to simply let go, to plunge into the abyss and end it all. And so, for a heartbeat or two, Beth ceased fighting, her body slackening as if to accept the fatal embrace of gravity below. Her arms relaxed as she ceased to claw at his hands, her legs refrained from kicking as she allowed herself to settle, the weight and pressure of the metal railing pressing into her as she felt the sharp pain coarse through her torso. The change in her demeanour didn't go unnoticed as Victor snorted, his amusement coated with disdain.

"Giving up so easily? How incredibly dull." With a vicious yank, he hauled her back over the railing, her feet finding the solid ground of the balcony once more. Beth crumpled onto the rough tiles, her hands instinctively curling around her pained abdomen. Victor towered over her, eyes alight with a cruel mockery of concern.

"I—" Her voice was hoarse and her breathing shallow as she clutched at her stomach.

"*You* what, wish for death?" He taunted as she raised her head just enough to lock eyes with him and nodded, her expression hollow.

"Yes." A simple, single word was all she would provide, but the tone for which she spoke was louder and more powerful than anything she had said in months. A flicker of victory crossed his face as he leaned down, his voice a venomous whisper.

"Then do it yourself, Beth, if you're so eager." He stepped away, leaving her huddled on the floor. She pressed her forehead against the cool tiles, the echo of his challenge pulsing in her ears. But even as despair gnawed at her resolve, a stubborn flame of hope refused to be extinguished. Her pause to end her own life was gripped daily by the ceaseless thought that tomorrow could be her rescue - the moment she took her own life could be hours away from Ben and

Austin gallantly arriving on the shore to rip her from her nightmare. With trembling hands, she pushed herself up, every fibre of her being resisting the dark whisper of surrender. She had to endure, had to cling to the chance however slim, that freedom still called her name from beyond the horizon.

"Are you envious? Sabrina has taken your place in a way you never could with Marcus." Victor's sneer cut through the air, startling her thoughts as he posed his question. Beth met his gaze, her head shaking with instantaneous dismissal.

"Envy is for those who want something they don't have. If I had wished to remain Marcus's pet, I wouldn't have killed him," her voice laced with deceptive calm, she saw a brief flicker of interest in Victor's eyes and seized the moment to weave her treacherous lie, "I can still feel the weight of the torch in my hand, the one I used to bash his skull in. His body thudded against the floor, life waning away, but I didn't stop. Even after his last breath had left him, I kept striking. His blood, it splattered across my face, warm and slick. It was almost beautiful, the way it painted the walls, how it felt seeping into the fabric of my dress." Her hands involuntarily clenched as she painted the gruesome picture with her words. The memory was Austin's, not hers, but she delivered each word with a chilling conviction that made it sound like her own experience. There was a perverse artistry in recounting the violence as if she relished it, knowing full well the horror belonged to someone else, despite her being there to witness it.

"You—"

"Every time I look at my hands," Beth interrupted, raising her palms as if they were still stained, "I remember that warmth and how it contrasted with the cold emptiness of his death, and I imagine what it will be like when I do the same to you, *Victor*." His name was like poison filling her mouth as her voice dropped to a whisper that held both promise and threat. He stepped closer, and for a moment, the air between them crackled with the tension of her words. The balcony seemed to grow colder, the ocean's roar below them a distant thunder as they stood in the eye of a storm made of lies and vengeance. Victor's hand hovered in the air, an unspoken threat that carried the weight of a dozen beatings past. Just as his fingers began to curl into the menacing promise of impact, the balcony door swung open with an urgency that halted his intent.

"Sir." Tim's voice cut through the tension, and Beth seized the momentary distraction to slip away from Victor's reach. She edged towards the doorway, her body taut with both fear and a desperate need to overhear the news that had spared her another bruise.

"What is it?" Victor's tone was brusque and filled with irritation at the interruption.

"Guards are back from the mainland," Tim reported, his voice gruff, the eye patch lending him an air of severity that matched the gravity of his words, "they've found something." Victor's gaze snapped towards his henchman, the violent urge momentarily forgotten as he stepped inside, beckoning Tim to follow. Beth lingered at the threshold, her every sense straining to catch fragments of their conversation over the sound of her own pounding heart. As they moved into the room, Beth's attention was torn away by a faint but distinct noise drifting across the water. She turned back to the railing and leaned forward, her eyes scanning the endless expanse of blue. The rhythmic hum of a distant motorboat teased her ears, a siren call that spoke of freedom or folly - she couldn't decide which. Her hands gripped the cool metal railing, knuckles whitening as she peered over the edge. The drop was steep, a sheer descent to the hard concrete and churning waves below. For a heartbeat, she allowed herself to imagine the fall, the wind tearing through her hair, the ocean rushing up to meet her. It would be so easy to let go, but somewhere between reality and wishful hearing, the sound persisted. Her chest tightened around a flicker of hope that refused to die. Beth's resolve hardened - she couldn't take the leap, not yet. Not when that glimmer of a chance remained that the sound wasn't just another trick of the mind, but a sign that help was on its way. She released the railing, stepping back onto the solid ground of the balcony, her eyes still locked on the horizon, searching for a salvation that might never come. Squinting against the glare of the sun on water, Beth thought she saw it, A distant shimmer, different from the relentless lapping of waves. It was a flicker, a reflection perhaps, but something that wasn't supposed to be there, something out of place in the monotony of the sea.

"What—"

"Thinking about taking a swim?" Tim's gruff voice broke through her concentration as Beth recoiled slightly, not having heard his approach. She turned, finding him closer than she had anticipated.

"I thought you'd rather have me dead." She snapped, her gaze still tethered to the spot where she had seen the glinting light.

"Dead doesn't suit you," he shrugged, an oddly detached gesture, "besides, I've got my reasons for keeping you around."

"Reasons," Beth parroted, her skepticism clear as day, "like what, guilt?"

"Maybe," his single eye, surrounded by scars and memories, held hers for a moment longer than comfortable, "let's just say I'm glad I can keep an eye on you. Can't forgive those who left though."

"Yes," she looked him up and down, "better keep your *eye* on me."

"Very funny." He scoffed at the slight, rolling his one eye at her while the eyepatch shifted underneath the muscle movement.

"Left," she echoed hollowly, attempting to change the subject, feeling the sting of abandonment anew, "they left us both behind, remember?"

"Ah, but if you'd gone with them, who'd come back for me," his tone was bitter, yet edged with a reluctant gratitude, "you being here, it gives us a ghost of a chance." Beth's throat tightened at his words, at the acknowledgment of their shared predicament. They were the unwanted, the remnants of a failed plan, yet still they clung to a thin strand of hope that stretched across the ocean, connecting them to those who had made it out.

"Ghost of a chance," she murmured, turning again to the sea, the possibility of rescue fanning the embers of her resolve, "you don't know Austin. He doesn't leave people behind." Beth's voice was steady, yet beneath it a tremor of unshed tears threatened to break through, her eyes locked with Tim's unwavering gaze.

"And yet, he left you." Tim replied, his voice devoid of warmth. The words hung there between them like a guillotine blade poised to sever the last thread of Beth's composure. Without another word, he turned on his heel and disappeared into the room. The echo of his departure was a stark reminder of her isolation. Beth squeezed her eyes shut, willing the sting of rejection and fear away, fighting against the surge of emotion that clawed at her throat. Her resolve wavered, but she refused to let the tears fall. Not here, not in front of them. She was pulled from her efforts by the slamming of the door as Tim and Victor left, followed by the faint rustle of sheets inside. Chantelle stirred in Victor's bed, the movement causing Beth's heart to clench. She turned, taking cautious steps into the room, her breath hitching ever so slightly as she approached the bed where Chantelle lay, a broken figure amidst the tangled luxury of silk and shadows.

"Chantelle," Beth's voice was soft, almost hesitant, "are you okay?" The response came not with words but a cold dismissal in Chantelle's eyes - a hardness Beth had come to recognise all too well. It was the same look that had settled over Chantelle since that fateful night on Alcatraz, when their plans to flee had crumbled to dust, leaving scars in place of freedom. Beth squeezed her eyes shut and the sound of loud, pounding footsteps echoed through her mind as the guards rushed towards them from across the courtyard. She could feel Chantelle's hand trembling in hers and hear her muffled sobs. Beth kept apologising to Chantelle, promising to protect her, but Chantelle didn't believe a word she said. Not since that night. Beth continued to apologise every chance she got, but her words had fallen on deaf ears.

"Do I look okay?" The sharp and disdainful words from Chantelle snapped Beth out of her daze. She inhaled deeply, licking her dry lips and swallowing the lump that had formed in her throat. Beth grappled with finding the right words to say. After a year of having the same sparse conversations, her apologies had become a monotonous and tiresome routine. She was getting tired of repeating herself, but she knew she had to keep trying until Chantelle believed her.

"I was just—"

"Just *what*," Chantelle snapped, "checkin' in? Makin' sure I'm okay? I don't need anyone lookin' out for me." Beth cautiously inched forward, her actions and thoughts carefully calculated to maintain composure.

"I'm trying to—"

"You can barely take care of yourself," Chantelle gestured towards the blood on Beth's arm, watching while it slowly trickled down her skin and tickled her elbow as Beth wiped it away with the hem of her shirt, "Val and Luis protected me for so long that I forgot how to do it myself. But I'm doin' just fine, so stop tryin' to look out for me. I don't need it, and I don't need you. I don't need anyone."

"Chantelle—"

"They left us, Beth," Chantelle's voice was sharp and harsh, her features twisted into an unfamiliar expression that Beth had never seen before, "when are you gonna realise that they left us to save themselves? If you'd been given the chance, you'd have left too." Beth chose not to mention that she could have escaped with Austin, and instead held onto the memory in silence.

"It wasn't my fault," Beth whispered, more to herself than to Chantelle, "I went back for you. I couldn't just leave you there alone."

"But *they* did," Chantelle's laugh was bitter, sharp enough to slice through the thick tension in the room, "look around, Beth. I am alone." The accusation lingered in the air, a ghostly reminder of their shared plight. Beth's hands clenched into fists at her sides, the weight of guilt anchoring her to the spot. She wanted to reach out, to offer some solace in this sea of desolation they'd been cast adrift upon. But the distance between them was a chasm now, one not so easily bridged. With no one else around to blame, Chantelle's anger had been directed towards Beth for the better part of a year. Her gaze lingered on the fading violet bruises that marred Chantelle's once unblemished skin. Her voice was a mere breath as she reached out.

"You shouldn't have to endure this. I tried," the bitter taste of fear and guilt lingered on Beth's tongue as she swallowed hard, trying to push away the overwhelming emotions, "I've tried hard to distract him, shift his focus." Chantelle's eyes met Beth's in the mirror's reflection as she stood, her movements deliberate and devoid of modesty. The bathroom light cast stark shadows over the contours of her body, revealing the full extent of her suffering etched in blue and black and red. Beth flinched inwardly at each mark, the visual testament to their shared torment under Victor's cruel hand.

"Maybe you're not as special as you think." Chantelle said, her tone laced with a harshness that didn't quite reach her eyes, a defence mechanism Beth recognised all too well.

"Oh God, Chantelle—" Beth's gaze travelled down her body. On the back of Chantelle's arms, she could see fingerprint bruises that told a story of violence. The red scratch marks on her shoulders had slowly healed over time, a bruise the rough size of a fist was still visible against her ribs.

"He likes it when I struggle," Chantelle's movements were like a painter's brushstrokes, tracing the lines and curves of her body with practiced ease, "he's more violent when I don't." Beth took a deep breath, trying to push down the fear and pain that were rising in her chest.

"They will come for us. Val, she wouldn't abandon us, she wouldn't abandon you." Beth's heart tightened, but she pushed forward, clinging to a desperate hope. A mirthless smile twisted Chantelle's lips as she vanished into the bathroom, her voice trailing after her.

"We were moved for a reason, Beth. So no one could find us here. The others left us because we're expendable. We're the dead weight." The words were like ice water dousing the fragile flames of Beth's resolve. But deep down, beneath layers of fear and resignation, a stubborn ember of defiance still glowed. She refused to be snuffed out, not by Victor nor by despair. They would be saved, they had to be.

CHAPTER 2

Beth's eyelids fluttered in rebellion against the weight of sleepless-ness, the dark circles beneath them testament to countless hours spent in vigilant unrest. Perched on the edge of a bed that offered no comfort, she leaned towards the open window, her ears strain-ing for any sign that could puncture the monotony of rolling waves. The briny scent of the ocean did little to soothe her fraying nerves as she mentally berated the relentless surf below.

"Quiet, dammit." She murmured under her breath, desperate for the silence that might herald the approach of a motorboat, a har-binger of hope. Echoes of memories played through her mind. Austin's determined strength, Ben's reassuring touch - she clung to the fantasy of their rescue like a lifeline, an escape from the cease-less nightmare that had become her existence. As fatigue gnawed at the edges of her resolve, Beth's thoughts began to blur into a dreamscape where salvation was but moments away. A sharp crack came slicing through the night's tranquility like a knife through silk, a sound so foreign and jarring against the rhythmic lullaby of the sea that it catapulted her back to full alertness. Her heart ham-mered in her chest, adrenaline surging with the thought that she had heard a gunshot. In a frenzied scramble, she lurched towards the promise of the outside world beyond her window. But the treacherous rug beneath her feet betrayed her urgency, sending her careening forward. Pain exploded across her forehead as it collided with the edge of a table, and then the world went black. Suddenly, sunlight pierced the room, prying Beth's eyes open against her will. The sting of a wet rag against her skin drew a hiss from her lips as she blinked into focus, finding Tim hovering above her with a look that mingled concern with something harder to read.

"Are you okay?" He asked, his voice gruff with worry that couldn't quite mask the undercurrent of frustration.

"Feels like my head's been split open." She groaned, pressing her hand against the throbbing ache that seemed intent on splitting her skull.

"Your head or your personality?" Tim quipped, though his hands were gentle as they continued to dab at the wound. His attempt at humour felt out of place, a stark contrast to the cold distance he'd maintained on most other days.

"Make up your mind, Tim," Beth snapped, pushing upright despite the room's insistent spin, "one minute you're patching me up, the next you're glowering like I'm the enemy."

"Maybe I can't forget that night as easily as you can." He retorted, his voice rising as he gestured to his eye.

"Your anger's misdirected," Beth shot back, the words acid-etched with sarcasm, "just like you told Ben, right? Or does that wisdom only apply when it's convenient to you?" Tim's jaw clenched, the muscle ticking in silent admission. He held her gaze for a moment longer before turning away, leaving the unsaid hanging heavy between them. Beth's eyes, stubborn and unyielding, locked onto Tim's with an intensity that belied her pain.

"What did the guards find on the mainland?" She demanded, the words slicing through her headache like a knife.

"Nothing for you to worry about," Tim responded curtly, his tone suggesting he was finished with the conversation, "you should be more concerned with getting to the doctor."

"Tell me," she insisted, a sharp edge of desperation creeping into her voice, "I heard something last night. I need to know if it wasn't just—"

"Stubborn bitch," Tim snapped, frustration breaking through his usually collected demeanour as he took a breath that seemed to carry the weight of untold secrets before continuing, "they ran into a military group. Very organised, heavily armed. They were talking about Fort Irwin. There's some sort of community there, near a military base."

"That's gotta be them," Beth felt a surge of hope so strong it almost overpowered the throbbing in her head, "Ben, and Austin and the others, they all must be there."

"Even if they are it doesn't change anything," Tim's face was etched with skepticism, "you think we can just stroll out of here?"

"Tonight," she pressed, her mind racing with possibilities, "we can make it to Long Beach and then to Fort Irwin. We can find them."

"Listen to yourself," Tim's laugh held no humour, it was a hollow sound that bounced off the walls of the small room, "Victor's got this place on lockdown. His men are loyal. The men here are *his* men, from before. We wouldn't make it past the beach."

"Then we have to try something else," Beth said, her determination not waning, "there has to be a way—"

"Listen to me, Beth," Tim interrupted abruptly, his gaze hardening, "there is *no* way. Victor isn't some two-bit thug you can outsmart with a bit of luck and planning. This isn't a story where the cavalry comes in at the last second. This is real life, and in real life, people like us don't get past people like him." Beth's heart pounded against her chest, her dream of rescue clashing with the cold, hard reality that Tim laid bare. Yet, she couldn't let go - the thought of reuniting with the others was the only spark in her sea of darkness. "Then we'll find another way. We have to." She whispered, more to herself than to Tim as tears brimmed in Beth's eyes while she clutched at Tim's shirt, her voice a desperate whisper, "I can't do this anymore. Every day it's like I'm drowning, and every night I think maybe it would be better if it just ended." Something in Tim's posture shifted, his face hardening into a mask of disdain. "You think this is some kind of melodrama? That you're the tragic heroine waiting for a hero to sweep in," his words were a venomous sneer, dripping with contempt, "the only joke here is you, Beth. Your fanciful dreams of Austin and Ben charging in to save the day, to save *you*, it's classic narcissism. It's probably what got you into this mess." The harshness of his rebuke struck her like a slap, the stinging accusation draining the fight from her limbs. Her hands fell away from his shirt as she staggered back, the weight of his scorn bowing her head.

"I'm sorry," she murmured, the fight seeping out of her voice leaving it empty and small, "just leave me then." With a final glance of frustration, Tim turned on his heel and strode out of the room, the door slamming shut behind him. The echo of the latch falling into place was a cold reminder of her isolation, and Beth collapsed onto the floor, her body curled protectively around itself as she surrendered to the desolation that enveloped her.

Chantelle's movements were sluggish as she rose from the tangled sheets of Victor's bed, her feet carrying her to the sanctuary of the

bathroom. As she approached the sink, the muffled sounds of conversation drifted through the slightly ajar balcony doors, carried by the persistent summer winds.

"Three of ours down, caught in the crossfire," Victor's gravelly voice carried an edge of irritation, "this complicates things. I think I should have a chat with *her* again."

"She might not know anything," the other guard suggested tentatively, "she could've been telling the truth."

"Are you telling me I'm wrong?" Victor's harsh voice cut through the air with a cadency ready for battle. Chantelle's heart pounded in her ears as she strained to hear more, gripping the edge of the bed to steady herself. The thought of another confrontation between Beth and Victor sent a shiver of dread through her. Outside, the wind continued its relentless howl, indifferent to the turmoil it witnessed, leaving Chantelle to ponder the fates that hung so precariously in the balance. The wind's fury abated momentarily, giving way to a sudden stillness that felt as heavy as the muggy air pressing against Chantelle's skin. She crept from the bedroom slowly, her bare feet silent on the cool tiles, each step measured and cautious. The voices outside had grown louder, more heated, sharp with the bite of confrontation, but failed to carry with the dying wind. She leaned closer to the balcony doors, the veil of curtains fluttering like ghosts in the waning gale.

"Victor, you can't just—" The guard's objection was cut short, his words replaced by the sickening scuffle of a struggle. There was a visceral grunt, a thud of bodies colliding with railing, and then a horrified scream tore through the silence, plummeting down with the weight of inevitability. The sound ended abruptly, culminating in a hollow crash far below that resonated up through the building's bones. Chantelle slapped a hand over her mouth to stifle the scream that threatened to escape her throat, her body recoiling instinctively as she stumbled backward into the bedroom, and further into the bathroom's false sanctuary. Her heart hammered against her ribs, echoing the guard's final cries as she doubled over the toilet. The contents of her stomach surged upward, expelling in violent heaves. Eventually, the spasms subsided, leaving her trembling and hollow. She grasped the edge of the sink and pulled herself up, her eyes meeting her reflection in the mirror. The ashen color of her face was gradually replaced by a rosy hue, signaling the return of vitality to her body. Her eyes, rimmed with red, held a haunted gaze as they traveled over the landscape of her body. Fingers brushed across bruises that painted her skin in shades of suffering, each one a story she couldn't forget. They lingered on the tender fullness of her breasts, a foreign sensation that sparked an icy dread deep within her. Her gaze drifted lower, to the subtle swell of her belly that had begun to assert its presence. The absence of menstruation that should have come and gone without notice now loomed large in her mind. A cold realisation washed over her, snatching the breath from her lungs. She looked into the mirror once more, her lips parting in a whisper that carried the weight of her new reality.

"Fuck." It was a quiet exclamation, laden with fear, uncertainty, and the nascent understanding of just how much more complicated her captivity might become.

Tim stood at the base of the hotel, his gaze fixed on the ocean's expanse as a pair of guards heaved the lifeless body onto a makeshift stretcher. The crimson pool on the concrete was a stark contrast against the sterile white of the linen draped over the corpse.

"Get him out of here." Tim said, his voice low, eyes not leaving the horizon. He had learned to mask his thoughts well - one did not survive long around Victor without acquiring such skills.

"Tim," the approach of another guard broke his reverie, a man of stocky build and few words, Josh was not one to question orders or linger on sentiment, "thinking about the mainland?" Josh queried, following Tim's gaze out to sea.

"Something like that," Tim replied, his mind racing through a maze of possibilities and fears, "just wondering about the growing presence on the other side."

"Come on, you know we were careful," Josh scoffed, leaning on the fence with a false sense of ease, "I was there. No tails, no traces."

"Yeah, but what about the men we lost," Tim prodded, his voice casual yet probing, "were they confirmed dead?"

"Even if they played possum, what of it? We've got the firepower, and Victor's got plans." Josh's brow furrowed, a flicker of confusion crossing his face before he laughed it off.

"Plans." Tim echoed hollowly, his gaze dropping to the bloodied concrete.

"Yeah, plans." There was a cold irony in Josh's confidence, one that resonated with a deeper, gnawing apprehension.

"Tell that to him." Tim said, motioning towards the shrouded figure being carted away. Josh followed Tim's gesture, and for a moment, his laughter died in his throat. The reality of their situation lay bare before them in the shape of a fallen comrade, Victor's wrath given form.

"Victor will keep us safe." Josh muttered, more to convince himself than to reassure Tim.

"Sure he will." Tim replied, his response devoid of conviction. As the stretcher disappeared from view, he turned his attention back to the sea, to the unknown threats that lurked beyond the waves, and to the tyrant behind them who held their fates in his volatile hands.

Beth's pulse throbbed in her ears, a staccato counterpoint to the ocean's incessant murmur. She stood before Chantelle's door, the grain of the aged wood rough under her fingertips. Her knuckles hovered mere inches from the surface, clenched tight enough to blanch the skin. Every imagined scenario played out behind her eyes, each one ending with rejection or anger. She could almost hear Chantelle's voice cutting through the silence, heavy with disdain, and the words she needed to say. Apologies, hope, a flimsy sighting of salvation, all twisted into knots in her throat.

"Going to knock sometime today?" Sabrina's voice sliced through Beth's reverie like a blade, sharp and uninvited. Beth's hand dropped to her side as she turned, facing the mockery in Sabrina's gaze.

"I don't have anything to make amends for," she insisted, the defiance in her voice belied by the quaver of uncertainty, "I went back for her that night when everyone else ran."

"Did you now," Sabrina arched an eyebrow, her lips curling into a knowing sneer, "ever think about what you were saving her from? Or maybe she doesn't resent being left behind as much as being kept alive for *this*." Her gesture encompassed the oppressive walls around them, the dystopian existence they'd been thrust into. The accusation struck Beth harder than any physical blow could. The sardonic edge in Sabrina's tone suggested a truth Beth had never allowed herself to consider - that rescue might not have been mercy but a prelude to a different kind of hell. Beth's gaze flickered down the corridor, seeking an escape from the weight of that realisation, but found only the closed doors and silent judgments of those who shared their captivity. The echo of Sabrina's departure left a hollow silence in its wake, punctuated only by the soft creak of Chantelle's door swinging open. The abruptness of it startled Beth from her vacillation, her breath catching at the sight of Chantelle's surprised gaze.

"Can we talk?" Beth's voice was barely above a whisper, but it carried the weight of months of unsaid words.

"Mmm." With a resigned sigh, Chantelle stepped back into the shadows of her room, granting passage with a weary gesture. Beth crossed the threshold, her eyes scanning the space that so starkly contrasted with her own austere quarters. Here, there were remnants of someone trying to stitch together a semblance of home. Piles of books creating makeshift furniture, sheets tangled in an abandonment of care. Yet, an unmistakable staleness clung to the air, as if the room itself had given up on pretending.

"Have you been taking care of yourself?" Beth asked, her concern laced with a hint of reproach. Chantelle's response came not in words, but in the studied avoidance of eye contact, her gaze fixed on some indefinite point in the room. It was clear that self-care had long since ceased to be a priority, the concept as foreign and distant now as freedom. Beth recognised the signs, the same ones she saw when she looked in her own mirror. A shiver ran through Chantelle as memories, unbidden and cruel, seeping into her consciousness. They were the residue of those early days after their escape attempt. She and Beth had been isolated, each other's existence confirmed only by the shared torment they endured. They sought solace in brief glimpses across rooms, in the muffled sounds of mutual defiance. But the day they were torn from their cells and dragged down the hill to the yacht waiting for them had severed even that fragile connection. Beth remembered reaching for Chantelle then, her hand trembling with the need to offer some sliver of comfort amidst the chaos. But before their fingers could touch, guards had intervened, prying them apart with cold efficiency. As they were herded onto the vessel, Beth's heart had thrummed with a terrible understanding - this journey was not a new beginning, it was merely a continuation of their purgatory. Chantelle's gaze drifted to the yawning space of the main living area on the yacht, a stark contrast to the cramped cells they had left behind. Hushed whispers were quickly stifled as Doctor Horn cast a warning glance over the group. Victor's voice, calm and authoritative, had echoed off the polished surfaces, promising return for those left behind once safety was assured. But the promise felt hollow in Chantelle's chest as Catalina Island's shores embraced them with an eerie silence. No one had departed for Alcatraz since their arrival, the notion of being forsaken prey to a planned assault by their former allies gnawed at her mind.

"Are you okay?" Beth's voice sliced through the thick air of reminiscence, pulling Chantelle back into the present.

"Fine," she replied mechanically, "just tired." Beth hesitated, searching for the right words that seemed to weigh heavily on her tongue. "I'm sorry for that night," Beth started as confusion flashed across Chantelle's features, prompting Beth to elaborate, "the plan, it wasn't supposed to be like this. Austin was meant to come for me, and the others for you. But everything went wrong. We got separated." Beth's eyes held a depth of regret, her shoulders bearing the burden of decisions made amidst chaos - a chaos that had torn their fates into shreds too tangled to piece back together. The hazy light filtered through the room's sole window, casting long shadows that seemed to entangle with Chantelle's words as she began to unravel the horrors of that night.

"Ben, Chase, and Tyler burst into the dinin' hall, their weapons singin' death," Chantelle murmured, her voice a mere whisper, thick with the memory of gunfire and screams, "Su, Sam, Stephanie. No one stood a chance." Beth's heart clenched at the recounting, her own guilt mirrored in Chantelle's grief-stricken eyes. She remembered the chaos, the panic, how the world had narrowed down to adrenaline-fuelled snapshots of terror.

"I saw them drag you away," Beth's voice quivered, her words barely audible as she struggled to get them out, "I was with Austin on the other side of the courtyard. I tried to scream for him, to get his attention, but it was like shouting into a storm, and I couldn't just leave you." Her hands twitched involuntarily, recalling the desperation.

"You were that close to gettin' out?" Chantelle's gaze lifted, meeting Beth's, an ocean of unsaid words swirling between them. There was something new in her voice, a tender realisation laced with pain.

"Close enough," Beth said with a bitter half-smile, "but we haven't really talked since then, have we? This is the longest conversation we've had in almost a year, Chantelle."

"Thank you, for comin' back," Chantelle's voice trailed off as a shadow of ambivalence crossed her features, "but sometimes, I wish you hadn't." Her eyes flickered with a pain deeper than regret, a secret teetering on the edge of revelation.

"Why would you say that?" Beth prodded gently, sensing the weight of unspoken truths pressing against the fragile atmosphere. Chantelle paused, her lips parting as if to release the burden she carried within. But instead, she pressed them shut, locking away the words that threatened to expose her deepest fear, a fear that tethered her to a future as uncertain as the haunted look that now took refuge in her eyes. The silence stretched between them, a taut thread ready to snap. Beth's gaze wandered back to the window where, hours before, she thought she'd heard salvation in the form of an engine churning through the sea.

"Chantelle," she finally broke the stillness, her voice barely above a whisper, "I think I might've heard a motorboat on the horizon last night, but I don't trust my own ears anymore." She looked down at her hands, knotted together in her lap. Chantelle, leaning against the wall with her arms folded, regarded Beth with a solemn nod.

"You've always been sharp, Beth. If you say you heard a motorboat, then you probably did." There was no mockery in her tone, only a steady affirmation.

"I feel like I'm losing my mind here," Beth wrapped her arms around herself as if to quell the shivers that weren't there, "this place, it's grinding me down to nothing."

"Or maybe," Chantelle countered softly, "it's forgin' somethin' stronger in you. We're all crackin' under the weight of this place, but you survived things before we found you. And now, even without the others, you're fightin'." Her eyes held a glint of respect. Beth's breath hitched as memories flashed to a time when fear had been her constant companion until they had pulled her into their fold.

"I don't know who I am without them." She admitted, her voice faltering.

"Then maybe it's time you find out," Chantelle pushed off from the wall and moved closer, "you can't live on hope alone. We may never be rescued, you have to come to terms with that." Beth nodded slowly, absorbing the hard truth in Chantelle's words. After a moment, she looked up, a wry smile curving her lips.

"Have you figured out who you are in all this mess?"

"Perhaps," Chantelle said, pausing as if searching for the right words within herself, "but there's so much more to understand." Her eyes flickered with a depth that hinted at internal struggles yet to be reconciled.

"When did you get so philosophical?" Beth asked, the jest lightening the heavy air between them. Chantelle offered a small, genuine smile.

"I've always had thoughts swirlin' in my head," she confessed, "I guess it took all of this to make me grow up and listen to them." Their shared laughter was brief but cathartic, slicing through the tension and offering a glimpse of camaraderie amidst the chaos of their captive lives.

The first light of dawn bathed the world in a gentle glow as Beth and Chantelle settled at a wrought-iron table nestled on the veranda. A spread of scant breakfast rations lay between them, untouched by the opulence that once characterised the hotel's facade. They had always been given permission to dine outside, a rarity they seldom embraced. But today, the open air felt like a stolen breath of freedom.

"Last night's talk really helped," Chantelle said, a tentative smile touching her lips as she forked a piece of stale bread, "it's like a weight's been lifted."

"Mmm." Beth nodded, her gaze lingering on the horizon where the sky kissed the sea. She remained silent, her ears straining for the familiar chug of an engine. Chantelle watched her for a moment before reaching across the table to cover Beth's hand with her own. "Don't do this to yourself," Chantelle advised gently, "if they're out there, they'll come." Beth allowed herself a small sigh, turning to offer Chantelle a grateful glance. Before she could respond, the crunch of gravel announced another's approach. Tim ambled towards them, his one remaining eye scanning the scene with a mix of curiosity and disbelief.

"What're you two doing out here?" He asked, his voice carrying a gruff note that betrayed his surprise.

"Since when do we need permission to eat outside?" Beth retorted, her tone edged with defiance. Despite the tightness in her chest, she met his gaze squarely, challenging him. Tim raised his hands in mock surrender.

"Just never seen you take advantage of it, is all," his expression shifted, "actually, I've got news. Victor's sent some guards to the mainland. He thinks your friends are the ones our guys have run into over there." Beth's heart skipped a beat. The possibility that their friends were close enough to warrant Victor's attention sent a ripple of both fear and hope through her. Beside her, Chantelle set down her fork quietly, the pallor of her face speaking volumes about the turmoil within.

"Is that supposed to be a warning or reassurance?" Beth asked, her voice steady despite the chaos of emotions.

"Take it as you will." Tim replied with a shrug, though his eye lingered on them a moment longer before he turned his attention towards the vast, unforgiving sea. The morning sun cast a warm glow over the beach as they watched Sabrina saunter along the shore, her arm linked with Josh's. The sound of Sabrina's laugh, dark and full of malice, carried over to where they sat. Chantelle shifted uncomfortably, her gaze fixed on the frothy waves lapping at the sand.

"I can't believe her," Beth murmured, her eyes narrowing slightly, "ever since she announced her pregnancy, she's been more—"

"Unbearable." Chantelle interrupted, a grimace touching her lips.

"If it is actually Victor's." Tim snorted, his words hung between them like a dare. Beth turned to him sharply.

"What do you mean?"

"Victor's bed has been a revolving door, a parade of women daily," Tim said, his voice low, "but only one pregnancy? Makes you wonder."

"I need to go back inside." Chantelle abruptly stood, her chair scraping against the patio stones before she hurried into the hotel.

"What's got into her?" Tim asked, watching Chantelle's hasty retreat.

"She's part of the parade," Beth said, though her mind was elsewhere, pondering Tim's insinuation, "I need a favour." After a moment of silence, Beth stood and faced Tim.

"Last time that happened, I lost an eye." He reminded her, touching the patch that covered his wound.

"Would you join the group going to the mainland? If you find our friends, maybe you could—"

"Escape and tell them where you are," Tim's skepticism was palpable, "you think Austin, Ben, Reece, Chase, Tyler, even Val, if they've joined some military outfit that they would be high enough in rank to mount a rescue for two insignificant girls?" Beth held his gaze. She needed him to understand, to see the desperation that fuelled her request. But in his one good eye, she saw only the hard truth of their situation reflected back at her. The gentle lap of the waves against the shore was a stark contrast to the turmoil churning within Beth as she gazed out over the water, Tim's words echoing in her mind. Her breakfast lay forgotten, the uneaten toast growing cold beside her half-empty cup of coffee. She drew in a deep breath, tasting the salt in the air, and let it out slowly, feeling a rising tide of frustration.

"Your manic emotions towards me," she began, her voice steady despite the anger simmering beneath the surface, "they're getting old, Tim. Either you blame me and hate me for what happened that night and everything since, or you need to get over it. Be angry at Marcus, at Victor, at every fucking person who's made us suffer since this pandemic began." Tim stood his ground, the flicker of surprise in his eye quickly masked by his usual stoicism. Beth stopped only inches away from him, her eyes locked with his, unflinching.

"Beth—"

"I killed Marcus," she lied, the weight of defiance heavy in her tone, "I ended his reign of terror, but I also handed us over to another tyrant. If I had the courage to kill once, don't think I won't have it again if I need to." A silence stretched between them, filled only by the distant cries of seabirds and the soft rustle of leaves in the breeze. Tim's gaze never wavered from hers, searching for something he hadn't seen before. Beth continued, her voice softer now, but no less determined.

"Every day since that night, I've thought about my own death.

But I haven't given in because I believe there's something else I'm meant to do first," she took a step back, her posture unwavering, the ocean air lifting strands of her hair like whispers of rebellion, "if I'm going down, I'm taking the whole fucking system with me, and it ends with Victor." Something shifted in Tim's expression then, a subtle change that softened the hard lines around his mouth. A smile, small and reluctant, tugged at the corner of his lips, revealing a glimmer of respect, or perhaps it was understanding.

"Damn, Beth," he said, the gruffness in his voice tinged with a new-found warmth, "I'm starting to see why Austin and Ben were both so caught up with you." For a moment, they stood there, two survivors on the brink of an uncertain future, bound by loss and the unspoken hope of retribution. The fire in Beth's eyes reflected the morning sun, signalling a new day and the promise of a fight yet to come.

Chantelle's hand trembled as she rapped softly on the weathered wood of Doctor Horn's door. It swung open with a creak, revealing the disheveled figure of the man who once commanded respect with his crisp white coat. Now, his shirt was unbuttoned at the collar, and dark circles underscored his bloodshot eyes.

"Chantelle," he said, his voice a husky whisper of its former authority, "it's been quite some time."

"Doctor." She greeted, stepping into the chaos of his quarters. Her gaze swept across the cluttered surfaces, over the medical journals turned confetti, the stained coffee cups sheltering mould gardens. Then her eyes fell upon the shackle, an ugly band of metal encircling his ankle, tethering him to the bedpost.

"Ah, that," he followed her line of sight, a bitter chuckle escaping him, "not for your sake, but for mine. Victor can't afford to lose his healer, even one as unpredictable as myself." She studied him, the erratic twitches, the laboured breaths, the once-sturdy pillar of sanity now seemed as fragile as the papers strewn about his floor.

"Doctor, I need your help," she began cautiously, her voice barely above a whisper, "I think I'm pregnant." The room seemed to contract around them, the air growing dense with the weight of her confession. His expression shifted from weary resignation to a poignant mix of sorrow.

"Victor isn't like Marcus, he won't kill you," his thoughts flashed to the memories of his own daughter briefly as a tense silence lingered, "when they brought us here, they brought everything from the prison. All the supplies should be in a storeroom on the bottom floor. There should be some tests with them." He mused, raising an eyebrow.

"Thank you," Chantelle said as she backed away from the room where madness and genius lay intertwined, where the ghost of the man he used to be still lingered in the shadows, "take care." She added, though the words felt hollow against the magnitude of his own personal hell. As she left, the weight of potential life within her fought against the gravity of despair that clung to the walls. Chantelle's shadow slipped through the corridor like a whisper, her footsteps muffled against the plush carpeting. The hotel, once a bastion of opulent vacationers now laid out like a mausoleum to silence itself - a stark contrast to the ever-watchful eyes of Alcatraz. She held her breath with each creak of the aged floorboards beneath her, aware that sound was now her greatest betrayer. Descending the staircase to the bottom floor, her hand grazed the cold banister, feeling the ghosts of past grandeur. She paused at the foot of the stairs, senses straining for any sign of movement. Nothing stirred, the stillness was as unsettling as it was reassuring.

"Chantelle?" The voice cut through the quiet, and she whirled around, heart leaping into her throat. Tim stood there, an eyebrow cocked in question, his one eye scrutinising her from the dim light cast by the exit sign. She hesitated, then her resolve solidified.
"I need something from the old medical supplies." She whispered.
"You shouldn't be wandering around like this. It's not safe." His gaze narrowed.
"I know," she breathed out, "but I have to find something important." Tim studied her for a moment longer before sighing and rubbing the side of his head.
"What is it you're looking for?" His voice simultaneously curious and cautious.
"I'm looking for a," the confession hung on her tongue, heavy and daunting, "a pregnancy test." Recognition flickered across Tim's features, and he nodded slowly, as if piecing together a puzzle he had only just been presented with.
"Come on then," he said, motioning for her to follow, "let's get what you need." They moved through the corridors with a practiced stealth, shadows flitting between the soft golden glow of the wall sconces. At last, they arrived at the storeroom, its door ajar and inviting secrets to be uncovered. Inside, rows of boxes lined the walls, labeled hastily in fading marker. Tim led her to the back, where dust motes danced in the sliver of light from the hallway. He crouched down, fingers deftly searching through the contents of each container until his hand emerged, triumphantly clutching a small box.

"You found it?"

"Here." His voice was softer now, tinged with an understanding that transcended their usual interactions as he handed her the box of pregnancy tests.

"Thank you, Tim." Chantelle murmured, her voice barely audible as she clutched the box close, the weight of potential life pressing urgently against the confines of her future. Chantelle's footsteps were hushed as she retreated to the sanctuary of her room, the box clutched tightly in her grasp like a lifeline. The door clicked shut behind her, sealing her within the confines of her own uncertainty and dread. She wasted no time, tearing into the packaging with trembling fingers that betrayed her cool exterior. With the test now in hand, she followed the instructions mechanically, her mind adrift in the sea of what-ifs that had plagued her since the suspicion first took root. Settling the test on the edge of the sink, she backed away, distancing herself from the catalyst that would either confirm or deny the new life charting its course inside her. The room seemed to contract around her, the walls pressing inward as the seconds ticked by. Each minute stretched into an eternity, mocking her with its slow crawl. Chantelle fixed her gaze on the back wall, the patterns on the wallpaper blurring into obscurity as her focus turned inward. In her mind, she counted the minutes, each digit echoing with a resonance that filled the silence of the room. Finally, the interminable wait drew to a close. Her breath held hostage in her chest, Chantelle approached the sink with hesitant steps. The test lay there innocently, its result displayed in stark clarity against the plastic window. It was a moment of truth that had loomed on the horizon for weeks, yet it still struck with the force of a revelation. As her eyes fell upon the positive result, a surge of emotions cascaded through her. Tears welled in her eyes, spilling over in silent streams that traced the contours of her face. There it was, the confirmation of her deepest intuition, a secret hope mixed with a paralysing fear. Holding the test gingerly between her fingers, Chantelle allowed herself a moment to absorb the reality of her situation. She was at the mercy of a future that felt both daunting and fragile, a delicate balance of life that she now carried within her. This piece of evidence, this tiny, plastic oracle, had sealed her fate, transforming the ephemeral into the tangible with just a few droplets and a waiting game. The tears continued their steady flow as Chantelle sat down heavily on the edge of her bed, the pregnancy test still in hand. It confirmed what she already knew to be true, but acknowledgment didn't ease the weight of it. Instead, it anchored her to a new chapter, one that would unfold with or without her readiness.

CHAPTER 3

The first light of dawn struggled to break through the thick curtains as Beth's door was pushed open with a sense of urgency that was all too familiar. Tim stood in the doorway, giving her a quick once-over before nodding towards the hallway.

"Victor's asking for you," he murmured, his voice low and laced with an unspoken warning, "and he's not in the best of moods today, so tread lightly." Beth quickly got dressed and followed him into the hallway, her heart beginning to race. She could feel the tension coiled in Tim's broad shoulders, even as he walked ahead of her down the opulent corridor.

"Why? What's happened?" She asked, trying to keep her voice steady.

"No time, I'll tell you later," Tim said without turning back, his steps quickening, "just don't antagonise him." She swallowed the lump forming in her throat and braced herself for what was to come. The moment Beth stepped into Victor's room, the air felt different, charged with a volatile energy. It took only a second for her to notice the figure in Victor's bed, the silk sheets draped over Jennifer's bare shoulders instead of Chantelle's usual delicate form. A flicker of surprise crossed Beth's face before she could mask it.

"Victor?" Beth called out tentatively, her gaze shifting from the bed to the balcony door left ajar. Victor turned at her voice, his sharp features twisted in a scowl that promised nothing good. Beth took a hesitant step forward, reaching the threshold of the balcony just in time to meet the sting of Victor's open palm across her cheek. The force of it sent her reeling, a hot flush of pain blooming across her face.

"Stay." Victor commanded sharply, his gaze fixed on Tim who had instinctively taken a step towards the exit.

"Yes, sir." Tim froze, his jaw clenching as he obeyed the command with a curt nod, resembling nothing so much as a trained dog under the heel of its master.

"Always lying Beth! Where are they hiding!?" Victor's voice thundered as he stalked closer to her. Beth's ears rang, her vision blurring with unshed tears. With every ounce of defiance she could muster, she raised her head to look him in the eye.

"I don't know!" She screamed, the truth raw in her voice as she faced the tempest of Victor's wrath. His silhouette loomed over Beth, a dark spectre against the rising sun that spilled onto the balcony.

"I don't believe you," his voice was like gravel laced with malice, "and when we do find them, with or without your cooperation, I'll make you watch as I pull out their teeth and their fingernails, one by one until they beg for death!" Beth met his gaze, her own eyes empty of fear, hollowed out by the horrors she had already endured.

"I look forward to the day," she said, her voice devoid of emotion, chilling in its steadiness, "when I feel your skull give way beneath whatever I hit you with." The words had barely left her lips when Victor's hand struck again, sending her sprawling to the cold floor. She felt the impact reverberate through her, yet it seemed distant, surreal, as if she were observing the scene from afar.

"Tim," Victor barked without looking at him, turning on his heel and striding into the room, "you're going to the mainland with the others." His command echoed with an undertone of threat.

"Sir—"

"Bring back a head or I'll take your other eye." Victor snarled as he stormed from the room. Beth lay still, listening to Tim's footsteps following Victor obediently, the sound fading away. All around her, the morning was waking up - the sky bled shades of orange and pink above her, a mockery of the beauty on a normal summer day. She rolled onto her back, the pain from Victor's blows lingering but secondary to the numbing coldness within her. Above her, the sky stretched vast and indifferent, and for a long moment, she watched the clouds drift lazily by, a stark contrast to the chaos of her world below. A single tear traced the contour of Beth's temple, disappearing behind her ear and into her hair.

"Ben, Austin," she whispered, her voice barely carrying over the whisper of the sea breeze as her eyes searched the sky, as if willing their silhouettes to materialise amidst the vast expanse of ocean, "if you're out there, you have to come. You have to save us." The words tumbled from her lips, a raw plea cast into the void. The sound of the sliding door interrupted her solitary vigil. Jennifer emerged, her figure casting a long shadow across the balcony. She leaned against the doorframe, arms folded, a sardonic smile twisting her lips.

"Praying are we," Jennifer's voice dripped with scorn, "or just talking to ghosts?" Beth's gaze lifted slowly, meeting Jennifer's mocking stare.

"I don't know what I'm doing anymore." She admitted, the desolation in her voice stark and unguarded.

"Useless," Jennifer spat out the word like it was poison, "just like all the faith you're pinning on those friends of yours." Beth's throat tightened at the accusation, her heart pounding a rebuttal she couldn't voice.

"Jennifer—"

"Your friends are the reason my sister is dead," Jennifer's voice hardened, each syllable a sharpened blade, "don't forget that. Even if they turn this whole island upside down to save any of us, it won't bring her back, and I will never forgive them for it." Her words hung heavy in the air, a shroud of unresolved grief and seething resentment. Beth remained silent, her thoughts a swirling maelstrom of hope and despair, unable to find purchase in the chaos of Jennifer's bitter reminder.

Beth trudged through the sterile corridors, her feet dragging against the hard floor as she returned to her room. The hotel once a haven for sun-seekers and lovers, now a gilded prison, bustled with a flurry of activity. Guards, including Tim, were gathering supplies and checking their weapons, their movements mechanical and predetermined. The air was thick with tension, anticipation hanging over them like a storm cloud. She reached her room and pressed her forehead against the cool glass of the windowpane, gazing out towards the mainland. The deep blue waters stretched between her cage and freedom. An hour by motorboat, a brief traverse across the undulating waves, yet that distance might as well have been a chasm of immeasurable depth. If Austin and Ben were there, plotting their next move, they felt like phantoms just beyond reach. A knock at the door snapped Beth from her reverie. It swung open to reveal Tim's imposing figure as he scanned around her room before settling his gaze on her.

"Time for me to head out." He said, his voice betraying a trace of something undefinable - regret, perhaps, or resignation. Beth turned from the window, her expression unreadable.

"So are you really going to do it," her voice was steady but her insides coiled tight, "bring back someone's head?" Tim's jaw tightened, the muscle twitching in the hollow of his cheek.

"Victor made it clear. Austin and Ben are off-limits," his voice was flat, the words delivered like a death sentence, "he wants that pleasure for himself." Beth clenched her fists at her sides, nails digging into her palms.

"And the others? Reece, Tyler, Chase, Val?" She pressed, each name a stone in her throat.

"Still on the table," Tim confirmed, his gaze unwavering, "Victor doesn't forget, and he certainly doesn't forgive." The silence that followed was a tangible thing, a chasm opening up in the small space between them. Beth felt the weight of the unsaid, the unacknowledged bond of shared horrors and the tenuous thread of hope that refused to snap. She held Tim's gaze for a long while as the silent tension in the room multiplied.

"Tim—"

"Goodbye, Beth." Tim muttered, turning on his heel to leave her alone with the ghosts of possibilities. Beth remained motionless, the view of the distant mainland blurring as her eyes stung with unshed tears. In her chest, her heart hammered a ferocious rhythm, a defiant drumbeat that whispered of survival and retribution. Beth's voice broke through the stillness of the room, each word laced with desperation, catching Tim as he was about to disappear.

"Tim, please," she begged, "whatever happens over there, don't hurt them." He stood with his back to her, shoulders rigid beneath the worn fabric of his jacket. His response came reluctantly, a gravelly murmur barely audible over the hum of tension that filled the space between them.

"I can't make any promises, Beth. It depends on what we walk into." He reached for the door handle as she watched on desperately, her heart pounding against her ribcage.

"Wait," she blurted out as he paused, hand resting on the cold metal, "Tim, there's a chance here. A chance for you to be more than Victor's enforcer. Tell Ben and Austin about us, about Chantelle and the others. If they bring help, if they free this island, you would be a hero." His silhouette faltered, an almost imperceptible softening in his posture. For a moment, Beth thought she saw the glimmer of possibility in his stance, the hint of a man who wanted to believe in redemption.

"No—"

"Listen to me," she pressed on, seizing the fragile thread of hope, "you could start over. You said there's possibly a community at Fort Irwin—"

"Start over," Tim interrupted, the bitterness in his voice was sharp enough to cut through her words as he turned to face her, his one good eye dark with unspoken pain, "there's no life for me beyond this, Beth. Not without them." His admission hung heavy in the air, loaded with grief.

"Your wife and sister?" Beth asked softly, the surprise evident in her tone.

"My daughter too," he said, the word like a stone dropped in still water, "she didn't make it past the outbreak. They're all gone, and I couldn't save them." Beth felt the sting of tears threaten her eyes, mirroring the sorrow etched deep into Tim's weathered face.

"Then save us," she whispered, her plea fervent and raw, "you have nothing left to lose." For a long moment, neither spoke. The silence was its own language, communicating a shared understanding of loss, of the relentless grip of the past. Then, without a word, Tim turned away, leaving Beth alone with the ghostly echo of what might be their last conversation. She watched his retreating figure until he vanished from sight, her whispered prayer lingering in the air behind him.

The low thrum of engines sent vibrations through Beth's head, a sombre lullaby that ebbed away into the night. She pressed her ear against the cool glass, catching the fading growl of boats as they cut through the water towards the mainland. The door creaked open without warning, and Sabrina's silhouette loomed in the doorway, the candlelight casting an ominous glow around her.

"Ever heard of knocking?" Beth turned, masking the tremor in her voice with feigned annoyance.

"Knocking is for guests, Beth. Not for prisoners," Sabrina replied, stepping inside with a casual saunter as her eyes scanned the room with a sense of ownership that set Beth's teeth on edge, "with Tim and half our men gone to the mainland, you'll be staying put. Can't have you stirring up trouble now, can we?"

"Was this your idea, or Victor's?" Beth asked, probing for a sliver of leverage in the tightened security around her.

"Let's just say I might have suggested it." Sabrina said with a sly tilt of her head. The half-smile that followed was neither warm nor comforting, but rather the satisfied curl of a cat that had caught a particularly elusive mouse.

"Good thinking," Beth conceded with a hollow laugh as she rose from her spot by the window, feeling the weight of her confinement settle in her chest, "because you know, given the chance, I'd burn this whole fucking place to the ground." Sabrina's laugh was sharp and cold as it sliced through the tension between them. "Oh, I know," she said, her laughter tapering off into a chilling silence, "and that's exactly why you're going to stay locked away." With a final glance, Sabrina turned on her heel, leaving Beth alone with the echo of her own threats and the distant promise of rescue she hoped was coming. The metallic click of the lock sealed Beth's fate as Sabrina's footsteps faded into silence. Beth turned away from the locked door and moved back to the window, her gaze drawn to the ocean outside. The once agitated waves were now settling into a gentle rhythm, the frothing whitecaps dissolving into the vast, blue-black calm. She watched, entranced by the slow dance of water reclaiming its tranquility, a stark contrast to the turmoil that churned within her. Days melded into one another, each indistinguishable from the last. The only markers of time were the visits from the two guards who delivered her meals with robotic efficiency. Breakfast and dinner arrived with punctuality that was both comforting and maddening in its constancy. She picked at the food they brought, appetite stolen by the gnawing anxiety for what lay beyond her walls. Each forkful was a reminder of her captivity, each untouched plate a silent protest she knew went unnoticed. As she sat on the hard wooden chair by the table, the monotonous tick of an unseen clock mocked her. She would close her eyes and let her mind wander back to the ranch where the winter had been long but life had been theirs. There, time had been marked by the changing skies, the difference in the snow-covered landscapes, and the laughter that filled the evenings after a good day. Here, it was just a languid, oppressive force, pushing her further into a solitary existence stripped of hope. The room, once merely a place to rest, had become a cell. The walls, adorned with fading wallpaper, seemed to inch closer each day, the air growing thicker and harder to breathe. Memories of freedom played behind her eyelids - images of verdant fields, the touch of the sun's warmth, and the comforting solidarity of her friends. Now, these recollections felt like relics from a life lived by someone else, someone who hadn't known the cold embrace of despair. She would stand at the window for hours, her fingers tracing the grain of the wood as if it could somehow transport her across the expanse of water that separated her from salvation. Her reflection in the glass, pale and ghostlike, gazed back at her - a constant reminder of the strength that had once coursed through her veins, now diminished to a whisper.

"Please, please let it be them." She'd murmur to the horizon, where the sky kissed the sea, begging for a sign, any sign, that rescue was imminent. But the horizon remained indifferent, offering no answers, only the vast stretch of emptiness that mirrored her isolation. In the quiet moments before sleep claimed her, when the darkness of the night seemed to seep into her bones, she clung to the hope that somewhere, beyond the reach of her captors, her friends were plotting, planning, and coming for her. This sliver of hope was the fragile thread that tethered her to sanity, to the belief that this nightmare would eventually end. And so she waited, the captive queen of her own dwindling domain, counting down the endless seconds until the world righted itself once more. The tray clattered onto the small table, the ceramic plate chipping at the edge as it collided with the metal surface. Beth's gaze lifted from the worn pattern of the floorboards to Jennifer, who stood rigidly by the door, her arms folded tightly across her chest.

"You need to eat," Jennifer's voice was flat, the usual sneer absent from her tone, "Victor's made it clear. If you don't, Chantelle will suffer for it."

"Chantelle," the name fell from Beth's lips like a stone dropped in still water, disrupting the calm she had desperately clung to, "she's fine. I saw her—"

"Things have changed," Jennifer interrupted, a cautious look flitting across her features, as if the madness she suspected in Beth might be contagious, "she's pregnant, Beth. Second trimester." A bitter laugh escaped Beth, disbelieving.

"That's impossible. I just—" Her protest died on her lips as realisation dawned, the hazy blur of days merging into weeks, possibly months. She moved to the window, the glass cool against her forehead.

"How long have I been staring out this window?" Beth whispered impassively.

"Too long," Jennifer replied, eyeing her warily, "Chantelle is doing fine, but you need to take care of yourself too."

"Why does Victor care if I don't eat? I thought he'd be happy if he were rid of me." Beth felt a tightness in her chest, one that compressed the air from her lungs and forced a small wheeze from her lips as she breathed.

"He feels that this is the closest he's ever been to catching your friends," she remarked with oily disdain, "he wants you around to see it."

"Does Victor know about the baby?" Beth asked, her voice barely above a whisper, the question laced with concern and an underlying current of fear.

"Of course he does," Jennifer said, stepping back towards the door, "and speaking of Victor, he's allowing you a walk tomorrow. Fresh air might do you good."

"Walk?" The word seemed foreign, yet enticing, a brief respite from the claustrophobic confines of her room.

"Yes, but I'll be accompanying you, along with some guards. Victor's orders." Jennifer snarled as Beth nodded mechanically, her thoughts already adrift, carried by the promise of open skies and the caress of the sun on her skin. It was a small mercy, a crack in the fortress of her captivity, through which she could glimpse the illusion of freedom.

"A walk." Beth repeated, almost disbelievingly, as a solitary tear slowly descended from her right eye and tickled her cheek as it fell.

"Try to get some sleep," Jennifer advised, though the glint in her eyes belied any genuine concern, "you'll need your strength." With that she took her exit, leaving Beth alone once more with her tray of untouched food and the pressing weight of reality. The possibility of Chantelle's condition wrestled with her own disbelief.

"Tomorrow," Beth murmured to herself, her fingers tracing the cold pane of glass as she searched the horizon for answers that lingered just out of reach, "just survive until tomorrow."

The first touch of the morning sun cast a golden hue across the sand as Beth stepped out onto the beach. The grains, cool and coarse, shifted under her bare feet, a sensation long forgotten during her confinement. She walked close to the water's edge, waves occasionally lapping over her toes, offering a briny chill that made her shiver with each step. Silent, she let the rhythmic sound of the sea fill the space where conversation would normally exist. Jennifer and a pair of guards had escorted her as she emerged from the room, their shadows stretching long and thin in the early light. But now, Jennifer and one of the guards had been whisked away by another guard. They both turned back towards the hotel, leaving Beth in the company of her individual escort. He was younger than the others, his face unmarred by the brutalities of the world they now knew. He watched her for a moment before attempting to pierce the silence with idle chatter.

"Beautiful day, isn't it?" He said, his eyes scanning the horizon as if expecting it to answer him instead.

"Yes." Beth could barely respond, continuing her measured pace along the shoreline, her gaze fixed on the delicate dance of the surf. The guard cleared his throat, undeterred.

"Never seen the ocean this calm before. It's like glass." He tried again, his words hanging in the air like kites without wind. She stopped then, the quietude enveloping her once more as she considered the vast expanse before her. A deep breath filled her lungs, and she finally turned to face him, her voice barely above the sound of the water.

"Can you take me to see Chantelle?" She asked, her eyes pleading more than her words. The guard hesitated, shifting uncomfortably on the spot.

"I can't do that," he said, regret lacing his tone, "you've gotta go back to your room after your walk." Her heart sank, a silent nod her only reply. She turned away, resuming her walk, letting the sea's whisper soothe the sting of disappointment. In her head, she rehearsed the questions she would ask Chantelle, the reassurances she would offer, all the while knowing the visit she yearned for remained just another unreachable horizon.

"What's your name?" The wind seemed to carry her words away, swirling them around before bringing them back to her own ears. Her voice was timid and weak, a mere echo of her former self.

"Stone." His tone matched the name, a stoic calm about him which seemed to cement him to the present moment.

"Stone," she repeated, the name rolling off her tongue as though it were a talisman that could grant her a modicum of safety, "is that a first name or a surname?"

"Neither." He said, his voice firm like the resolve in his eyes. Beth sensed a rigidity about him, an unyielding nature reflected in the nickname he bore. All the while he had tried to make small conversation but his tone had remained devoid of any emotion, as if talking to her were more of a chore than a want. She wondered, if talking to her had in fact been a chore, that perhaps Victor had instructed him to try to get close to her in Tim's absence. Probably to extract information she didn't have, potentially to gain her trust and get close to her so he could learn of her secrets and report them back to Victor. Conceivably, it was something she could use to her advantage, playing the player.

"Did Victor instruct you to make conversation with me? Make sure my mind wasn't melting from spending so long in isolation?" She pressed slowly, her jaw set tight and eyes fixed on his stoic gaze.

"Not particularly," he raised his eyebrows and stared back at her before looking out over the water, "but there was some concern you may have become a little—"

"Unhinged?" Beth mused, interrupting him with a coy smile.

"Not exactly the word I'd use," he smiled slightly, the first sign he had displayed of any emotion other than imperturbable contemplation, "but yes, something along those lines." Beth paused, her eyelids fluttering slightly from the brightness she was not yet used to. Pleased with herself that she had slightly seeped through the armour that had thus far encased his demeanour, she tested the waters of his diminishing walls.

"May I?" She gestured towards the ocean with a look of yearning, her heart longing for more than just the confines of her room and the company of guards.

"Fine," Stone conceded after a pause, his gaze fixed on her, "but not too long."

"Thank you." She whispered, her feet carrying her closer to the embrace of the sea. The ocean stretched out before her like a pathway to freedom, each step forward etching a temporary mark upon the wet sand – a fleeting testament to her existence in this place. She ventured deeper, the water cool against the warm sun on her skin. The waves, gentle and rhythmic, almost seemed to beckon her further away from shore. Beth had finally concluded that she must have been in that room for almost a month, now that the summer sun was in its full force.

"Stop right there." Stone commanded, a note of caution edging into his voice. Beth halted, turning back to face him with a half-smile that didn't quite reach her eyes.

"What am I gonna do? Swim to the other side?" She asked, the jest hollow but her spirit rebellious against the invisible chains that held her captive.

"Very funny," Stone replied dryly, but there was a begrudging admittance in his stance that allowed her this small reprieve, "just don't make me come in after you." She nodded, lowering herself until the water kissed her neck, enveloping her in its salty caress. For a moment, she felt weightless, untethered from the anguish that had become her constant companion. Here, in the ocean's vast cradle, she could almost imagine a world untouched by torment, a breath of life amidst the suffocating grip of her captivity.

Stone watched her closely, a sentinel between her and the unfathomable depths that whispered of escape. But even he couldn't keep the water from casting its soothing spell over her troubled soul, if only for a fleeting moment. Beth closed her eyes and let the soft swells of the ocean rock her. The water muffled the world, and for a moment she could pretend. The memory bloomed before her - sunlight dappling the surface of a mountain lake, the air crisp with the scent of pine and earth. She felt Ben's hands again, gentle yet strong around her waist, pulling her close in the tepid embrace of the water. His body was a solid presence against hers, a promise whispered without words. The memory was so vivid, she could almost feel the brush of his lips on her forehead, a tender gesture that had anchored her to a time when they seemed invincible, when the future was something to be met with smiles and linked hands, not tear-streaked faces and clenched fists. The recollection stirred a longing so acute it clawed at her chest, demanding release. A sob broke from Beth, surfacing from a well of grief she'd kept sealed beneath layers of anger and defiance. Tears mingled with the saltwater as she allowed herself to weep openly, the ocean a silent confidant to her sorrow. There was a purity in this sadness, a cleansing sorrow that stripped away the facade she'd built to survive. She submerged then, letting the water envelop her entirely. Her hair fanned out around her, caressed by the sea's unseen fingers. For a heartbeat, she imagined dissolving into the depths, becoming one with the rhythm of the waves, untouchable by any hand that sought to harm. Resurfacing, Beth tasted the brine on her lips and did not wipe her eyes, letting the sting remind her that some part of her remained undulled by pain, capable of feeling something as simple and human as sorrow. It was a small rebellion - to cry, to mourn, to remember love in a place that had tried to strip her of hope. But in that moment, as she faced the indifferent expanse of the sea, Beth claimed it as her own. Salt clung to her skin, the grains of sand adhered to her wet calves as Beth trudged alongside Stone, leaving a trail of damp footprints on the bleached concrete leading away from the shore. The sea's whispers faded into the background, replaced by the hollow echo of their steps. Stone paused at the weather-beaten door that marked the threshold between the open beach and the oppressive confinement of the hotel.

"Wait here," Stone instructed, his voice devoid of emotion, "I'll get you a towel." Numbly, she nodded, her thoughts still adrift in the memories that the ocean had momentarily revived. As Stone disappeared inside, the briny breeze tugged at her sodden hair, offering an illusion of freedom that mocked her with each gust.

"Looking like a wet dog won't help your cause." Sabrina's sneer cut through the solitude, her voice dripping with disdain as she surveyed Beth's soaked form. Beth turned slowly to face her, the remnants of her earlier vulnerability hardening into a sharp retort. "I'd take being a wet dog over a cold bitch any day." Beth smirked, her callous disdain something neither of them had seen for a while. Sabrina cocked an eyebrow, her lips twisting into a smirk that didn't quite reach the chill in her eyes.

"Welcome back, Beth," Sabrina laughed slightly, her tone was laced with malice but her eyes were filled with something else, "I thought your month in solitude had broken you." Beth took a moment to analyse Sabrina's expression, trying to decipher what it meant. It wasn't her typical intimidating or sarcastic look. Instead, there was surprise and a hint of fear creeping onto Sabrina's face. Beth could feel herself starting to come back to life, and it seemed like Sabrina's plan to isolate her hadn't completely broken her after all.

"Victor's affections are as fleeting as his temper," Beth scoffed, a bitter laugh breaking free, "and now Chantelle's pregnant too. You're not so special anymore." She let the words hang between them, a challenge and a revelation all at once. The air grew heavy, laden with unspoken threats and the weight of secrets untold. Sabrina's expression flickered, a momentary lapse that betrayed her cool facade before she regained control, her gaze narrowing on Beth.

"Chantelle, huh," Sabrina's voice was a low purr, tinged with dark amusement, "something tells me she won't be a problem." The promise of menace in her words left a chill that even the warm island sun couldn't dispel - something in her voice was confident and laced with happiness, and it made her uneasy. Beth wrapped her arms around herself, fighting off the sudden cold as she waited for Stone to return.

"You're not worried," Beth threatened callously, "because you should be." Sabrina's laughter sliced through the humid air, a sound devoid of genuine mirth. She caressed her abdomen with an exaggerated tenderness that did not reach her eyes. Those eyes, cold and calculating, now held a glint of something else - something dark and troubling.

"Worried? Oh, Beth," she drawled, her voice silky and scornful, "I've got nothing to worry about."

"Meaning what, exactly?" Beth pressed, frowning at the ominous tone lacing Sabrina's words. A slow, chilling smile crept across Sabrina's face.

"You'll find out soon enough." She said, leaving those words to hang ominously in the air as she turned on her heel and strode away, her steps measured and cold. Beth's thoughts churned with unease, but she had little time to ponder Sabrina's cryptic message. Stone was approaching, his expression stern as he handed her a rough towel.

"Thank you," Beth murmured, though her mind was elsewhere, wrapped around the well-being of another, "Stone, I need to see Chantelle, *now*." She said urgently, the towel forgotten in her hands. Stone's face was impassive, like a mask carved from granite.

"That's not going to happen." He replied flatly.

"Please," Beth implored, desperation sharpening her voice, "let me see her. You can come with me. I just, I really need to check on her." He regarded her for a moment, his stance unyielding.

"Victor's orders are clear. You're not to wander the grounds without supervision, especially not to visit Chantelle."

"Then supervise me," Beth countered swiftly, locking eyes with him, "escort me there. I have to know she's okay." Stone hesitated, his gaze searching Beth's face as if weighing the sincerity of her plea against his own orders. After a tense silence, he gave a curt nod.

"Alright," he conceded begrudgingly, "but I'm with you every step of the way."

"Thank you." Beth breathed, relief mingling with the knot of apprehension in her stomach. Together, they made their way back through the hotel's opulent yet oppressive corridors, each step taking Beth closer to Chantelle. Beth wrapped the towel around her shoulders, the gesture mechanical, her mind racing ahead to Chantelle. She moved quickly, urged on by a gnawing dread, while Stone's grip on her arm was unyielding - a human shackle ensuring she stayed the path he allowed. They reached the door to Chantelle's room, and Beth felt her heart hammer against her ribcage.

"Wait." She whispered, halting Stone's hand mid-motion.

"What now?" His eyes narrowed, irritation etched into the lines of his weathered face.

"Something's not right," Beth said, her voice barely above a breath, trying to still the tremor in it while her instincts screamed, a visceral alarm that clawed at her insides, "I need a moment." Stone's jaw clenched, his impatience a palpable force, yet he held back, granting her the briefest respite. Beth closed her eyes, bracing herself, seeking an inner bastion of strength for whatever lay beyond the threshold. With a grunt of frustration, Stone turned the handle and pushed open the door. The sight that greeted them halted Beth's breath - a silent tableau macabre and surreal. Chantelle dangled lifelessly from the ceiling fan, her body a pale spectre of the vibrant soul she once was. Her eyes, wide and vacant, fixed on a point in eternity only she could see. The gentle sway of her suspended form seemed almost serene, a cruel contrast to the violence of her end, driven by the capricious whim of the coastal breeze that meandered through the open window. Beth's heart splintered, shards of grief piercing her with cold precision. Chantelle was lost to a world that had already taken too much. Stone's silhouette vanished into the corridor, his footsteps echoing a frantic rhythm that matched Beth's racing heart. She edged into the room, her feet betraying her with their slow, unwilling advance. The air felt dense, charged with an unspeakable truth that clung to her skin like a second, suffocating layer. As she moved closer to Chantelle, her gaze transfixed on the horrifying stillness of her friend, Beth's thoughts tangled into a silent scream of denial. Each beat of her heart was a deafening drum in her ears, threatening to drown out the distant clamour of guards scrambling up the staircase. A flutter at the edge of her vision drew her attention to the table where a solitary sheet of paper lay - Chantelle's final words, perhaps a confession or a plea. With trembling hands, Beth reached out, the note cold and accusing under her touch. She folded it with a reverence born of despair and tucked it close against her, a secret now shared between them.

The world outside the room erupted into chaos as the guards burst through the door, but Beth remained anchored in place, a lonely figure shrouded in the aftermath of tragedy. She watched them, detached, as they worked to lower Chantelle's body, her friend's ethereal dance with the wind coming to an abrupt end.

CHAPTER 4

Beth's hand pressed against the cool glass of the window pane as she peered out at the horizon where the sun dipped low, its fiery trail smudging the sky with embers of orange and red. It seemed impossible that almost two months had whittled away within these four walls, yet the late summer glow, with its warm hues melting into dusk, whispered the undeniable truth. She exhaled softly, her breath fogging a tiny circle on the glass before it dissipated, much like the memories she tried to hold onto. Her mind wandered to the previous summer on Alcatraz, the salt-tinged air, the desperation they felt and the torture they had endured, and then even further back to the summer in Australia where she had exchanged vows, the laughter and promises still rang clear, despite the tyranny of time and distance. But home was a siren's call Beth refused to heed. With a mental shove, she pushed thoughts of her husband and her family to the shadowy corners of her mind where she wouldn't have to face their worried faces or the weight of their unanswered questions. The ocean before her absorbed the dying light, transforming from a vibrant turquoise to the dark, impenetrable blue-black of night - a void that called to Beth with an eerie, seductive promise of oblivion. The glass remained cold under her fingertips, a barrier between her and the vast, darkening sea. She longed for it to consume her, to wash away the days of captivity and uncertainty, leaving behind nothing but the purity of endless depths. Yet, as the last sliver of sun vanished, leaving the world to twilight, Beth knew the abyss also held secrets far more chilling than the ones she sought to escape. The sudden rap at the door shattered the calm of twilight like a stone through glass, and Beth jolted from her reverie. With a soft creak, the door swung inward, revealing Jennifer, whose presence felt like a ripple in the stagnant air of confinement. She carried a tray heavy with the scent of roasted meat and vegetables - a stark contrast to the sterile atmosphere of the room.

"Mind if I join you?" Jennifer's voice carried an unspoken plea for unfamiliar companionship that Beth heard loud and clear.

"Sure." Beth murmured, motioning towards the small table set against the wall. As Jennifer entered, she gave a curt nod to the guard who lingered at the threshold until he retreated with a clink of keys and a thud of the closing door. Jennifer set down the tray, the clatter of ceramic on wood slicing through the silence. She took a seat opposite Beth, her eyes reflecting a tumult of emotions.

"I'm sorry about Chantelle," she began, her voice barely above a whisper, "I really did like her." Beth pressed her lips together, feeling a pang in her chest.

"I keep thinking there's something more I could've done." She confessed, her voice strained with regret.

"Chantelle was off, after she found out she was pregnant," Jennifer continued, her gaze drifting away, "I should've seen it too."

"Seen what?" Beth asked, a flicker of anger igniting within her.

"Her despair, her fear," Jennifer shook her head, a strand of hair falling across her face, "I see it in myself every day. I should've been able to recognise it in someone else."

"Speaking of not right," Beth stabbed a piece of meat with more force than necessary, attempting to hastily change the subject, "Sabrina is parading around here like she's won some twisted prize."

"She's been unbearable," Jennifer's expression soured, "more smug than usual."

"Let her come to me with that smugness," Beth warned, her voice low and dangerous, "just one word about Chantelle and I swear, I'll lose it." They shared a look, an understanding that transcended words - a silent vow that they would not let Sabrina's callousness go unchecked. The room felt smaller suddenly, filled with the weight of their shared grief. The clink of utensils against plates and the soft murmur of their voices created a bubble of intimacy in Beth's otherwise cold and austere room. They spoke of Chantelle with tender reverence, each memory surfacing like a cherished photograph fading at the edges. It was as if speaking her name could somehow bridge the gap between this world and the next, keeping her spirit alive just a little while longer.

"She was always kind," Jennifer said, the hint of a smile gracing her lips despite the sorrow in her eyes, "sometimes she was snappy, but that was understandable given the situation. But she was always just kind."

"Yes," Beth nodded, her own smile fragile, "when they found me, I remember—" A sudden shout from outside cut through their reminiscences, bringing them back to the grim reality of their confinement. Jennifer cocked her head, trying to listen.

"Probably just the guards being idiots again." She finally dismissed, but her voice lacked conviction. Before Beth could reply, a series of sharp cracks ripped through the air - a staccato punctuation that brought an immediate tension to the room. The unmistakable sound of gunfire echoed from the other side of the hotel. Both women froze, the resonance of their shared laughter now replaced by the pounding of their hearts. Abruptly standing, Jennifer's chair scraped against the hardwood floor. The table shook under her sudden movement, dishes clattered, and their evening meal tumbled into disarray. A bowl of thick soup overturned, its contents splashing across the white linen like dark blood. Beth reached out, her hands latching onto Jennifer's trembling arms. Adrenaline surged through her veins, fear and survival instincts meshing together in a sharp rush. Without needing to speak, they both understood the gravity of the situation - their private sanctuary had been shattered.

"Come on." Beth's voice was calm but carried an undercurrent of urgency as she tugged Jennifer away from the exposed doorway. She guided them both around the side of the wall, pressing their backs against the cool surface. Here, they were hidden from immediate view should anyone burst in.

What's going on?" Jennifer's voice was hushed, her tone a mix of confusion and fear.

"Stay down." Beth whispered, her eyes locked on the door, expecting it to fly open at any moment. Jennifer nodded, her breathing shallow, her gaze mirroring Beth's own mix of terror and determination. They listened to the chaos unfolding beyond their walls, the intermittent gunfire telling a story neither of them wanted to read to the end. Their dinner lay forgotten on the floor, the room a testament to how quickly life could turn from mundane to mayhem. But there, against the wall, they found a semblance of safety in the closeness of one another, ready for whatever came next. Jennifer's question pierced the tense air.

"Do you think it could be your friends?" Her eyes searched Beth's face for some semblance of hope, a lifeline amid the tempest that had engulfed their lives. Beth's jaw set with resolve, her mind whirling with possibilities and the slimmest chance of salvation.

"I'm not just gonna sit here and find out." She stated flatly, the edge in her voice cutting through Jennifer's apprehension.

"Wait—" Jennifer's plea was cut short as Beth sprang into action, her feet carrying her across the room with a determination born of desperation. The door swung open with a force that echoed down the empty hallway as Beth emerged, her strides long and rapid. The thick carpet muffled the sounds of her urgency as she barrelled towards the staircase. Every instinct screamed at her to move faster, to escape the confines of the room that had been both her prison and her sanctuary. Reaching the foyer, she burst forth from the shadows of the corridor, expecting to see the source of the commotion. But there was nothing. Only the ghostly echoes of gunfire betraying chaos somewhere in the darkened expanse outside. Then, with a suddenness that stole the breath from her lungs, the main doors flew open. A solitary guard stood silhouetted against the fading light, his eyes locking onto Beth with a fury that seemed to eclipse the world itself.

"You!" He bellowed, voice brimming with accusation and something darker, more personal. He charged towards her, boots thudding ominously against the polished floor, his intent clear. Before she could react, his hand clamped around her arm with vice-like strength, pulling her along in his wake. Confusion and fear collided within her, urging her to resist, but the iron grip forced her compliance. They ascended the stairs, each step an eternity, as he hauled her relentlessly through the labyrinthine halls. She caught glimpses of familiar doorways, darkened alcoves, all blurring together in a nightmarish procession towards a destination she dared not consider. But fate, or perhaps fortune, intervened. Stone materialised before them, his presence commanding and immovable.

The guard halted abruptly, his momentum broken, his captive released as if by some unspoken command. Stone's eyes met Beth's for a fleeting second, long enough for a silent exchange fraught with questions and the barest flicker of hope. Stone's reaction was swift, the edge of his hand striking with precision at the guard's neck. The man crumpled to the ground in an unceremonious heap, his grip on Beth instantly gone as he succumbed to unconsciousness. Beth stumbled back, her heart pounding in her chest, her eyes wide with shock and gratitude.

"Come on." Stone urged, his voice a harsh whisper as he reached for her arm. But their fleeting moment of respite shattered like glass as a door flew open along the corridor. Victor emerged from the shadows of his room, his face twisted in rage. In one fluid motion, he raised his gun and fired. The sound of the shot echoed through the hallway, a harbinger of dread. Stone grunted, his body jolting forward from the impact, and then he was falling, hitting the floor with a thud that seemed to reverberate through Beth's very bones.

"Stone!" Beth screamed, her voice tearing from her throat as she dropped to her knees beside him. His eyes met hers, filled with an unspeakable pain, and then they glazed over, his breaths coming in short, ragged gasps.

"Move and you're next." Victor snarled, stepping forward, his gun trained on Beth. His eyes were cold, devoid of any humanity as he loomed over her, the barrel of the weapon promising death with its silent, black mouth. Beth could feel the weight of his gaze, the inevitability of her fate hanging between them. Time slowed, each heartbeat a thunderous drum in her ears. Suddenly, the radio at Victor's hip crackled to life, a voice urgently calling out for him.

"Victor, respond! We have a—" It was the distraction she'd been praying for. Her instincts screamed at her to move, to flee the dark

promise in Victor's eyes. As he glanced down at his radio, she darted back around the corner. The heavy footsteps of Victor pursuing her were almost drowned out by the cacophony of her own frantic pulse. She raced down the other hallway, the carpet muffling her steps. Behind her, Victor cursed, his shots ringing out and hitting the walls, leaving pockmarks in the plaster. The dim light filtered through arbitrary windows, casting strange shadows that danced just as frantically as Beth herself. The stairwell loomed ahead - a beacon of hope, a gateway to potential freedom. Beth took the stairs two at a time, her breaths coming in sharp bursts. The metallic scent of gunfire and fear lingered in the air, mingling with the musty odour of old wood and disuse. As she descended, the sounds of Victor's pursuit grew fainter, his impaired vision and the inadequate lighting hindering his aim. She glanced over her shoulder, seeing only the ghostly outline of his figure at the top of the staircase, his gun still spitting fire into the void between them. Every sinew in her body protested the pace, but she didn't dare slow down. Not when freedom was within reach, not when survival hung on the speed of her feet and the will driving her forward. Beth's feet skidded across the polished floorboards as she threw herself into the nearest bedroom, her heart racing with exertion and fear. The door closed with a soft click, far too quiet not to mask her entrance. She heard Victor halt at the distant end of the corridor, his footsteps imposing even from afar. As he stood in the hallway, his head turned sharply from side to side, predatory eyes scanning for any sign of her.

"I know you're here," Victor's voice boomed, bouncing off the walls with chilling authority, "you couldn't have made it far, Beth!" His heavy boots thudded against the plush carpet as he moved from one room to the next. Each kick against a door was like a thunderclap, announcing his violent search. The rooms were violated one by one, the brief silence between each intrusion filled only by Beth's shallow breathing.

"Just stay calm," she told herself, whispering into the void, "breathe." Inside the sanctuary of her temporary hideout, Beth crept towards the window, her fingers trembling as they worked the latch. It didn't budge. Panic clawed at her throat, and she forced it down with a silent curse. Her gaze swept the room, hunting for an impromptu tool or a means of escape. In the corner, the ornate handle of a hairbrush glinted in the moonlight filtering through the curtains. She snatched it up, weighing it in her hand. She wondered if she could shatter the glass without alerting him. A heavy footfall sounded outside her door, and her decision was made for her.

"Come on, you coward!" Victor's taunt slithered through the woodwork, igniting a spark of defiance within her. Gripping the brush like a lifeline, Beth backed away from the window, resolute that the glass would remain whole. She wouldn't give herself away, not now when every second mattered. Her breath hitched as another door down the hallway caved under Victor's onslaught. Beth's muscles tensed, ready to react, the hairbrush held aloft. She would not go down without a fight - she could not afford to be Victor's victim any longer. Her survival instincts blazed, fuelling her resolve as she prepared to confront the menace that was sure to come through her door next. The sudden boom of the door across from her shattering under a vicious kick sent shockwaves through Beth's frame, her heart thundering in response. She whirled towards the sound, the primal fear of being cornered flashing bright and urgent. But as Victor's grunts and curses filtered through the splintered wood, a fierce determination overrode her panic. Beth's eyes locked onto a heavy-duty torch resting innocuously on a nearby table, the metallic surface promising more than illumination. With swift, purposeful strides, she seized it, its weight reassuring in her grip. She positioned herself next to the bedroom door, her back to the wall, gripping the torch like a baton, ready to strike. Her plan shifted - no longer was escaping through the window her priority, but confrontation. She would wait for him as he tumbled through the door and then she'd unleash the full force of her bottled fury. She was determined to fulfil her promise to him, breaking and cracking his skull with all of her force, or dying in the process. Her breath stilled, muscles coiled tight as she heard another door buckle and crash down the corridor. Victor was close, too close, and his shadow loomed large against the fractured light slicing into the hallway. "Come and fucking get me." Beth braced, every nerve ending alight with adrenaline as she whispered, her voice cracking as she shook uncontrollably.

"Where are you, Beth?" Victor's voice slithered under the door, oily and menacing. She tightened her hold on the torch, a silent promise that he'd regret finding her. But before fate could bring Victor through her doorway, an eruption of chaos shattered the building's deceptive calm. Gunfire resounded like a violent storm, concussive and relentless. Shouts fragmented the air, sending guards scrambling past her door, their footsteps a frenzied tattoo on the hardwood floor.

"Victor! Move your ass!" The urgency laced in the guard's voice was unmistakable. A new threat had entered the fray, shifting the balance.

"Damn it, Beth!" Victor's roar echoed down the hall, the name torn from his throat in a mix of frustration and fury. His footfalls receded rapidly, the thud of his boots mingling with the clamour of conflict. Beth edged closer to the door, her fingers twitching around the torch's handle. Silence crept in, a haunting void following the cacophony. She peered through the crack where the door met the frame, her pulse thrumming in her ears. The coast was clear - the guards and their leader were ghosts in the dark. She took a fraction of a second to gather herself before bursting from the room, feet pounding against the floor, propelling her towards the staircase. The previous terror morphed into a rush of survival instinct as she navigated the deserted hall, each turn bringing her closer to an uncertain fate lying in wait below. Beth's heart hammered against her ribcage as she descended the staircase with caution, each step an echo in the tense silence. The air was thick with the scent of gunpowder and fear, a stark contrast to the once opulent atmosphere of the hotel. Shadows danced along the walls, playing tricks on her vision. A gun barrel slammed into her line of sight, halting her mid-step. Instinctively, her hands shot up, a silent testament to her surrender. Her breath hitched in her throat, eyes locked onto the cold metal that promised oblivion. Her gasps for air quickened as she fought to replenish her lungs after the exhausting run through the hallways. Her health and endurance had been severely weakened after a year of constant torture and malnourishment. The only sounds in the air were her ragged breaths and the occasional gunfire from outside.

"Not her," grunted a man clad in tactical gear, his voice rough like gravel, "we're not here for them." The soldiers, their faces obscured by masks of anonymity, brushed past her without a second glance. Their boots thudded heavily, a deadly rhythm as they continued their pursuit. Beth's arms trembled as she lowered them, grateful yet unnerved by the recognition that she wasn't their target. She pressed herself against the wall, allowing the soldiers to pass, their mission singular, yet unclear.

The sound of splintering wood reverberated through the lower levels as Chase made his entrance. The back dining room, which had been converted into the guards dining area, now bore the scars of forced entry. He stormed through, his presence commanding and purposeful.

"Clear the bottom floor!" He barked orders to his men, who dispersed with military precision. His gaze swept the room with practiced vigilance before he advanced towards the kitchen. There, amidst stainless steel and the lingering aroma of cooked meals, cowered Sabrina. Her once-impeccable appearance was marred by fear, her eyes wide and reflecting the chaos that had usurped her world.

"Come on." Chase said firmly, reaching out to grasp her arms and pull her to her feet. Despite the situation's gravity, there was a gentleness in his touch, a reminder that he was there to protect, not harm.

"Please don't hurt me." She whispered, her voice low and soft.

"Remember me?" He asked, peering into her face, searching for recognition. His eyes scanned down to her swollen abdomen as Sabrina nodded, her movements slow and deliberate. Innocence played across her features, a mask worn so often it had become second nature. But the facade didn't sway Chase, experience had taught him the art of discernment.

"We," Sabrina stumbled slightly, pretending to be exhausted and traumatised, "we didn't think you'd come."

"Let's get you out of here," he said, ushering her out of the kitchen, away from the danger that had infiltrated the very walls of what had become her prison, "where are the other girls?" Chase's eyes narrowed as he fixed Sabrina with a scrutinising gaze, his voice low and urgent. The dim lighting of the corridor cast ominous shadows across her face, but she managed to maintain her composure under his intense scrutiny.

"In their rooms, maybe," Sabrina murmured, her voice barely above a whisper, "or elsewhere, depending on which bed they find themselves in." Her words trailed off, her eyes darting nervously as if expecting another threat to materialise from the shadows. Chase opened his mouth to press further - to ask about Chantelle, to ask about Beth - but the sudden eruption of gunfire from the bottom floor cut him off. Instinctively, he reached out, his hand closing around Sabrina's arm with a firm grip, propelling her forward.

"We need to move, now!" They dashed through the maze of corridors, the cacophony of chaos echoing behind them. Chase could feel the reverberations of each shot in his chest as he guided Sabrina towards the relative safety of the outdoors, where the boats bobbed quietly on the water, awaiting their return.

On the second floor of the hotel, Reece was a whirlwind of action as his boots thudded heavily against the carpet while he barrelled down the hallway, his team flanking him. They met resistance - a line of guards with fear etched into their faces, but Reece was relentless. With a flurry of tactical manoeuvres, he sent the opposition scrambling backward, his men efficiently pushing the guards back as they fired down the corridor.

"Check every room," Reece commanded, his voice carrying over the din of retreat, "stay sharp. We don't know who or what we'll find." He paused by a door, its wood grain pattern stark against the sterile walls, listening for a moment before moving on. His men nodded, their movements a symphony of disciplined searches as doors were thrown open and rooms were quickly cleared. Reece pushed forward, determined, his mind racing with the possibilities of who they might encounter next in this labyrinthine hotel turned war zone. His stride was a rhythmic thunder, each footfall punctuating the tension that hung thick in the air. The second floor had become a maelstrom of desperation and violence, guards and intruders clashing with an intensity that made every second critical.

"Sir, someone's here!" One of the men yelled out with urgency. He veered towards the voice, his path a calculated weave through the dark hallway. The door to the room was ajar, and inside the bathroom bled into the dimness, painting a stark contrast between sanctuary and battlefield.

"Clear." One of his men called out, stepping aside as Reece entered. In the small space of the bathroom, Jennifer cowered against the cold tile, her arms wrapped around her knees. Her eyes, wide with a mix of fear and recognition, met Reece's with an almost palpable relief.

"Jennifer," Reece kept his tone level despite the adrenaline that coursed through him, "are you okay?" She nodded, her response a silent flutter of movement, like a bird trapped against a window pane.

"I remember you, from—"

"Are the others here?" He crouched down, bringing himself to her eye level, the professional mask he wore as a shield showing a hairline fracture of personal concern.

"I don't know," she whispered, as if the words were a lifeline thrown between them, "Beth was here with me, but she ran off into the hall when the gunfire started."

"And Chantelle?" His voice softened with the inquiry, but the tightening of his jaw betrayed his anticipation of bad news. Jennifer's gaze dropped, and her silence filled the room with a sorrow that needed no words. She shook her head slowly, confirming what Reece had feared but hoped not to hear.

"I'm sorry." Jennifer whispered finally, her voice filled with desolation.

"Damn it," Reece's hand went to the back of his neck, squeezing as if he could wring out the sudden weight that had settled there, "do you know where Beth would've gone? Where's her room?"

"This *is* her room," Jennifer's voice broke through his thoughts, "we were having dinner when everything started. She ran off, thinking she might find one of you. If it really was you."

"Of course she did." Reece muttered under his breath, frustration lacing his tone. He straightened up, casting a final glance at the overturned remains of their meal - a mute testament to the abrupt shift from normalcy to chaos. With renewed purpose, he stepped back into the fray, his mind singularly focused on finding Beth amidst the turmoil. Reece exhaled a mix of frustration and concern, the edges of his mouth turning down as he shook his head.

"Did you come for us? Or to kill Victor?" Jennifer queried, her eyes darting between Reece and the open door, worry set upon her brow at the thought of someone coming to kill them at any minute.

"She can't stay put for more than five minutes?" He grumbled as he ignored her line of questioning, unsure if he was more irritated at Beth's recklessness or impressed by her unyielding spirit.

"Reece," Jennifer's voice pulled him from his musing, her arm in his grasp firm but trembling slightly as her eyes held a glimmer of something that might have been admiration or fear, perhaps both, "Beth went outside, towards the gunfire. She's probably on the ground floor by now."

"Outside?" His brows knitted together as he processed this new information, his grip unconsciously tightening before he gently released her. He signalled to one of his team members, a sturdy man with a stern face softened by concern.

"Your orders?" The man stood straight, his rifle pressed firmly to his chest, hands clasped tightly around the firearm.

"Get her to the boats, make sure she's safe." Reece commanded as the man nodded, understanding the gravity of his task, and took Jennifer's arm with a careful respect. Reece watched them for a moment, the protector in him wanting to ensure every civilian's safety, but the soldier in him knew priorities had to be established.

"Reece—" Jennifer's voice trailed off as she was led away, but her expression held a message clearer than words.

"Victor is my priority right now." Reece admitted, though the declaration tasted like ash in his mouth. He didn't have the luxury of yielding to personal quests.

"Reece!" Jennifer's plea rang out like a bell as the guard let go of her arm.

"What?" Reece walked towards the trembling girl, his eyes set with frustration.

"Victor won't be in his room," Jennifer looked between Reece and her escort, "he's been hellbent on finding you for months. If he thinks it's all of you who've come for him, his first instinct will be to kill Beth."

"Why?" Reece pressed.

"Pride, anger, take your pick," Jennifer turned to the door as her escort ushered her away slowly, "Beth's been interrogated repeatedly for information on where you'd gone. He won't let her go easily."
"My objective is to find Victor," Reece nodded, looking out the window, "Chase is here to evacuate civilians. Hopefully she runs into him before anyone else." Jennifer's smile was a fleeting thing, a spark of hope against the backdrop of gunfire and chaos, and then she disappeared down the stairwell with her escort. Reece turned back to his mission, the image of Jennifer's tentative smile etched into his mind as he moved swiftly to carry out his orders.

Beth crouched low, her breaths shallow and controlled behind the weathered half wall. The staccato of boots against concrete sent jolts through her nerves as the guards hastened past, unknowingly missing their quarry by mere feet. Through the clamour, Beth could discern the distant thrum of engines - the boats that brought her potential rescuers were so close she could almost taste the salty promise of freedom. With a surge of resolve, she bolted from her cover, darting towards the chaos erupting on the other side of the once-opulent hotel. Her bare feet slapped the cold ground, each step a rough bite against her skin, but Beth pushed the discomfort away, focusing only on the urgent need to move towards the gunfire, to see if it was who she thought it was, who she thought it *had* to be. But as she raced out onto the gravel road, the world exploded in sound and pain. A shot rang out, impossibly loud, and a searing heat lanced through her arm. Beth stumbled, her momentum grinding to a halt as she clutched at the burning sensation that wrapped her limb. She whirled around, every nerve ending screaming, to see Victor emerging from the shadows like some vengeful spectre, his gun raised and eyes ablaze with fury.

"Stop!" He commanded, his voice cutting through the ringing in her ears. He advanced slowly, deliberately, the weapon an unyielding statement of intent in his trembling hand. Beth stood rooted, her mind racing as she assessed the man before her - Victor, whose ambitions had twisted into something monstrous, whose grip on power was slipping away amidst the crackling gunfire and encroaching forces of retribution. There was no mistaking the desperation etched in the lines of his face, the wild edge to his usual composure now shattered beyond recognition.

"Victor." She said, her voice steady despite the tumult within and without.

"This ends now." He said through gritted teeth, the sharpness of his words pressed against her skin and briefly stole Beth's breath, a momentary distraction from the throbbing in her arm. Her fingers worked quickly, tearing at the hem of her dress sleeve with a desperation born of survival instinct. The fabric gave way, and she wrapped it tightly around the wound, the makeshift bandage soaking through with crimson almost instantly.

"Victor," she gasped out, her eyes lifting to meet his, searching for any sliver of humanity that might have survived his descent into madness, "what do you want? You've lost, let me go." His laugh was devoid of humour, a hollow sound that echoed off the barren road.

"Your friends," he spat the word as if it left a foul taste, "they've destroyed everything!" His arms swept wide, encompassing the chaos that had become his empire in ruin.

"Destroyed what? What are you talking about?" Beth's voice was steady, but inside, her heart hammered against her ribs, each beat a clock ticking down to an unknown end. For a fleeting second, pain flitted across Victor's features, the pain of a man watching his dreams turn to ash.

"A trade," he said, and the word hung heavy in the air between them, "with an evangelical group on the mainland. They wanted to repopulate, start anew. The children—" He trailed off, the implication clear and horrifying in its stark reality. Beth's stomach turned, revolted by the depths of his scheme.

"You can't be serious," she whispered, the gravity of their plight settling upon her like a shroud, "for *what*?"

"For supplies, and manpower," he snarled, shaking his head at the thought of his loss, "how do you think we had so much food recently? We were starving on this island, Beth. The decision was an easy one." Children bartered for supplies, and the promise of power - it was unthinkable. But the truth was there, laid bare in the moonlight that bathed Victor's twisted visage, in the fervent glint of conviction in his eyes. This was the world he had crafted, one where innocence was currency, and Beth knew then that there could be no redemption for a soul so lost. Gritting her teeth against the sting of her wound, Beth took measured steps closer to Victor, her mind racing with disgust and fear.

"And Sabrina," she asked, her voice a low drawl laced with skepticism, "did she know about your twisted trade?" Victor's laughter crackled through the tension like dry ice, cold and unsettling.

"Sabrina," he scoffed, as if the name left a bitter residue on his tongue, "that foolish bitch was merely a pawn in my game. She thought she'd sit by my side, and she gave me her loyalty while her delusions of grandeur fed my plans." He said, his eyes alight with derision. Beth's pulse thrummed in her ears, a rhythm of impending doom. With each step she drew nearer, her free arm raised in a mock surrender that veiled her true intent.

"You're insane," she spat out, the words sharp like shards of glass, "what you've done, you deserve every ounce of retribution that's coming for you." The moonlight glinted off Victor's eyes, revealing a depth of madness and regret.

"My only regret," he growled, the muscle in his jaw twitching with fervour, "is not being there to see your face contorted in agony while I broke each one of your friends before your eyes."

"I guess that means I win," she smiled sourly as the bright moon cast a shadow on her face that made her look as menacing as he did, "you will never get to see me watch them break at your hands." In the shadowed dance of predator and prey, Beth held his gaze, unflinching, the fabric pressed against her bleeding arm now soaked in red. She knew the monster before her revelled in pain, but she would not give him the satisfaction of seeing hers. Her heart beat a silent vow - this man would fall, and she would not be the one to break. The night exploded into a singular, deafening crack that shattered the tense silence. Beth's gaze locked onto Victor, his eyes widening in disbelief as time seemed to slow. A dark red bloom appeared on his forehead, spreading like ink in water. His knees buckled and he fell backwards, a lifeless marionette cut from its strings, hitting the ground with a thud. The gun slipped from his fingers, clattering across the concrete, its metallic echo a grim punctuation. Beth stood frozen, her breath caught in her throat, the acrid smell of gunpowder biting at her senses. Her arm throbbed in time with her racing heart, but it was the sudden stillness of Victor's body, twitching only once in its final protest against death, that held her captive. Then, movement in the periphery - a shadow detached itself from the cloak of darkness, a figure solidifying under the silver wash of moonlight. Beth's eyes darted towards the source of salvation, the silhouette becoming clearer, more defined. The gun in his hand lowered, his posture relaxed from the poise of an executioner to one of concern. He stepped forward, each footfall a deliberate echo in the quiet aftermath. His face, usually a mask of stoic resolve, softened as the moonlight played upon his features, revealing a mix of relief and urgency. As he approached, she saw the familiar determination set in his jaw, the same unspoken promise that had been their anchor in countless moments of despair. Beth felt a surge of something beyond pain or fear - it was hope, reignited by the sight of him, her steadfast ally in this chaos. Despite the burning in her arm and the gravity of all that had transpired, she felt an inexplicable calm settle over her, as if his mere presence could mend more than just the wounds of battle.

"Beth." The figure took another step towards her, as she smiled at his familiar, reassuring face, whispering into the evening summer air.

"Austin."

CHAPTER 5

The first whispers of dawn crept over the horizon as the boat's engine hummed to life, slicing through the still waters between Catalina Island and the mainland. The crisp ocean air was laced with a metallic tang, a lingering reminder of the night's bloody work. Military precision had turned chaos into eerie calm - guards lay motionless in grotesque repose as the hotel, once a gilded cage, sat hollowed out by violence. Reece towered among the huddle of rescued women, his gaze vigilant, sweeping from face to face. His duty was clear – protect Beth, Jennifer, and Sabrina, along with the others they'd pulled from the brink of hell. Austin and Chase were a heartbeat away, yet worlds apart, scouring the island for secrets left behind by their enemies.

"You sure you've taken everything you need? We won't be coming back after this." Reece's voice cut through the silence, his eyes settling on Beth.

"I don't have anything to take," Beth replied, her voice a rasping whisper that belied the steel within, "these clothes aren't even mine." Her fingers curled inside her jacket pocket, clasping the scrap of paper that bore Chantelle's last words like a talisman against the future. Beside her, Sabrina's sobs sliced through the pre-dawn stillness, raw and unrestrained. A soldier nearby attempted consolation, his words clumsy but well-intentioned.

"Don't worry, you're safe now." He said quietly. Beth turned her head, casting a glance as sharp as shattered glass towards Sabrina. "She's not weeping for joy or relief," she said, her tone devoid of warmth, "she's mourning everything that can't be reclaimed." The man fell silent, and the mournful serenade of Sabrina's grief became the sole score to their shared journey. Each woman sat encapsulated in their own cocoon of thoughts, the unspeakable weight of loss and liberation bearing down upon them. The boat cleaved through the water, carrying them forward into an uncertain dawn. Behind them, the island shrank, taking with it a chapter of horrors best left adrift in the churning sea. The chill of the morning air bit into Beth's skin as her shoes hit the solid ground of the Long Beach Shoreline Marina. The journey's end brought no comfort, only a shift in her captivity from one form to another. Reece's steady hand guided her away from the throng of survivors and towards an army medic who waited with an expression that managed to be both severe and indifferent.

"Let me see that." The medic muttered, barely looking up at Beth as she extended her injured arm. With deft movements, he wrapped it tightly as the gauze pressed into her flesh. As soon as he was done, he moved on without a word, his attention already snatched away by another wounded soul.

"Back there, on the boat. What did you mean about Sabrina?" Reece's voice was low, just for her, his eyes searching hers for truths unsaid. Beth leaned in closer, the urgency clear in her hushed tone. "Sabrina was Victor's favourite, and she was determined to run the world with him," her gaze flickered with the effort of dredging up painful memories, "she's upset because she's no longer in charge."

"Noted. Anything else?" Reece's jaw tightened, the lines of his face hardening.

"Val," Beth's voice cracked like dry earth begging for rain, "is she safe?"

"Safe as any of us can be these days. She's back in town at Fort Irwin." Reece replied, his affirmation doing little to ease the tightness in her chest.

"Reece," there was a plea in Beth's voice, a need to be the bearer of her own heartache, "can I be the one to tell her about Chantelle?" Reece's eyes softened, the soldier in him receding for a fleeting moment.

"It should be you, but it's not my call to make," he clapped a hand on her shoulder, a brief anchor in the storm of change they found themselves adrift in, "come on, let's get you moving." Beth's gaze lingered on the horizon where Catalina Island was now just a shadow beneath the rising sun. She turned back to Reece, her eyes tracing the lines of his uniform before she spoke.

"Austin," her voice barely above a whisper, "is he in charge?"

"Nope," Reece's lips quirked into an amused smile as he shook his head, scratching at the stubble on his chin, "we've got a whole operation at Fort Irwin. Austin's a Major now. And Chase climbed up to Captain alongside me." A sense of relief mixed with curiosity washed over Beth. The chain of command had shifted, but life, it seemed, had carried on without her.

"And Ben," her voice faltered slightly, the name stirring a blend of hope and anxiety within her, "is he—"

"Ben's been up north," Reece cut in, his tone even, eyes tracking the activity around them, "his unit's been clearing out Alcatraz. They should be rolling back any day now." Beth nodded, the information sinking in like stones in water. She cast her eyes towards the bustle of soldiers and rescued civilians disembarking from other boats. Each face told a story of survival and loss. But none were

Ben's, and for now, that had to be enough. The marina was a symphony of chaos and order as the military conducted their precise ballet of rescue and recovery. Amidst the orchestrated movements, Beth's attention snagged on a solitary figure being eased onto a stretcher - Stone. Without thought, she dashed through the crowd, her feet pounding against the concrete until she reached his side. She grabbed his hand, the roughness of his skin a stark contrast to the sterile gloves of the medic attending to him. Stone's eyes flickered open, a glimmer of recognition passing between them before he was hoisted into the back of a waiting military truck.

"Do you know him?" Reece's question pulled her momentarily from her concern.

"Not really," she said softly, watching as the truck's doors closed, cocooning Stone in its metal embrace, "but Stone, he tried to help me." A shudder of uncertainty passed through her, the weight of countless untold stories pressing on her chest. She turned to Reece, the morning light casting his features in sharp relief.

"It seems we'll need some time to figure out who was helping Victor because they wanted to, and who was helping just to survive." Reece gazed out at the still water, then turned to observe the group of guards now seated and under arrest on the benches behind him.

"Stone took a bullet for me," Beth examined Reece closely, then observed as the truck drove off with her rescuer safely inside, "I'll vouch for him."

"You'll all most likely be questioned." Reece turned to walk along the marina with Beth in tow a few steps behind him.

"Is Tim alive?" Her words tumbled out, laced with hope and fear.

"Yeah, he is," Reece met her gaze squarely, nodding once, "gave us the intel we needed." Beth raised a curious eyebrow.

"Intel?"

"Major General at Fort Irwin had Marcus on his radar since before we were all taken. We knew about a new group stirring trouble on Catalina recently, but we had no idea," his voice trailed off, the revelation still fresh, "it was Tim who confirmed it was Victor, and that you and Chantelle were there." Beth's heart raced, piecing together the puzzle that had been their captivity and rescue. Relief at Tim's survival warred with the bitterness of betrayal and the sour taste of what-ifs.

"Thank you." She whispered, though whether to Reece or to the fates that had aligned to bring them this far, she wasn't quite sure. Beth's fingers curled into fists at her sides, her nails digging into her palms as she searched Reece's face for any hint of further information.

"There has to be more." She demanded, her voice low and insistent. "Beth, I've probably told you too much already," Reece's gaze remained steady, but his lips pressed into a thin line, "you're a civilian. It's better if you don't know the full scope of military intel." His words were measured, his posture rigid with the discipline of his role.

"Since when did you start following the rules?" Beth shot back, her frustration seeping through. The man before her seemed like a stranger compared to the Reece she remembered - the one who would bend the rules, who wore his heart on his sleeve. The one who randomly spoke Korean and slept on a sleeping bag under the stars.

"Things are different now, Beth," Reece's voice held a note of finality, "you know that as well as I do." Before she could argue, a soldier beckoned her towards an idling truck where several other women had already taken their seats. She climbed aboard, the metal beneath her shoes cold and unforgiving. Inside the truck, the air was thick with a mixture of fear, relief, and the faint scent of diesel. Beth found a spot on the bench and settled in, pulling her jacket tighter around her.

"Where are you taking us?" In the back, a woman shivered and huddled under a blanket, trying to keep warm.

"Fort Irwin," the soldier responded in a dry tone, before quickly checking himself and relaxing his posture, "you'll be safe there."

"Listen to me," Reece said, stepping up to the truck's open back as his eyes locked onto Beth's, a silent promise flickering within their depths, "I have to go back to the island, but you're in safe hands here. I promise." He gestured to the soldiers around them, a crew of stoic faces and watchful eyes.

"Sure." She replied, though the word emerged as barely a whisper. Reece offered her a brief nod, a shadow of a smile tugging at the corner of his mouth before he turned away, his figure retreating into the growing light of dawn. As the truck rumbled to life and began to move, Beth leaned back against the cool metal wall. She closed her eyes, feeling the vibration of the engine through her bones, and tried to imagine what *safe* might mean in a world where everything familiar had been stripped away.

The air within the medical tent was suffocating, a stark contrast to the cool breeze that occasionally lifted the flap at the entrance. Beth's legs swung lightly, her bare feet tapping against the metal frame of the cot that served as her temporary sanctuary. Dust danced in the shafts of light piercing through the canvas walls, and the murmurs of the base outside filtered in, a reminder of the world that continued to turn. A woman entered, her white coat crisp, her short black hair falling neatly onto her shoulders hovering slightly over her stethoscope. She carried the air of someone who had seen enough trauma to last several lifetimes but still held onto the hope that came with healing.

"Hi there," she began, her voice a soft balm in the harsh reality of the military encampment, "I'm Doctor Major, but you can call me Anne." There was an edge of weariness to her smile, the kind that came from hours of tending to the wounded.

"Hi." Beth nodded, her throat tight, unable to muster the strength for pleasantries. Anne seemed to understand, her apology for the delay coming with a sincerity that reached beyond professional courtesy.

"Sorry it took me so long to get to you. Had to tend to others first, the more critical cases," she said, moving closer to Beth with a tray of medical supplies, "let's see what we've got here." Anne's hands were gentle yet firm as she unwrapped the bandage around Beth's arm. The wound beneath was angry, a jagged line marring her skin.

"Just another injury to add to the list." Beth winced slightly as the bandage pulled off some dried blood as it was removed.

"You're going to need stitches," Anne murmured, her fingers working with practiced ease, "are you allergic to anything?"

"No." Beth shook her head slowly. As the needle pierced her skin, she felt a strange detachment.

"I've heard quite a bit about you Beth," Anne's hands moved with precision, threading her flesh back together, "Val, Austin, they all talk about you and Chantelle. It's good to finally meet you."

"Is Val here?" Beth's jaw tightened at the mention of Chantelle. Memories, fresh and raw, clawed at her insides. She forced them down, focusing on the sensation of the thread pulling through her skin.

"Val's been working at the clinic in town," Anne continued, seemingly oblivious to Beth's inner turmoil, "Austin, Ben, Reece, Chase, and Tyler, they've all been invaluable to our efforts here. We owe them a lot." Beth let out a breath she didn't realise she'd been holding. The names were familiar, a litany that tethered her to a past life, to a time before everything had spiralled into chaos. She could almost picture them - her protectors, her friends out in the world, fighting battles just as she fought hers. The only difference being that she had been fighting for herself and Chantelle, while they had been fighting someone else's war.

"Thank you." She managed to say, her voice a mere whisper, but it was enough. Gratitude, like a fragile bridge, connected her to the woman who sewed her back to wholeness. The final loop of the stitch pulled tight, and Anne snipped the thread with a pair of surgical scissors that gleamed under the harsh white light of the medical tent. Beth's eyes wandered, taking in the small space that was both a haven and a cage. Metal trays held an array of medical instruments, their sharp edges and pointed tips laid bare, a vivid reminder of the violence that had been a constant shadow in her life. The open display of scalpels and needles, so carelessly out in the open, seemed almost obscene compared to the meticulous sterility of Alcatraz and Catalina Island's clinical precision. There, they had made sure no weapons were within reach of anyone daring enough to utilise them. Here, it seemed everyone was trusted to do the right thing. She suppressed a shudder, feeling the weight of vulnerability settle into her bones. These tools had cut away the fabric of her reality, piece by piece, leaving her exposed and raw. Yet here they were meant to mend, to close wounds rather than inflict them. The dichotomy was not lost on her, nor was the irony that she found a semblance of safety amidst such blatant reminders of pain.

"Alright, that should do it." Anne said, her voice pulling Beth back from the precipice of her thoughts. The doctor's tone was gentle but there was a steeliness behind it, a strength born from necessity. Before Beth could muster a response, the flap of the tent lifted, and Austin stepped through the threshold. His presence filled the space, a stark contrast to the fragility of the makeshift infirmary. He looked different - cleaner, more composed than the last time she'd seen him a mere twelve hours earlier. In all the madness of the evening, she had hardly spoken to him. After Victor fell, he had quickly directed her to the boats before darting back into the midst of gunfire and shouting. Now, he radiated a sense of order amidst the chaos, a pillar in the swirling storm that had become their lives. Beth's heart skipped a beat, a jolt of comfort surging through her at the sight of a familiar face, even if that face belonged to someone who represented a complex tangle of emotions. She shot him a glance, the corners of her mouth twitching in a feeble attempt at a smile. Without missing a beat, Anne crossed the short distance between them and stood on her toes to place a small kiss on Austin's lips. It was an intimate gesture, one that spoke of shared moments and private understanding. Beth felt a pang of something bitter twist in her stomach - confusion or jealousy, she couldn't tell. Her fingers curled into the thin blanket beneath her, the fabric bunching up as she tried to anchor herself to the present, to this new reality that kept shifting under her feet.

"I need to grab some more bandages." Anne said, brushing past Austin, her hand lingering for a fraction longer than necessary on his arm. Beth watched her go, the flap falling back into place behind her. Alone with Austin now, she felt the air shift, charged with the unspoken words that hung heavy between them. She drew in a deep breath, trying to prepare herself for whatever came next, aware that the stitching of her wounds was far simpler than the mending of her fractured world. Austin approached Beth with deliberate steps, his boots scuffing the ground, the sound almost too loud in the tense silence of the tent. His shadow fell across her cot, and she could feel his presence before she even looked up. When she did, the sight of him, so well-groomed and unmarred, struck a jarring note against her own battered reflection she imagined.

"Are you okay?" He asked, his voice tentative as if he were reaching across a chasm that had opened between them. Beth simply nodded, her throat tightening against the words that threatened to spill out. The nod was a lie - it was all she could muster. She searched for something, anything to say, but all that came was the cold, hard truth.

"I hope you've enjoyed playing house," her words were like ice shards cutting into the still air, "while we were on Catalina being, being—" She couldn't finish the sentence. It was a darkness she wasn't ready to face, not out loud. Austin's jaw clenched visibly, his eyes darkening with an emotion he quickly quashed.

"I'm sorry," he said, and there was a weight to his apology, the acknowledgment of her pain and his powerlessness to have prevented it, "leaving that night, it was the only way. Otherwise we would've all been dead." The admission hung between them, heavy and undeniable. He stood there, a soldier clad in guilt, while she lay fractured, trying to piece herself back together. They were survivors, but survival came at a cost neither had fully counted yet. Beth's eyes, still clouded with the residue from a year of torment, followed the lines of Austin's uniform. The fabric seemed too crisp, the edges too sharp for the crumbling world they inhabited. She wrapped her arms around herself, as if holding together the fragments of her spirit that threatened to scatter.

"I understand why you did it," she murmured, the words scraping out from a place of raw honesty, "but understanding doesn't mean I can forgive. Not yet." Her voice was a whisper of her former self, a ghost haunting the silence between them. Austin's features softened, his own battle scars hidden beneath the surface.

"We tried, Beth. We pushed for a rescue every damn day. But the brass wouldn't move. Said there was no strategic incentive," his fists clenched involuntarily at his sides, "until Victor started taking shots at us. He ambushed a patrol, killed a few soldiers. That's when the orders came down to take him out." A bitter laugh escaped Beth's lips, devoid of humour.

"So Victor's own stupidity was our salvation. If he hadn't turned into a bigger monster, we'd still be on that island," the irony was not lost on her, but it provided cold comfort, "too bad he hadn't cracked sooner. Then maybe—" Silence stretched between them, filled with the unsaid and the unforgettable. Austin's gaze dropped to the floor before finding its way back to her face.

"What happened to Chantelle?" The question hung heavy in the air, his brows furrowed with concern.

"*Chantelle*," Beth's heart clenched at the name, pain flickering behind her eyes, "I'll tell you about her, but first I need to speak with Val. It's not fair if she's not the first to know what happened to her daughter." In that moment, their shared history and the weight of their separate griefs wove a fragile thread of understanding. They were bound by what had been endured, by the hope of what might be salvaged from the wreckage of their past. The muted clink of metal against metal announced Anne's return, her hands deft as she unfurled a roll of fresh bandages. Austin stood by the tent flap, his posture rigid, the lines of his face etched with a subtle discomfort.

"I should go." He said, voice edged with a cool detachment that hadn't been there moments before. Beth's eyes followed him, a faint tightening in her chest. There was a history between them, a depth of emotion that had once been acknowledged but now felt like a secret kept in shadow - a love confessed but left to wither in the harsh light of survival. She wondered how much of their story had been shared with Anne and how much remained confined to the silent spaces between her and Austin. Anne approached the cot, busying herself with Beth's arm, wrapping it with practiced care. The touch was clinical, impersonal, yet not unkind.

"You should take a shower once we're done here." She suggested, the hint of a routine smile on her lips.

"A shower?" The word was foreign on Beth's tongue, an echo from another life. The weight of years' worth of grime and trauma seemed to press against her skin.

"Of course," Anne laughed lightly, readying a knot on the bandage, but her laughter faded as she met Beth's earnest gaze, "you haven't had one in—"

"Years." The admission hung heavily in the air, and for a moment, Anne's expression mirrored the realisation of what such deprivation meant.

"Sorry, I—" Anne trailed off, the levity drained from her features, "we have a fully functional hot water system here at the base." Beth nodded, the information settling within her. It was a luxury that felt as distant as the concept of safety or normalcy. She glanced up at Anne, curiosity threading through the weariness.

"How long have you been here at the base?" Beth bit her bottom lip gingerly.

"Since the initial outbreak." Anne replied, her tone a mix of pride and something else - something that didn't quite reach the surface. "Must be nice," Beth commented, a trace of bitterness edging into her voice, "to have been safe all this time." Anne paused, her eyes flickering away for an instant before returning to meet Beth's steady look. She said nothing more, but in her silence, there was an acknowledgment of the divide between them. The gap between those who had weathered the storm from a distance and those who had faced its fury head-on.

Guided by the steady hand of a soldier, Beth stepped into the communal showers, the steam from the hot water wrapping around her like a gentle shroud. She paused for a moment, soaking in the warmth that radiated from the tiled walls. It was then she noticed Jennifer, her eyes tracing the familiar lines of her friend's face - a face that had shared every hardship, every fear.

"Jennifer." Beth whispered, her voice cracking with the weight of emotions held at bay. Jennifer's smile was a beacon in the foggy room as they moved towards each other, their embrace a solid affirmation of survival.

"Are you okay?"

"Safer now." Beth responded, echoing Jennifer's sentiment as she pulled back to look at her. Jennifer nodded, a flicker of relief passing through her gaze. Together, they stepped under the streams of water, laughter bubbling up between them as it cascaded over their heads, sluicing away layers of grime and the remnants of terror. Their hands found the bottles of shampoo and conditioner - luxuries long forgotten - and they marvelled at the scents, so ordinary yet so incredibly foreign after what felt like an eternity of absence. "Can you believe this?" Jennifer asked, her light laughter mixing with the sound of falling water.

"Feels like a dream." Beth agreed, her eyes shining with a mixture of joy and disbelief. The simple act of lathering and rinsing became a rite of restoration, washing away not only the physical filth but also some of the emotional residue that clung to their battered souls. As night fell, they retired to a large tent that had been erected to house all the women rescued from the island. Rows of cots offered a promise of rest that seemed too good to be true. Sitting cross-legged on her cot, Beth accepted a plate piled with food, the aroma tickling her senses and reminding her of a life where such things were taken for granted. Their meal was interrupted by the arrival of another man, one they had yet to meet. His uniform was immaculate, the badges and ribbons denoting his rank and service. He cleared his throat before addressing the group.

"Ladies," he began, his voice carrying the weight of authority softened by genuine concern, "I'm Major General George Bishop. I just want to express my gratitude for your courage, for surviving, and for letting us bring you home." Beth watched him, taking in his stance - the set of his jaw, the air of authority about him. He looked the part of a leader, one who had made hard decisions and carried the burden of command. Yet amidst the strength, there was a glimmer of something paternal, a hint that behind the medals and the title, he understood the trauma that had been inflicted upon them. Yet something about him set Beth on edge.

"Thank you." Someone called out, and a murmur of agreement

rippled through the tent. Beth joined in the chorus, her voice a mere whisper in the collective swell of appreciation.

"In the morning, you'll be taken to town. We have housing arranged for you all," he declared with an encompassing gesture that seemed to wrap up each and every one of them in a protective embrace, "you will have food, a place to stay, and as you recover we'll find the right roles for you to contribute to our community." His voice was steady, almost reassuring. The words should have been comforting, a balm to the raw wounds of their past. They were promises of normalcy, of routine, of safety - the very things they had been starved of for so long.

"Thank you God." Jennifer whispered from the cot next to Beth, wrapping her arms around herself as she closed her eyes. Beth's gaze drifted between Jennifer and George.

"Everyone will be taken care of." He concluded, his eyes sweeping across the faces of the rescued women, pausing as if to offer a silent vow to each. As the murmurs of gratitude faded and George exited the tent, Beth felt a shiver run down her spine despite the warmth of the evening. This sense of dread crept into her, uninvited and insidious, whispering doubts and fears into her ear. For the first time in a long while, as she lay down on her cot surrounded by the soft sounds of others settling in, Beth allowed herself the luxury of feeling a sliver of hope. Maybe, just maybe, they were truly safe now. Her fingers traced the edge of her cot as George's promises lingered in the air. Jennifer, catching the change in Beth's demeanour, leaned closer. Her voice was gentle yet firm.

"You need to stop looking for trouble where there isn't any," she touched Beth's arm lightly, the contact meant to ground her, "we're safe and secure here. For once, let's just accept the good." Beth offered a tight smile, but it didn't quite reach her eyes. Jennifer was right, they were out and they were free. But as she lay back on her cot, staring up at the canvas above, the shadows cast by the outside lights seemed to dance menacingly. Beth closed her eyes, willing sleep to come and bring respite from this gnawing dread. Tonight, at least, the spectres of the island would have to wait until dawn.

The engine of the Humvee hummed a steady rhythm as it rolled to a stop in front of the Sleepy Hollow Neighborhood Center. The crisp morning air carried a sense of purpose and routine that seemed foreign to Beth. She stepped down from the vehicle, her feet touching the pavement with an unfamiliar ease. Around her, people bustled with a quiet efficiency, their expressions unreadable. Smooth masks of contentment that felt eerie to eyes accustomed to fear and sorrow. The sound of Beth's name, a distant echo against the backdrop of subdued chatter, snapped her from her observations. Beth approached the designated desk where a neatly dressed woman with a clipboard waited, her smile practiced and unflappable.

"Bethany Taylor?" The woman queried, though she already knew the answer.

"Yes," Beth confirmed, her voice barely above a whisper, "just Beth, please."

"Welcome, Beth. You've been assigned a house on Blackhawk Drive, just across from here." The woman pointed to a map laid out on the table, her finger tracing a line to a small dot labeled '29'. Beth hesitated, the knot in her stomach tightening.

"Is there something further out?" Her words were tentative, laden with a yearning for solitude, for a space untouched by the ghosts of others. The woman glanced up, her smile unwavering.

"I'm afraid not. All assignments are final, and it's important we keep everyone close for safety."

"Of course." Beth murmured, taking the map with a nod. The word *safety* left a hollow echo in her mind, a reminder of how much she had changed and how much she still longed to be disconnected, to heal in the quiet expanse of her own thoughts.

"Welcome to your new beginning." The woman said, but to Beth it sounded more like a rehearsed sentence than a promised salvation. The parade of escorts stood outside in the grassy area behind the community centre. Beth watched as her fellow survivors were met by their escorts, each one a face she barely knew, yet was expected to trust. A woman approached her, a hesitant smile on her face, her eyes betraying a youthful innocence that felt almost distant to Beth now.

"I'm Mary," she said softly, extending a hand that Beth took, noting the lack of calluses, a lack of any sign of hard work, "I'll show you to your house." As they walked across the grass towards Blackhawk Drive, Mary attempted conversation about the weather, the community activities, and the local amenities. Her voice was light, but it skimmed across the surface of Beth's attention like a stone across water, barely making an impact before sinking away. The house stood solitary, its facade oddly immaculate, the lawn meticulously trimmed. Beth hesitated on the threshold, the weight of the key in her hand feeling disproportionate to the space beyond the door. Mary took the key hesitantly and pushed the door open, stepping inside. She led Beth through the living room which was furnished with a few couches and a coffee table, along with an empty fruit bowl and random decorative items, and then into the kitchen where stainless steel appliances gleamed under fluorescent lights.

"This is for me?" Beth noted the oddly stale appearance, almost like a display home.

"Yes. We've put some clothes in the closets for you," Mary pointed towards the hallway, "anything that doesn't fit or anything you don't like, just bring them back to the community centre. And there's food in the fridge for you as well" Beth nodded, following Mary's gestures mechanically. On the counter lay a manila envelope, bulging slightly with its contents.

"This is your welcome pack," Mary continued, "everything you need should be in here."

"Thank you." Beth managed, her voice a hollow echo in the spacious kitchen.

"You're welcome." Mary's presence was a gentle warmth, but Beth couldn't help but feel disconnected from the girl's well-meaning attempts at hospitality.

"Can I ask—" Beth began, her gaze wandering to the hall that led to more rooms than she could use, "why do I have such a large house all to myself?"

"Oh," Mary answered, shifting her weight from foot to foot, "we actually have quite a few houses available. The population here is small, so there's plenty of room for everyone." Her explanation came out rehearsed, a line recited too many times to count.

"Right." Beth murmured. The idea of so much unused space felt indulgent, almost wasteful after so long in confinement.

"Anyway, if you need anything else just let someone at the community centre know." Mary's voice was bright, but her eyes didn't meet Beth's. With a final awkward smile she turned and left, closing the door behind her with a soft click that sounded like finality. Alone,

Beth ventured further into the house, taking in the unoccupied rooms with their neatly made beds and empty closets. It was quiet, too quiet, and the vastness of the place enveloped her, a stark contrast to the cramped, controlled existence she had endured. Each step echoed, bouncing off walls that seemed to wait expectantly for a life to fill them. Beth ran her fingertips along the smooth countertops, the reality of her new freedom settling around her like a heavy cloak. She glanced back at the door Mary had exited through, the silence amplifying the absence of the young woman's shy chatter. There were no orders here, no threats lurking in shadowed corners. Just the unfamiliar promise of a beginning that felt as daunting as any challenge she had faced before. Beth paced through the living room, the soles of her shoes pressing against the plush carpet. She felt like an intruder in a stranger's home, surrounded by an eerie stillness that seemed to press in on her from all sides. The past years had been a cacophony of fear and survival. Now, confronted with silence and solitude, she was adrift. She looked at the folder Mary had mentioned, its edges perfectly aligned with the countertop. Hesitantly, Beth reached out and opened it, her fingers brushing against the crisp paper. Her eyes skimmed over the printed words, each line a tether to this new reality. A curfew of 9pm - she wrinkled her nose at the thought of being governed by time once again, even in freedom. The guide to using food stamps was a reminder of just how long it had been since she had needed money for anything. The maps detailed the layout of Fort Irwin's military base and the surrounding town, a geography she would have to learn. The rules were clear and numerous, dictating everything from waste disposal to community gatherings. *No unauthorised firearms*, one section began, a rule that seemed both comforting and constraining. Another instructed residents to report any suspicious activity immediately. Beth wondered how many times she would be able to sleep through the night without hearing phantom footsteps outside her door. Turning the page, she found the census - a list of names and addresses, neatly ordered by surname. It was a snapshot of life continuing despite the chaos that had reigned outside these walls. Her finger trailed down the list until it paused on a familiar name, assigned to a house just a street behind her. A mix of relief and apprehension washed over her. Ben was close, yet she wasn't ready to face him, not until she understood the contours of her own fractured psyche. Continuing down the list, Beth's breath hitched when she saw another name. Her heart skipped, then sank as she noted the address Austin shared with Anne. Something twisted inside her, a complex knot of emotions - betrayal, longing, bitterness. She clutched the edge of the folder, the paper creasing under her grip. Closing her eyes briefly, she attempted to quell the turbulence within. This was the hand she had been dealt, and there was no use railing against it. Not here, not now. With a deep, steadying breath, she closed the folder. Tomorrow, she would have to face this community and carve out a space for herself among its ranks. But tonight, she was allowed to grieve, to rage quietly against what had been lost and what could never be reclaimed.

CHAPTER 6

Beth lay motionless, the crisp sheets and bright room a stark contrast to the darkness she had grown accustomed to. Her eyes, wide and unblinking, stared up at the unfamiliar ceiling of her new room. It was silent, the kind of silence that hums in your ears. But within it, Beth could hear the tumultuous beat of her own heart - a relentless reminder that safety was an elusive spectre, not quite grasped. She shifted under the covers, trying to convince herself that the walls around her were real, that the softness of the mattress wasn't just another deceitful comfort destined to be ripped away. The moonlight slithered through the blinds, casting eerie shadows that danced across the room. Shadows that seemed to whisper secrets of a life once lived, of normalcy that now felt like a distant myth. Somewhere in the pit of her stomach, a coil tightened with the thought of Val. The words she needed to vocalise to her friend twisted like barbed wire in her throat. Val deserved the truth, yet she wondered how someone could convey a message draped in such despair. She wasn't sure how to articulate a grief that was as much Chantelle's as it was hers. Her hand slipped to the drawer of the bedside table, fingers trembling as they found the edge of the paper she had hidden away - the last testament of a soul lost too soon. With a breath that felt like it carried the weight of the world, she pulled Chantelle's suicide note out and unfolded it delicately, as if it might crumble to dust at any moment. The lamplight flickered on, its glow harsh after so many nights softened by candle flames. She squinted, giving her eyes a moment to adjust to this abrupt brightness that seemed to mock her longing for the familiar dim. In the warm light, every word written on that piece of paper screamed of finality, of a choice made in the depths of despair. Beth's fingers traced the looping letters of Chantelle's handwriting, each curve a tangible echo of her friend's voice. The paper trembled with the quiver of her hands, resonating with the silent sobs that threatened to escape her lips. There, in the stillness of the night surrounded by the trappings of a life reborn, Beth held onto the note - a frail bridge to a past that refused to release her from its cold grasp. The words swirled in her mind, a mantra of despair that clung to the air around her.

"I can't do this anymore, and I will not bring his baby into this world. Val, I love you. Forgive me." Beth whispered them aloud, her voice barely audible as if speaking them might somehow lessen their power. The note crinkled under her fingers as she folded it, the sound deafening in the quiet room. She slid the paper back into its dark confines, away from the accusing light. Her eyes pressed shut, but the darkness behind her lids was far from empty. It conjured an image, a haunting tableau of Chantelle, lifeless, suspended in a grotesque dance with death. Beth's heart lurched, the fresh memory like a physical blow driving the breath from her lungs. A knock from downstairs startled her, echoing in the eerie quiet of the night. Beth swung her legs over the side of the bed, her pulse a staccato against the silence. She reached the top of the stairs, each step cautious and deliberate. The weight of potential danger sat heavy on her shoulders as she descended, guided by the faint moonlight filtering through the windows. In the hallway, her hand found the cold metal of a candlestick. An absurd choice for defence, yet comforting in its solid heft. Approaching the door, her grip tightened, muscles tensed for the unknown. Swallowing hard, she unlatched the door and pulled it open. The figure was shadowy in the night's embrace as his eyes locked onto the weapon in her hands, he couldn't help but let out a laugh, albeit tinged with concern. In the darkness, Beth squinted as she tried to make out his features. She couldn't believe how much he had changed since the last time they saw each other. The memories of his scruffy appearance and unkempt beard faded away as she took in the sight of him now. His beard was much shorter with neatly groomed hair that was styled at the top, except for a few strands that fell delicately across his forehead. His coy smile was a striking contrast to the pain and suffering she had witnessed during their last encounter, imprisoned together in a cramped storeroom with the smell of blood and sweat and despair filling the air. For a fleeting moment, those haunting memories were replaced by a cleaner image of the man she once knew. Memories that she had clung onto for over a year to survive through each day were now being replaced by a different version of him.

"A candlestick? Really?" Humour dissipated as quickly as it had appeared when Ben saw the torrents of emotion threatening to spill from her gaze. The candlestick felt suddenly foolish in her grasp, a symbol of her vulnerability rather than strength. Her arm fell to her side, the candlestick clattering to the floor, forgotten. Tears welled as she met Ben's eyes, silently pleading for understanding amidst the chaos that churned within her.

The amber liquid swirled in Austin's glass as he leaned back into the worn leather of the armchair. The dim glow from the lamp cast a warm hue over the living room where he and Phillip Major sat enveloped in an uneasy quietude. Phillip, a pillar of strength with his commanding presence, watched Austin over the rim of his own glass, his eyes softening.

"It must be some relief to have Beth back," Phillip remarked, breaking the silence with a note of genuine concern, "but Chantelle, that's a tragedy no one should have to endure." Austin nodded, the ice clinking against the sides of his glass as he took a slow sip.

"Beth's not the same person we lost, Phillip. You can see it in her eyes," he set his drink down on the side table with a gentle thud, "when I saw her today, I could see the mania behind them. She looked like a caged animal. I've seen that look a thousand times during deployment."

"Then you know she probably has post traumatic stress," Phillip nodded, setting his own glass down gently, "which is something she may be able to come out of, with a little help from her friends."

"Friends," Austin scoffed lightly, "we were apart far longer than we were together."

"Strangers become friends in the blink of an eye when they face the same storm," Phillip tapped his fingers together as he pondered, his brow wrinkling in deep thought, "there's no bond stronger than the one forged in fire. And from what you've told me, everything you all went through would have bonded you all for life." Austin leaned forward in his chair, burying his face in his hands as he rubbed his temples indefatigably.

"She wants to break the news about Chantelle to Val herself."

"Understandable," Phillip conceded, his voice a low rumble, "Val still doesn't know, then? About the missions to the islands I mean."

"No," Austin replied, his jaw tightening just enough to betray the weight of unspoken thoughts, "it's going to hit her hard. All of it."

"You seem troubled, son. More than the situation warrants," Phillip studied him for a moment, the lines on his weathered face deepening with concern, "what's really on your mind?"

"Beth being back. It complicates things." Austin's gaze flicked away, settling on the faint pattern of wear in the carpet before returning to Phillip's probing stare.

"Complications of the heart?" Phillip ventured, a knowing edge to his voice.

"Something like that," Austin murmured, thinking how easily everything could unravel, choosing his next words with care, "Ben and Beth had something. It wasn't simple before, and it won't be simple now." Austin offered, omitting his own entanglement of feelings for Beth from the narrative. Phillip nodded slowly, as if piecing together a puzzle only he could see. Austin picked up his glass once more, the facade of calmness as fragile as the surface tension of the whiskey inside. Austin continued to idly swirl his drink in the glass, a silent partner to the tension that hung between him and Phillip. The older man's eyes, always keen and discerning, seemed to pierce through the layers of Austin's carefully maintained composure.

"Are you talking about the complications with Ben and Julia?" Phillip's voice cut through the stillness, his question direct. Austin's grip tightened on the glass, an involuntary reaction.

"How'd you know about that?" He asked, though the answer was clear even as he spoke.

"Anne and I have known Julia's family for years," Phillip offered a half-smile that didn't quite reach his eyes, "we were all on the base together. Julia's like a daughter to me, and when her parents died in that car crash she lived with us. She doesn't have many secrets from Anne, or myself." Nodding, Austin felt the edge of the lie prick at his conscience as he played along with Phillip's assumption.

"I'm worried about Ben and Julia, and what Beth's return means for them." His statement was flat, the falsehood heavy on his tongue. He wasn't ready to delve into the deeper complexities of his own feelings for Beth, nor to reveal the truth behind his earlier omission. Before the conversation could continue any further, the front door creaked open and Anne stepped inside, her posture weary yet resolute after a long day's work.

"I think Stone will pull through," she announced with a sigh of relief, "his surgery was complicated, but he's strong."

"Good." Austin managed, his attention snapping to Anne's presence. There were questions he needed answers to, and Stone might hold some of them. But those would have to wait until the man was conscious and able to talk.

"Ready to go home?" Anne's gaze shifted from her father to Austin, the fatigue etched into her features drawing forth a nod from him.

"Let's go," Austin set down his empty glass with finality, the sound marking the end of the night's discussions as he offered a brief, respectful nod to Phillip, "thanks for the drink. And the talk."

"Anytime, son. You know where to find me." Phillip responded with a warm yet knowing look. With that, Austin followed Anne out into the cool embrace of the evening, the weight of untold stories and unresolved emotions trailing after them like shadows in the waning light. The night air held a crispness that hinted at the change of seasons, wrapping around Austin and Anne as they left the comforting glow of Phillip's porch light behind. Gravel crunched under their boots, the rhythmic sound marking their progression towards the sanctuary they called home.

"You seemed pretty keen on discussing Ben and Julia," Anne mused, breaking the comfortable silence between them, "I heard you from outside while I was fumbling for my keys." Her voice was low, carrying only to Austin's ears amidst the quiet of the base housing area. His gaze lingered on the path ahead, his mind replaying the earlier conversation.

"Yeah. We were talking about how Beth's return might shake things up." He admitted, the words tasting bittersweet as Anne's brow furrowed in thought.

"Ben and Julia," she started, her tone contemplative, "they were casual. Convenient for both of them, I suppose." She glanced at Austin, her eyes reflecting a depth of understanding.

"Convenient is the word for it." Austin's face was cold, and Anne tried to decipher the trail of thought behind his blank eyes.

"But Julia," she paused, replaying recent conversations in her head as she thought, "I think she's caught feelings for him." He nodded slowly, acknowledging the truth in her observation. The streetlights cast shadows across his face as he spoke.

"Ben never really got over Beth. For him, it was always her. It will always be her," he paused, considering the entanglement of emotions that awaited them all, "I feel for Julia, but Beth was something else." A soft sigh escaped Anne's lips as she looked up at the star-speckled sky.

"I just hope this doesn't disrupt our calm too much," she said, the weight of potential drama pressing upon her words, "we have more important things to worry about." They reached their front step, the familiar sight offering a semblance of stability in the uncertainty of what lay ahead.

"We'll manage." Austin reassured her, though his heart echoed her sentiment. The door clicked shut behind them, the sound a definitive end to the day's outside concerns. Anne's gaze lingered on Austin, a silent question in her eyes.

"You and Ben painted such a vivid picture of Beth," she murmured as she slipped off her shoes, "I just hope I recognise the woman you spoke of with such reverence." Austin leaned back against the cool wood of the door, a flicker of unease crossing his features.

"What do you mean?" He asked, though he already sensed the answer curling up between them.

"Heroic and strong. Unyielding," Anne said, her voice trailing through the dim hallway like a wisp of smoke, "sounded like no one could ever match up to her." He looked down, a shadow of guilt darkening his expression.

"We might've embellished a bit," he confessed, his words slow and heavy, "leaving them there, at Alcatraz. I think we felt so guilty that we'd idealised her a bit. We tried to remember all the good stuff to make ourselves feel better." His voice was barely above a whisper, the ghost of that day clinging to him still. A small, understanding smile tugged at Anne's lips.

"We tell the stories we need to." She reached out, her hand brushing against his arm, grounding him.

"I didn't tell you everything."

"And there are some things you're allowed to keep to yourself," she offered gently, "you're allowed to have secrets, Austin. Even from me." Austin shut his eyes tightly, taking a deep breath and trying to suppress the lump forming in his throat. He fought back tears that threatened to fall from his eyes.

"I never thought we'd see her again." He confessed, the guilt hitting him harder as the past two days finally settled upon him. Exhaustion clung to Anne, a tangible shroud that seemed to dull the vibrant energy she usually emanated.

"But she's here, and she's safe," stifling a yawn with the back of her hand, Anne shook her head lightly, "I should turn in. Early morning tomorrow. Stone and the others won't check on themselves."

"Of course." Austin replied, his concern for her well-being momentarily pushing aside the tumultuous thoughts of Beth and Ben. He watched as Anne made her way upstairs, each step measured and weary.

"Goodnight, love." She called over her shoulder, her voice a soft lullaby in the quiet of the house.

"Goodnight." He answered, but remained where he stood, rooted by more than just the evening's chill. The house felt too empty, too silent with only his own thoughts for company. He would stay up a while longer, the night's conversations replaying in his mind, the spectre of the past looming close.

Ben's silhouette filled the doorway, the dim porch light outlining his figure as he stepped over the threshold into Beth's house. He didn't wait for her to speak, to break the icy stillness that seemed to have claimed her. Instead, his movements were deliberate and quiet, bending to pick up the candlestick as he walked past her. She watched him place it back on the hallway table, its metallic base making a soft clink as it met the wood, now paired with its twin once more. Beth drew in a shaky breath, finally finding her voice, though it emerged softer than she intended.

"When did you get back?" Her eyes, large and searching, followed his every move as he turned back to face her.

"Few hours ago. Had to debrief at the base first." Ben replied, his voice steady but with an undertone of something else. A weariness, perhaps, or a relief that was too profound to be named.

"Have you been home yet?" She asked, the question hanging between them like the faint echo of distant thunder. He shook his head slightly, the shadow of a smile touching his lips.

"No, I came straight here." His admission hung heavily in the air, charged with unspoken words and shared memories.

"How did you know where to find me?" The curiosity in her voice was tinged with vulnerability, her gaze flicking away before locking back onto his.

"Got a copy of the new housing assignments," he answered simply, his eyes never leaving hers, "a friend helped me out." In that moment, standing in the tight space of her new reality, Beth felt the weight of everything unsaid pressing down upon her chest. Ben's presence was both a balm and a reminder of scars still fresh, of wounds unseen that lay beneath the surface. Beth shuffled into the kitchen, the cold tile a stark contrast to the warmth of Ben's gaze that followed her every movement. She paused in front of the refrigerator, an alien behemoth compared to what she'd been accustomed to since the pandemic had started.

"Can I get you something to drink? I think I have sodas, or water." Attempting to infuse some normalcy into the surreal night, she avoided his gaze. Ben laughed awkwardly, a soft sound that bounced gently off the kitchen walls.

"I know what they stock in there when you first arrive," he said, leaning against the door frame with a casualness that seemed out of place in the tense atmosphere, "there should be some juice hiding in the back too."

"Right, of course you do," Beth's cheeks flushed with embarrassment as she cracked open the fridge, allowing a sliver of light to spill out and illuminate the array of beverages, "it's just so new to me. A fridge full of food, a house with power, a king-sized bed, couches. It's overwhelming." She confessed, her voice barely above a whisper as she grabbed a can of lemonade for herself. He offered her a sympathetic smile, one that didn't quite reach his eyes before it faltered, the humour slipping away as if it were never there. The air grew thick with unspoken thoughts, each breath seemingly magnified by the silence. Beth's fingers traced the cool aluminium of the soda can, her mind racing for a pretext to break the stillness, to find an excuse that would justify asking him to leave. But then, with a few measured steps, Ben closed the gap between them.

"Could I—" his voice was tentative, almost hesitant, "can I hug you?" The request hung there, delicate and laden with a history that stretched back further than their present uncertainty. Beth's heart hammered in her chest, and for a fleeting moment she considered refusing. But something in his eyes, the raw vulnerability compelled her to consent.

"Okay." She managed to say, her acquiescence sounding more like a question than permission. Ben's arms encircled her tentatively, the contact a strange mixture of familiarity and foreignness. In the shelter of his embrace, Beth stood rigid, her body betraying the turmoil within. They were two survivors adrift in the same sea of memories, seeking an anchor in each other even as the waves threatened to pull them under once again. The warmth from his arms felt alien against the coolness of her skin, a sharp contrast to the chill of solitude she'd grown accustomed to. Beth's breath hitched as she felt moisture prickling at the corners of her eyes. She hadn't expected to be so undone by this simple gesture, an embrace that spoke of shared pasts and unvoiced promises. Ben felt the rigidity in her posture, the way she held herself as if bracing for a blow rather than a touch born of tenderness. With a gentleness that seemed at odds with the strength in his hands, he released her and stepped back, giving her space.

"I'm sorry." He moved to perch on one of the stools, his figure a silent sentinel against the backdrop of her kitchen.

"No, I'm sorry." She murmured, her voice barely louder than the hum of the refrigerator. Her hands gripped the edge of the counter as if anchoring herself to this moment, to the reality of his presence. The apology hung awkwardly between them, unnecessary yet instinctive.

"Hey, there's nothing to apologise for Beth," Ben said softly, his tone careful not to disturb the fragile atmosphere, "I shouldn't have pushed, not when you're not ready." His gaze was earnest, seeking her forgiveness for overstepping boundaries that neither fully understood anymore. Beth shook her head, a wistful smile touching her lips as she glanced away.

"It's not about being ready," she confessed, the words tumbling out with a vulnerability she had not planned to reveal, "It's just, I haven't felt a kind hand since that day they took us. Since before everything—"

"Turned to shit?" Ben mused as an uncomfortable silence fell between them. Unable to articulate the darkness that followed, there was a pause filled only by the ticking of the clock on the wall before she continued.

"The last good thing I remember is waking up beside you. That morning in that motel room, before everything went wrong." The memory surfaced with a clarity that stole her breath. Sunlight filtering through curtains, the weightlessness of oblivion, and his face, the first thing she saw upon opening her eyes that day. Beth noticed the shadow that passed over Ben's expression, a silent storm of self-reproach and regret. He was still for a long moment, his jaw clenching as if he were grappling with internal demons. Finally, he drew in a deep breath and his voice cut through the quiet.

"What happened on Catalina?" His question was cautious, the words weighted with an understanding of pain she'd endured. She hesitated, the memories crowding her mind like spectres she couldn't elude.

"Nothing like what Marcus did," she replied, her voice barely above a whisper, "he didn't touch me. Not like that." Her hands gripped the edge of the counter, knuckles whitening. The chill of the stone beneath her fingers served as a stark reminder of the warmth she craved, the warmth that was once offered by human touch before cruelty became her constant companion.

"Good." Ben's resolve was firm and protective, almost as if he had finally received the answer to a question he had been longing to ask. Beth's eyes narrowed in on Ben's softened face, a flash of anger sweeping across her features.

"Don't get me wrong Ben," her previous attempts to remain delicate had been abandoned at the slight notion of Ben's ignorance, "just because Victor didn't rape me doesn't mean his actions were any less violating." Ben's lips parted slightly, his face a mix of empathy and apology. His gaze met hers, silently hoping he had not made her any more upset and angry than she already was.

"Beth, I'm sorry—"

"Victor," she interrupted, her voice steadying with the effort to remain composed, "he would summon me to his room, demanding answers. There wasn't one time I left that room without a new bruise or scar." Ben's eyes darkened, reflecting the torment of imagining her pain. His fists clenched involuntarily at his sides.

"Beth—"

"Almost every morning," she continued, her gaze fixed on a distant point past the walls of the kitchen, "I'd barely had a chance to wake up before someone would come for me. That was the only touch I knew after Alcatraz, after everything changed." The room seemed to shrink around them, the air thick with unspoken apologies and shared traumas. Ben remained silent, his presence a hushed vow against the shadows of their past. The silence in the kitchen seemed to stretch, a tangible entity that pressed upon both of them with the weight of unsaid words and shared histories. Ben's gaze lingered on Beth with an intensity that spoke of regret and yearning. With each tick of the clock, the memories of Alcatraz loomed over him like spectres in the dimly lit room - the damp, oppressive air, the sound of waves crashing against the rock, the occasional muffled scream.

"Leaving you behind, I never wanted that," he finally broke the silence, his voice laced with a bitter edge of self-reproach as he looked away for a moment, pain etched into the lines of his face, "Austin, he made the call. Said we'd be dead if we stayed." The words came out strained, as if it pained him to admit their helplessness. Beth's response was a soft exhalation, a whisper woven with the thread of understanding that only those who had faced darkness together could share.

"I know." Her eyes held a faraway look, haunted by the memory of the speedboat's engine fading into the night, the figures aboard slipping away into the black void of the ocean. A heavy breath escaped Ben's lips as he absorbed her quiet acknowledgement. It did little to assuage the guilt that gnawed at him, but it was a start - a small step towards reconciliation.

"And Chantelle?" The name hung between them like a delicate

shard of glass, threatening to shatter under the pressure of unspoken truths. His question was hesitant, a careful probing into a wound still raw. Beth's hands stilled, her fingers pressing into the hard counter.

"I want to tell you everything," she said, her voice steady despite the turmoil that churned beneath her calm exterior, "but Val deserves to hear it first." It was a matter of honour, a debt of the heart owed to a friend lost in the labyrinth of their past battles.

"That's a reason I can accept," Ben nodded slowly, "I won't push you further until you're ready."

"I'm going to the clinic tomorrow morning," she informed him, a fragile determination in her tone, "after that I'll tell you everything."

"Okay." Ben nodded, acknowledging the bond that tethered them all to Chantelle's memory, respecting the pact of friendship that demanded such loyalties. They were a constellation of souls marked by the same tragedies, and in that shared darkness they sought out the faint light of healing and redemption. Beth traced the brand on her forearm, a nervous habit that she had developed during long nights of solitude. She glanced at the clock on the wall, its hands pointed accusingly past midnight.

"Why are you out so late? Isn't there a curfew?" She asked Ben, shifting the topic away from their shared grief.

"Curfews are for civilians," he replied with a half-smile, "military personnel are exempt." In the dim light of the kitchen, his uniform seemed to blend into the shadows.

"Are we safe though?" Her voice was smaller than she intended, betraying the vulnerability she fought so hard to keep hidden.

"Tonight is the safest I've felt in a long time," there was a sincerity in Ben's voice that wrapped around her like a blanket, "now that I know you're alive. Now that I know you're okay." Her laugh was a bitter sound, startling in the quiet of the room.

"*Okay*," Beth echoed, her gaze dropping to the floor as if she could see through it, back to the island that had been her prison, "I'm not okay, Ben. Alcatraz, and then Catalina. It destroyed me." She looked up at him, her eyes glistening with unshed tears. He took a step closer, instinctively reaching out before stopping himself. They were two people bound by trauma, yet separated by an invisible chasm of pain.

"Beth—"

"Victor tormenting us," Beth's voice cracked as she continued, "being trapped in that storeroom, thinking we were gonna die. What Marcus did to me—" She trailed off, unable to give voice to the horrors that still haunted her dreams. Ben's jaw clenched, his body tensing as if ready to fight demons that had already claimed their pound of flesh. He remained silent, offering no platitudes, knowing that some wounds were beyond the reach of words. The muscles in Ben's arms tensed, his hands balling into fists.

"I'm sorry Beth," his voice was raw and straining with a blend of rage and regret as he paced the kitchen floor, the tight line of his mouth revealing an internal battle, "I am so fucking sorry that I couldn't protect you from him."

"Ben—"

"Thinking about what he did to you. When I watched him brand you, I think my heart literally broke."

"Ben, stop." Despite her firmer tone, Ben's rage and revulsion consumed him and he refused to acknowledge her plea.

"And when he took you from that storeroom and brought you back, bleeding and broken, I couldn't get the image of what he did out of my head," Ben's pacing had increased, his breath quickening as he relived their final moments alone together, "how he—, it makes me want to—"

"Ben!" Beth yelled angrily, her tone firm enough to slice through the tension.

"What!?" He turned towards her, the torment evident in the set of his broad shoulders. As if propelled by a force outside himself, Ben's fist connected with the wall, the impact echoing in the space between them as plaster and paint chips shattered into the void.

"Marcus is dead. Victor is dead," she reminded him gently, moving closer while her gaze held steady on his storm-tossed eyes as she reached out and placed a calming hand on his arm, "you're not responsible for the ghosts of the past." His breath hitched, and his eyes shut for a moment, a shudder passing through him. When they opened again, the anger had ebbed slightly, replaced by a haunted vulnerability. Beth's touch lingered on his arm, a lifeline in the swirling current of their shared despair.

"But it was supposed to be me," he uttered, his voice barely above a whisper, "that night, I wanted to be the one to get you. Austin wouldn't let me. He gave the command, and I've resented him for it ever since. If I'd gone, I would've been the one to kill Marcus. And after that, I never would've let you leave my sight. Never." Her fingers tightened around his arm, grounding him.

"But we're here now, Ben," she met his anguish with a resilience that belied her own suffering, "and it's over. They can't hurt us anymore." Beth's heart raced as she stood in the dimly lit kitchen, her gaze locked with Ben's. The tension hung between them like a physical barrier, each lost in their own whirlwind of emotions and memories.

"There's always gonna be someone who wants to hurt us," his voice grew low and angry, laced with a hint of sorrow, "it's just the way the world works now."

"Then we won't let them," she said, her voice a brittle whisper that seemed to carry the weight of the world, "I want to know everything that happened after you left. I need to understand." Ben's jaw tightened, a storm brewing in his eyes as he nodded, the faintest glimmer of pain etched across his features.

"Okay," he agreed, his voice steady despite the tempest within, "but only if you tell me everything too, and you can leave out anything you don't want to tell me about Chantelle. Not until you've talked to Val." She swallowed hard, feeling the sting of unshed tears and the clawing fear of reliving those dark days. But she owed him this much - she owed herself the release of truth.

"Yes," Beth whispered, her commitment sealing a pact between them, "it's gonna be hard to tell you what happened to me without revealing too much about Chantelle, but I'll try." The silence that followed was abruptly shattered by a knock at the door. Both startled, they exchanged a tense look. Ben's hand instinctively went to his side where a weapon would normally rest, but found nothing. Beth crept towards the door, her every muscle tensed for fight or flight. She reached out with a trembling hand and pulled it open as she peered at the silhouette framed against the soft glow from the streetlights outside. In his hands, he carried an offering - one bottle of whiskey and another of rum.

"Thought you might like a drink." Austin said, his voice betraying the casualness of his words. Ben stepped into view, his presence causing a flicker of shock to pass over Austin's face before it settled into an expression that wasn't quite surprise. A long history shadowed the space between the two men, a history full of command and resentment, decisions made under duress, and the heavy burden of survival.

"Come in." Beth said, breaking the momentary stand-off, her tone weary yet welcoming. She couldn't bear any more secrets or silences. Tonight was about unraveling the past and perhaps finding a path forward through the honesty shared in the telling of their stories.

"Your timing is actually perfect," Ben started, a half-smile briefly lifting the corner of his mouth as he gestured to the bottles in Austin's hands before shifting his gaze back to Beth, "we were about to dive into the past year, and having you here might fill in some gaps." Austin stepped over the threshold but hesitated as he glanced between them. The weight of the bottles seemed to anchor him to the spot.

"This kind of recounting should have everyone present. Reece, Chase, Tyler—" Austin's voice trailed off, his eyes searching Beth's for guidance.

"Val shouldn't be part of this, not yet," Beth interjected firmly, her voice steady despite the tremor she felt within, "she doesn't know about Chantelle yet, and I need to be the one to tell her. But not with everything else she went through filled in."

"What do you mean?" Ben searched her stoic expression for a hint.

"I—" Beth started, trying to choose her words carefully, "I might not have endured the same punishment that I went through on Alcatraz, but Chantelle's experience is a little different. This won't be the right environment for Val to hear what happened to her daughter." Understanding flickered in Austin's eyes, and he nodded slowly.

"Alright, then. We'll leave Val out of it for now." He said with a note of deference that acknowledged the gravity of Beth's responsibility.

"Let's go grab the others." Ben said, glancing at Austin with a newfound camaraderie formed through shared experience rather than rank. They moved towards the door as Austin handed her the bottles, their footsteps muted against the wooden floorboards.

"Be quick." Beth called after them, her voice laced with a mix of anticipation and dread. Once alone, she exhaled a breath she hadn't realised she had been holding and made her way to the kitchen. The clink of glass against countertop echoed in the quiet house as she poured herself a drink, watching the liquid amber steady in the glass. She wrapped her fingers around it, the cool surface grounding her swirling thoughts. With each tick of the clock, she prepared herself mentally for what was to come - truths laid bare and wounds reopened. She sipped slowly, allowing the warmth to spread through her chest, bracing against the chill of memories that would soon flood into the light.

CHAPTER 7

The boat's hull scraped against the gravelly shore with a finality that echoed in Ben's chest. The grey waves behind them whispered of the past, the decisions made, and the souls left behind. As Austin killed the engine, they all stepped off onto the damp earth just north of San Jose. Their boots sank into the wet sand, the night sky pressing down on them with the weight of their choices. Ben couldn't tear his gaze from the churning water, something inside him ripping apart with each retreating wave. His thoughts were with her, with what he'd left behind, the promise broken. The light drizzle began to thicken, mingling with the salt on his lips. It was as if the sky understood, weeping for their predicament.

"Beth!" The name tore from his throat, raw and filled with a pain that clawed at his insides. Austin's voice cut through the mist, attempting to anchor him to the present.

"Ben, we can't—"

"I'm going back!" Ben's declaration was fierce and desperate, his voice cracking under the strain of grief. Before he could take a step towards the boat, Austin lunged, his body colliding with Ben's with the inevitability of a storm surge. They hit the ground hard, the mud an unforgiving bed beneath them. Austin's hands gripped Ben's arms, pinning him down as the struggle kicked up clumps of earth.

"Listen to me," Austin's eyes bore into Ben's, fierce and unyielding, "it's not possible."

"No!" Ben's voice broke, his muscles flexed against the restraint, seeking freedom. Austin pressed closer, the fight between them as much a battle of wills as it was physical. The rain intensified as it washed over them, turning the ground to sludge beneath their grappling forms. The rest of the world faded into the background, leaving only the two of them and the relentless downpour. Reece's brow furrowed as he watched the chaotic thrashing of limbs before him, the sky weeping over the scene. Tyler stood silent, his jaw clenched, eyes tracking each movement with a soldier's discipline. Chase's hands were balled into fists at his sides, a silent testament to the frustration boiling within him. Beside them, Val's face was a canvas of pain, her eyes shimmering pools reflecting the turmoil playing out on the bank. She knew her voice would be lost amidst the sounds of battle and betrayal - it was an echo of her own heartache, the silent scream for Chantelle that she couldn't vocalise. The ground churned under the two men as Ben's muscles bulged in protest, his frame a testament to strength now compromised by grief. He knelt, the fight ebbing from him not by choice but by sheer exhaustion, his breaths coming in ragged gasps.

"Ben," Austin said, his tone low and steady, chin resting heavy on his friend's shoulder in a gesture meant to ground rather than restrain, "we can't turn back now, not yet." His words were soft but carried the weight of command, a promise etched between the lines. Ben's voice was strained, each word infused with a blend of desperation and defeat.

"Beth, I promised—"

"We will," Austin assured him, his grip firm but gentle on the arms of the man he'd called brother in more ways than one, "but we survive first." The rain painted them both in strokes of sorrow, the droplets mingling with the mud, staining them with the reality of their situation. Ben's cries tore through the sombre quietude of the shore, raw and shattering. Tears streamed down his dirt-streaked face as he writhed under Austin's grip, each sob a stark echo of the heartache he bore.

"I shouldn't have left her!" He wailed, the words a guttural howl against the injustice of their retreat. Chase exchanged a glance with Tyler, a silent communication that spoke volumes of their collective dread. With heavy steps, Chase approached the pair ensnared in their struggle, his voice cutting through the tension.

"Keep it down. We've gotta move," he urged, eyes darting to the encroaching darkness, "or all of this is for nothing." The next lash of rain struck then, heralding a downpour that drenched them in an instant. The heavens opened with merciless intent, washing the scene in a deluge that felt almost purgatorial. Thunder growled in the distance, a natural tumult mirroring the storm inside each of them. Ben's once ironclad resolve now lay shattered at his feet, mingling with the rivulets of water that sought the lowest ground. Austin, his own face pelted by the relentless rain, tightened his hold on Ben, not in restraint but in support. He hoisted Ben up, the act a display of solidarity forged in shared suffering. They trudged through the darkness towards San Jose as the cold seeped into their bones. Unarmoured against the elements and the world, each step was an effort against the pull of despair. Forward they moved, a pact without words between them, driven by necessity and the faintest ember of hope that refused to be extinguished by the storm. The *Homewood Suites by Hilton San Jose North* loomed ahead, its facade a ghostly silhouette against the pale dawn light. They moved cautiously, their silhouettes hunched and weary, scanning for any signs of danger.

"Keep it tight." Austin whispered as they approached the entrance, his voice betraying none of the fatigue that clawed at his limbs. The door gave way with a reluctant creak, granting them access to the once welcoming lobby, now silent and desolate. Inside they dispersed wordlessly, each claiming a space in the dust-covered refuge. Exhaustion hung heavy on their shoulders, but a deep sleep was a luxury they couldn't afford. With the first hint of morning light they were up again, headed to the nearby Walmart. The store stood picked over, a carcass of necessity, yet they managed to arm themselves with what could only be described as a motley arsenal. Baseball bats, kitchen knives, anything that could be wielded against an unforeseeable threat, as well as some rations for the journey, and a tattered map. They headed southward, their path a winding serpent through abandoned streets and overgrown avenues. They walked in silence, each step a testament to both their determination and the haunting solitude of their journey. A week passed - a tapestry of endless highways and the relentless California sun beating down on their vulnerable forms. Finally, Bakersfield's skyline broke the monotony of the road. They settled into the *Holiday Inn Express & Suites Bakersfield Airport* as night began to cloak the world once more. Here, amidst the stale linens and echoes of absent travellers, they allowed themselves a momentary reprieve.

"Tomorrow we'll check the guard post," Austin announced, breaking the stillness, "it's about a five hour hike. Probably more in our condition." His words were met with nods - there was nothing more to say. They needed something tangible. A radio call, a safe haven, a sign that they were not alone in this new desolation. The dim light of the evening filtered through the blinds, casting long shadows across the map sprawled on the table. Val's eyes were fixed on it, her brow furrowed with a mix of concern and determination. "Are we just going to hope that we find somewhere with a group of geared up soldiers who have extra guns and hope that they agree to help us rescue two girls trapped on an island inside a prison?" She asked, breaking the heavy silence that had settled over the group. Austin's hand hovered over the map, tracing the jagged coastline as if the answer might be etched there. He looked up at Val, his expression unreadable. The weariness in his eyes, however, betrayed the toll of their journey. Beside him, Ben stood rigid, the muscles in his jaw working silently.

"Val," Austin began, his voice carrying a weight that seemed too heavy for the room, "I wish I had a solid plan. But let's face it, heading back now with no guns, no gear, and no backup is suicide." His words hung in the air, stark and unyielding. Ben shot Austin a glance loaded with silent despair. For a moment, he seemed to be wrestling with an invisible adversary, caught between the urge to act and the knowledge of their dire reality. Their gazes locked, a beat passed, and then another, until the stillness became an unbearable presence. With a guttural cry, Ben's control snapped. His fist came down hard on the table, the sound of shattering glass echoing through the room like the crack of a rifle. A vase, forgotten decor from a world that no longer existed, lay in pieces around his knuckles. The group flinched as one, the sudden violence jarring them from their thoughts. Chase's eyes darted to the shards scattered across the wood, while Tyler shifted uncomfortably, his hand instinctively reaching for a weapon that wasn't there.

"Fuck!" Ben's voice was ragged, laced with pain and frustration. The others remained silent, the sound of Ben's laboured breathing filling the space between them. They knew all too well the depth of his anguish - the haunting guilt of leaving loved ones behind, the gnawing hunger that had become a constant companion, the exhaustion that clung to their bones. Val's sobs rose, small and heartbreaking in the heavy air of the room. She trembled visibly, clutching at her arms as if to hold herself together. Reece's face, etched with lines of concern and weariness, crossed to where she sat huddled on a threadbare couch.

"Val," he said softly, his voice a gentle command amid the tension, "let's get you to bed." His hand extended towards her, an offer of support that seemed to carry more weight than just the promise of rest. She looked up at him, her eyes glistening with tears that spilled down her cheeks, leaving trails in the grime that marked days of hardship.

"Okay," with a nod, she took his hand, allowing him to guide her to her feet, "thank you." Reece cast a glance back at the others, his gaze lingering on Austin and Ben for a moment before he spoke.

"I'll stay with her tonight and make sure she gets some sleep." There was an unspoken understanding in his words, a silent plea for them to settle their own turmoil while he tended to Val's fragile state. Chase and Tyler exchanged weary looks, the day's events weighing heavily on their shoulders. Without a word they rose in unison, their movements stiff from both physical exhaustion and the mental toll of their journey. They made their way to another room, leaving their companions behind to find solace in whatever rest they could muster. In the dim light Austin turned to Ben, his gaze drawn to the fresh cuts that marred his friend's hand - a testament to the fierce outburst that had shattered more than just glass. He moved closer, retrieving a damp rag from a nearby counter. The fabric was stained but clean enough for the task.

"Was this really necessary?" Austin asked quietly as he took Ben's injured hand in his own, dabbing carefully at the blood that welled from the shallow lacerations.

"I love her Austin," Ben's jaw clenched, a myriad of emotions flickering across his face as he found his voice, "and I know she loves me too." Austin paused, the rag hovering over a particularly deep cut as he processed Ben's words. A pang of envy gnawed at him, yet he pushed it aside, masking it with a steady expression.

"I'm not surprised," he replied, his tone even despite the tumult within, "you two had something real." The confession hung between them, a fragile truth in a world that had grown accustomed to lies. Austin continued his treatment, cleaning away the blood with meticulous care. For now, it was enough to tend to the wounds they could see, leaving the deeper ones for another day when strength and hope might be renewed. He carefully wrapped a makeshift bandage around Ben's hand, securing it just tight enough to hold the dressing in place without causing discomfort. The room was dimly lit by a single flickering candle that cast long shadows against the barren walls.

"If anything happens to her, if she doesn't make it because we left her behind," Ben's voice broke, raw with guilt and fear, "I'll never forgive myself." Austin met his gaze, seeing the torment etched deeply into his friend's features.

"We will go back for Beth *and* Chantelle. We need to be smart about it, brother. That means taking care of ourselves first," he placed a firm hand on Ben's shoulder, grounding him with the weight of his resolve, "and don't forget, we left two people behind. Try to remember that, especially around Val."

"You're right," Ben nodded, the fight draining from him as he accepted Austin's words, "I'm sorry." They both knew the risks involved in returning, but the unspoken promise hung heavy in the air - a silent vow that they would not abandon their own.

"Let's get some rest," Austin suggested, his eyes lingering on Ben's exhausted face, "we'll need our energy for whatever tomorrow brings." They silently walked to their separate beds. As sleep claimed them, neither man noticed the hours slipping into days, their exhaustion deeper than either had imagined. When consciousness finally returned, it took Austin a moment to orient himself. The candle had long since burned out, leaving them cloaked in darkness save for the slivers of light that dared to creep through the holes in the curtains. He nudged Ben awake, and together they stirred the others.

"Wake up." Ben called out softly, his voice hoarse from disuse. One by one, they came to life, each sharing fragments of consciousness during their extended slumber. Reece had woken for water sometime on the first day, and Val recalled stirring to distant thunder sometime later, while Chase and Tyler had no recollection of waking at all. They recanted their moments of lucidity, their brief dances with consciousness that brought forth a timeline they struggled to comprehend.

"Three days," Chase said, disbelief colouring his tone, "I think we've been out for three full days." The group exchanged weary glances. Their bodies had demanded rest, and perhaps in this rare instance the ruins of the world had granted them a brief reprieve.

"Guess we needed it more than we thought." Tyler mused, stretching his stiff muscles.

"Rest up for today then," Austin decided, authoritative yet gentle, "we start fresh at dawn." Silence fell over them, a shared understanding that no further discussion was needed.

As the first streaks of light heralded a new day, they made for the *California Army National Guard* post. Hope, fragile and unspoken, drove them onward, but as the high midday sun settled over them their exhaustion caused them to cave, needing another night of rest. The hiss of a can opening punctuated the hush that had settled over them as twilight embraced the desolate highway. The group sat in a loose circle, their backs to each other, eyes scanning the horizon with an instinctual vigilance. Austere meals were claimed from backpacks, the clatter of utensils against metal containers echoing softly in the stillness as they sat on the road where they had collapsed hours earlier. They watched as Val carefully rationed out the food, her movements methodical and precise - a stark contrast to the turmoil that churned within them. Reece maintained a steady gaze into the distance, his posture betraying none of the fatigue that tugged at his bones. Tyler's hands trembled ever so slightly as he unwrapped a granola bar, the wrapper crinkling loudly in the silence. They ate without words, sustenance over sentiment. The food tasted of preservatives and tin, but beneath the blandness there was the faintest hint of vitality returning to their weary bodies. Austin took inventory of their supplies, noting the canned goods, the bottled water, the dwindling medical kit. Beside the provisions lay their modest arsenal, a collection of handguns and a rifle they'd secured from an abandoned police station days prior.

"More than we had a week ago." Chase muttered, catching Austin's assessing eyes.

"True." Austin acknowledged, feeling the weight of the firearm at his side. It was both a burden and a lifeline. As darkness yielded to dawn, the road ahead promised no kindness, only the relentless march towards an uncertain future. They were up with the first sliver of light, shouldering their packs and stepping on the asphalt with renewed determination. The morning air was crisp, laced with the scent of rain. They marched in formation, a habit drilled into them long before the world had frayed at its edges. Austin led them, his eyes fixed on the path ahead, while the others kept pace, their footfalls a rhythmic drumbeat on the pavement. As they approached the post, the tranquility shattered. Soldiers in military uniforms materialised from the tree line, weapons trained with practiced ease on the small band of travellers.

"Hands where I can see them!" One of the soldiers barked, his voice cutting through the morning calm. Instinctively, the group raised their arms, the familiar cold rush of adrenaline surging through their veins. Austin stepped forward, locking eyes with the man who seemed to be in charge.

"Captain Austin Williams, US Army," he declared, his tone steady despite the thumping of his heart, "this is First Lieutenant Ben Molina, retired Colonel Reece Griffin, Sergeants Chase Matthews and Tyler Blake of the National Guard, and our nurse, Val Mendez." Silence hovered as the soldiers took in the information. Austin could feel the tension coiling around them like a spring ready to snap. But behind his identification lay an unspoken plea for recognition, for camaraderie in a world where such things had become rare currency. These were not civilians playing dress up, Austin was sure by their movements and stature. The brief standoff stretched into an eternity, the two groups sizing each other up under the scrutiny of a wary sun. Then, slowly, the soldiers lowered their weapons. The one with the air of authority, a hint of grizzled experience in his eyes, stepped forward and offered a hand.

"Major Mickey Alvarado," he said, his grip firm as Austin reciprocated, "and this is First Lieutenant Chris Barnett." He gestured to the man behind him. Austin nodded to each of them in turn as they introduced themselves, noting the distinct patches and the wear on their uniforms that spoke of their own trials.

"Second Lieutenants Neil Howard, Eddie Ly, Dustin Webster, and Shauna Reed," Barnett looked to the others, motioning to the younger officers who relaxed their stances but remained alert, "but please call me Barnett." Mickey's gaze lingered thoughtfully on each member of the group.

"What's your story?" He asked, the lines on his face deepening with genuine curiosity.

"It's a long one." Austin exchanged a glance with Ben, whose eyes bore the weight of unspoken tales, his words heavy with exhaustion and the ghosts of past horrors.

"Try us." Barnett encouraged, motioning for them to lower their arms completely.

"Is there somewhere else we can talk," Reece cast a concerned glance at Val, "somewhere we can sit?" As the sun climbed higher, the battered sign of the base loomed ahead, a beacon to Austin and his weary group. They followed Mickey's lead, each step an effort against the inertia of their fatigue. The base had the look of a fortress in repose - sandbags still piled against walls, but with the relaxed air of soldiers no longer on high alert.

"Inside." Mickey gestured, ushering them through the entrance where the remnants of sunlight strained through the dust-covered windows. The interior was sparse, utilitarian, with a long table at the centre surrounded by chairs that seemed to have seen better days. It was here under the buzz of fluorescent lights that the two groups convened, a makeshift council of war-weary survivors.

"Water?" Shauna offered, breaking the silence with the clink of bottles set upon the table. As they settled the air filled with the sound of gulps and sighs, the simple act of hydration momentarily grounding them in the present. Once the immediate need was sated, attention turned to the task at hand - sharing stories that weighed heavily on their souls. Austin started, his voice steady despite the gravity of their tale. His recap of their last few months felt distant as he told their story.

"We didn't just survive, we clawed our way through hell," he finished, locking eyes with Mickey, "it wasn't just about staying alive. We watched the world rot by people who enjoyed tearing it apart." Ben leaned forward, his face lined with the burden of his own story. "We've seen things," he paused, collecting himself, "shit no one should ever have to see."

"It wasn't chaos. It was designed, all of it," Reece chimed in, his military bearing unshaken despite the horrors recounted, "we were tools. Toys. They ran the show, and we danced for them. Bloody pawns."

"They hoarded supplies, kept us starved, weak." Chase's hands clenched into fists, the knuckles white.

"Control," Val whispered, the single word hanging heavy, laden with the sorrow of a mother torn from her child, "that's what they wanted. Control over everything and everyone." The soldiers across the table listened, their expressions a mix of empathy and steely resolve.

"We've been tracking movements along the coast for a while," Eddie admitted, "heard rumours of stockpiles, but nothing concrete."

"Your story fills in a lot of gaps," Barnett acknowledged, folding his arms as he processed the information, "it helps to know what we're up against."

"More importantly," Mickey added, his tone shifting to one of grim determination, "you're not alone anymore. We're part of something bigger, a community further south that's working to rebuild some semblance of order."

"Survivors," Neil interjected, "we're tasked with bringing them back. You'll be safe there, provided your intentions align with ours." Austin met Mickey's gaze, a silent understanding passing between leaders. In a world fractured by chaos, the promise of unity sparked a faint glimmer of hope, however fleeting it might be. Austin offered a small smile, leaning back in his chair with a renewed sense of purpose. The rest nodded in agreement, steeling themselves for the next leg of their journey. Here, in this bastion of faded glory, they found a new directive. One that might eventually lead them back to those they had left behind. The late afternoon sun cast an orange glow over the military base as Austin and his weary companions settled into a corner of the mess hall, their bodies slouched in fatigue. The scent of coffee and the clatter of utensils provided a backdrop to their ongoing conversation with Mickey and his team.

"Who's running the show there?" Austin asked, his voice a low rasp. He needed to know who held the reins of power in this patchwork of survival they had stumbled upon. Mickey took a slow sip from his mug before responding, his eyes scanning the faces around the table.

"Major General George Bishop commands the base," he said, setting his cup down with a soft clink, "his brother, Henry, acts as the mayor. They're trying to keep military and civilian leadership separate, but it's a small town. Everything's intertwined." Austin nodded, filing away the names. Leaders mattered in places like that, they set the tone and decided fates. He glanced at Ben whose eyes flickered with a determination that belied his exhaustion.

"We left people on the island," Ben's voice was steady but carried an undercurrent of pain, "we can't just abandon them." His gaze was distant, as if he could see the island they'd left behind through the walls of the mess hall.

"My daughter," Val's face was etched with sorrow, her lips trembling as she added softly, "she's one of them." Around the table, expressions softened and eyes lowered. Shauna reached out, placing a comforting hand on Val's shoulder. The group fell into a companionable silence, punctuated only by the occasional clink of cutlery. As the day stretched into evening, stories of Fort Irwin filled the space between them, tales of close calls and narrow escapes, of lost friends and new alliances. It was a tapestry of shared hardship and fragile hope, woven together by the voices of those who refused to be broken by the world's cruelty. The dust of the desert clung to everything - the buildings, the vehicles, even the people. As Austin stepped out of the truck, the fine grit found its way into the folds of his worn clothes. Fort Irwin sprawled before him, a military sanctuary amidst the desolation, its fences promising security and its barracks offering respite from the chaos they had traversed.

"Right this way." A voice called out, guiding them through the processing routine with practiced ease. They were poked and prodded by medics, handed meal rations that smelled faintly of preservatives, and shown to quarters that felt alarmingly like a luxury. Exhaustion weighed on Austin's shoulders as he trudged to his assigned billet. But it was there, in the shadow of normalcy, that he met Anne. Her smile was gentle, her eyes bright with a hope that seemed incongruous with the world outside these walls.

"Quite a place you've got here." Austin said, barely managing to acknowledge the small talk she offered about the weather, the food, and the comforts of a bed after so long.

"Never really left since the whole mess started," Anne replied, tucking a stray lock of hair behind her ear, "born and raised here, except for medical school back in LA."

"So you haven't seen what's really going on out there," Austin snorted dismissively, "living the dream." Her cheeks coloured slightly, caught between embarrassment and the desire to empathise.

"I can't even begin to understand what it's been like for you all," she admitted, "but if there's anything I can do to make your stay more comfortable."

"*Comfortable*," Austin laughed, the sound harsher than he intended, "you think we're just going to settle in, plant some flowers, and wait for the world to right itself?" She flinched, apology quick to her lips.

"I'm sorry, I didn't mean—"

"Save it," Austin interrupted, his own grief and frustration bleeding into words that could wound as he took a breath, rubbing a hand over his tired face, "sorry, that was out of line. It's been a long couple of weeks and kindness, well, it just feels so strange now."

"It might feel strange, but you'll find plenty of it here," Anne's expression softened, a hint of relief in her nod, "so try to get used to it." Austin watched her walk away, her figure becoming part of the busy backdrop of soldiers and survivors finding their way. As he turned towards his new temporary home, he allowed himself a sliver of hope that Fort Irwin might offer more than just shelter - it might offer a chance to heal. Days passed, and housing assignments and jobs had been assigned. In the shadowed confines of a briefing room on the military base, Austin leaned forward, elbows braced against the cool surface of the steel table. He watched as Major General George Bishop paced before them, detailing the threat, or lack thereof, posed by a radical evangelical group.

"Keep clear of their path and they won't trouble us here." George concluded, his words clipped and certain. Austin straightened, the creases of concern etching deeper into his forehead.

"There's another group you need to worry about," he said, voice steady despite the whirlwind of memories threatening to disrupt his calm, "on Alcatraz Island."

"We've heard rumours, but they're no immediate threat to our operations." George halted mid-stride, turning to face him with a furrowed brow. Ben's hands clenched into fists at his sides, knuckles whitening.

"They're torturing innocent people!" His voice, laced with righteous fury, bounced off the walls and challenged the complacency of the room.

"I understand your anger," George admitted, his gaze locking with Ben's, "but San Francisco is 600 clicks away. We don't have the resources for a rescue mission based on sentiment."

"*Sentiment*," Ben's voice rose, sharp as shattered glass, "this is about life, about doing what's right!" The muscle in his jaw twitched, the weight of decisions made and unmade bearing down upon him.

"Ben—" Austin started, reaching out an arm. But Ben was already storming out, boots thudding heavily against the concrete floor, leaving behind a palpable wake of frustration and helplessness. George's gaze lingered at the door through which Ben had departed, his expression a concoction of sympathy and resolve. He turned back to face the four men, each bearing their own brand of exhaustion and quiet determination. The air in the room felt heavier, saturated with unspoken understandings and the ghosts of personal battles.

"Look," George started, his voice softened, "my wife, she's been gone for months now, presumed dead. Every part of me yearns to sweep across the wastelands to find her, but we have to think about the greater good." He sighed, his eyes searching those before him, seeking an echo of his own resignation. Austin's jaw tightened, the flicker of conflict crossing his features. He met George's gaze and after a moment and gave a slight nod, the action seeming to draw a line under the conversation.

"I understand." He said, his voice barely above a whisper but laden with reluctant acceptance. The moment hung between them, a silent pact made amidst the ruins of the world they once knew.

The scent of antiseptics mingled with the faintest whiff of medicinal herbs. Val trailed behind Anne, taking in the rows of neatly organised supplies, the cleanliness a stark contrast to the chaos that had become their norm. Phillip stood to the side, his watchful eyes missing nothing as he oversaw the impromptu tour. Anne's hands gestured fluidly as she spoke, pointing out the various stations within the clinic.

"I spend much of my time on base, but dad here runs things when I'm away," her smile was warm, comforting even, yet it carried the weight of responsibilities far beyond her years, "you'll be primarily stationed here, especially on days when we're both needed at the military base." Anne concluded, her voice tinged with both authority and kindness. Val nodded, the knowledge that she'd be the clinic's mainstay settling in her stomach like a stone.

"Thank you," she replied, her tone steady, "I'll do my best." Phillip offered her a brief, approving nod. With that, Val took her first steps into a role that promised not just work, but a semblance of hope in the continued fight for life. Her fingers lingered over the bandage wrappers, each one a small promise of healing she could offer in this broken world. Phillip glanced at his watch, a subtle nod indicating it was time to leave. With a final sympathetic look, they exited, leaving Val alone amidst the quiet clinic. The door clicked shut, echoing through the pristine space. Alone now, Val felt her resolve crumbling. Her shoulders shook as she succumbed to sobs, the sound muffled by the walls meant to heal and protect. Months unfurled like a dusty road, marked by the rhythm of survival rather than the passage of time. Val became a fixture within the clinic, her hands moving with practiced ease as she took temperatures and soothed fears, offering comfort where she could no longer find it herself. Outside the clinic's confines, Austin, Ben, Reece, Chase, and Tyler embraced their new roles with a grim tenacity. They patrolled and scavenged, their eyes always scanning the horizon, keeping vigilant for any sign of unrest. Reports of other survivors in Los Angeles trickled in, whispers of potential threats that required their attention. But through the ceaseless cycle of duty and watchfulness, Val's heart remained anchored to the island, to the daughter she longed to embrace once more. Each day she donned her white coat was another day spent yearning for a rescue that never seemed to come. The sun dipped below the smog-stained horizon of Los Angeles, casting an orange pallor over the broken city. Austin led his unit through the skeletal remains of downtown, his eyes sharp and movements deliberate. They had been scouting for months, tracing the faint whispers of hostility that fluttered through the desolate streets like wayward spirits.

"Contact!" Reece's voice was a low growl, barely above a whisper, but it cut through the stillness with the urgency of a gunshot. In an instant, the quiet was shattered by the staccato rhythm of gunfire.

A group of men, hunkered down behind the carcass of an over-turned vehicle, returned fire. Austin recognised the cold efficiency in their movements - these were not just survivors, they were trained, disciplined.

"Push forward," he commanded, the words terse as he and his team advanced, using the debris for cover, "Chase, Tyler, flank left!" Austin yelled, noting how Chase's eyes were narrowed, his jaw set. Tyler nodded, his own resolve mirrored in the firm set of his shoulders as they peeled away from the group, disappearing between the fractured buildings. Ben was at Austin's side, his face a mask of determined fury. The two men moved in tandem, clearing a path through the hostile territory. Bullets whizzed past, and the sharp scent of gunpowder mingled with the acrid air. The exchange of fire was brief but intense. When it ended, the street fell eerily silent save for the distant wail of a siren that would never come. Several bodies lay motionless on both sides. Austin's heart hammered against his ribcage as he surveyed the casualties - this loss was senseless, unnecessary.

"George won't let this stand," Ben said quietly, his voice heavy with a mixture of grief and unspoken determination, "this group, they're organised, dangerous." Austin nodded, feeling the weight of leadership pressing down on him. Their presence here spoke of a larger threat, one that could not be ignored. Weeks passed, the tension mounting like the crescendo of a storm. They continued their patrols, ever watchful, until the coast revealed the confrontation they had been bracing for.

"You're outnumbered, stand down!" Austin called out as his unit cornered the two guards against the backdrop of the night.

"Go to hell!" A man spat, defiance etched across his features even as the reality of his situation began to sink in.

"Secure them." Austin ordered, and in moments the men were disarmed and restrained, the fight leaving their bodies along with the adrenaline.

"Tim," Austin stared down at one of the men, narrowing his gaze, "talk." He demanded, his eyes fixed.

"Okay, okay!" Tim's resistance crumbled under the weight of the cold metal cuffs around his wrists. As Tim recounted details of the defences and routines of Catalina, Austin felt a flicker of hope ignite within him. But it was the news that Beth and Chantelle were alive that sent a jolt through the entire unit. Ben's face, always stoic, broke into an expression of raw, unabated relief. A look that spoke volumes of the love and guilt that had been his silent companions for far too long - Austin knew the stakes had risen once again.

As the last words of the story hung in the air, Beth shifted uncomfortably in her chair, her gaze lost somewhere beyond the confines of the room. There was a heaviness about her, a weariness that seemed to go beyond the physical toll of their journey. They had told her everything, save for a few minor details including Ben's confession of his feelings to Austin.

"That's quite a story." She finally said, her voice tinged with a mix of awe and skepticism. Her fingers idly traced patterns on the arm, avoiding the expectant looks from the others.

"Your turn." Ben reminded her gently, though the intensity in his eyes betrayed his own anticipation. She pulled a blanket tighter around herself as if bracing for the weight of the memories she was about to unearth.

"Okay," she conceded after a long silence, lifting her gaze to meet Ben's, "but I'm only going up to the events of Chantelle's death, after that—" She paused, her lips pressing into a thin line.

"Of course." Reece agreed, nodding solemnly. They understood all too well the gravity of what Beth was holding back. The others settled in more comfortably, readying themselves for Beth's account. As her story unfolded, the warmth of the plush surroundings did little to ease the chill that crept into her bones with each word spoken - a chilling reminder of the time lost and the pain endured.

CHAPTER 8

Beth stood motionless outside the *Mary Walker Clinic*, her gaze fixed on the pavement that stretched from the sliding doors to where she was rooted. The crisp autumn air nipped at her cheeks as a mother, clutching her child's hand, emerged from within. They were wrapped in light jackets, the little one's laughter floating up like a kite on the breeze. As they approached, Beth caught the child's bright eyes and tousled hair, which stirred something poignant deep inside her chest. The mother, sensing the sombreness in Beth's stance, offered a small nod of acknowledgment before guiding her child past and into the day. With the pair now gone, the weight of the moment settled upon Beth, pressing her with the gravity of what was to come. She took an involuntary breath and began her approach towards the clinic's doors. Each step felt laden as though her boots were mired in unseen sludge. Her mind spun, dredging up fragments of conversation, searching for the right words to convey a truth that seemed impossible to articulate. The walk from her new home should have been a brisk 15 minutes, but today it had stretched on indefinitely. She had meandered, taken detours, and explored the town a little as if her feet betrayed her urgency to face Val. Beth's thoughts spiralled back to Chantelle - sweet, vibrant Chantelle - whose life had slipped away in the sterile solitude of a world far too cruel. The image of her friend, swinging alone with only shadows for company in those final moments, clawed at Beth's resolve.

"Focus." She whispered to herself, shaking her head as if to cast out the haunting images. But they clung like cobwebs, each thread a reminder of a promise unfulfilled, a protection not given. Resolute yet heavy-hearted, Beth reached for the door handle, steeling herself for the conversation she dreaded. Inside awaited Val, and with her the need for answers that Beth feared she didn't possess. Beth's palm pressed against the cool metal of the door, resisting for a moment before giving way to her gentle nudge. A familiar antiseptic scent of the clinic greeted her, yet it did nothing to cleanse the turmoil that churned within. Val, stationed behind the reception desk, looked up as Beth crossed the threshold. Their eyes met, locking in a silent exchange more piercing than words. There was an intense scrutiny in Val's gaze, a searching that probed beneath Beth's surface, seeking something - some inkling of what had transpired. Then just as quickly, her attention dropped away, the click of her pen and the rustle of paper reclaiming her focus. Confusion furrowed Beth's brow. Not a single query about Chantelle's whereabouts escaped Val's lips, no shadow of concern crept across her features. It was as if the question had been answered before it could be formed, leaving Beth adrift in uncertainty. The air between them grew thick with tension, each second elongating into an eternity of unspoken dread. Beth's throat tightened, words like boulders too heavy to lift. She willed herself to break the silence, to speak of Chantelle, but found her voice ensnared by an invisible force. Val let out a weary sigh, the sound slicing through the quiet like a scalpel. She turned slightly, facing Beth.

"If you're here to tell me about Chantelle," she said, her tone carrying the weight of resignation, "I already know." Beth's heart stumbled over its next beat, the revelation pricking at her insides. There was a bitter comfort in not having to voice the sorrowful news, but it was swiftly overshadowed by the sting of being robbed of the chance to offer a personal touch to such a cold fact. The depth of their shared loss seemed trivialised, reduced to mere information passed along without ceremony or care.

"How," Beth's voice faltered as she absorbed the news, "how did you find out?"

"Shauna, one of the second lieutenants," Val replied curtly, her fingers tapping a staccato rhythm on the clipboard, "she briefed us after you all arrived." The words hung in the sterile air of the clinic, their sharp edges cutting into Beth's resolve. It was supposed to have come from her lips, a careful delivery of a fragile truth.

"I wanted to tell you myself." Beth said, the hurt evident in her tone.

"We don't get the luxury of personal courtesies here," Val began, not lifting her gaze, "you don't get to call the shots, Beth." Her voice held an edge that suggested this was not up for debate, a protocol woven into the fabric of their existence. Beth's hands clenched at her sides, the need to share, to *explain* swelling within her chest.

"I need to tell you what happened, about Chantelle—"

"I'll ask when I'm ready." Val cut her off with a raised hand, her eyes finally meeting Beth's. There was a coldness there, a barrier erected against the onslaught of pain.

"Val—"

"And honestly, I'm not surprised that you made it back and Chantelle didn't." The accusation, veiled though it may have been, landed like a punch to the stomach. Beth staggered under its weight, her apology a whisper lost in the void between them.

"I'm sorry. I—"

"Sorry," Val echoed, her lips twisting into a semblance of a smile that didn't reach her eyes, "Beth, I thought at the very least that you'd try to protect her." Beth stepped back, feeling the chasm of unspoken blame widen. She had failed Chantelle, failed to be the shield she promised to be. Val's words were a confirmation of her own deepest fears, and in that moment, the clinic walls seemed to press in, suffocating her with the enormity of her guilt. Beth's fingers trembled as they traced the creases in the paper, each fold a stark reminder of Chantelle's final words. The note felt like lead in her hands, heavy with unsaid goodbyes and unshed tears. She hesitated, her mind warring with the impulse to share this last piece of her friend and the fear of opening old wounds anew.

"Val," Beth's voice was barely audible as she stepped forward, the note extended between them like a fragile truce, "this is for you." Val's eyes flickered down to the crumpled paper in Beth's outstretched hand, her expression unreadable.

"What is it?" She asked, though her tone suggested she already understood its grim nature. Beth swallowed hard, her throat tight with emotions she couldn't afford to release.

"You know what this is," she said, her voice laced with the weight of truth and sorrow, "please just take it." Val maintained her cold stance, staring at the note in Beth's hand. With a few tentative steps forward, Beth placed the note on the desk and met Val's gaze, her eyes dark with curiosity and bereavement. Without another word, Beth turned on her heel and left the clinic, the door closing behind her with a soft click that echoed the finality of her departure.

The sound of leather smacking against pads echoed through the walls of the *Memorial Fitness Center*, punctuated by the occasional grunt or shout. Reece, with his quick footwork and agile dodges, was a force to be reckoned with as he sparred against the much younger Tyler. The two men moved with fluidity and grace, despite the sweat glistening on their brows and their heaving chests. Age seemed to have no impact on Reece's endurance and skill, as he laughed and taunted Tyler, proving that experience was truly the greatest teacher in the ring.

"Come on kid," he jeered playfully, "did you hit the bottle too hard last night? Got lost in Beth's story?" Panting slightly from the exertion, Tyler shook his head, but his smile was strained.
"Probably a few too many," he echoed Reece's laughter, wiping sweat from his brow, "do you ever miss it?" Reece's laughter faded into a smirk, a shadow of something darker crossing his features for a moment before it passed.
"Nah," he replied, his voice firm with conviction, "I'm better off sober." The two exchanged a few more blows in silence, the only sounds their controlled breaths and the muffled impact of fists on training gear, and the occasional escape of laughter. Each man lost in his own thoughts, yet bound by a shared understanding that some battles were fought within, far away from the physicality of the sparring ring. Reece's fists were precise, each strike a testament to years of discipline. He could feel Tyler's gaze on him, heavy with unspoken questions that lingered in the air like the scent of sweat and leather.
"Man," Tyler finally exhaled, "you've got more reasons than most to fall back into old habits." Reece's next punch hit the pad with a snap, his eyes never leaving Tyler's.
"It's about what I've lost," his voice was low, almost reverent, "Chantelle, she was too good for this world. If I let myself slip, I'd lose her all over again, you know, in my head. I can't dishonour her

memory like that." Tyler nodded, understanding flickering in his eyes before they diverted to the entrance as Chase sauntered in. He had a cocky grin plastered across his face, a silent challenge as he clapped Tyler on the shoulder.

"I'm tapping you out, let's see if the old timer has any fight left in him." Chase quipped, cracking his knuckles. Reece welcomed the change, stepping lightly on the mat as Chase advanced. They circled, two predators sizing each other up before Reece saw his opening. Quick as lightning, he executed a manoeuvre, pinning Chase to the mat with a grunt of satisfaction.

"Looks like age before beauty still stands." Reece laughed, helping Chase to his feet only to take him down again moments later when Chase attempted a sly move that failed spectacularly. Laughter erupted from the trio in the centre of the ring while Austin and Ben watched from their post by the weights. Ben shook his head, letting out a low whistle.

"Should we tell 'em we're not even trying anymore?" Ben called out, amusement lacing his tone. Austin simply grinned, leaning back against the rack of weights, their laughter mingling with the sounds of camaraderie that filled the gym. The clink of weights punctuated the air as Austin watched Ben rack a barbell, his form strained from the effort. Sweat beaded on Ben's forehead, a physical testament to the turmoil that seemed to radiate from him like heat from a flame.

"Everything okay?" Austin asked, his voice low enough not to carry over the grunts and thuds of exertion around them. Ben wiped his brow with the back of his hand, exhaling sharply.

"Overwhelmed," he admitted, his eyes briefly flitting towards the door through which Julia might enter at any moment, "it's complicated, with both Julia and Beth here."

"I can imagine," Austin leaned against the wall, his gaze following Ben's, "but you knew it wasn't just casual for Julia, right?"

"And what about you and Anne? You're one to talk about being careful." A muscle twitched in Ben's jaw, his glare sharp as it landed on Austin.

"Hey, I'm not the one who was pining for someone else." Austin retorted defensively, though the lie felt heavy on his tongue. He had felt something for Beth once, something he still couldn't fully explain away.

"Right," Ben said, sarcasm dripping from each word as he picked up a towel and draped it over his neck, "forgive me for seeking some comfort while grieving. We all have our ways."

"Beth wasn't dead, Ben. And if you really loved her, maybe you would've shown a bit more restraint instead of jumping into bed with the first girl you saw." Austin's response was immediate, a reflex born from guilt and self-defence. Ben's expression hardened, the hurt clear in his eyes before he turned away, the conversation hanging unfinished and heavy in the air between them.

"You know what Austin," Ben angrily stuffed his gym bag with his towel, snatching it from the weight bench, "I dealt with my demons the way I needed to. You left her there that night. You left *them* behind. *You* made that decision. Deal with that how you please, and I'll do the same." With those final words, Ben stormed out of the gym, leaving Austin alone with his thoughts and a heavy sense of guilt weighing on his chest. The slam of the fitness centre door echoed off the walls as Ben's heavy footsteps receded. He knew Ben was right, he had left Beth and Chantelle behind that night without even a second glance back. Once that decision had been made in his mind, there was no going back, not when they would have been killed. He had been consumed by grief and anger, unable to process or face the reality of it. Austin watched the exit, his hands clenched around the cold steel barbell. The weight of his own accusations pressed down harder than the iron plates he was about to hoist. He couldn't shake the gnawing doubt that had taken root - if his feelings for Beth were as dormant as he claimed, he wondered why every mention of her stirred such turmoil within him. With a grunt, Austin returned to his bench press, attempting to channel his frustration into physical exertion. The weights ascended steadily at first, propelled by his pent-up energy. But as his mind wandered back to Beth, his focus wavered. The rhythm faltered - once, twice, until finally on the third rep a sharp jolt of pain seared through his upper arm.

"Fuck!" Austin's cry cut through the gym's bustling ambiance. The barbell clattered onto the safety catches, the sound reverberating through the room. Reece, Tyler, and Chase turned in unison towards the source of the noise. In an instant, they were at Austin's side, their expressions etched with concern.

"You okay?" Reece asked, eyeing the contorted grimace on Austin's face.

"Something in my arm," Austin gasped, cradling the injured limb, "it just popped."

"Come on," Chase helped Austin to his feet, grabbing his uninjured arm in the process, "let's get you to Anne."

As the warm rays of the early morning sun danced across the horizon, casting long shadows along 1st Street, Anne and Julia jogged side by side. Their synchronised breaths created a rhythmic puffing sound, perfectly matched to the soft thudding of their feet against the pavement. The *Fort Irwin Quadraplex* athletic field loomed beside them, a sprawling green oasis in the midst of the dry and barren landscape. They continued on, their bodies moving in harmony with each other and the serene surroundings around them.

"Have you talked to Ben since he got back?" Anne asked, her tone casual but probing. Julia's stride didn't falter, though her lips curled into a slight frown.

"Not yet," she admitted, annoyance flickering in her eyes, "but I'm not surprised. Ben has this pattern. Usually comes straight to me after missions. There've been times though, when he heads home instead. Especially when it's been a rough one."

"Must be tough," Anne commented, keeping pace, "the unpredictability."

"Maybe," Julia laughed, shaking off any hint of discontent, "but there are perks to dating a soldier. No curfews mean late-night visits aren't out of the question." Anne glanced at Julia, noting the carefree shrug of her shoulders. They continued their run, the rhythm of their footfalls and the easy conversation masking the storm brewing just beyond the horizon of their awareness. The rhythm of their jog had brought them to a slower pace, allowing for the conversation to weave between breaths. Anne's concern creased her forehead as she turned towards Julia, the early light casting a soft glow on her face.

"Julia," Anne started, a cautious tone underpinning her words, "you do know that you and Ben, you're not really dating, right? You need to be careful with how you frame things." Julia's stride remained confident, her gaze fixed on the path ahead, unfazed by the warning.

"So, what's Beth like?" She asked, artfully sidestepping Anne's advice. Her curiosity about the woman who seemed to occupy so much of Ben's past, and Austin's thoughts, was genuine if not tinged with rivalry.

"Truthfully, I haven't really gotten to know her," Anne admitted, her voice reflecting a hint of regret for the missed connection, "our paths have crossed, but it was all too brief for any real conversation."

"Still, you've spent more time with her than I have." Julia pointed out, recalling the formal interaction she'd had with Beth over her housing assignment. It had been brief and impersonal, a procedural necessity rather than an introduction.

"It wasn't exactly a heart-to-heart," Anne shook her head slightly, "look, if you want to know about Beth, you're asking the wrong person."

"Could you ask Austin for me?" Julia's request came with a hopeful lilt, an attempt to delegate the task to someone already in Beth's orbit.

"No, I don't think I want to get involved in that." Anne replied firmly, unwilling to play intermediary in the delicate dynamics at hand. She knew better than to stir the pot of an already simmering situation. They continued their jog, each lost in thought as the field fell behind them, and the conversation shifted like the desert sands around them - unpredictable and uncontainable. The sun was beginning to dip towards the horizon as Anne and Julia rounded the bend onto Inner Loop Road, their sneakers crunching in unison against the gravel. A solitary figure approached in the distance, shoulders squared despite a weariness that seemed to cling to her like a second skin.

"Who is that?" Julia squinted into the distance, shielding her eyes against the sun with her palm.

"Or better yet, get to know her yourself," Anne murmured, slowing her pace just enough for implication, "Beth is right there." Julia, her curiosity piqued ever since the housing assignment hand-off, nodded silently.

"I barely recognised her." Julia lowered her hand as they came to a halt, waiting as the gap between them and Beth narrowed with each measured step.

"Hi." Anne called out as she drew near. Beth slowed her pace, finally halting in front of the two women. Beth nodded towards Anne before settling her gaze on Julia.

"I'm Beth." She offered her a faint smile, the kind worn by those who have learned to mask their true feelings after a difficult confrontation.

"Of course, I remember you," Julia replied with a friendly tilt of her head, recognising the woman before her, "I gave you your housing assignment."

"Right, sorry. My mind has been elsewhere. The last few days have been a lot." Beth's voice was threaded with apology as she brushed a strand of hair from her face, a futile attempt to push away the fatigue that dulled her eyes.

"Well, I'd imagine this is all pretty overwhelming after what you've been through," Julia let out a light laugh, one that fluttered awkwardly between them, "sounds like you've had quite a rough time out there from what we've heard."

'Yes, it was quite a *rough time*." Beth responded through gritted teeth. Her frustration seemed to grow with every passing second in this new community, especially every time she came across someone who hadn't spent one moment out in the real world.

"Beth," Anne took a step towards her gingerly, "is everything alright?" Beth's response was a slow nod as an acknowledgment of

Anne's concern, but one she couldn't ascertain was genuine or not. Beth's gaze, once filled with the weariness of recent events, sharpened as it locked onto Julia. Her blank expression was a canvas upon which confusion and curiosity warred for dominance.

"Jobs," the change of topic was sudden, Beth's tone betraying a hint of frustration, "do you handle those assignments too? Because I haven't received one yet." Anne's eyes darted between the two women, the tension palpable. With a disapproving glance at Julia, she stepped in, her voice smooth but firm.

"Julia distributes them, but she isn't responsible for the actual assignments," Anne explained quickly, "no one from Catalina has been assigned a job yet. They thought you should all rest first. You know, ease back into things before taking on professional responsibilities." Beth's nod was slow, the information settling in like sediment in still water. It made sense, yet another part of her desired something, *anything* that could anchor her to normalcy. Julia, seemingly oblivious to the undercurrents of the conversation, chimed in cheerily.

"Austin and Ben have told us so much about you." The statement was like a pebble dropped into the calm waters of Beth's mind, ripples distorting her thoughts. She arched an eyebrow, silently pressing for more as Anne's gaze darted towards her friend.

"Julia—" Anne interjected.

"Your name came up often during our date nights," Julia continued, a smile playing on her lips, seemingly proud of her inclusion in these intimate gatherings, "it's nice to finally put a face to all those stories."

"Date nights?" The words fell from Beth's mouth before she could catch them, laced with incredulity.

"Yep," Julia beamed, as if announcing a well-kept secret, "I'm Ben's girlfriend. It's so nice to finally meet you. I know you're like a sister to him, so it's nice to put a face to the name." A delicate breeze played with strands of Beth's hair as she processed this new piece of the puzzle. The revelation hung in the air, mingling with the scents of the fading day. Beth studied the lines of Julia's face, the expression she had maintained the entire time they were talking. No hint of malice swept across her expression, just one of naive understanding of the state of the outside world. Beth finally concluded that Julia wasn't trying to be cruel, she was just asinine and clueless. "Come on, we need to get going." Anne said curtly, her face a shade paler than usual. She gripped Julia's arm with a firmness that brooked no argument, pulling her away from the awkward encounter with Beth. A sheen of sweat glistened on Anne's forehead, remnants of their interrupted run. Julia tossed her hair back with a nonchalant shrug.

"I didn't do anything wrong." She insisted, matching Anne's brisk pace reluctantly.

"That was cruel." Anne scolded her sharply.

"What was?" Julia hurried along beside her friend, pulling her arm from Anne's grasp.

"Ben never explicitly said you two were together." Anne pointed out, the edges of her words sharp as if trying to pierce Julia's bubble of nonchalance.

"And he never said we weren't," Julia countered, her voice light but carrying an undertone of defiance, "the more it's put out there, the more he'll come around to it." The two women's sneakers crunched against the gravel path, their stride hurried by necessity and discomfort. Beth turned away as they disappeared around the corner, her mind a whirlwind of emotions she couldn't quite name. The weight of the conversation pressed down on her as she approached the familiarity of her own front steps.

"Beth!" Ben's voice cut through her reverie, causing her to pause just shy of her door. He jogged towards her, his expression a mix of concern and something else she couldn't quite place. She offered him a half-hearted shrug in lieu of a greeting.

"Ben." She whispered softly, wanting nothing more than to disappear inside and lock the door behind her.

"Did you chat with Val? How did she take it?" He asked cautiously, noting the exhausted expression on her face as he buried his hands in the pockets of his sweatpants.

"Val already knew about Chantelle," Beth replied, feeling a twinge of disappointment at having been robbed of the closure she had sought, "I wanted to tell her myself."

"It doesn't really work that way here." He sighed, a note of apology in his voice.

"So everyone keeps telling me." Beth felt a surge of emotions clawing for release - disappointment, anger, sadness. When Ben reached out, as though his touch could somehow make things better, she instinctively recoiled, wrapping her arms around herself instead.

"Beth—"

"Please," she whispered, taking a step back, "don't." He withdrew his hand quickly, letting it hang awkwardly by his side. There was regret in his eyes, but he respected her boundary, nodding slowly as she turned away from him and towards the solace of her house. Beth's fingers traced the raised edges of the brand on her arm, her anxiety bubbling to the surface as she paused. She could feel Ben's eyes on her, waiting for her to speak, to explain the sudden distance she put between them.

"Beth," his eyes narrowed cautiously, "what's wrong with you?"

"I met Julia." She said quickly, not looking at him, focusing instead on the pattern she drew around the scar. He hesitated, his posture shifting as he searched for an answer.

"I hadn't found the right moment to tell you about her." Ben finally said, his words sounding hollow even to his own ears. Beth shook her head, dismissing the excuse with a faint glimmer of irony touching her lips.

"I don't care about the *right moment*, Ben. I promise you I am far from angry about that," she paused, searching for the words to accurately explain how she felt, "I'm annoyed at everyone here. I can't help how angry I feel all the time that while we were being beaten and battered and Chantelle was being raped *repeatedly* these people were just naively living their lives here without a second thought. Dating, exercising - the whole concept seems so foreign to me now and I'm fucking mad that while you were going on date nights with your girlfriend and Austin and Anne, we were waiting for you guys to come and save us."

"Julia is not my girlfriend." Ben interjected quickly, his voice firm yet laced with an undercurrent of frustration.

"Really," Beth replied, her tone flat, "because she certainly thinks she is." She finally lifted her eyes to meet his, and he could see the detachment in their depths. Ben let out a weary sigh, rubbing the back of his neck.

"I know," he admitted, "it was just a physical thing, nothing more." Beth returned her attention to the brand on her arm, the motion soothing yet detached. Her voice was calm, but there was a sharpness to it that betrayed her true feelings.

"I'm not interested in this drama, Ben. And judging by today's little performance, Julia seems more focused on dating you than anything else. Did you tell them what happened on Alcatraz?"

"Anne knows some things," Ben confessed softly, "I know Austin told her a bit, but Julia knows nothing."

"I wonder if she would be less inclined to stress about her love life if she really knew what was going on out there," Beth said sharply, looking up at him with fury in her eyes, "I wonder if she would've survived Alcatraz, or Catalina. Anne would've been fine because she's necessary, but people like Julia and people like me are good for one thing and one thing only."

"Beth, I—"

"See, I was eased into it back in Washington," she interrupted, her voice a hushed and angry whisper, "if I'd started out with someone like Marcus it would've killed me. But these people here have been living behind walls of normalcy and it's fucking infuriating." He struggled to find the right words, but they seemed to escape him as he faced her intense gaze. All of his carefully constructed words had crumbled under her scrutiny, forcing him to confront uncomfortable truths that he had buried deep within himself. The silence stretched between them, tension mounting with each passing second.

"Beth, I'm sorry." His words fell flat like wilted flowers, once full of vibrant colour and life, now shrivelled and lacking any impact.

"Ben," she started, her voice steady but cold as steel, "after everything we've been through, it's hard to believe that *normal* life is supposed to be this easy. You talk about relationship drama as if it's the end of the world. But that? That's delusion." Ben shifted awkwardly on his feet, the sound of the footpath crunching beneath his gym sneakers as the wind rustled leaves softly nearby.

"Chantelle suffered every night," Beth continued, her tone now laced with a venomous sarcasm that made the air around them feel thinner as her hand dropped from the brand and fell limp by her side, "while I faced the horrors of Victor's hand and she faced the horrors of Victor's bed, you all enjoyed your double dates and your dinner parties, and went on about your daily lives as if the world hadn't fallen apart. Maybe for you, life moved on. But for me it's going to take a bit more time to get used to this semblance of civilization you're all so enamoured with."

"Beth, I don't know what to say," Ben stammered, his mouth formed the words but his eyes were downcast and his shoulders sagged, his body language betraying the heartache in his words, "what can I do to make this easier?" Beth shook her head, a bitter laugh escaping her lips. She turned on her heel, the gravel beneath her boots crunching softly as she strode towards the sanctity of her house.

"Please," she said over her shoulder, her voice almost lost amidst the sound of her retreating footsteps as she refused to look back at him, "just leave me alone." Ben stood still, the silence enveloping him like a thick fog as he watched her retreat. With a soft click, the door closed behind her, the finality of the lock slotting into place echoing in his ears. He was left standing outside, grappling with a reality that felt more complex and unforgiving than any battlefield he'd ever known. Ben watched her go, realising that the scars they both carried weren't just physical - they were etched deep within, shaping the chasms that lay between them. Beth's fingers lingered on the raised skin of her brand as she leaned against her front door, tracing the edges as if they held some hidden answer. She stood rigid, a statue with eyes that held centuries of pain, and drew in a deep breath. Beth closed her eyes, trying to push back the onslaught of memories that threatened to engulf her. She could still feel Victor's hands on her, his cruel words searing into her mind. But she refused to let him have power over her anymore, not now that he was dead. She took another deep breath, and with a final touch to her brand, she opened her eyes and let go of the past. As she walked through the unfamiliar halls of her house, Beth couldn't help but feel a sense of emptiness. The vast home felt too big for just one person. The walls seemed to mock her, reminding her of all the happy memories in her life that were now tainted by pain. The childhood home she knew so well, the one she had made a life in with her husband, and now this new house that was given to her, expected to be her fresh start - all these houses had come and gone, just like this one would inevitably be ripped from her as well. Beth's thoughts turned to Chantelle, her fellow captive and friend who had endured so much at Victor's hands. She wondered where Chantelle was now, if she had found some semblance of peace in a place beyond pain and suffering, where the weight of the past was lifted and only tranquillity remained. Beth longed for peace of her own - it was always elusive, hovering just out of reach like a shimmering mirage, a place of pure joy and contentment where all pains and sorrows were washed away like sand castles by the tide. She shook her head suddenly, pushing her intrusive thoughts from her mind. It was a dark path she had begun to walk along, and Beth wasn't ready to give up on the world she lived in, not when she'd barely given her freedom a chance.

Anne's practiced fingers probed the tender flesh around Austin's swollen bicep, her brow furrowed with concern. The sterile scent of antiseptic hung in the air of the infirmary, a stark reminder of the vulnerability even the strongest faced.

"Okay, talk to me," she said, her tone gentle but insistent, "what happened here? Because this doesn't look like a simple miscalculation." Austin winced under her touch, not just from the pain, but also from the realisation that he couldn't mask the truth from Anne. She knew him too well, and she could read his body language like an open book.

"An argument," Austin admitted, his voice betraying a hint of embarrassment as he shifted uncomfortably on the edge of the cot, "with Ben. I should've stopped lifting after that, but I was pissed off and lost focus." Anne exhaled slowly, taking in the information while continuing her examination.

"You let your emotions get the best of you." She retorted flatly, pressing her fingers carefully at his arm before stepping back and withdrawing her hands.

"My diagnosis?" Austin met her annoyed gaze, mirroring her body language.

"Looks like a tendon rupture," Anne concluded, her clinical eye assessing the damage as she reached for an ice pack and placed it gently against the bulging skin, "you're going to need rest, Austin. And ice, lots of it." She helped him to his feet, guiding his arm into the support of a sling.

"Sure." He replied angrily, more towards himself than anyone or anything else.

"You'll be wearing this for a while." She instructed, making sure the fabric sat snug but not tight, allowing for healing without restricting circulation.

"Thanks." Austin's gratitude was genuine, though his pride smarted. As a soldier, he was trained to push through pain, but Anne's care reminded him that sometimes the bravest thing to do was to acknowledge when to stop.

"Take care of yourself," Anne said softly, locking eyes with him for a moment, "that goes for more than just your arm, okay?"

"Okay." Austin nodded solemnly, the weight of her words settling in. The fabric of the sling brushed against Austin's skin, a constant reminder of his lapse in judgment. Anne's fingers worked deftly, securing it around his muscular torso, her touch both professional and comforting. The infirmary's sterile smell mingled with the faint scent of her shampoo, and Austin found himself focusing on that rather than the tightness enveloping his injured arm.

"What was the fight about?" Anne asked, her voice low as she stepped back to examine her handiwork. She had always been able to read him like an open book, but there were chapters he preferred to keep closed - this being one of them.

"Anne, I'm allowed to have some secrets from you," Austin began, his tone carrying a note of finality that he hoped would deter further questioning as he met her gaze, imploring silently for her understanding, "just drop it, okay?" She pursed her lips but nodded, accepting his boundary for now. It was then that she shifted topics, her expression turning pensive.

"I ran into Beth earlier with Julia," she said, her eyes flickering with concern, "and Julia told her that she's Ben's girlfriend."

"Julia isn't his girlfriend." Austin corrected automatically, the words slipping out with a hint of irritation. He knew the complications that little lie could brew within their tight-knit community.

"That's what she told Beth." Anne's eyebrows lifted, a silent question hanging between them.

"Great," Austin muttered, massaging his temple with his good hand, "that girl is going to cause drama."

"Julia or Beth?" Anne probed, her curiosity piqued.

"Both." He replied quickly, the word laced with resignation. He knew all too well how quickly sparks could ignite into a blaze amongst people who lived and worked so closely together.

CHAPTER 9

Phillip's living room was steeped in a comfortable silence, the kind only old friends could share without discomfort. The tick of the grandfather clock and the soft crackle from the fireplace filled the space between them. Austin sat sunk deep within the plush folds of an armchair, his injured arm cradled protectively against his chest.

"You've been unusually quiet tonight." Phillip observed, breaking the stillness as he set down his glass with a soft clink on the wooden coffee table. Austin exhaled a heavy sigh, shifting uneasily.

"Had a row with Ben a few days back," he admitted, eyes fixed on the dancing flames, "haven't spoken since, and with my arm I can't exactly bump into him around the base, what with the medical leave and all. I don't really have an excuse to go there and *accidentally* run into him."

"You are close friends. Doesn't seem like you need an excuse to seek him out to talk," Phillip nodded, understanding the weight of unresolved conflict, "what was the fight about, if you don't mind me asking?"

"Concerns about Beth," Austin confessed, dragging a hand through his tousled hair, "she's struggling to find her footing here." Phillip leaned forward, resting his elbows on his knees. His gaze was both earnest and empathetic.

"You've all had your share of demons to wrestle with since arriving here," he said softly, "but none of us have walked the path she has. Her journey's been different, harsher."

"*Harsher.*" Austin's jaw clenched, the muscles working silently as he processed Phillip's words. He knew his friend was right - they'd all seen darkness, but none quite like Beth's. Phillip shifted in his seat, the leather of the couch creaking under him. He studied Austin's troubled expression with a piercing intensity that seemed to reach beyond the surface.

"You know, Austin," he began, voice low and steady, "Beth's ordeal, it was likely more about being a pawn in someone else's sick game than about survival." The shadows cast by the flickering firelight played across Austin's face, accentuating the furrows of concern etched deeply into his brow.

"A pawn?" He echoed, the word tasting bitter.

"Think about it," Phillip pressed on, his eyes never leaving Austin's, "if everything you told me about Alcatraz and Catalina is true, she'd have been subjected to atrocities we can't even begin to comprehend." His voice was a gentle prod, urging Austin to confront an uncomfortable truth.

"Everything I told you was true. Worse, actually. Probably left out the really nasty shit to spare you." Austin's gaze faltered, falling to his hands, and for a moment he seemed to grapple with an invisible adversary.

"Well then," Phillip tilted his head to the side, his eyes searching for Austin to come to his own conclusion, "she's clearly been through a lot."

"To be turned into nothing but some *thing* for men to use," Austin struggled with the concept, feeling anger simmer beneath the surface, "it's sick. It makes me sick. They would've ripped everything from her."

"Exactly," Phillip affirmed, leaning back as if giving room for the gravity of his words to land between them, "she needs more than just safety now. She needs a reason to wake up in the morning, something to make her feel human again."

"You're probably right." Austin met Phillip's gaze once more, his eyes blank slates reflecting a storm of unspoken thoughts. Before he could articulate any of them, Phillip cut through the silence with a pointed observation.

"Consider this," Phillip said, gesturing vaguely at the modest comforts of the living room around them, "this place might seem like a haven. But for Beth, the monotony of doing nothing is possibly a cruel reminder of her time spent waiting in confinement. Waiting in a cell or a hotel room, never knowing when she'd be collected next." A shudder ran through Austin as he imagined the uncertainty and fear that must have gnawed at Beth during those endless hours of captivity. The safe walls of the living room suddenly felt oppressive, the quiet too reminiscent of a calm that promised storms. Phillip let the words hang heavy in the air, a solemn tribute to the resilience of a soul who had endured far beyond what was fair. Austin knew he couldn't undo the past, but the resolve hardening within him was clear - it was time to help Beth reclaim her life, one small step at a time. Austin's fists finally released, a physical manifestation of the decision taking shape in his mind.

"She needs control over her own life again," he said, the words etched with newfound purpose, "freedom to come and go as she pleases. A job could be the key."

"I know you wanted to give her time to settle into normalcy, but I don't think the monotony of having nothing to do is helping her." Phillip nodded in affirmation.

"Tomorrow," Austin concluded, his voice steady despite the turmoil roiling within him, "I'll see what can be arranged."

Days slipped away, marked only by the slow traverse of sunlight across the walls of Beth's seclusion. The routine was numbingly familiar, yet each morning she woke to it with a shiver of dread. No longer did the threat of violence loom over her, no insidious footsteps echoing down a sterile corridor towards her door. But the ghost of fear remained - a spectre haunting the quiet corners of her new home. Sitting for hours, her gaze fixed on the door, flinching at every creak and groan of the settling house. Though the silence should have been a solace, it thrummed against her skull, a relentless drumbeat that echoed the pounding of her heart. She longed for the warmth of the sun on her skin, the whisper of the wind through leaves, but the thought of stepping outside, of facing the world beyond her four walls, anchored her to the safety of her solitude. The stillness of the house became her sentinel, guarding against a past that clawed at the edges of her peace. Yet, in its vigil, it also held her captive to the memories that surged like tides within her - memories of waiting, always waiting, for the next horror to befall her. It was in this self-imposed isolation that Beth found both her sanctuary and her prison, day bleeding indistinguishably into day. The abrupt rap at the door cleaved through the silence, jolting Beth from her reverie. Her heart lurched in her chest, a familiar surge of adrenaline prickling at her nerves as she peeled herself from the couch's worn fabric. She paused, breathless, catching the reflection in the hall mirror of a woman she scarcely recognised. The mirror held no kindness for her dishevelled state - hair knotted and lifeless, the pallor of her skin accentuated by the dark circles that had taken residence beneath her eyes. The same threadbare clothes hung on her frame, a testament to days spent cocooned in the linen confines of her bed seeking refuge in sleep's elusive embrace. With a leaden arm she turned the lock, opening the door with trepidation. The daylight seemed intrusive, too bright against her dull senses. Two figures stood there, an odd contrast to each other - one familiar, one not - a juxtaposition of past and present.

"Reece." She whispered, voice hoarse with disuse, acknowledging the man whose presence had become a sporadic comfort in this new existence.

"Hey Beth." Reece offered a tentative smile, his expression tinged with concern. Beside him stood a figure straight from the mould of military propriety, uniform crisp and posture rigid.

"Second Lieutenant Chris Barnett," the man introduced himself, his voice carrying the timbre of authority softened by a semblance of warmth, "just Barnett will do." His eyes met hers, searching, perhaps, for the person he had been briefed about. Beth nodded, a motion stiff with caution.

"What are you doing here?" The question emerged more brittle than intended, the words laced with the instinctive wariness of a creature cornered one too many times.

"Your new job," Reece chimed in before Barnett could respond, "we're here to take you there." The concept of a *new job*, a purpose beyond her own survival was foreign, almost alien in its simplicity. Yet, it stirred something within her. A flicker of curiosity, of hope cautiously rekindling in the desolate landscape of her mind.

"Okay," she said, the word tasting strange but not entirely unpleasant, "give me a moment?"

"Of course," Barnett replied, his stance relaxing marginally, "we'll wait." As they stepped back, allowing her to retreat and gather herself, a sliver of resolve edged out the remnants of fear. Maybe this time, stepping out into the world would not be another descent into chaos, but rather a stride towards something resembling a future.

"Can I," Beth cleared her throat as her eyes darted between the two men, uncertainty clouding her gaze, "may I have some time to change?"

"Sure," Barnett responded with an ease that felt foreign to the tension in her chest, "you don't need permission from us to take the time you need. I'll come back for you in an hour." With those words, he turned on his heel and strode away, his uniform crisply outlining his departure. The silence that settled was punctuated by Reece's lingering presence. He stood there, a sentinel against the backdrop of a life that Beth could scarcely remember being part of. "Why wasn't I allowed to tell Val about Chantelle?" She caught his eye, a question burning behind her lips.

"Things work differently here, Beth. None of us are in charge. It's just how it is." Reece's face softened, but his stance remained firm and resolute. Beth wrapped her arms around herself, feeling the chasm of change gaping beneath her feet.

"Things really are different." She murmured to herself as much as to Reece.

"Look, I know it's tough," Reece offered, his voice threading empathy through the firm fabric of his words, "you might not think it now, but give it some time. Working might make things feel more normal. Go get yourself cleaned up, okay?" With a final nod, Reece departed, leaving her alone with the vast expanse of possibility that lay beyond her threshold. Beth watched him go, then turned her gaze out over the field towards the community centre. People moved with a freedom she couldn't yet grasp, their lives unfolding in a rhythm unmarred by the sharp staccato of fear that still pulsed in her veins. Taking a deep breath, she stepped back into the quiet sanctuary of her home to prepare for the unknown, her heart clinging to the fragile tendril of hope that maybe, just maybe, Reece was right.

Beth lingered by the door, her fingers tracing the grain of the wood as she waited. Time ticked heavily, each second a weighty echo in the silence of the room. She had been ready to leave - ready to be collected - for ten full minutes, yet that sliver of time felt stretched and boundless. A sharp rap at the door cut through the stillness and she straightened herself, brushing imaginary creases from her jeans. Barnett stood on the threshold, his smile easy and disarming.

"Looks like you're all set for work." He observed with a nod of approval. She managed a half-smile, uncertainty shadowing her features.

"I wasn't sure what to wear," she confessed, "neither of you really explained anything. I don't even know where I'm going."

"It's okay, Beth," Barnett reassured, his voice carrying a casual authority, "this isn't the kind of place where appearances matter much. Unless you're in uniform, of course."

"Of course." Beth smiled lightly, locking the door behind her before leaving. As they walked down the road, an oppressive silence settled between them, filled only by the crunch of gravel underfoot. Beth's gaze flitted across the landscape, taking in the mundane normalcy of a world trying to rebuild itself. Barnett cleared his throat, breaking the quietude.

"Heard quite a bit about you," he said, casting a sidelong glance her way, "glad we've finally met."

"Seems I'm somewhat famous," Beth remarked dryly, the words tasting bitter, "or infamous, depending on how you look at it." It was strange to be known without knowing, to be a topic of conversation amongst strangers.

"Your friends talked about you two a lot. You and Chantelle." Barnett's voice held a note of something unspoken, a reverence perhaps, or a shared grief.

"Chantelle," her voice trailed off, the name hanging heavy in the air as she corrected herself with a formality meant to distance, "it seems my past is more present here than I am." Barnett nodded, accepting the boundary she set with a respectful tilt of his head. They continued their walk, the silence now a comfortable companion as Fort Irwin unveiled itself before them, one step at a time. The cool metal of the doorknob turned under Barnett's hand as he gently pushed open the heavy door to the town hall. Beth paused on the threshold, her heart thumping in a rhythm that echoed the uncertainty in her eyes. She entered with a careful step, her gaze sweeping across the foreign space.

"Beth." Came a warm voice, cutting through the stillness of the room. Mary stood across the hall, her smile like a beacon in the sombre mood. The corners of Beth's lips twitched, an involuntary response to the kindness in Mary's greeting.

"Mary," Beth acknowledged, remembering her from the first day, her voice steadier than she felt, "do you work here?"

"Oh, no. I'm just visiting my uncle," Mary replied, the casualness of her tone belying the purpose in her stance, "but you're going to be helping us with housing reassignments and expanding our little community while Sarah goes on maternity leave."

"Who?" Beth's question was more of a reflection than an inquiry, her mind racing to assemble the pieces of this new role she'd been thrust into.

"The lady who worked here before you," Mary affirmed, the certainty in her voice attempting to transfer confidence to Beth, "now I really must be going." Before another word could pass between them, Mary glanced at the clock on the wall and excused herself. Beth watched Mary's retreating figure, her presence leaving an imprint of normalcy in the wake of chaos. Slowly, Beth turned back to face the expanse of the town hall, her new reality waiting to unfold before her.

"Welcome," the firm handshake from a man who had emerged from another room brought a moment of clarity to Beth's foggy thoughts, "Henry Bishop, lovely to meet you." His voice a gravelly echo as Barnett nodded towards them both before exiting the room, leaving Beth alone with the mayor.

"Bishop." She thought aloud, piecing together the family tree in her mind as she surveyed her new surroundings. The office was pragmatic, outfitted with the bare essentials. Trestle tables stood like soldiers at attention, papers and folders piled atop them in an order known only to those who created the chaos. A lone laptop perched on one, its screen dark and inscrutable. Henry's laughter filled the space, a rumble that seemed too large for the small office. "Not much to look at, I know," he admitted, gesturing around the room with a sweep of his hand, "but we make do. It keeps us going." Beth offered a polite nod, her eyes continuing their inventory of the space. She noticed the maps pinned haphazardly to the wall, their edges curling like dried leaves. Her gaze lingered on the topography lines and handwritten notes scrawled in the margins - stories and strategies compressed into cartographic symbols.

"Maternity leave." She mused inaudibly, the concept feeling alien in this new world they were all stitching together. As if drawn by a magnetic force, her steps carried her closer to the stacks of paper that teetered on the edge of order and chaos. Each sheet was a life, a decision, a piece of the future they were all trying to reclaim.

"Anyway," Henry continued, pulling her attention back, "I could really use your help. It's been a one-man show since Sarah left to have her baby." His eyes held a spark of something Beth recognised, the same determination to persevere that she saw when looking in the mirror.

"Of course." Beth replied, her voice more confident than she expected. The task ahead felt monumental, but the structure and purpose it promised seemed to be the anchor she desperately needed. She approached the desk, her hand hovering over the laptop - a portal to a role that might just redefine her place among these people in this fragmented yet hopeful world. Beth picked up a stapled packet of papers from the nearest stack, her fingers brushing against the coarse surface. Her eyes skimmed the top page, numbers and addresses pin-balling around her mind as she sought to make sense of the logistics detailed in front of her.

"Prescott has been holding on," Henry said suddenly, breaking through her concentration as he leaned back against the corner of the desk, arms crossed, "my sons and my nephew, they've made it work, but it's time for them to come here."

"Here?" Beth echoed, placing the papers back down with precise alignment to the edge of the table.

"Fort Irwin," he clarified with a nod, "we're bringing the whole community. 116 souls looking for a fresh start."

"116," Beth mumbled, trying to visualise the influx of people, "how many are here now?"

"192 residents," Henry replied with a pride that seemed to swell his chest, "and we're well-equipped. The military presence is robust, and housing, well we have more than enough to accommodate everyone comfortably. It's the sensible choice, really."

"Seems reasonable." She nodded, absorbing the information.

"Children, the elderly," Henry went on, gesturing towards a map dotted with various coloured pins, "they need stability. It was an easy decision once we weighed the pros and cons."

"Your family," Beth asked, turning to face him fully, "why were they in Prescott?"

"Ah," Henry's expression softened, tinged with the weight of memory, "when the outbreak hit, I was visiting George here. I'm originally from Prescott, but duty called. I stayed to help secure the place. Only after everything quietened down could I head back to check on the rest."

"And they were all okay?" Beth's words were quiet, tentative.

"Alive and kicking," he confirmed with a slight chuckle, though his eyes betrayed the sobering truth of what *okay* meant in these times, "we've all lost something, or someone to get to this point." Beth nodded silently, a flicker of empathy passing between them. She understood loss, the shape it carved into your life, how it hollowed out spaces you didn't even know existed until they echoed with absence.

"What exactly will my job entail?" Beth inquired, her voice steady despite the churn of uncertainty within her.

"Yes, let's get back to it. There's much to do before everyone arrives, and I could use your sharp mind to help sort this all out." Henry cleared his throat, straightening up.

"Right." Beth agreed, the purpose he offered anchoring her once again. She reached for another stack of papers, her resolve hardening like the concrete walls that encased them, ready to build upon the ruins of yesterday. Beth's fingers danced across the worn edges of the town map, tracing the grid-like pattern of streets that now represented her new realm of responsibility. The census forms lay scattered around her, a patchwork quilt of names and lives waiting to be stitched into the fabric of Fort Irwin's future. She raised her gaze to Henry, who was watching her with an expectant look.

"You'll be at the heart of our resettlement efforts," Henry began, gesturing broadly towards the documents spread before them, "housing assignments, job allocations. You'll ensure we have the right balance of skills and people to keep this place functioning. We're not just rebuilding homes here Beth, we're rebuilding lives. That means setting up a new school, a church, establishing a routine." Beth arched an eyebrow as she glanced at the existing community centre marked on the map. It stood there, unassuming yet prominent, a question in the shape of a building.

"Don't you already have a school and church set up?"

"We do have a functioning school but the older children are currently being taught by a middle school teacher. We have a high school teacher coming from Prescott, which is pretty exciting. Oh, and my son, he's a pastor," Henry's eyes twinkled with a mix of pride and practicality, "been leading his flock back in Prescott all through the chaos. They need a space, a sanctuary to gather, to heal. He needs a place to work, to preach. A church is more than walls and a roof. It's hope for many, a beacon in these dark times." Beth nodded slowly, absorbing the weight of the task ahead. The idea of a church as a vessel of hope resonated with her. The notion that amidst the rubble of their old world, they could erect symbols of faith and community. Her gaze returned to the map, already envisioning where each piece of this intricate puzzle might fit, laying the groundwork for tomorrow on the foundations of today.

"When will they be arriving?" She asked, her voice threading the silence that had settled in the office.

"Within a month," Henry replied, folding his hands atop the desk, "we want them established before the winter sets in. To provide some semblance of stability." She nodded, mentally calculating the tight schedule.

"What should I start with first?" Beth's gaze shifted from a calendar to the older man, seeking direction.

"Take a look at this stack here," he gestured towards a pile of papers on the corner of the desk, "file away those recent housing assignments. It'll give you a feel for how we've been organising things." Beth approached the desk and gathered the stack with a measured motion, her eyes scanning the top page. As she flipped through the documents, a particular file caught her attention - a file branded with her own name. She paused, thumbing open the cover. Inside, a list of skills was bullet-pointed alongside notes on her medical history.

"Shouldn't these be private?" She asked, a frown creasing her brow as she lifted her gaze to meet Henry's.

"Ah, it's not what you're thinking," Henry leaned back in his chair, an air of reassurance about him, "that's more for our internal use. Just a formal assessment of mental state and general well-being. Helps us understand where you're at, how we can support you. The actual medical records are kept confidentially, either at the clinic for civilians or at the base for military personnel." Beth mulled over his words, still clutching the file. She understood the necessity of such assessments in their fragile post-pandemic society, yet the sight of her vulnerabilities laid out in ink was unsettling. With a reluctant nod, she closed the file and added it back to the stack, burying the unease under the task at hand.

"Alright," she said, pressing the weight of responsibility onto her shoulders like a mantle, "I'll get these filed away."

"Good," Henry responded with an approving nod, "and Beth, you're not just your record. You're much more than what's on paper. Remember that."

"So you've read it then," she raised an eyebrow at him curiously, "can't be good if you're making that statement."

"I have read every single file that has come through this office," he said with unwavering confidence, "and yours isn't the only one with a harsh experience, just rougher than most." With a small, grateful smile, Beth acknowledged his words and walked towards the filing cabinet, each step steadier than the last, her determination growing with the knowledge that her role here meant something more than the past that haunted her. Beth's fingers worked methodically through the stack of papers, each file a life distilled into bullet points and checkmarks.

"Okay, I'm done." She slotted the last of the Catalina Island arrivals into the cabinet, then turned to face Henry who was holding out another sheaf bound by a single rubber band.

"Here," he said, passing the list to her, "these are the folks from Prescott. You'll find everything you need to get started." She took it from him, feeling the slight give of the paper, the promise of lives about to intertwine with their own community. She settled into the chair by the trestle table, the list sprawling before her like an open road. Beth scanned the lines, each name a stranger's story waiting to be woven into the fabric of Fort Irwin. The aforementioned high school teacher, a retired nurse, a carpenter, all reduced to words on a page but all essential threads in the tapestry of survival they were stitching together. Her gaze lingered on a particular entry, a social media manager, and she felt a twinge of nostalgia for a world where such professions thrived. How quaint and distant those jobs now seemed, relics of a society that had no place in this new, stark reality.

"What am I supposed to do with a social media manager?" She murmured, half to herself, half expecting Henry to have some repository of wisdom to draw from. Henry leaned back against the edge of his desk, arms folded as he considered her question. There was a momentary silence, the kind that often preceded insight.

"Every skill can be adapted Beth," he said finally, the hint of a smile playing at his lips, "think about the essence of the job. Communication, organisation, perhaps a bit of creativity. We may not have social media anymore, but we still have messages to spread, people to unite. Maybe there's something in that?" Beth nodded slowly, absorbing his words. He was right, of course. The roles they once played were shadows of what was needed now, yet the core skills remained valuable. It was just a matter of repurposing them, of finding where they fit in the puzzle that was their burgeoning society.

"Communication," she echoed thoughtfully, her mind already racing with possibilities, "we could use someone to help coordinate announcements, manage information flow between different areas—"

"Exactly," Henry straightened up, approval evident in his eyes, "you'll get the hang of this before too long."

"Thanks." She allowed herself a small, satisfied smile. This was more than just assigning jobs, it was giving people a sense of identity, a role in their new world. And in doing that for others, perhaps she was also edging closer to redefining her own. Henry's laugh echoed lightly in the sparsely furnished office as he rummaged through a drawer, searching for the elusive list.

"We've got an array of jobs that need to be filled," he said, pulling out a crumpled sheet and smoothing it over the wooden surface, "but if a specific skill seems redundant, we find other ways for contribution. The warehouse for food distribution is always looking for hands. And the barracks, well, they could certainly use more help with upkeep." Beth watched his movements, the way his fingers traced the lines of text on the paper, categorising lives into columns of utility. She bit her lip, a crease forming between her brows.

"And if someone isn't useful?" She asked, her voice smaller than she intended.

"Useful? Beth, everyone is necessary," Henry glanced up at her, his eyes softening as he met her uncertain gaze, "it's not about being useful in the old sense. It's about contributing to the community, finding a place where you fit in." His voice was firm and resolute, a stark contrast to the uncertainty that seemed to perpetually cloud Beth's thoughts. A shiver ran down her spine as a memory surfaced, unbidden. Victor's cold, dismissive tone echoed in her mind - *unnecessary*. The word had been like a death sentence, stripping away humanity with clinical efficiency.

"Excuse me." Beth murmured abruptly, standing up so quickly that her chair skidded back. Her heart pounded, the ghost of terror that Victor had instilled in her flaring up once more. To Henry she might have appeared just a little pale, a bit unsteady. But inside she was fighting the surge of panic that threatened to overwhelm her.

"Of course." Henry responded, nodding with a mixture of concern and confusion as he watched her stride towards the door, her shoulders set in a rigid line that spoke of an inner turmoil he couldn't fully comprehend. Beth needed air, space - anything to clear the remnants of her past that clung to her like cobwebs. As she pushed open the door and stepped out into the sunlight, she sucked in a deep breath, trying to anchor herself in the present and far away from the dark shadows of her memories. Stepping out of the town hall, Beth blinked against the bright afternoon glare, her eyes taking a moment to adjust from the dimly lit interior. Panic set in as the weight of the word *unnecessary* played over again in her mind. Victor's voice was cold and unfeeling as she saw Alex's lifeless body on the ground in the recreation yard. She heard Su's screams as her child was ripped from her arms and dragged behind the motel, the gunshot ringing out in her ears. Children were unnecessary. The elderly were unnecessary. She almost missed Barnett as her breathing intensified. He leaned casually against the weathered doorframe, his presence an unexpected silhouette against the brightness of day. Her gaze locked onto him, and she instinctively tightened her grip on the files still clutched in her hand.

"Done already?" He quipped lightly, breaking her focus on her memories.

"Waiting for someone, lieutenant?" She asked, her voice steady despite the tremor that lingered within her chest. Barnett pushed away from the door with a slight smile that didn't quite reach his eyes.

"You could say that," he replied, "I'm keeping an eye on you."

"Me? Why?" The question emerged sharper than intended, cutting through the mild air between them.

"Orders. I've been assigned to make sure you're okay, help you find your place here," he said simply, his tone matter-of-fact before pausing to scratch the back of his neck awkwardly, "and, uh, when you're done for the day I'm supposed to escort you to the football game."

"Football game?" Confusion laced her words. The concept felt foreign, out of place amidst her whirlwind of duties and haunting recollections.

"Yep. It's a weekly thing. The military team versus the civilian team," Barnett's explanation came with an easy shrug, as if such trivialities were commonplace in this new reality they found themselves in, "everyone shows up. Fort Irwin Warhounds versus the Irwin Dust Devils."

"Seriously," Beth's fingers dug into the paper edges, crinkling them slightly, "I'd rather go home." She admitted, her voice a quiet confession. The thought of being surrounded by cheering crowds and the thud of boots on grass left her longing for the quiet refuge of her own space.

"Come on Beth," Barnett's voice softened, the friendliness in it somehow more disarming than his earlier official tone, "just give it a shot. If you don't like it, I'll personally walk you back home before the game's over." She hesitated, torn between the safety of solitude and the possibility that maybe, just maybe, something as normal as a game could ease the relentless anxiety that hummed beneath her skin.

"Okay," Beth murmured, the word barely more than a breath as she cast her gaze downward, shadows playing across her face, "but only for a little while." There was something about Barnett's earnestness that convinced her. At least enough to try.

"Deal," his grin was genuine this time, and it sparked a flicker of hope that perhaps things could be different here, "it's a date." Barnett quipped, his attempt at lightening the mood slicing through the air between them like a misaimed dart. Beth's eyes snapped up, and her eyebrow arched in silent reprimand. The corners of her mouth twitched. Not quite reaching a smile, but softening the sternness of her features for an ephemeral moment.

"Don't." She warned, though the hardness in her tone was tempered by an undertone of weary amusement.

"Sorry," he said, rubbing the back of his neck, a flush creeping up his cheeks, "bad joke." She gave him a nod that was both dismissal and acknowledgment of his apology.

"I should get back inside." She said, turning away from the light that spilled out from the open door behind him and stepping back into the dimmer confines of the town hall. The task that awaited her was systematic, almost soothing in its straightforwardness. Beth moved methodically, drawing lines through names and assigning houses with a steady hand. Families were grouped together, single individuals slotted into smaller units. Each line on her list represented a life, a story, a fragment of the world they were all trying to rebuild. Her eyes flicked over the occupations listed next to each name, searching for the skills that were vital to the community's survival. She circled doctors and nurses, underlined those with military experience, and put stars next to lawyers and teachers. These were the pillars on which they could lean, the people who could stitch together the fabric of society that had been so violently torn apart. As she worked, her mind absorbed the details, the connections forming between names, professions and needs. For a moment, the spectres of her past receded, their whispers drowned out by the clarity of purpose. Here, in these lists and maps, was a semblance of order in the chaos. A promise that life could be more than just an endless cycle of fear and waiting. Beth reached for another file, her movements slowing as the reality of her role settled upon her. She was no longer merely a survivor, she was becoming a weaver of the community, threading together the lives of others in a tapestry of hope. A far cry from the pawn she'd once been, helpless in the games of others. With each assignment, she fortified her place within these walls, and perhaps in time, within herself. Beth slid the last sheet into place, a soft exhale escaping her lips as she surveyed the stacks of paper that now covered the desk. There was something almost soothing in the order she'd created from the chaos, the neat rows of files and lists providing tangible evidence of her day's labor. She leaned back in the chair, her gaze tracing the outlines of empty houses on the map, plotting out her strategy for when morning came. The room around her had grown quiet, the bustle of earlier hours fading into a hush that seemed to press against the windows. For once, Beth found herself adrift in the present, her thoughts not snagged on the barbed wire of memories from Catalina or Alcatraz. It was as if the intensity of her focus had built a temporary shelter around her mind, warding off the ghosts that so often breached its defences. As she pondered this newfound calm, the door creaked open and Barnett stepped through, his frame momentarily blocking the waning light of the setting sun.

"Beth," he said, his voice firm but not unkind, "it's time to head to the game." She blinked, drawn abruptly from her reverie. The idea of attending the football match, with its clamour and crowds, seemed suddenly daunting - a stark contrast to the cocoon of paperwork she had wrapped herself in. But there was a promise she had made, albeit reluctantly, and Beth knew better than most the value of keeping one's word, especially in times like these. She stood slowly and smoothed the front of her shirt. Her movements were automatic, betraying none of the trepidation that fluttered beneath her composed exterior.

"Alright," she glanced at the piles once more, a silent affirmation of the day's progress, before turning to face Barnett, "let's go."

CHAPTER 10

Val leaned in close, her stethoscope pressed gently against Sabrina's swollen belly. She could hear the rhythmic thumping of the foetal heartbeat echoing through her ears. The air was heavy with the scent of antiseptic, and Val's heart raced with anticipation as she listened for any changes or abnormalities in the sound.

"It won't be long now." Val murmured, her voice a blend of professional warmth and detached concern. Sabrina, cradling her abdomen with tender pride, allowed a satisfied smile to play upon her lips. Her eyes reflected a glint of self-absorption as she met Val's gaze.

"If it's a girl, I think I'll name her Chantelle." She said, a touch of vanity lacing her tone. Val straightened up, pulling away the stethoscope. There was a slight tightening around her eyes, a subtle shift in her demeanour that suggested discomfort.

"That's very kind," she replied, her words measured, "but I'd rather not have the constant reminder."

"I think it would be nice to have a little girl named Chantelle running around," Sabrina tilted her head, feigning innocence, "if Chantelle's baby had been a girl, she probably would've named her after you, don't you think?"

"Chantelle's baby," Val's expression faltered for a moment, a frown creasing her brow as she tried to piece together Sabrina's implication, "what do you mean?" Sabrina's smile thinned as she observed Val's reaction, her eyes narrowing with a flicker of something cold and unreadable. Val's hands trembled slightly as she withdrew the stethoscope from her ears, the soft thud of Sabrina's heartbeat still ringing in the background. The chill that had crept up her spine seemed to freeze her in place for a moment.

"You didn't know?" Sabrina asked, an edge of ice lining her voice.

"That Chantelle was pregnant?" Val managed, her shock splintering her professional composure. Sabrina's cold laugh was devoid of humour.

"You mustn't have read her note then." The remark, tossed carelessly into the air, settled heavily on Val's shoulders.

"Her note? No, I—" Val stuttered, her mind racing. She glanced over to her desk drawer where she had placed the note Beth had given her days prior, unable to bring herself to open it, until now.

"Yes," Sabrina tilted her head coyly as she leaned back on the cot, gently rubbing her abdomen, "It was—"

"I think we're done here." Val said abruptly, her voice firm despite the quiver of emotion threatening to break through as she interrupted and dismissed Sabrina in one fell swoop. She could feel the walls of the clinic closing in around her, suddenly oppressive. She gestured towards the door, a clear signal for Sabrina to leave.

"If you say so." Sabrina hoisted herself off the examination table, her movements deliberately slow, as if she was savouring the turmoil she'd instigated. She exited, leaving a palpable silence in her wake. Alone now, Val's fingers found the envelope tucked away in her desk drawer - Chantelle's last words that she hadn't dared to face until this moment. Her heart pounded in her chest as she opened it, unfolding the paper with shaking hands. The words blurred as tears welled in her eyes. She hastily wiped them away, but they kept coming, relentless in their flow.

"Damn it, Chantelle." She whispered to the empty room, to the void where her daughter should have been. There was no time to process, no time to grieve anew. With the note clutched tight in her grasp, Val locked the clinic behind her and set off, her pace quickening to a run as she headed towards Beth's house, driven by an urgency that bordered on desperation.

On the other side of town, Austin lounged in the stillness of his living room, an ice pack enveloped in cloth placed gently on his throbbing shoulder. Recollections of Anne's cautious advice reverberated through his mind, urging him to rest and not push himself too hard. But the persistent soreness was an ever-present reminder of his physical limitations and the fragility of his body's endurance. The sharp and frantic knock at the door jolted him from his thoughts. Wincing, he set the ice pack aside and shakily rose to his feet. Each movement was a negotiation between pain and necessity as he repositioned his arm within the sling. He cursed under his breath, his jaw set against the discomfort.

"Coming!" He called out, more to steel himself than to inform whoever waited on the other side. It took a concerted effort to cross the room, each step measured and deliberate. When he finally reached the door, he used his good hand to swing it open, bracing himself for the flood of outside light and whatever storm had come knocking. Val's arrival was like a whirlwind, her face etched with lines of panic and distress as she stood at Austin's threshold.
"Where's Beth? She's not at home." Val demanded, her voice trembling with urgency. Austin managed his discomfort, replying

through gritted teeth.

"She's likely at the town hall, probably working," concern furrowed his brow as he took in Val's agitated state, "what's going on, Val?"

"I need to talk to her, now!" Val's eyes were wild, haunted almost, and without waiting for any further response she turned on her heel, her determination clear.

"Wait up." Austin called after her, moving awkwardly but as swiftly as he could to follow. The pain in his shoulder protested with each jarring step, but it was eclipsed by a growing sense of alarm. The town hall loomed ahead, its doors open wide as if inviting the coming storm. Val burst into the reception area, her breath coming in quick gasps. Without preamble, she found Beth and thrust the crumpled note towards her.

"Why didn't you tell me about Chantelle?" Val's howl cut through the hushed murmur of the hall, turning heads and halting conversations. Henry, who had been sorting through paperwork at a nearby desk, stood up and discreetly exited the room. His presence suddenly felt intrusive amidst the private agony unfolding. Beth's face blanched, her own shock mirroring that of Austin, who stood just behind Val, his good hand gripping the back of a chair for support.

"You didn't want to talk about it Val, I thought," Beth said, her voice low and filled with regret, "I thought you'd have read the note." The tension was palpable, an unsaid accusation hanging heavy in the air between them. Silence fell, save for the rustle of paper still clutched in Val's trembling hands. Val's voice was a raw, ragged thing, shredding the air between them.

"How could I have read it, Beth? How? I wasn't ready to face," her eyes were glassy with unshed tears, her knuckles white where they gripped the damning sheet of paper, "to face any of it until Sabrina blurted out about the pregnancy!" Beth's expression fractured, the pieces of her composure scattering like shards of dropped porcelain. She had always been the one with answers, the one who held others up when they faltered. But now she was struggling to absorb the blow of Val's words, to understand the depth of her friend's pain.

"I'm sorry." She whispered, the apology inadequate against the tide of Val's grief. Austin moved closer to Val, his good arm reaching out to offer a semblance of comfort.

"Val," he touched her shoulder gently, a silent promise of support, "this isn't Beth's fault." But Val was beyond the reach of consolation, caught in the whirlpool of betrayal and heartache. She shrugged Austin's hand from her shoulder indignantly as she took a quick step towards Beth.

"Unless," Beth's voice trailed off as her gaze locked onto the note, a flicker of doubt creeping into her eyes as she seemed to retreat for a moment into her own thoughts, "Sabrina couldn't have known what was inside the envelope, or what was written on it. It was sealed when I found it." She muttered, more to herself than to Val or Austin.

"What do you mean?" Val's anguish turned to confusion, her voice laced with suspicion.

"Sabrina must've found Chantelle. I don't have any doubt about that, the way she hinted at it one day on Catalina."

"Hinted at it?" Austin's face filled with confusion, his eyes darting between Beth, Val and the note.

"Yeah. They finally let me out of isolation, and Stone took me for a walk on the beach. I got drenched and when we got back to the hotel, he went to grab me a towel. And then Sabrina," Beth's face twisted like a knot, a sharp contrast to the smooth and calculated movements of her lips as they formed a mocking smile, "she came out of nowhere. Walking up to me like she had a secret. That fake-sweet sarcastic voice."

"What did she say?" Val's voice was much calmer than her earlier approach as her face had softened and her eyes were no longer filled with rage, only sadness as Beth recounted her daughter's final day. "I told her that Victor's affections would have to be shared now that Chantelle was also pregnant. Sabrina, she hinted that Chantelle might no longer be a problem. Something in the way she spoke, I knew something was wrong and I begged Stone to take me to Chantelle's room. But even if she'd found Chantelle first, even *if* she had seen her and left her there to come and tell me so I would have to see her body hanging there, she couldn't have seen that note. I might have lost my mind a little when I was on that island but I will remember that day clearly for the rest of my life and that note was sealed. Think about it," Beth urged, her analytical mind clicking into place as she spoke with conviction, "there's no way Sabrina could've seen what was inside unless—"

"Unless she saw it before it was sealed." The realisation dawned on Val, a cold tide that threatened to sweep her away. The sealed envelope, the private words meant only for the eyes of those left behind - it all pointed to an unsettling possibility that neither woman wanted to entertain.

"Jesus." Austin stood between them, a rock amidst the swirling chaos, instinctively knowing that this revelation could unravel far more than just the mystery of a sealed note. Val's hand trembled as she unfolded the crinkled paper, her movements delicate and fraught with a gravity that seemed to pull the very air taut around them. Her eyes moved slowly across the page, absorbing each word as though it were written in an alien script. The silence stretched into eternity, punctured only by the sound of her ragged breath.

"That's not Chantelle's handwriting." Val finally murmured, almost to herself. The words hung in the charged atmosphere, heavy with implication.

"I didn't know," Beth whispered softly, almost silently, "I'd never seen her handwriting before so I didn't pick up on it." She leaned over, peering at the scribble that sprawled messily across the paper. Her face was a mask of concentration, then realisation. She met Val's gaze, a silent communication passing between them, laden with fear and suspicion. Time seemed to slow as they both contemplated the impossible.

"Stop it," Austin's voice cut through the stillness, firm yet edged with concern, "whatever you're thinking, it's not possible. Sabrina couldn't have—"

"Couldn't have what, Austin," Beth snapped, turning towards him with a flash of anger in her eyes, "you didn't see her on Alcatraz like we did. You don't know what she's capable of. You didn't see what she became on Catalina." Austin held her gaze, his jaw set in defiance, but there was a flicker, a shadow of doubt that crept into his eyes. He knew their shared past was a dark tapestry woven with threads of survival and desperation, but he clung to the belief that Sabrina, in her current vulnerable state, was beyond such acts.

"Alcatraz changed me," Val added quietly, her voice laced with an edge of steel, "I'm sure Sabrina was different before she got there."

"And Catalina made us all worse versions of our already broken selves," Beth interjected, "it changed me, and Chantelle. We saw sides of each other that—" She trailed off, the unspoken horrors lingering in the space between them. Austin looked from one woman to the other, his protective instincts warring with the dawning realisation that perhaps he hadn't seen the full depth of

Sabrina's darkness after all.

"What happened to her?" Val's fingers trembled as she clutched the deceiving paper, her gaze still locked with Beth's.

"Sabrina was different on Catalina," Beth murmured, the words heavy with implication, "she would've done anything to make sure no one else had Victor's child." Austin paced, his gait uneven due to his healing shoulder.

"That doesn't mean she killed Chantelle." He argued, his voice strained with the effort to maintain reason amidst the tempest of suspicion. Val's outburst sliced through the tense air like a shard of shattered glass.

"What else does it look like, Austin?" Her eyes blazed with the fire of conviction, and in that moment doubt became tangible, wrapping its cold fingers around the room.

"Maybe she saw the note after you opened it." Austin's suggestion hung between them, desperate and fragile. His eyes sought theirs, pleading for sanity in a situation slipping beyond control. Beth shook her head, her expression unreadable.

"It was hidden," she said, "no one knew about it. I kept it close until I gave it to Val."

"Perhaps Sabrina found Chantelle and, and she wrote the note out of spite." Austin ventured, his hope waning in the face of their shared history, a past marred by survival's cruel games. The idea loomed before them, monstrous in its potential truth. But even monsters can wear masks, and in this twisted tale of loss and betrayal nothing was certain. Beth took the paper from Val, her hands trembling slightly as she clutched it. Her eyes darted between the scrawled lines and Val's anguished face.

"No one writes something like this just because they found a body," her voice was edged with incredulity and pain, "there's nothing here that's taunting. Nothing malicious. If Sabrina forged Chantelle's suicide note, she'd make it sting. This? It's too plain. The only goal was to make it look like Chantelle ended things herself, not that someone else did it for her."

"Sabrina killed her," Val stood rigid, her posture a testament to her resolute belief, her gaze unwavering as the truth she perceived cemented itself within her, "she knew about Chantelle's baby, about Victor."

"Let's not jump to conclusions," still nursing his injured shoulder, Austin interjected with caution thick in his tone, "we need to dig deeper, get more information. I can talk to the guards from Catalina. They're locked up but might know something we don't." The air hung heavy with tension, the weight of suspicion and fear pressing down on them. Val nodded after a moment's consideration, her jaw set in a hard line of reluctant acceptance.

"Fine," her voice softened, revealing the conflict within, "but I won't be near Sabrina, not until we know more. Phillip will have to take over my prenatal duties. I can't, not right now."

"Agreed." Austin said, his relief audible. He understood the gravity of the situation and the need for caution.

"Val," Beth gingerly held out her hand, handing the note back to her, "I—"

"We should let Beth continue her work." Austin interrupted, giving a supportive nod towards Beth who seemed rooted to the spot, the note still clutched in her grasp.

The incessant clicking of the handcuffs against the cold metal rails reverberated through the sterile room as Stone shifted, his features contorting with discomfort. The thin mattress offered little relief to his battered body, and the constraints served as a constant reminder of the precariousness of his position. Anne, clad in her crisp white coat, entered the room with the practiced steps of a doctor who had seen too much within the confines of the community but had little idea what really went on outside their refuge. Her hands worked methodically, inflating the blood pressure cuff with an efficiency that spoke of routine. The stethoscope's cold metal seemed to listen to the secrets of Stone's heart, as Anne's brow furrowed slightly, reading the tale the beats told.

"Your vitals are stable," she announced, her voice tinged with professional detachment, "and you have a visitor." She added as her gaze flickered briefly to the doorway where a shadow loomed. Stone's expression hardened, the anticipation of the conversation ahead drawing a veil over his previous discomfort.

"Could use some more painkillers before we start." He grunted, nodding towards the door.

"I'll bring them shortly." Anne replied, her voice softening just a touch as she made her way out, leaving the promise of temporary respite in her wake. Austin stepped into the room, the subtle wince as he moved betraying the pain in his own shoulder. His eyes, sharp and probing, locked onto Stone, taking in the sight of the man who held pieces to a puzzle Austin was desperate to solve. As he drew near the air between them charged with unspoken questions.

"Stone, I need to ask you about what happened before the rescue," the request hung in the air as Austin clasped the back of a chair, his grip betraying the tension that knotted his muscles as he leaned forward, "but first, I owe you thanks. Beth made it clear how much you did for her that night."

"I didn't do much." Stone shifted, the handcuffs clinking against the metal rails with a sound that seemed to echo in the stark room. His brows gathered in a mix of pain and concern.

"You took a bullet for her," Austin cocked his head lightly, "I imagine that was more than anyone had done for her in a long time."

"Is Beth," Stone paused, looking down at his handcuffed wrist and clenching his fist, "is she okay?"

"Better than okay," Austin assured, with a nod that carried more relief than mere affirmation, "she's settling in. Slowly, but she is—"

"That's a surprise," Stone shifted on the cot slightly, adjusting his back as he winced, "she doesn't seem like the type to play well with others." A moment passed, heavy with shared understanding before Austin's gaze sharpened, focusing on the matter at hand.

"But there's something I need from you," he paused, measuring his words carefully, "the dynamic between the women on the island, what was it like?" The question hung in the air, charged and waiting. Stone's face registered surprise, the lines of his rugged features deepening.

"What exactly do you want to know?" He asked, skepticism etching his voice.

"I've got Beth's perspective," Austin straightened but didn't release the chair, the wood under his fingers feeling like the only anchor in a sea of uncertainty, "and I'll need Jennifer's too. But you, you saw things differently. You weren't involved in their personal circles. Your objectivity is what I'm after." Stone studied him for a long, silent moment, his eyes probing, searching for the intent behind the inquiry. Eventually, Stone nodded, a slow and deliberate movement that signalled his acquiescence to the unspoken gravity of Austin's request. Stone's eyes narrowed, a glint of understanding sparking within as he shifted against the constraints that bound him to the hospital bed.

"You're not here for small talk," his voice was gruff, the rasp of it betraying a weariness that went beyond the physical, "you can easily ask Beth and Jennifer and all the others for their take. So I'm guessing this is about Sabrina." Austin's nod was firm, an unspoken confirmation hanging between them.

"You're smart."

"Smart? No, I'm observant. There's a difference," Stone acknowledged, his gaze momentarily drifting off as if he were sifting through a mental archive of unpleasant memories, "Sabrina, she wasn't about to let Victor choose her fate. Took matters into her own hands."

"What do you mean?" The room seemed to contract around Austin as he processed, the weight of Stone's words pressing in on him from all sides.

"Made sure to be the first to share his bed," Stone continued, his expression darkening, "guess in her mind, carrying his child would make her untouchable. Queen of the fucking island or some twisted shit like that." Austin's lips drew into a thin line, his thoughts racing.

"But Victor," he observed quietly, "he probably didn't see it that way." Stone's laugh was humourless, a bitter sound that filled the sterile space.

"Care? That man cared for no one but himself," he paused, locking eyes with Austin, "you know about Chantelle, don't you?" At the mention of Chantelle's name, a cold shiver traced its way down Austin's spine. He remained silent, allowing Stone's question to linger, an echo of darker truths yet to be revealed.

"Mmm." Austin's nod was a silent cue, the go-ahead for Stone to delve deeper into the abyss of past events. The heavy air around them seemed to thicken with anticipation as Stone's voice broke the stillness.

"She found out about Chantelle," Stone began, his eyes narrowing as if the memory caused him physical pain, "went straight to Victor. All fire and brimstone, demanding what he planned to do." He shifted, the discomfort in his posture mirroring the unease of the recollection.

"Do with what? The baby?" Austin's confusion made Stone laugh, a bitter sound with a hint of mockery.

"Victor was ice-cold, told her there was nothing to be done. Sabrina was nothing to him. No wife, no partner. Just another pawn in his sick game." Stone shook his head as a muscle twitched in Austin's jaw, his mind painting vivid strokes of the confrontation. Sabrina's fury would have been a sight - her dreams of dominion challenged, her status on the island threatened by the mere existence of another carrying Victor's child.

"Then what?" Austin pressed, needing to hear the sequence of betrayal unfold. Stone's gaze dropped to his shackled wrists before meeting Austin's eyes again.

"She lost it. Shouting, cursing him, blaming him for not choosing her above everyone else. Victor, he," Stone hesitated, swallowing hard as if the next words were shards of glass in his throat, "he hit her. One slap, so hard it knocked her flat. She landed bad, cradling her stomach when she went down. Made this sound I'll never forget." The image seared into Austin's brain. Sabrina, sprawled across the unforgiving floor, pain and shock etched onto her features as the dream of being queen shattered against the cold reality of Victor's cruelty.

"Was the baby hurt?" Austin's question was barely a whisper, dread clinging to each syllable.

"Couldn't say," Stone replied, a haunted look passing over his face, "but she cried, right there at his feet. And Victor, he just screamed at her, telling her she was nothing. That she'd failed to learn where she stood with him."

"Learn her place." Austin echoed grimly, the very idea leaving a bitter taste.

"Exactly," Stone's voice was a low growl, "in Victor's world, everyone was disposable. Sabrina thought she was different, but that day she learned just how wrong she was." In that moment, Austin understood the depth of Sabrina's desperation, the lengths to which she might go to reclaim a semblance of control, to rewrite the narrative once more in her favour. Austin felt the weight of suspicion settle over him like a shroud, knowing full well the tangled web of deceit and power that had ensnared them all. The sterile scent of the infirmary mingled with the faint tang of antiseptic, wrapping around Austin as he stood by the bedside where Stone lay, a study in pained resignation.

"Unnecessary." His eyes were fixed on Stone's face, searching for any flicker of deception or misdirection. But all he found was a hollow weariness as Stone's voice cut through the heavy silence.

"Exactly. Victor never planned to keep any of them," Stone murmured, his gaze drifting away towards some unseen point in the memory, "he had deals, trades set up with a group on the mainland."

"Trades?" The word caught in Austin's throat, a revolting concept that made his stomach churn.

"Kids," Stone clarified, his voice dropping to a conspiratorial whisper, "we were just pawns to him, and none of us were meant to stick around. He fucked every single one of those women, except Beth. He needed her head on one thing, where you guys had gone."

"Why kids?" Austin clenched his jaw, the muscles there working as he processed this new, grim layer to Victor's twisted world. It was a puzzle with too many missing pieces, but even these fragments painted a picture so dark it threatened to swallow the light.

"Who the hell knows," Stone shook his head and furrowed his brows in bewilderment, "what kind of person would trade kids? For what? He was picky. Only ever told people what he wanted them to hear. Kept us guessing. Kept us apart."

"Control through chaos." Austin muttered, an understanding dawning that felt like cold water trickling down his spine.

"Exactly." Stone's confirmation was punctuated by Anne's return, her presence like a soft breeze as she moved to Stone's side with the quiet competence of a seasoned nurse.

"Here, this should help with the pain." Anne said gently, holding out the painkillers to Stone, who accepted it with a nod of gratitude.

"Thank you." He rasped, relief evident in the sag of his shoulders as the medication promised a respite from the ever-present ache.

"You're welcome." Anne offered a small smile before making her exit once more. Stone turned his head back to Austin, his eyes now clouded with a different kind of pain. The metal cuffs clinked against the rail as he shifted, the sound a stark reminder of his confinement.

"So, does this earn me any goodwill? Any chance these can come off?" He rattled the handcuffs against the railing. Austin met his gaze, seeing the raw hope there, and he felt the weight of responsibility settle deeper on his shoulders.

"We'll see." He said, the words deliberate and noncommittal, yet not without empathy. With a last look at Stone, Austin turned and walked away, the echo of the cuffs in his ears. As he left the infirmary behind, the gravity of Stone's revelations pressed down on him, the pieces of the puzzle still scattered and elusive, but the edges becoming sharper, more dangerous with each step he took.

Sunlight draped over the community centre's courtyard, bathing everything in a warm glow that belied the chill of recent events. Austin's shadow stretched long and thin as he approached Tim, who was ensconced on a bench, the pages of his book flickering gently in the breeze. Tim had quickly gained the trust of Austin, Reece, and Chase when he had aided them in their mission to infiltrate Catalina. He had even disguised himself in their uniforms, concealing his true appearance. However, despite earning their trust, Tim had still been denied the pleasure of venturing outside without an escort. Austin gestured towards Eddie, who was casually leaning against a nearby tree only ten feet away from where Tim was seated.

"Tim." Austin called out gently, his voice betraying none of the weariness that clung to his bones.

"Austin," Tim glanced up with a nod, his eyes quickly assessing Austin's slumped posture before he placed a thoughtful finger between the pages of his book and closed it, "didn't expect to see you walking around. Nursing that arm still?"

"Something like that." Austin muttered, easing himself onto the other side of the bench with a wince. His injured shoulder protested, but he masked the discomfort with a tight-lipped smile. The bench's wooden slats felt solid beneath him, grounding in their unyielding support.

"Looks painful," Tim observed, his tone neutral yet not devoid of concern, "you need something? Or just walking by?"

"Information," Austin replied, meeting Tim's gaze squarely, "I was wondering if you could share some insight into the dynamic on the island."

"Dynamic?" Tim placed his book gingerly on the bench between them.

"The relationships between the women at Catalina," Austin stared out across the grass, "specifically Sabrina, Chantelle, and Beth."

"Ah," Tim leaned back, resting his elbows on the backrest, his posture open, almost relaxed, "well, you know how it was. Victor, he played things close to the chest. But he thought I was bitter enough about being left behind to play ball. Trusted me more than he should've." Austin nodded, absorbing his words with a furrowed brow.

"And did you see much? About the women, I mean." Austin pressed lightly.

"Coming and going, yeah," Tim shrugged, his lips pursing for a moment as if tasting the sourness of the past, "Victor had this idea that everyone had their price or their breaking point. He talked to me, sure. But always in riddles and shadows, thinking he could twist loyalty from my resentment towards you all."

"Did he ever talk about any plans for the kids?" Austin pressed, his voice low but laced with a hint of urgency.

"Plans? No explicit details," Tim's face took on a contemplative expression, a flicker of something unreadable passing through his eyes, "but there were whispers, rumours. You know how it is. Walls have ears, but they don't always hear clearly."

"Right," Austin's hand unconsciously drifted to his shoulder, pressing lightly against the fabric of his shirt as if to soothe the ache by sheer will, "and the relationships between everyone?"

"Look," Tim sighed heavily and leaned forward, pressing his elbows into his knees, "the girls weren't exactly friends. Chantelle hated Beth, Beth hated Sabrina, and Sabrina hated everyone."

"Chantelle hated Beth?" Austin repeated, his previously toneless expression shifting suddenly.

"Of course," Tim looked over at him cautiously, "Chantelle was angry that Beth saved her that night on Alcatraz. Beth went after her when she saw her being dragged away, and Chantelle thought that if Beth hadn't done that then she might have been killed, and wouldn't have gone through what they went through on Catalina. At least, that's what she told me."

"I know some of that story," Austin admitted, looking down at his feet in an attempt to hide his shame, "Beth told us some of what happened to them after we escaped."

"Mmm," Tim furrowed his brow slightly, frowning as he thought about the last year, "Jennifer blamed all of you for the death of her sister, but Beth was the only one around for her to take it out on."

"What do you mean?" Austin raised an eyebrow, meeting his gaze.

"Austin, you need to understand that Beth had no one on Catalina," Tim shifted in his seat, turning his body towards him slightly, "Chantelle and Beth only fixed their friendship days before she killed herself. Jennifer avoided her at all costs, and when they had to be in the same room she glared at her as if her eyes could melt her on the spot. Sabrina took every chance she could get to either belittle her or intimidate her. Hell, even I'll admit that I resented you all for escaping and not taking me with you when I did so much to help you, and I took it out on Beth because I had no one else to blame." The silence stretched out like a taut rubber band, the seconds ticking by as if each one carried the weight of an eternity. The air hung heavy with unspoken words, the stillness so profound that even the faintest rustle seemed deafening in comparison. Austin shifted uncomfortably - he knew that leaving Beth and Chantelle behind had been hard, but the last year had been marginally easier knowing that they had each other. The realisation that neither of them had a friend, or even an ally, hit him like a ton of bricks.

"Thanks Tim," Austin eventually managed to utter, "every little piece helps."

"Does it? Or does it just make the puzzle more complicated?" Tim asked, a hint of skepticism creeping into his voice.

"Complicated or not, it needs to be put together." The sun was waning, casting a warm glow on the side of Austin's face as he leaned forward, elbows resting on his knees. He watched Tim for a moment, trying to gauge the man's sincerity from his relaxed posture and the casual way he had discarded his book.

"Your loyalty," Austin said, voice steady despite the twinge in his shoulder, "was it ever with Victor?" Tim's eyes held a glint of something hard to read. He ran a hand through his hair, pushing back the strands bleached by the sun.

"Survival doesn't always choose sides, Austin. But if there is a *good side* as you call it," he paused, tipping his head slightly as though considering the weight of his next words, "I haven't decided yet where the good side is." Austin's brow creased. He noted the evasiveness, the noncommittal shrug that followed. It was like trying to hold water in a net. Nothing substantial, nothing solid. Tim exhaled, looking off into the distance, where the rays of sunlight stretched across the ground.

"You're asking the wrong person," Austin finally conceded, meeting Tim's gaze with a level stare, "none of us are good." He leaned back on the weathered bench, his injured arm resting awkwardly in his lap. The sun was slowly descending behind the community centre, casting long shadows that stretched out like fingers across the grass.

"You mentioned that Beth told you some of this story?" Tim shifted uncomfortably, the man's eyes darting away before they settled back on Austin.

"Mmm." Austin acknowledged with a nod.

"I get the feeling she might've left out a few key elements," Tim looked down at the ground, "especially if you didn't know that Chantelle barely uttered a word to her for the better part of a year. It wasn't just about surviving Victor for those girls, it was surviving each other too." Austin narrowed his eyes, sensing the undercurrents of resentment and turmoil in Tim's words.

"What do you mean *surviving each other*?" He probed further, his curiosity piqued by the implications.

"Exactly what it sounds like," Tim's hands clenched into fists, then relaxed again, "we were all pitted against each other, fighting for scraps of favouritism, or just to stay alive another day. Beth and Chantelle? Their relationship was just as broken. Everyone's was. It was hate, yeah, but the kind that was created because of the situation, out of desperation, not genuine anger at each other." The revelation gave Austin pause. He had seen fractures, but to hear the depth of animosity laid bare was unsettling.

"And Sabrina?" He ventured cautiously, pressing for more detail.

"Cunning, manipulative, and just as much a victim of that place as the rest of us," Tim exhaled sharply, his expression twisting into a grimace, "but she embraced the chaos, used it to her advantage. She was no saint. None of them were, not even Beth, not even Chantelle. Keep in mind, while we were all fighting for Victor's approval, Beth knew where she stood. I believed that she had no idea where you'd gone, but Victor didn't. She couldn't change that, even if she'd provided a false story to where you'd gone, Victor would suss it out and find out she'd been lying. There was nothing Beth could say that would change his mind, and she knew it. Sabrina did too, and she used that to her advantage." Austin absorbed the words, a chill settling in his chest despite the fading warmth of the day. He had come seeking answers, but with each new piece of the puzzle revealed, the image grew darker, more complex. Sabrina, a nightmare - it was a descriptor that would haunt him as he delved deeper into the web of secrets and lies woven around her. Austin rose from the bench, nursing his arm as he did.

"Thank you for your honesty." He managed, before walking off suddenly. Tim watched him go, the sunlight casting a long shadow that trailed behind Austin like a silent echo of his resolve.

CHAPTER 11

The mattress groaned softly as Austin tossed and turned, his arm throbbing in time with his racing thoughts. Anne's gentle snoring seemed to mock his wakefulness, an audible reminder of rest he couldn't grasp. He winced, adjusting the sling that cradled his injured limb, a constant dull ache pulsing through him. Above the physical discomfort, it was the image of Beth and Chantelle's strained silence on Catalina that clawed at his mind - two friends marooned amidst unspoken grievances, the kind of emotional isolation that gnawed deeper than any physical wound. With each tick of the clock, sleep slipped further away, receding into the shadows that danced across the ceiling. Finally, the futility of his attempt at rest became too blatant to ignore. His feet found the cool floor, and he stood with a resigned sigh. Clothes gathered in the ambient light spilling from the half-open bathroom door, he dressed quietly, sparing a glance at Anne who was undisturbed and blissfully oblivious to the turmoil next to her. Austin eased the bedroom door open and stepped into the stillness of the night. The chill outside clung to his skin as he made his way down deserted streets, guided by the pale wash of moonlight. Houses stood silent, sentinels to his clandestine journey until he arrived at Beth's doorstep. His knock sounded heavy in the quiet, and moments later the door creaked open. Beth's face appeared in the gap, her hair tousled from restlessness, eyes questioning the interruption.

"Seems like you've all got a bad habit of visiting me at the worst times." She remarked dryly.

"Sorry. It's just," Austin managed, his voice barely above a whisper, "I needed to talk to you. I can come back tomorrow if this is a bad time."

"I'm awake now," Beth stepped aside, her expression softening, "you might as well come in."

"Thanks." Austin shuffled into the dimly lit kitchen, a space that had once been the heart of many late-night conversations and confessions. Now, it was just a hollow echo of the past, much like the rest of the world outside. Beth moved ahead to flick on a small lamp, casting a warm glow over the countertops.

"Can't sleep?" Beth inquired, leaning back against the counter as she rubbed her eyes.

"Time doesn't seem to matter anymore, does it?" Austin forced a smile, trying to lighten the mood but his attempt fell flat. The muscles in his arm throbbed in protest, reminding him of the reality they all faced. Beth's face was tired and her features were slightly drawn with dark circles under her eyes. There was a hint of worry in her expression, and lines of stress etched on her forehead.

"I have to be up early for my job tomorrow," she said, the word *job* laced with a hint of irony, "you know, the one you all assigned me so I can pretend to be normal again."

"Sorry." Austin sighed, the humour draining from his voice. She stepped away from the counter to grant him full access to the kitchen. His gaze followed her as she moved, noting the subtle changes in her demeanour since their world had been turned upside down. They settled at the old wooden table, an island of worn familiarity in a sea of uncertainty. For a long moment Austin remained silent, his thoughts swirling. Beth watched him, her arms wrapped around herself as if bracing for impact.

"What's on your mind?" She finally asked, breaking the silence that seemed to stretch between them like a chasm. He exhaled, feeling the weight of his guilt pressing down on his chest.

"Beth, I'm sorry," he began, his voice unsteady, "for leaving you there. With everything going on, I never considered—" The words caught in his throat, tangling with emotions he hadn't anticipated. This wasn't just about the physical distance that had separated them, it was about the emotional gulf he had allowed to widen by ignoring the signs of her struggle. Beth's expression softened, her protective stance loosening ever so slightly.

"Austin, you don't have to—"

"I should've tried harder," he said, the words tumbling out with a rawness that surprised even him, "I thought you and Chantelle had each other on Catalina. But now I know you were completely alone. My guilt for leaving you there was softened by the thought that you had each other but now I know—" Beth watched him, her eyes reflecting the kitchen's dim light, a pool of sympathy amidst her own unresolved pain. She didn't need him to apologise for leaving them there, but she desperately wanted him to apologise for having some semblance of a life while she and Chantelle suffered, even though she knew it was selfish. He had to make it right, or at least try. Their world might be broken, but perhaps some shards of what had been could still be pieced together. Austin's hands found the edge of the table, gripping it as if to anchor himself in the storm of his own remorse.

"Fuck Beth," Austin continued, a tremble creeping into his voice that betrayed the depth of his emotion, "I've been so wrapped up in my own survival, my own grief, that I didn't think. You both had no one." Her gaze never wavered, taking in the man before her, seeing the friend who had also been swept along by the tide of chaos that was their reality. The silence that followed was filled with a thousand unspoken words, a testament to the fragmented lives they were trying to rebuild piece by piece. Austin swallowed hard, feeling a tightness constrict his throat. Beth opened her mouth to speak, a mere ghost of a whisper crept from her lips.

"Austin—"

"After all the things you've told us, the light you've shed on the situation," his eyes glistened with unshed tears as he reached for words that felt woefully inadequate, "I never actually told you how incredibly sorry I am. For everything." In that moment, something shifted, and the distance that had grown between them seemed to collapse. Beth rose from her chair, the motion fluid and instinctive. She crossed to where Austin stood, her arms encircling him in an embrace that was at once fierce and gentle. Austin returned the hug, wrapping his arms tightly around her. Their bodies pressed together in a silent acknowledgment of shared loss and regret. He felt her breath against his neck, warm and steady - a counterpoint to the cold uncertainty of the world outside. They remained locked in the embrace, two souls seeking solace in the midst of darkness, finding a moment of connection surrounded the ruins of what had once been familiar. It was a testament to their enduring humanity, a whisper of hope that even amidst the desolation they could still find the strength to comfort one another. The subtle shudder that ran through Beth's frame subsided into a deep exhale as her body finally relaxed against his. Her tears, once restrained, now flowed freely as they soaked into the fabric of Austin's shirt where her face was buried. He winced slightly at the pain in his arm but he tightened his hold nonetheless, understanding the necessity of this release for her.

"Thank you." She whispered between sobs, her voice muffled against his shoulder. The raw honesty in those two words spoke volumes of the burdens she had carried alone. Austin nodded, his own eyes damp with empathy. Slowly, she pulled back just enough to meet his gaze, their faces mere breaths apart. In the dim light of the kitchen, her green and gold eyes shimmered, a mosaic of sorrow and gratitude reflecting back at him. For an instant, the air between them charged with an intensity that neither had anticipated. They hovered in that delicate space, the world beyond the walls of the kitchen ceasing to exist. Their mutual pain and understanding wove an invisible thread, drawing them closer still. But as their lips nearly touched, a tremor of realisation quivered through Beth. She halted the momentum, her hand pressing firmly against Austin's chest, a silent plea for pause.

"Beth—"

"I appreciate your apology. More than you know," she said softly, her voice steady despite the turbulence within, "but I can't do this." He searched her face for a sign of reproach, but found none - only the gentle firmness of a boundary being set. With a nod of respect, Austin leaned forward and placed a tender kiss on her forehead.

"Goodnight, Beth." He murmured, the words carrying the weight of unspoken promises and regrets. He stepped away from the warmth of her embrace and out into the cool night that seemed all too eager to swallow up the fragile moment they had shared. As he closed the door behind him, he left behind not just Beth, but a piece of the turmoil that had gripped him since leaving them that night on Alcatraz.

Beth's fingers fluttered over the last manila folder, heavy with its contents of lists and notes, before she allowed it to settle onto the towering stack. With a weary sigh, she stepped back and crossed her arms as her gaze swept across the room that now resembled a war table more than a town hall. The walls were adorned with maps, each speckled with colourful pins marking housing assignments and professional placements. Papers formed neat rows and columns on every surface, the product of countless hours of meticulous labor.

"Is that for us?" A voice cut through the silence like a stray bullet, causing Beth's heart to leap into her throat. She spun around, her hand instinctively clutching the edge of the table for support. Standing in the doorway was the figure of a man, his presence commanding yet not ostentatious. His hair, dark and controlled, traced the contours of his head before ending just above the collar of his white shirt. The beard on his face was neatly trimmed, lending him an air of scrupulous grooming. His attire was casual but deliberate, with suspenders clasped firmly to the waistband of his jeans, the tweed jacket adding a touch of scholarly distinction. Behind thick-framed glasses, his dark eyes held a spark of keen intelligence, or perhaps curiosity. For a moment, Beth could only stare at him, taking in the incongruity of such a well-put-together individual appearing unannounced in their humble, work-strewn hall. She cleared her throat, recovering from the initial shock of his sudden appearance.

"It's all for the Prescott arrivals." She managed to say, her voice steadier than she felt. The man stepped forward with unhurried grace, his gaze sweeping over the landscape of documents and maps spread before him.

"Abraham Bishop." He introduced himself, extending a hand not in greeting but as an accompaniment to his perusal of Beth's work. His fingers hovered above the meticulous arrays of paperwork as if admiring a well-curated exhibit.

"Beth Taylor." She said quietly, her eyes never leaving his gaze as he scrutinised her, almost as if he were assessing her worth.

"Quite the setup you have here," he remarked, pausing at one particular map adorned with colour-coded pins, "I'm impressed."

"Thank you." Beth whispered, almost silently.

"Is that my new church?" Abraham leaned in, tracing a route with his index finger before pointing out the window towards the steeple rising in the near distance. Still on edge from his sudden intrusion, Beth crossed her arms defensively, maintaining the width of the table between them.

"You must be Henry's son." She surmised, trying to infuse her tone with a warmth she didn't feel. The nod he gave her was curt, affirming her guess with a polite detachment that seemed to widen the space between them. Though the room was silent save for their conversation, Beth could almost hear the weight of Abraham's presence pressing against her senses. There was something about the set of his shoulders, the assuredness in his stance, that marked him as someone accustomed to occupying space authoritatively. His eyes, sharp and assessing behind the panes of his glasses, seemed to take in more than the visible effort she had put into preparing for the newcomers. They seemed to appraise her, and in that moment, Beth felt uncomfortably transparent under his scrutiny. Abraham's fingers brushed the edge of a manila folder, his touch deliberate as he flipped it open, revealing the lists and notes Beth had meticulously compiled. She watched, her hands gripping the back of a chair for support, as he scanned the contents with an unreadable expression.

"I was told I could find my father here." Abraham glanced back to Beth, his eyes intense and unblinking.

"We weren't expecting anyone until next week." She said, her voice steady despite the fluttering in her stomach. His gaze lifted from the papers, meeting hers with a calm that felt almost invasive.

"Merely a preliminary visit to observe the preparations." He replied, his interest returning to the files before him. As he rifled through the pages, Beth's sense of order began to fray at the edges. Each shift of paper was a dissonant note in the symphony of her organisation. The room seemed to shrink around her, the air thick with the scent of ink and anticipation.

"It might look like chaos," she ventured, her words rushing out in an attempt to reclaim some semblance of control, "but everything is accounted for. It just needs to be filed properly now." Abraham closed the folder with a soft thud, his eyes never leaving her face.

"I didn't ask." He stated plainly, and something about his dismissiveness sent a shiver down Beth's spine. She nodded, her mouth suddenly dry, chastising herself silently as she wondered why had she felt compelled to justify her work to a stranger. Abraham's presence loomed large in the small space. Beth retreated a step, feeling inexplicably vulnerable in the face of his quiet dominance. The door to the town hall creaked open, and Henry's familiar form filled the doorway. Beth's heart leapt into her throat as relief momentarily washed over her. The mayor's eyes crinkled with surprise as he approached Abraham, who stood like an imposing statue among the sea of papers.

"Abraham!" Henry exclaimed, his voice echoing in the high-ceilinged room. He reached out to his son with a warmth that seemed to thaw the air around them, pulling him into a robust embrace.

"Father." Abraham said with an undertone of unfamiliarity, as if greeting a stranger.

"I had no idea you were coming," Henry looked between his son and Beth, "what a surprise."

"Surprise has always been a favoured ally." Abraham replied, his tone dry but his lips curving into a half-smile at his father's delight. "This is Beth, she's taken over for Sarah while she's out on maternity leave." Henry gestured towards Beth, introducing her with a proud tilt of his head. At the mention of children, a genuine smile broke through Abraham's stoic exterior, softening the lines around his eyes.

"Ah, children," he mused, quoting scripture with a reverence that seemed to come naturally to him, "a heritage from the Lord, offspring a reward from him." Beth felt a flicker of kinship at the biblical reference, despite the unease that clung to her like a second skin. It was a sentiment that echoed deeply within the community's values - values that had become even more precious in these trying times.

"Let's not keep Beth from her important work," Henry suggested, motioning towards the exit, "how about we go grab some lunch? You must be hungry after your journey."

"Of course." Abraham agreed, turning his attention back to Beth. His gaze held hers with an intensity that made her feel as though he was reading chapters of her life she'd never spoken aloud.

"Nice to meet you." She forced a smile, though she was certain he could easily read the insincerity written all over her face. With a respectful nod he recited another verse, his voice resonant in the almost-empty hall.

"Then God blessed Noah and his sons, saying to them, 'Be fruitful and increase in number and fill the earth.' It was lovely to meet you

Beth." He looked her up and down as he exited the room.

"Thank you." Beth managed, her tone polite but guarded. There was a beat of silence where their eyes locked in a silent exchange laden with unspoken thoughts before Abraham pulled away, following Henry out of the town hall. Beth exhaled slowly, feeling the weight of Abraham's presence lift as the door closed behind them. His parting words hung in the air, both a blessing and a reminder of the monumental task that lay ahead for them all. Her fingers trembled as they brushed against the cold, metallic edge of a binder, sending a stuttering echo through the cavernous space of the town hall. The files before her had transformed from organised chaos into an ominous reminder of the encounter she had just endured. She wrapped her arms around herself, trying to quell the shiver that wasn't entirely due to the room's chill. There was something about Abraham Bishop's voice - a subtle timbre or perhaps it was the cadence of his speech - that set her nerves on edge. His eyes held a sharpness that seemed to slice through the pretence of civility. Beth couldn't articulate why, but she felt exposed and scrutinised, as if he'd leafed through her soul like one of the many pages scattered across the table. Involuntarily, her gaze flitted to the door, now closed, which had offered him entry into her meticulously ordered world. Sighing in an attempt to release the tension coiling within her, Beth forced her attention back to the task at hand. She needed to regain composure - the people from Prescott were depending on her precision and care. With deliberate movements, she began to re-stack the papers, her hands gradually steadying as she immersed herself once more in the familiar task.

Austin stepped inside the dimly lit warehouse at the base, his eyes quickly adjusting to seek out Ben. He found him hunched over a workbench littered with maps and supply lists, his focus unwavering as he inventoried what appeared to be medical supplies. Ben glanced up at him before he could say a word, watching as he slowly approached. He grunted in acknowledgment of Austin's presence before returning his attention to the items before him. Austin walked slowly, as if approaching a caged animal, unsure about the unpredictability of what would happen next.

"Ben, I'm sorry about what happened," Austin ventured, his tone earnest, "about what I said."

"It's fine." Ben offered in return, his tone passive and insincere. It was clear Ben hadn't fully moved past their last exchange, but Austin's need to talk was pressing.

"I really need to talk to you about something. Can you stop for a minute?" Austin pressed, his frustration simmering as Ben continued his meticulous work.

"There's nothing to talk about." Ben merely shifted another box closer, his hands methodically checking off items from his list, each tick a pointed indication of his current priorities. Austin realised he would not easily garner the full attention of his friend, not while the spectre of their previous conflict lingered unresolved in the air. He sighed, recognising the conversation would have to wait, but the urgency of what remained unsaid gnawed at him as he watched Ben prepare for the journey ahead. Austin's patience frayed as he watched Ben meticulously fold a sleeping bag, the methodical movements grating on his nerves. His jaw clenched, and a sharp edge crept into his voice.

"Ben, stop! I need you to listen to me." He demanded, louder than intended. The sleeping bag thudded softly onto the concrete floor as Ben complied, his arms crossing over his chest. The raised eyebrow was a silent challenge, a barrier as formidable as any wall. Austin dropped into a nearby chair, the metal creaking under his weight. He leaned forward, elbows resting on his knees, and focused on the grounded figure before him.

"Something's going on with Sabrina," Austin began, the gravity of the situation seeping through his words, "Beth and Val, they think she's involved in Chantelle's death." Ben's posture remained unchanged, but something flickered in his eyes - a mixture of concern and skepticism.

"What've you found out?" He questioned, his voice betraying no hint of judgment or disbelief. Austin's hands flexed open and closed, the frustration tangible.

"I was gearing up to take it to Henry, but then Sabrina went into labour," he paused, the facts of the case tangling like wires in his mind, "and now I'm at a standstill. We've got suspicions, and hunches, but nothing solid. No proof."

"Have you considered confronting her directly?" Ben's suggestion was straightforward, unembellished by emotion.

"Confront Sabrina," Austin scoffed lightly, almost bitterly, "she's a damn good liar, Ben. Too good. She could run us in circles all day, and we wouldn't even see it." Ben's silence lingered, heavy and thoughtful as he absorbed the complexity of the dilemma laid bare before him. Ben's folded arms seemed to convey an unspoken understanding of the bleakness that had settled like a fog over their conversation.

"You're giving Sabrina too much credit for being subtle. If she's as narcissistic as we think she is, she might *enjoy* the attention. Someone discovering her secret? That could feel like validation to her. Twisted, but still validation." He finally spoke, his tone carrying a hint of resigned certainty. The words hung in the air between them, and Austin found himself nodding, the idea unsettling yet strangely fitting with the image of Sabrina he held in his mind.

"Yeah," he murmured, more to himself than to Ben, "I'll have to bring this to Henry. See what he thinks about it all." The two men fell into a prolonged silence, the tension of the room dissipating slightly as they both retreated into their own thoughts. The base's ambient noises - a distant hum of machinery, the occasional muffled voice - filtered through the quiet.

"Why are you here then," after minutes had passed, Ben broke the stillness with a question, "if the one you should be telling is Henry?"

"I wanted your advice," Austin spoke slowly, attempting to counter Ben's disinterested and impolite tone with his own passiveness, "I needed your input."

"Well," Ben bent down to collect the sleeping bag he had dropped on the floor, "you've got it. So if there's nothing else—"

"Where are you off to anyway?" Austin's curiosity was piqued by the supplies scattered around them.

"Supply run," Ben replied curtly, his gaze shifting towards the window where the fading light hinted at the encroaching evening, "some of the scouts stumbled upon a couple of Walmarts in Idaho. Twin Falls and Pocatello. They're not completely picked over so we're taking a handful of trucks to load up on whatever we can find."

"Idaho, huh?" Austin mused, picturing the distance and the potential risks involved.

"Yep," Ben affirmed, his eyes returning to meet Austin's, "gotta

keep this place stocked up." Austin leaned against the heavy workbench, his injured arm aching as he watched Ben sort through
the equipment, methodically checking each item before packing
it away. The room was filled with a sense of urgency. Outside the
world was fading into twilight, and inside, preparations for survival were underway.

"Idaho's not exactly next door," Austin said, casting a glance at the
maps sprawled across the table, their routes highlighted in neon
markers, "that's a fair hike." Ben paused, his hands stilling on the
straps of a backpack.

"The towns close by might as well be ghost towns now. We've
scavenged them to the bones, and who knows what other groups
have been through," he secured the strap with a firm tug and then
faced Austin with a grave expression, "might want to talk to Henry
about setting up some kind of farming. Sustainability's going to
become our best friend soon enough."

"Right," Austin replied, a wry smile tugging at the corner of his
mouth despite the seriousness of the situation, "because farming's
a breeze in acres of sand."

"Guess we'll have to make it more than sand then," Ben retorted,
his tone carrying an undercurrent of determination that Austin
had come to respect, "we can't keep banking on these supply runs.
They take days, put everyone in danger, and fuel isn't getting any
easier to find. I can't talk to George about it because he doesn't
want to hear it. Maybe he'll listen to his own brother."

"I hear you. I'll bring it up with Henry," Austin nodded, absorbing
the logic in Ben's words, "see what the old man thinks." It was true,
they were living on borrowed time if they couldn't adapt.

"Good." Ben acknowledged, returning his attention to the tasks at
hand. Austin pushed off from the bench, feeling the pull of his

muscles as he moved.

"Are you," he hesitated, a question forming in his mind, "are you gonna say goodbye to Beth before you leave?" Ben froze momentarily, his face impassive as he looked up.

"She's got her hands full. No need to add to it." He said, but there was a hint of something unspoken in his eyes - a mix of regret and resolution.

"Alright." Austin said softly, recognising the boundaries that friendship demanded he respect. Ben's fingers moved deftly, securing the straps around a tightly rolled sleeping bag with a practiced efficiency. Austin lingered by the door, watching his friend prepare for the journey ahead. The silence that had settled between them was heavy, punctuated only by the occasional snap of canvas and the rustle of supplies.

"Look, about Beth—" Austin started, breaking the quiet with a hesitant voice. Ben didn't look up from his task, but the tension in his shoulders was palpable.

"She made it clear," he said, the words tight as the bindings he was fastening, "she wants to be left alone."

"Ben," Austin caught the slight edge in Ben's voice, a mixture of hurt and stubborn pride, "I don't think she does. Especially from you. All she needs is time."

"She's mad about Julia."

"She's not mad about Julia," Austin pressed, "she's mad that we seemed to move on. Why don't you tell her what you did? Tell her that you stole guns and ammo and everything else and snuck out into the night to look for them before you were caught." Ben stopped for a moment, turning suddenly to face Austin and slamming his clipboard onto the table. Pens scattered, and a pile of canned food toppled and rolled onto the floor.

"Because I didn't help them!" Ben's voice was shrill, broken, his pain and torment seeping into the void to be swallowed by the silence that followed. Austin studied his face, his frustration and anger painting an image onto what had previously been a blank canvas.

"Ben—"

"I hate Eddie and Barnett for turning me in. I hate George for suspending me for six whole months. I wasn't allowed anywhere near the base. I couldn't even—"

"It might be the thought that counts," Austin interjected, attempting to sooth his anger, "Chantelle's dead. We can't change that. But Beth's here, and she's alive. You can tell her what you tried to do."

"Maybe," with a resigned sigh, Ben collected his clipboard from the table and looked at the mess of pens and cans, "I need to get back to work." Austin knew better than to push further, the unspoken boundaries between them were as clear as day. With a nod that carried more empathy than could be voiced, Austin stepped back, signalling his departure with a soft clearing of his throat.

"Stay safe out there, brother." Austin said, offering a supportive nod as the weight of their strained camaraderie lingered in the air. With a nod that carried the weight of a thousand unspoken words, Ben returned to his preparations. Austin turned and made his way out of the room, the echo of his footsteps mingling with the distant sound of life continuing amidst uncertainty.

The quiet of the room was a stark contrast to the noise of his thoughts. Ben lay still, the warmth of Julia's body against his chest an undeniable comfort, yet his eyes remained fixated on the ceiling above. The soft rise and fall of her breathing was a soothing rhythm in the darkness, but sleep eluded him. His mind raced with the upcoming mission, the roads they would travel, the risks they'd face. Each thought was a thread pulling him further from the solace of slumber. In just a few hours they would be departing at dawn, and the night was slipping away like sand through his fingers. He cursed himself silently, knowing full well he needed the rest, but restlessness had claimed him entirely. In these moments, the reality of their existence pressed down on him with a crushing weight - the constant fight for survival, the dwindling resources, the gnawing fear of what each new day might bring. It was a life measured in the currency of risk and resolve, and tomorrow's ledger was already demanding its toll. A sudden shift in the bed sent a ripple of unease through the stillness of the room. Ben swung his legs to the floor, sitting on the edge as if the mattress were a raft floating away from the shore of an inevitable conversation. His hands clasped together, knuckles whitening with the grip of decision. Julia's movement behind him was gentle, a quiet stirring that pulled at the edges of his resolve.

"Ben," her voice, soft and laced with sleep, reached out to him in the darkness, "what's wrong?" He turned slightly, enough to see the concern knit across her brow.

"I need to go back to my place. It's going to be an early start." He said, the words heavy and freighted with more than their simple meaning.

"You could stay." She murmured, reaching out a hand towards where he sat, her fingers brushing the air. But he shook his head, a small gesture that cut through the space between them.

"No, I can't," the finality in his tone was like a door closing, and he felt it shut within him too, "I don't want to."

"Then why did you come—"

"I shouldn't have," the words were like ice escaping his lips, his gaze fixed on the wall in front of him, "this was a mistake."

"What do you mean?" Her eyes widened as her lips parted softly, her attention fully on him now as she was startled awake from his comment. He paused, rubbing the back of his neck where tension had taken root.

"Julia, I really do like you. You're sweet, and kind, but it's just," the sincerity in his voice did little to soften the blow, "you're not what I want. I can't keep pretending that you are, or that this is enough." The silence that followed was filled with the sound of her breath hitching, a prelude to tears that threatened to spill. He wanted to reach out, to comfort her, but knew it would only serve to muddle the clarity of his confession.

"Then why did you come here tonight?" She pressed, her voice was soft and determined followed by a hint of anger.

"I don't know," he confessed, "familiarity, or habit I guess. It was the wrong thing to do and I'm sorry."

"You're *sorry*," a bitter laugh escaped her lips, "so you think you can just come here before your missions so you can get one last good fuck in just in case you die?" Ben quickly turned his head to face her, shock written all over his face as it was the first time he had heard her use profanity.

"Julia—"

"No," she sat up properly on the bed, the sheets falling from her form and exposing her trembling, naked body, "you love me. You know you do. You just need time—"

"I don't love you," his response was flat and clear, "I never said I did. We've never been alone unless we're in bed together. Every *date* we've ever had has been with Austin and Anne. You knew what this was." Her sobs grew louder, and a sense of guilt washed over Ben as he turned back to the wall. He had never intended to be this cruel, but perhaps cruelty was what she needed to see his rationalisation.

"Ben," she managed through a muffled sob, "you're not thinking clearly—"

"Take some time while I'm away. Process this, and when I come back," he hesitated, his voice low but steady as every word was another stone in the foundation of their parting, "I'm going to come back for Beth." Her hands moved to her face, fingertips pressing against her eyelids as if trying to hold back the tide of emotion. He stood then, the divide between them now a gulf filled with truths unspoken and shared moments fading into memory.

"It's a little too late for that." Julia's voice cracked as she whispered, her hand gravitated towards the gentle swell of her abdomen, eyes glistening with unshed tears. She watched Ben's features shift from confusion to concern in the dim light of the bedside lamp.

"Are you—" His question trailed into silence, the unspoken word hanging between them, palpable yet unspoken. She nodded, a single tear breaking free as she reached into the drawer beside her bed. The plastic test emerged, its result clear and unmistakable.

"I didn't know how to tell you," she confessed, her voice a mere breath, "you were pulling away and I thought if I could show you how much I love you, maybe your attention would return to me. Not because of this. Not like I've trapped you with *this*." Ben's jaw tightened, the weight of the revelation settling upon his shoulders like an iron yoke. It was the first time she had used that word - *love*. He stood motionless, the distance between their hearts stretching with each second of silence.

"This doesn't change how I feel about her." He finally spoke, his voice steady but distant. The words hung heavy in the air, a funeral dirge for what might have been. He glanced at the clock, its ticking a reminder of the impending dawn and the duties that awaited him.

"Ben—"

"We'll talk when I get back," his tone was final, the words more an evasion than a promise, "I need to sleep." He turned towards the door, his back now to Julia's tear-streaked face. Her sobs filled the room as he exited, closing the door behind him with a quiet click that echoed through the hollow space they once shared. Alone, she curled into herself, cradling the burgeoning life within her as the reality of their fractured future settled in like an unwelcome guest.

The dust billowed behind the convoy as it rumbled towards the community centre, a caravan of hope in a world starved of it. Beth's gaze flitted over the gathering - Henry with his stoic calm, George's hands clasped behind his back, Anne's fingers tapping a nervous rhythm on her thigh. Phillip stood slightly aloof, his eyes scanning the horizon as if waiting for something more than just the newcomers. Julia was there too, her presence subdued, a shadow of her usual vibrancy. She stood a little apart from the others, her hand occasionally brushing her abdomen in a gesture so fleeting it might have been mistaken for a trick of the light. Austin, whose restless energy often matched the tempo of his thoughts, shifted beside Beth as he kicked up small puffs of the dry earth. Val, ever the sentinel, surveyed the scene with a calculating gaze, her mind undoubtedly running through a hundred different scenarios.

"Looks like they made good time." Austin murmured, a hint of forced cheer in his voice.

"Let's hope it's a sign of good things to come." Beth replied, her voice betraying none of the turmoil that had churned within her these last few days. The first truck rolled to a stop, the brakes sighing as if in relief. Doors creaked open and new faces emerged, squinting in the bright desert sunlight. The school bus followed, its faded yellow paint a stark contrast against the muted colours of the desert. The masses peered out from behind the dusty windows, their curious eyes wide at the sight of their new home. Beth felt her heart lurch with a mixture of empathy and responsibility. These were people uprooted by necessity, seeking sanctuary in a world where safety was a luxury. Now, they looked to her, to all of them, to provide it.

"Welcome," Henry called out, his voice carrying the weight of his leadership, "welcome to Fort Irwin!" One by one, the people from Prescott stepped forward into the embrace of this new community, their future unwritten but for now filled with the promise of belonging. And as Beth watched them, she couldn't help but feel the stirrings of hope - fragile and delicate - unfurling in the vastness of the arid landscape.

CHAPTER 12

The setting sun cast a warm, orange glow across the sky as Beth handed over house keys to the last newcomer. The woman took them with a grateful nod, her fingers tracing over the metal notches with her fingers. Beth smiled, a sense of peace washing over her as the woman's eyes met hers with an appreciative smile.

"Mary will take it from here." Beth said, her voice carrying the weight of a long day. She watched as the woman before her stood slowly, a faint smile emerging despite the fatigue etched into her features. Mary stepped forward and gestured towards the door, her presence reassuring.
"This way." She said softly, her tone imbued with a practiced warmth. With the pair's departure, an enveloping stillness settled over the room that had buzzed with anxious energy just hours before. Beth let out a sigh, allowing herself a moment to absorb the quiet that now blanketed the space. Her gaze swept across the empty chairs, each one a silent testament to the tide of humanity that had flowed through this very hall. Her respite was brief. Turning back to her makeshift desk, Beth's attention fixed on the unruly stack of files yet to be addressed. They loomed behind her like an accusation, a reminder of the day's unresolved business. With a sense of duty propelling her forward, she reached for the pile, her fingers brushing against the cool surface of the paper as she fanned

them out before her.

"Brian Phillips, Taylor Rich," she murmured under her breath, her eyes scanning the names while a crease formed between her brows as she continued, "Lee Chung, James Stanton, Rocky Alvarado, Max Nunez, Jacob Riddle." The last name fell from her lips, tinged with uncertainty. Each name was a puzzle piece, and as she laid them out in her mind she realised some vital pieces were missing from the day's mosaic. No notice had been given of their absence, no word of delay or defection. Beth's intuition gnawed at her, a familiar unease that clung to her thoughts like a persistent shadow. These men were more than just names on a page, they were individuals who had survived the chaos of a fractured world, only to be swallowed by a new kind of obscurity. The descending dusk seemed to mirror her growing concern, the fading light casting long shadows across the walls as if to echo the darkening of her own contemplations. With the files clutched in her hand, the urgency of the unanswered question propelled her from the desolation of the empty hall, the mystery of the missing men fuelling her resolve to uncover the truth. Beth's footsteps echoed against the gravel as she approached the trio of men huddled outside, their voices a low murmur dissipating into the cooling air. The sky was painted with strokes of orange and purple, dusk settling over them like a heavy blanket, the day's weariness starting to show in the shadows under her eyes.

"Good evening." Henry welcomed her with a smile that was as warm as the day's sunshine.

"Evening Henry." She greeted, her gaze drifting across the faces before landing on the stranger among them. Abraham's stern countenance broke into a rare, cordial smile as he gestured towards the newcomer.

"Beth, this is my brother Adam." Abraham said, his voice carrying that usual characteristic firmness.

"Nice to meet you," Beth offered dryly, though her mind was elsewhere, a tangle of names and unanswered questions lingering at the forefront of her thoughts, "I'm looking for some men, they didn't show for placement today. Phillips, Rich, Chung, Stanton, Alvarado, Nunez and Riddle." Her eyes narrowed slightly, reading the quiet exchange of looks between them. Henry's face remained impassive, a mask of neutrality common to him.

"They've been on assignment for the last week," Abraham replied evenly, "not expected back any time soon."

"Assignment? What kind of assignment keeps seven people away without notice?" Beth's brows furrowed, her voice tinged with concern and curiosity. Adam, the new face with eyes as guarded as his brothers, stepped forward just enough to claim a subtle authority.

"That's not your concern, Beth." His tone was dismissive yet not unkind. Beth reeled slightly at the brusqueness, about to retort when Abraham interjected with a recitation that seemed almost reflexive.

"All hard work brings a profit, but mere talk leads only to poverty." Abraham cocked his head slightly as he gazed at her, his expression impassive as the platitude hung in the air.

"Proverbs, chapter 14 verse 23." Adam remarked, as if the words themselves justified their silence. Beth regarded Abraham with a mix of skepticism and exasperation.

"Do you do that often?" She pressed, unable to hide the edge in her voice. Abraham's features etched into lines of genuine confusion, or perhaps well-practiced innocence.

"Do what?"

"Quote scripture like it explains everything." Beth clarified, her stance firm despite the growing chill.

"Only when it is necessary." Abraham replied, his voice carrying the weight of his conviction. There was no trace of irony or jest - this was a man who wielded his faith like an ancient sword, unyielding and sharp. Beth took a moment to measure her next words, aware that the conversation was veering into territory she had neither the energy nor the desire to explore under the watchful eyes of the dying day. The missing men were still a puzzle, and Abraham's cryptic references to scripture did little to shed light on the matter.

"Right," she murmured, nodding once as if conceding to a point she didn't fully grasp, "well, let me know when they're back. We need to get them settled." Beth's response was met with Abraham's steady gaze, his presence as unyielding as the desert that bordered the settlement. He held a small, well-worn Bible in his hand, its pages fluttering ever so slightly in the evening breeze.

"Wives, submit yourselves to your own husbands as you do to the Lord. For the husband is the head of the wife as Christ is the head of the church, his body, of which he is the Saviour. Now as the church submits to Christ, so also wives should submit to their husbands in everything." Abraham placed his hand over his bible cautiously, straightening his posture and maintaining his gaze at Beth. She couldn't mask her incredulity, her brow furrowing at the unexpected turn.

"I don't have a husband," she cut in sharply before he could continue, "and I won't be submitting myself to anyone."

"Don't take it so literally Beth," Adam chuckled lightly with a dismissive wave of his hand, "my brother is only suggesting that these men know what they're doing and you shouldn't worry yourself."

"Maybe you shouldn't take the Bible so literally." Beth retorted, locking eyes with Abraham. Her defiance was palpable, her stance rooted like the earth beneath her. Abraham's lips pressed into a thin line, a slight nod acknowledging her words.

"The only way forward is the word of God." He stated with an unwavering certainty. A smile tugged at the corner of Beth's mouth, but it was devoid of warmth.

"I think your God abandoned everyone when the pandemic broke out." She pointed out, her voice laced with a bitterness she didn't bother to hide.

"God didn't abandon me." Abraham responded simply, almost inaudibly, his faith a fortress around him. He turned then, his silhouette stark against the dimming sky, and walked away without another word. The statement lingered in the air, a testament to a belief that seemed as immovable as the mountains themselves. Beth watched Abraham's retreating figure until he was swallowed by the shadows that crept along the ground as dusk began to settle. She turned her attention back to Adam, who was observing his brother's departure with a curious tilt of his head.

"Look," Adam said, breaking the silence with a casual ease, "don't mind Abraham's seriousness too much. His faith has kept him going through all of his hardships, including those before the pandemic." She crossed her arms, the chill of the evening prompting a shiver that she fought to suppress.

"I'll do my best to avoid it altogether," Beth's tone was edged with a determination that matched the steel in her eyes, "if he plans on sticking to his church, then we definitely won't run into each other."

"Fair enough." Adam conceded with a slight shrug, as if the weight of his brother's convictions was something he had learned to navigate long ago.

"Just let us know when the other men are back," Beth conceded with a defeated sigh, "they need to be assigned to their houses and their duties." At that moment, Henry stepped forward. His presence was like a balm, smoothing the ruffled air between them. He addressed Adam with a fatherly authority, effectively shutting down any potential for the conversation to loop back to unease.

"Yes," he nodded slowly, "you will let Beth know when they return. That's an order, son."

"Will do." Adam nodded as he turned on his heel to follow the path Abraham had taken, leaving behind a trail of dust that danced in the fading light. Beth let out a breath she didn't realise she had been holding as she watched Adam disappear into the lengthening shadows. The quietude that followed felt fragile, like the calm before a storm she wasn't sure how to prepare for. The evening air bit at her skin as she turned to Henry, the frustration evident in her furrowed brow.

"I don't like this Henry. This *secret mission*, it's not sitting right with me," she folded her arms across her chest as she clutched the files against her, "and Abraham's cryptic bible verses aren't helping. I'm not a child to be talked down to." Henry's face softened with understanding, his eyes reflecting the last glimmers of twilight.

"Abraham means well, even if his words come off stern," his voice carried an undercurrent of reassurance that was familiar and comforting, "but if it bothers you, I'll have a word with him."

"Thank you." Beth replied, though her eyes still held a spark of defiance. Without another word, she turned on her heel and strode towards the town hall, the weight of the files in her hand a tangible reminder of the unfinished business that lingered like a bad aftertaste.

Clinks of ice against glass punctuated the silence as Julia sat rigidly, her hands clasped in her lap, as Anne held out a tumbler filled with amber liquid.

"Come on, Julia. It'll take the edge off." Anne coaxed, pushing the drink closer. Julia shook her head, pressing her lips into a thin line. "No. I can't." Her gaze was distant, troubled. Anne's brows knit together in concern.

"What's going on?" She asked, retracting the glass and studying Julia's pallor. It took a moment for Julia to find her voice, and when she did it was scarcely more than a whisper.

"I'm pregnant," she confessed, her eyes brimming with unshed tears as Anne's expression shifted from concern to shock, and then quickly to empathy, "and Ben told me he'd be coming back for Beth." A tremor ran through Julia's words. The admission hung heavy between them, a spectre of complications yet to unfold. Anne reached across the space, her hand squeezing Julia's in solidarity.

"We'll figure this out," she murmured, but the certainty she tried to convey didn't quite reach her eyes, "but I did warn you about Ben. You knew he didn't share your feelings." Anne's words were frank, the kind of truth that cut through illusions like a sharpened blade. Julia's face crumpled, eyes glistening with the sting of reality.

"But I love him." She whispered, a stubborn edge to her tone.

"Love doesn't change the fact that he doesn't feel the same," Anne's gaze was unwavering, "you need to move on, Julia."

"Move on," the word came out choked and desperate, "how can I just move on when I'm carrying his child?"

"Like people did before all this," Anne replied, gesturing vaguely to the world outside forever altered by pandemic and chaos, "they break up, they move on. They share custody. We live with our choices, Julia. It's harsh, but it's life." Julia rose abruptly, her chair scraping against the wooden floor.

"I don't feel well." She said, her voice hollow. Without another word she turned and fled, the door slamming behind her with a finality that echoed in Anne's chest.

"Henry, we need to talk." Austin's voice was grave, brooking no delay. The town hall had loomed like a silent sentinel in the fading light as Austin hurried towards it, finding Henry inside poring over a map littered with notes and markers.

"It's been a long day," Henry glanced up, his weathered face creasing with concern at Austin's expression, "can it wait until morning?"

"No. It can't," Austin said flatly, "I think Sabrina had something to do with Chantelle's death." The words spilled from him, each one heavy with implication. Henry straightened, his eyes narrowing.

"Yes, I suppose your concern is something we should discuss. What proof do you have?"

"None," Austin admitted, his hands clenching into fists, "but there's enough to warrant questioning. Patterns, behaviour, we can't ignore it. I want to question her." Austin continued demandingly.

"Absolutely not," Henry took a small step towards him, "you're too close to this, and you will let your emotions run high. We'll proceed carefully, and if there's even a shadow of truth to this I will get to the bottom of it. But *that* can wait until tomorrow. She's just had a baby. She isn't going anywhere." Henry's resolve was a wall but the cracks showed when Austin's voice filled the room, thick with the weight of unspoken deeds and sacrifices.

"I've stood back when needed, Henry. When we arrived I accepted that George wouldn't allow us to go after Beth and Chantelle, and Chantelle's dead because we were too late. I've supported this community without fail," his unyielding gaze locked onto Henry's, "so if Sabrina is responsible for Chantelle's death then let me be there when you question her, at least give me that." The older man's eyes dropped to the map again, as if seeking counsel from its web of lines and scribbles. Silence stretched between them, taut like a bowstring. Finally, Henry exhaled, his shoulders slumping ever so slightly in resignation.

"Alright," he conceded, the words drawn out and reluctant, "first thing in the morning, we will go and see Sabrina. You can be there." Satisfied at Henry's reluctant agreement, Austin gave a curt nod, the line of his jaw softening just enough to signal his gratitude.

Beth's arrival at Reece's was less of an intrusion and more a silent understanding shared among old friends. As she knocked and was welcomed inside, the door was already unlocked when she pushed against it, the scent of liquor and the mellow sound of laughter greeted her as Chase's laughter mingled with Reece's deeper tones. They sat opposite each other, glasses poised in midair, conversation momentarily suspended by her entrance.

"What's up?" Chase glanced over his shoulder at her.

"Where's Tyler?" Beth's inquiry came casually, but her eyes were sharp, scanning their faces for any sign of evasion.

"He's on assignment with Ben." Reece replied with a nonchalant shrug, his fingers drumming against the glass.

"Well we need Austin and Val here." She stated, her tone taking on a new urgency, that familiar undercurrent of determination threading through her words.

"Val's upstairs." Chase mentioned, gesturing vaguely towards the ceiling with his drink. As if summoned by the mention of her name, Val appeared at the top of the staircase, descending with a grace that seemed unburdened by the world's newfound chaos.

"I thought I heard your voice." Her tone was soft, almost tender, belying the steely resolve that had carried her through the worst of times. A brief, affectionate kiss graced Reece's cheek as she passed through the living room into the kitchen - a fleeting moment of intimacy in a landscape starved of such warmth. Val moved past them, her hand trailing along Reece's shoulder before she reached into the cupboard for a glass. The clink of ice and the splash of liquid held a comforting rhythm, a small reminder of life's continuance amidst uncertainty. Beth's gaze lingered on the soft kiss Val had placed on Reece's cheek, her mind piecing together the subtle shifts in their dynamic.

"When did this happen?" She asked, her voice laced with genuine curiosity. Chase leaned back in his chair, a knowing grin etching across his face.

"It was a long time coming," he said, his eyes flicking between Reece and Val, "everyone saw it before these two did."

"Congratulations." Beth offered warmly, her eyes meeting Val's. In response, the corners of Val's mouth curved upward ever so slightly, a hint of a smile breaking through. A rarity these days, and the first semblance of happiness Beth had seen from her since her arrival.

"Thanks." Val murmured, her voice carrying an unspoken gratitude.

"Let me go grab Austin." Chase said as he rose to his feet, his movements fluid with an undercurrent of resolve.

"I'll get you a drink." Val extended her hand for another glass as Beth lifted a hand in polite refusal.

"I'm good, thanks." She said, her eyes darting to the half-empty glasses already at play on the table. Her thoughts needed to remain sharp, undiluted by the haze of alcohol. As Val shrugged and settled into her seat, an awkward silence fell over them, filled only by the occasional clink of ice against glass. Reece attempted small talk about the state of repairs around town, but the conversation felt stilted, each word hanging heavier than the last. The door swung open and Chase returned, shadowed by the figure of Austin, whose presence seemed to break the uneasy quiet.

"Found him." Chase announced, gesturing towards Austin with a nod. Austin's gaze immediately found Beth, a silent question in his eyes.

"Thanks for coming." Beth said, acknowledging both Chase's effort and Austin's swift compliance. The room shifted subtly, the air charged with the weight of unspoken concerns. Austin stepped into the dimly lit room, his eyes scanning the faces before settling on Beth's. The tension in her stance was palpable, even from a distance.

"What's going on?" He asked, crossing the room to join the uneasy gathering. Beth took a deep breath before her words came tumbling out.

"Something's not right. Seven guys are unaccounted for from today's intake," she began circling the scars of her brand, a telltale sign of her distress, "and Abraham, there's something off about him." Chase leaned back against the wall, arms folded across his chest.

"Haven't met the guy yet." He said, casting a sidelong glance at Austin who was half-hidden in the shadows.

"Neither have I." Reece chimed in, his curiosity piqued.

"Trust me," Beth continued with an edge to her voice, "you're better off not crossing paths. There's an unease around him that sets my teeth on edge."

"Maybe you're just too quick to judge," Val let out a scoff from where she lingered in her chair, the sound sharp in the mounting silence, "these people are new, Beth. We should give them a chance to settle in before casting suspicions."

"Val, my gut has a pretty solid track record," Beth retorted, frustration creeping into her voice, "I'm telling you, there's something *off* about him."

"Look, if all you wanted to discuss was your feelings about some guy most of us haven't met," Val said with a dismissive wave of her hand, "then I'm off to bed." She turned away, her silhouette receding towards the staircase.

"Wait, please," Beth pleaded as she stepped forward, the urgency in her tone rooted Val in place, "you need to hear me out. Something's wrong, I can feel it." The room fell silent as the gravity of Beth's words settled over them, the tone in her voice placing them into a sense of unease. Even Val paused halfway up the stairs, the doubt clear on her face despite her earlier skepticism. Chase stretched his arms above his head, an easy-going yawn escaping him as he stood up from the worn sofa.

"Beth, can you at least give us a chance to meet him? If it makes you feel any better I promise I'll keep an eye out for anything odd," he said with a relaxed tone that belied the tension that had knotted the air moments before, "been one hell of a day though. I need some rest." He ambled towards the door and with a casual two-fingered salute, he disappeared into the night, the sound of his boots fading away. Reece followed Chase's departure with a lingering gaze out the window before turning back to the room.

"I think I'm gonna hit the hay too." His voice was soft, yet there was an unmistakable firmness to it, signalling the end of the meeting. The glance he cast towards Austin and Beth was subtle but pointed, a gentle nudge towards the exit.

"I'll walk you home." Austin offered, standing and stretching his legs. There was a protective undertone to his words, a silent acknowledgment of the weight that hung between them after Beth's unsettling disclosures. Beth nodded, grateful for the company yet frustrated at their dismissal of her concerns. As they stepped out into the cool night, she glanced at the sling cradling Austin's arm.

"How's the arm healing?" She asked, steering the conversation towards safer waters.

"Slowly but surely," Austin replied, flexing his fingers within the confines of the fabric, "not fast enough for my liking. I'm ready to be back at full strength."

"Patience was never your strong suit." Beth said with a small smile, the lines of worry around her eyes softening momentarily. The silence that settled between them wasn't uncomfortable, but it was filled with unspoken thoughts. Beth broke it first, her voice dropping to a murmur.

"Something's not right about Abraham." Her eyes searched the shadows as if half-expecting to find answers lurking there.

"Let's take it one step at a time," Austin suggested, though his furrowed brow betrayed his own concern, "I still have to figure out what to do about Sabrina."

"Oh fuck Sabrina, Austin," she raised her hands up and squeezed at her face, pressing her eyes hard before rubbing her eyebrows, "she's not going anywhere."

"Not here." Austin chastised her, grabbing her arm and quickening their pace towards her house. As they neared Beth's front door, her pace slowed slightly, each step heavy with dread.

"Abraham, he recites the bible like it's the only way he can communicate, and he keeps talking about women knowing their place," she stopped, facing him squarely in the dimming light, "and I think, no, I'm almost certain that Abraham is the one Victor had that trade deal with. For the kids." The gravity of her words hung between them like a spectre, and for a moment they simply stared at one another, the chilling implication setting into their bones. Beth leaned against the worn wood of the door, pressing her forehead to its rough surface. Her breath came in ragged pulls, the fear she'd kept at bay now clawing its way to the forefront.

"Are you okay?" Austin's voice was soft, but it shattered the fragile calm she had been grasping at.

"Okay," she spat out, her voice escalating as she jerked upright, eyes flashing with a mix of anger and terror, "no Austin, I am not okay. We're all in danger and no one will listen to me!" Her shout broke the stillness of the night, her words an ominous echo in the quiet street before them. Beth's heart drummed in her ears, the palpable sense of impending doom wrapping around her like a shroud. As she stood there with Austin's concerned gaze locked on hers, she realised that this was just the beginning. Austin's hand found her shoulder, a gentle but firm pressure guiding her into the safety of her home. The door closed with a decisive click, and the muffled sounds of the outside world fell away, leaving them wrapped in an uncomfortable silence.

"You need to keep your voice down while you're out there making accusations like that." His voice carried the weight of caution. Beth turned sharply, her eyes alight with a fiery defiance.

"Maybe it would be better if someone did hear me," she retorted, the edge in her tone like the blade of a knife, "maybe then someone would actually listen."

"Listen to what," Austin leaned against the closed door, crossing his arms, "conspiracy theories?"

"I need you to believe me." Her plea was almost a whisper, desperate and raw. The room seemed to contract around them as their gazes locked, and for a moment neither moved. Then the tension broke as they stepped away from the door and the argument between them flared to life like a match struck in darkness.

"Why?"

"Look, I get it," Beth began, pacing the room with agitated steps, her boots thudding against the wooden floor, "everyone's settled into this, this domestic bliss or whatever, while Chantelle and I were struggling to survive, and I should be over it, right? Moving on, living my life." Austin watched her, his jaw clenched, the lines of his face drawn taut by the stress of their conversation.

"Beth—"

"I can't just ignore what I've seen, what I *feel*," she continued, her voice escalating with each word, "do you have any idea what it's like to sit in captivity for over a year with nothing but your own thoughts and your gut feeling for company? I sat, and I waited, and I listened, but more importantly I *learned*. I've spent the better part of two years being strung along in someone else's game and it's time someone listened to me. Men like Abraham, they have an agenda and it's never good for people like us."

"Us," Austin echoed, his voice rising to meet hers, "what do you mean *like us*?"

"Survivors, fighters, women," Beth shot back, her frustration boiling over, "you weren't there, Austin. There is something so familiar about his voice, and you didn't hear the way he talked about children, about women. He has plans, and I'm telling you, they're not good. We can't just sit back and—"

"*Enough*," Austin's shout cut through her tirade and the room fell silent again, the echo of his voice hanging in the air, "I'm here now, aren't I? Trying to understand, trying to help, but you're acting fucking crazy, Beth. I thought this place would heal you but you're too far gone. You're making it fucking hard when all you do is push everyone away." Beth's breath hitched, her chest heaving as she fought to control the anger that threatened to consume her. She knew he was right, in her heart she knew it. But admitting it out loud was another battle entirely.

"Austin—"

"Let's *pretend* I believe you. If everything you say is true, you don't have a shred of evidence," Austin admitted after a moment, his voice softer now, "we need more than just gut feelings. We need something solid to act on."

"Then help me find it," Beth pleaded, her voice breaking with the strain of her emotions, "help me show them that we're not just paranoid. That there's something genuinely wrong here. I can feel it, Austin. The first moment I met him, he assessed me. He spoke about children and women as if they were objects. Victor was trading babies with an evangelical group on the mainland and he fits that profile perfectly. I don't know how, but I know it's him." Austin nodded, the fight draining from him as he took a step towards her.

"We'll find proof Beth. But for now lower your voice and keep your head clear, and trust that you're not alone in this. I'll help you, I promise, but please don't have a breakdown over this." The air crackled with tension, Beth's nostrils flaring as she drew in shaky breaths.

"I can't just trust things will be okay!" She spat out, her voice a serrated edge cutting through the silence as her hand shot out, colliding with the vase on the side table. Porcelain exploded into shards, the impact resonating through her bones.

"Jesus." Austin lurched forward as crimson bloomed across her knuckles. Pain seared through her hand, but it was distant compared to the anguish that clouded her mind. She barely registered the warmth of her own blood as it dripped down her wrist.

"I didn't mean to—"

"Let me see." Austin's voice was calm, but his hands betrayed a sense of urgency as he unwound the sling from his arm and pressed it against her wound. The fabric darkened where it soaked up the blood. Beth tried to pull away, her instincts to fight any form of constraint kicking in.

"I don't need—"

"Stop being so fucking stubborn and calm down," Austin growled, his grip surprisingly gentle as he wrapped the makeshift bandage around her hand, "let me take you to Anne."

"I've been through worse," she shook her head vehemently, her gaze fixed on the drops of blood hitting the wooden floor, "this is nothing." With a heavy sigh he guided her towards the kitchen, the scent of iron following them. She sat down heavily at the table, her injured hand laid out before her like a grotesque still life. Austin rummaged under the sink, pulling out the first aid kit with a clatter. His movements were methodical as he retrieved antiseptic wipes and gauze, his training taking over.

"You might need stitches." He muttered more to himself than to her as he dabbed at her wounds. The sting of the antiseptic snapped Beth back to the present, a hiss escaping her lips.

"Just get it done." She said through clenched teeth. He worked quickly, cleaning and wrapping her wounds with an efficiency born of necessity. Despite the pain, despite the anger that still simmered within her, there was an odd comfort in the familiarity of it all - the care given and received in moments of vulnerability.

"Done," Austin announced, securing the final strip of gauze, "I'll sit with you for a bit and if it bleeds through this, you're seeing Anne. No arguments." Beth nodded, unable or unwilling to muster further protest. Her eyes traveled from the neat bandaging to Austin's face, finding something similar to concern etched into his features. It was enough to soften the edges of her anger, enough to remind her that battles were rarely fought alone. In the dim light of Beth's kitchen, the shadows danced across Austin's intent face as he scrutinised her bandaged fist.

"Okay." She murmured, steeling herself against the throbbing in her hand. The weight of her own fury sat heavily in her chest, an unwelcome companion that had been with her for far too long. Silence enveloped them for a moment before Austin broke it with a question that seemed to echo off the walls.

"Why are you so angry all the time?" He zipped up the first aid kit gingerly and pushed it aside on the table, turning back to face her. Beth's gaze met his, a tumult of emotions swirling within her.

"I don't know," she admitted, her voice barely above a whisper, "it's like there's this fire inside me and it just won't go out. It burns hotter whenever I feel like I'm shouting into the void and no one's listening. I feel like I'm losing my mind. When I'm here, alone, I'm almost okay. But when I'm out there in the world, I just feel like everything's going to fall apart all over again." She could see the concern in Austin's eyes and the way he paused, considering her words.

"Sounds like PTSD," Austin sighed, "I wish we had someone here you could speak to but unfortunately we haven't rescued any psychologists."

"It's fine." She wished she could reach inside herself and extinguish the blaze that consumed her peace, but every day seemed to fan the flames more fiercely.

"Remember when I got into that fight with Luis at the campsite? I was so full of anger, and you were the one patching me up back then," a faint smile crossed his lips, tinged with nostalgia, "seems we've switched roles now." A small laugh escaped Beth, despite herself.

"Yeah, I remember," she said, allowing herself a brief respite from the anger as her thoughts drifted to the past, "sometimes I wish we'd just stayed there. It was peaceful, before everything came crashing down." Their days at the campsite felt like a lifetime ago, simpler times when the world was less complicated and less cruel inside their bubble.

"We would've frozen solid in those tents come winter." He pointed out as he gave a soft laugh, but there was a seriousness to his reply. A half-hearted attempt at a smile graced Beth's features. They fell silent once more, lost in memories of a time that seemed both close enough to touch and yet impossibly distant.

"Still," Beth murmured, her gaze drifting to the half-curtained window where a sliver of moonlight fought its way through, "we almost froze at the ranch anyway. But those days at the campsite, we had our own little slice of the world. Just us and the serenity." She sighed, the weight of their current predicament pressing against the walls of her chest. Austin nodded, understanding the unspoken yearning for peace that hung between them.

"Isolation had its perks, didn't it?" His voice was a low thrum in the dim kitchen, carrying with it an undercurrent of shared hardship and camaraderie.

"Definitely wouldn't have worked with tents though." She added, the ghost of a teasing tone beneath her words. They both knew survival wasn't about comfort, it was about making the hard choices when you had to. Still, the idea of seclusion, of a time when troubles were simpler, held a certain allure. The room grew quiet again, the air thick with contemplation and the faintest hint of antiseptic. Beth's wounded hand throbbed gently, a reminder of the present and all its complexities.

"Hey," Austin said suddenly, his voice barely louder than a whisper as he leaned forward in his chair, "do you remember our sparring sessions? How you'd never back down, always ready to go another round?" Beth's eyes met his, a spark of the old fire igniting within them.

"How could I forget?" Her response was immediate, almost instinctual. Those moments encapsulated so much of who she was - determined, resilient, unyielding.

"That's what I loved about you," Austin confessed, his words hanging heavily in the air, "your eagerness to learn. Your willingness to grow from every experience. What happened to her?"

"Loved?" Beth echoed, emphasising the end of the word, seeking clarity in his gaze - the past tense didn't escape her.

"Beth." Austin's eyes, darkened by the twilight of the room, locked onto hers with an intensity that stirred something deep within her. It was a connection that transcended their current turmoil, reaching back to a foundation built on mutual respect and survival. Austin's breath was warm as he leaned in closer, pressing his face against her cheek before his lips met hers, tentative at first, as if testing the waters they had both silently agreed to navigate. The hesitation that flickered across Beth's face vanished as quickly as it appeared, and she found herself kissing him back - a desperate need for connection overriding her initial reluctance.

"Make me feel something else," she implored as she pulled away just enough to gaze into his eyes, her voice laced with urgency, "please. I'm so tired of being angry." Understanding, or perhaps the same need flared in his expression. With a raw intensity that matched the turmoil inside her, Austin swept her up, the strength in his arms leaving no room for argument as he ignored the pain pressing into his shoulder. He pushed her onto the kitchen table, his fingers skillfully working to unfasten the button of her jeans before pulling them down in one quick motion. The cool surface of the table pressed against her heated skin, a stark contrast to the fevered pace of their movements. She reached for his pants, disregarding the pain in her bandaged hand as she quickly tried to tug them over his broad hips. Drawing her close with an urgent intensity, he leaned in to kiss her and she felt herself being pulled back into the safe harbour of their connection, calmed by the familiar pulse of his heartbeat and the deep rumble of his groans in her ear. The world outside the walls of this small room faded away, replaced by nothing but their ragged breaths and the groaning of the table beneath. All the pent-up frustration and the lingering fear and confusion that had haunted her since her return began to melt away under the fervour of his touch. The moment, shattered as abruptly as it had ignited, was halted by a knock on her door that jolted them out of their heated embrace, the sound like a bucket of ice water.

"Shit." Austin scrambled to right himself, his brow furrowed in annoyance, or perhaps regret. Beth propped herself up on her elbows, staying still for a split second longer. Her breaths came in ragged gulps before she too forced her body to cooperate as she jumped off the table and pulled up her jeans. Whoever stood on the other side of the door had no idea of the storm they had just interrupted.

CHAPTER 13

Beth's hand trembled slightly as she drew the door open, her mind still a whirlwind from the intense moments with Austin. The figure before her was both familiar and imposing, his tall frame crowned by a mess of dark hair that seemed too wild for the solemn expression he wore. Abraham stood on her doorstep, his eyes searching hers with an intensity that made her recoil inwardly.

"May I come in?" His voice held a quiet steadiness that belied the late hour. Beth hesitated, the air between them thick with unspoken tension. As she stepped aside, her gaze flickered to Austin who leaned against the wall with arms folded like a silent sentinel ready to intervene. She was grateful for his presence, a comforting solidity in the midst of her confusion.

"Of course." Beth managed, her voice not quite as steady as she had intended. Abraham entered, his movements deliberate and respectful of the space as if aware of its sanctity to her.

"Thank you," he said, closing the door gently behind him, "I won't beat around the bush and I won't overstay my welcome. I came here to apologise." There was a note of something genuine in his voice that gave Beth pause.

"Apologise?" Her brow creased in puzzlement, the word hanging awkwardly in the air. Abraham nodded, the shadow of regret passing over his features.

"Yes. My father, he mentioned that I may have caused you discomfort earlier. It wasn't my intention. I value harmony among us, especially now. I'd like for us to start tomorrow with a clean slate if possible." Beth searched his face, trying to discern the sincerity behind the carefully chosen words. The apology seemed at odds with the man she had come to briefly know - one driven by firm beliefs and divine certainties. Yet here he was, extending an olive branch, however unsteady it might be.

"Alright," she said steadily, the word a cautious acceptance, "thank you." Abraham inclined his head, an acknowledgment of the fragile truce they had woven in that brief exchange. There was much left unsaid, questions lingering like ghosts between them. But for now they would let them rest. Beth shifted from one foot to the other, a tinge of unease colouring her stance as she regarded Abraham. The room lay steeped in an uncomfortable silence until Austin cleared his throat, stepping forward with an extended hand.

"Name's Austin," he said, his grip firm as their hands met, "I don't think we've been properly introduced." Abraham's eyes flickered with recognition, and for a brief moment his lips parted as if to quote scripture.

"Forgive me. I was about to be discourteous." A self-aware smile tugged at the corner of his mouth.

"Discourteous?" Beth whispered softly, raising an eyebrow between him and Austin.

"I was about to cite something, but I think that might be too much for the moment. God speaks through me often," Abraham confessed, releasing Austin's hand, "my convictions run deep, though they sometimes stir the waters around me." Beth watched the exchange, noting the restraint in Abraham's tone - a stark contrast to his usual fervour. She remembered the men who had vanished without a word, their absence a growing hole in their community fabric.

"Abraham," she interjected, her voice steady despite the current of anxiety beneath it, "where are the missing men? The ones who were supposed to arrive with you."

"Ah, yes," Abraham's expression sobered, his gaze momentarily distant, "before I settled here, I paid Fort Irwin a few visits. Whispers of dwindling supplies were already in the wind. The men, they've been sent on a supply run. Food, medicine, just essentials. It's a perilous task, but necessary for our survival." Beth's brow furrowed, skepticism etched into her features. Supply runs weren't uncommon, yet something about Abraham's explanation didn't sit right. It was too easy, too rehearsed, but she held her tongue. There would be time for probing questions later.

"Thank you Abraham," Beth replied with a measured politeness, hoping her face didn't betray the doubt gnawing at her, "that's good to know." Abraham nodded, sensing perhaps that his words had not entirely convinced her. But he left it at that, the unspoken tension lingering like a fog between them. Beth shifted uncomfortably, an awkward smile straining her lips as she glanced at Austin.

"Well, if that's all—" Her voice trailed off, the sincerity in her tone forced and brittle. She was a poor liar on the best of days, and this certainly wasn't one of them.

"Of course. And now I'll leave you. I've overstayed my welcome," Abraham's gaze softened as he clasped his hands before him, solemnity etching itself across his brow, "I must apologise once more if I've caused you any distress. It is not my intention. I truly believe that our world succumbed to its end due to the sinners' influence. We are now tasked with laying the foundation for a future cleansed of such corruption. One that our children can thrive in. Let us put our past encounters behind us. I do hope we can move forward as friends." His words hung heavy in the small space of the doorway, an invisible weight that seemed to press upon Beth's shoulders. She felt Austin's presence beside her like a pillar, silent yet supportive.

"Friends." Beth echoed, and there was a note of finality in the way Abraham nodded, accepting her response as though it were an unspoken pact sealed. The door closed with a muted thud after Abraham's departure, leaving Beth and Austin enveloped in a silence that was thick with unvoiced thoughts. They exchanged a look, a silent conversation passing between them. A shared uncertainty of a mutual wariness.

"Sinners." Austin murmured eventually, echoing Abraham's earlier sentiment. The word rolled off his tongue with a hint of irony, but it struck a chord in Beth's memory.

"His voice," she said suddenly, the realisation dawning like a slow sunrise, "It sounds so familiar."

"Sinners." Austin repeated, meeting her gaze as a flicker of recognition sparked in his own eyes.

"The radio—"

"Along the coast a few years back," Austin finished for her, a sense of nostalgia mingling with the shock, "when we were making our way to Mountain Gate—" Beth looked back at the door Abraham had disappeared behind. Their pasts, once thought to be separate threads, had been intertwined long before their paths had physically crossed. She turned from the hallway, pacing the length of her sparse living room, the worn carpet muffled under her restless steps. Each pass before the window framed a view of Fort Irwin, a compound that had promised refuge but now felt like a cage. She stopped abruptly, turning to face Austin who leaned against the wall, his arms folded as if to shield himself from the weight of her gaze.

"Do you believe me now? We can't stay here," she insisted, her voice low but exigent, the words tumbling out like an avalanche she could no longer hold back, "there's no way in hell we're staying here." Austin pushed off from the wall, his jaw set in a hard line.

"It's impossible Beth," he replied, his tone level but firm, "we don't have the resources for a clean escape. Not enough food, not enough weapons, no transport. Not to mention, we're in the middle of the desert." She shook her head, frustration knotting into her brow.

"So what then? We just wait for things to implode?"

"No. We stay and we sort through the mess." He stepped closer, his presence a solid reassurance despite the chaos swirling around them. Beth hesitated, her resolve wavering at his conviction. Memories of abandonment tugged at the edges of her mind, resurfacing fears she thought she'd buried deep.

"Last time I let someone else take control, I was left behind." She said, her voice barely above a whisper, each word laced with the sting of betrayal. Austin reached out, his hand finding her arm, a touch meant to anchor her to the present.

"You asked me to believe you, and now I do. So I'm asking you to trust me," his eyes locked onto hers, a silent plea etched into his expression, "I will never leave you behind again. I swear on my life I'll protect you." Something shifted inside her, a fragile hope taking root amidst the doubt. Beth nodded slowly, the motion more acquiescence than agreement.

"Fine. I trust you," she murmured, her voice steadier than she felt, "you should probably go." He lingered for a heartbeat, searching her face for something - forgiveness, understanding, maybe strength. Before he turned towards the door, he shot a last glance over his shoulder. Pulling the door open, the moonlight framed him for an instant before he stepped out, leaving her alone with her thoughts and the ghosts of voices long gone.

The low murmur of conversation ceased as Austin and Henry neared the threshold of Sabrina's house, the wooden door slightly ajar. Phillip emerged, his physician's bag in hand, offering them a solemn nod as he passed by on his way out. The air was thick with the scent of antiseptics mingling with the faint, underlying note of fresh linen, suggesting a meticulous cleanliness maintained even amidst the chaos of new life.

"Go ahead." Henry murmured, and Austin pushed the door open fully, every muscle in his body tensed for what lay beyond. Inside, the light filtered through gauzy curtains, casting a serene glow over the small room where Sabrina cradled a swaddled bundle in her arms. Her hair was swept back, exhaustion etched into the fine lines of her face, but her eyes sparkled with pride as she looked down at the child.

"This is Victoria." Sabrina said, her voice soft but clear, an undercurrent of strength belying her recent ordeal. Henry stepped closer, peering down at the infant with a genuine smile.

"She's beautiful," he commented, his gaze flitting between mother and child, "may I sit?" He gestured towards the edge of the bed, seeking permission to encroach upon this intimate space. Sabrina nodded, shifting to accommodate him.

"What brings you here?" Her question hung in the air, tinged with both curiosity and caution. Standing sentinel by the bedroom door, Austin's jaw was set firm as he let no word escape his lips. The silent tension betrayed his inner turmoil - a storm of emotions he dared not unleash. Henry settled on the edge of the bed with a cautious ease, his presence a tentative intrusion into the sanctity of the new mother's domain. He studied Sabrina for a moment, taking in the pallor of her skin and the subtle tremble of her hand as it rested protectively around her daughter.

"Rescue must feel strange when it's from a place you were beginning to call home," he started, his voice gentle yet probing, "how are you holding up after everything that happened at Catalina?" Sabrina's lips twisted into a wry smile, one that didn't quite reach her eyes.

"Rescued," she echoed, her tone laced with a bitter note, "no, Henry. I wasn't rescued. They took me from what I had made my new home, without asking if any of us wanted to leave." Her gaze was steely and defiant as her arms cradled Victoria closer. From his position by the door, Austin shifted, the wooden floorboards creaking beneath his weight. His face remained an impassive mask, but his clenched jaw betrayed his effort to maintain control. Henry caught the movement out of the corner of his eye and acknowledged it with a slight nod before redirecting his attention to Sabrina.

"And Victor," Henry hesitated, the name hanging heavily in the air, "his passing must have hit hard. How are you feeling about all of that?" The question seemed to pierce through Sabrina's armour, and for a fleeting second vulnerability flickered across her features. "She'll grow up never knowing her father," she murmured, her fingers brushing over the soft crown of Victoria's head, "I wanted a different life for her." Sabrina lifted her gaze, meeting Henry's eyes with a raw honesty.

"A different life?"

"I grew up surrounded by luxury in Hollywood, thanks to my parents' success. It couldn't have been more different from this," she glanced around the modest room, a stark contrast to her past opulence, "but I'll raise her to be strong and independent. To thrive in this new world just like I did. It's the least I can do for her." Henry nodded, understanding etched into his expression. The resilience in Sabrina's voice resonated with him - the determination to forge a better future from the ruins of the old.

"Thank you for sharing that," Henry said softly, "it's clear you'll be a guiding force for Victoria, no matter what lies ahead." As the conversation lapsed into silence, Austin remained immobile by the door as the void in the room hung heavy, a shroud over the raw emotions that had just been laid bare. Sabrina's confession about her privileged upbringing still lingered in the air when Austin's voice cut through the quiet, sharp and accusatory.

"That's why," his gaze pierced as it fixed on Sabrina, "because you couldn't stand not being at the top, like in your old life?" Henry's stern expression was a visual reprimand to Austin for the sudden interruption.

"Austin." He warned, his tone leaving no room for further outbursts, but Austin's question hung unanswered. The spectre of implied motivations hovering in the room.

"Why what?" Sabrina merely tilted her head, a ghost of a smile playing on her lips, seemingly unfazed by Austin's challenge.

"Chantelle's death," Henry redirected, trying to steer the conversation back on course, "how did it affect you?" The playful smile widened fractionally.

"It would've been lovely for Victoria to have a sibling to grow up with, one so close to her in age," she mused, her eyes drifting down to her arms where her baby lay sleeping, "but I can't say I missed the competition for Victor's affection, despite the brief time between both of their deaths."

"You—" Austin started, but Henry shot Austin a cautionary glance before allowing her to continue.

"Shame, what happened to poor Chantelle," she added, the words dripping with feigned sympathy as her eyes fleetingly met Austin's and the subtle taunt behind them was clear, "if only someone had been there to stop it." Austin's jaw tensed visibly, muscles working as he clenched and unclenched his fists at his sides. The restraint it took for him not to react more violently was palpable in the way his knuckles whitened from the force of his grip. Austin leaned forward, his gaze piercing as he scrutinised Sabrina.

"How did you know what was in the suicide note," his voice was low and steady, a controlled calm that belied the tension in his frame, "Beth found it sealed." Sabrina's composure wavered. The flicker across her face was brief but telling - a crack in her facade as she searched for an explanation.

"I saw it. That night at the base before we were assigned housing." She attempted to recover quickly, her words tumbling out in a stammer.

"You're lying," Austin shot back instantly, the accusation sharp, "Beth kept that letter close to her. It never left her sight." He stepped closer, his presence filling the room with an unspoken challenge.

"Maybe Beth isn't as vigilant as you think," Sabrina retorted with a forced lightness, trying to deflect the tension, "you're just looking for someone to blame." Her eyes darted between Austin and Henry. Without a word, Henry slowly and calmly reached into his pocket and produced a notepad and pen.

"Write something for us, Sabrina." He held them out to her with a deliberate motion. Her hand hovered over the items for a second, a momentary hesitation before taking them. Their eyes locked, an exchange charged with unspoken accusations and doubts, as the pen met paper with one hand while she cradled her newborn baby in the other.

"What do you want me to write?" Her voice was a thin veneer of innocence over a well of unease.

"Anything," Austin said, his eyes never leaving hers, "just so we can compare it." She poised the pen above the paper, her right hand hovered in an awkward dance of indecision. Before the first stroke of ink could mar the page, Austin stepped in, his observation sharp and unyielding.

"Here, let me help you." Austin took a few steps forward to take Victoria from Sabrina's arms.

"Excuse me?" She relented, moving her baby away from him as he approached her bed.

"I remember at the base, Sabrina. You were left-handed when you filled out those forms," he leaned over and took Victoria from her arms, placing her gently in the bassinet next to her bed, "you smudged the ink with your palm as you wrote and I remember Anne being frustrated over some of your medical history being un-readable." The spite in his voice was unhidden, accusation hanging heavily as he stared down at her.

"We already have your handwriting, my dear," Henry closed his eyes and shook his head, "why don't you tell us what happened." A beat passed, heavy with implication. The silence grew dense around them. As she attempted to maintain a semblance of her composure, Sabrina cursed under her breath. The pen clattered softly as she set it down, her movements now devoid of their earlier pretence. She looked up, her eyes brimming with tears that threat-ened to spill over. They gave her an almost childlike vulnerability that stood in stark contrast to the gravity of her next words.

"I was jealous," her confession was barely audible, "Chantelle, we got into a fight." Austin watched her, his face hardening as he pro-cessed the admission.

"Go on." Henry urged gently, though the stern note in his voice betrayed his need for answers. Sabrina wiped at her eyes, her breath hitching in her throat.

"I didn't mean for it to happen. I just, I lost control and," she stumbled on the words as she spoke, "and I wrapped my hands around her neck until she stopped fighting. She stopped breathing, and then she was dead." The final word hung between them, a grim punctuation to her statement. In the stillness that followed, Sabrina's tears flowed freely, yet the room felt colder as if the warmth had been leached by her chilling revelation. Austin's frame was rigid, his mind reeling from Sabrina's confession. The air felt thick, and the room seemed to close in around him. He watched her with an intensity that bordered on disbelief, his fists clenched at his sides. His voice, when he finally found it, was brittle with suppressed emotion.

"How," he croaked softly, "how did you get her up there?" Sabrina's gaze flickered to the floor, her hands twisting in her lap.

"Josh," she whispered, "I convinced Josh to help me. We strung her up and made it look like she did it herself." She swallowed hard, and the tears that had been threatening to overflow now streamed down her cheeks in earnest. Her voice cracked as she spoke the last words, and she buried her face in her hands, her body shaking with sobs. Henry, ever the composed leader despite the horror unfolding before him, stepped forward.

"Thank you for being honest with us Sabrina." He said, his tone measured but not without a hint of coldness. Austin spun on his heel, disgust etched into every line of his face.

"Don't thank her," he spat out, his voice laced with contempt, "those tears are as fake as the note she left. There's no remorse there, Henry. *None.* She's not crying because she's sorry, she's crying because she got caught." Without waiting for a response, Austin strode towards the door, each step heavy with fury and betrayal. But before he could escape the suffocating atmosphere of the room, Henry's authoritative voice called out to Sabrina, pausing his march down the hallway.

"Until we figure out what to do with you, you'll stay confined to your home," Henry declared, his gaze fixed on Sabrina who peeked through her fingers, her sobbing quieting to sniffles, "a soldier will be posted here with you day and night." Sabrina lifted her head, her eyes red-rimmed but her crying subdued, as if she'd suddenly regained a measure of composure. Sabrina's gaze lifted from her trembling hands, the remnants of her performed sorrows slipping away like a discarded mask. Her eyes rolled dramatically, an exasperated sigh escaping her lips as she shifted in the chair, the weight of her recent childbirth apparent in the pained expression that crossed her face.

"Look at me, Henry," she said with a flicker of defiance, "I can barely shuffle my way to the bathroom without feeling like I'm being torn apart. It's not like I'm planning some great escape." Henry, whose stoic demeanour had been unflinching throughout the ordeal, leaned against the wooden frame of the door, his arms crossed over his chest.

"Even so, Sabrina," he replied firmly, the timbre of his voice brooking no argument, "the community will rest easier knowing you're under watch." A twisted smile curled the corner of her mouth, a bitter chuckle following suit.

"Probably for the best I have a guard or two around," Sabrina mused aloud, her voice tinged with sarcasm, "given what I've done, there'll be more than a few clamouring for my head on a pike." Henry gave Austin a pointed look, urging him to leave the matter in his hands for the moment. Austin hesitated, his anger a palpable force, yet he recognised the necessity of order in their precarious existence. Walking briskly through the house, he pushed the door open and stepped out into the uncertain world beyond, the weight of Sabrina's betrayal and the task ahead pressing down on him like a shroud. The room fell into a heavy silence, the air thick with unspoken tension. Henry gave a curt nod, acknowledging her words with a neutrality that betrayed none of his thoughts. He turned and left, leaving her to stew in the bed she had made.

The afternoon light began to trickle through the blinds of the town hall as Austin stood before a large map of their settlement pinned to the wall, tracing routes with his finger, his brow furrowed in concentration. Henry approached, his footsteps echoing through the sparsely furnished space.

"Any word on Beth?" Austin asked without looking up, the concern in his voice thinly veiled. Henry shook his head, a frown etched into his features.

"Barnett swung by earlier. Beth's taken ill, needs a sick day." He informed, his gaze lingering on the map and searching for something only he seemed to understand. Austin's hand paused mid-gesture, the news striking an uneasy chord within him. Beth's absence felt like another thread unraveling in the tightly knit fabric of their community, now frayed and strained to its limits.

"Let's hope it's just a day." Austin's voice was low, betraying the unease that settled in the pit of his stomach, cursing himself for hoping she was actually unwell and not avoiding him. Henry nodded, his eyes meeting Austin's with a shared understanding.

"We'll manage." He said, though his tone suggested it was more a hope than a certainty. Together, they turned back to the daunting task at hand, the fate of their fragile society resting precariously on the decisions they were about to make. The door to the town hall swung open with a purpose, and Val strode in alongside Anne, their faces masked with uncertainty and a hint of confusion. The moment they entered, Austin and Henry ceased their deliberations over the settlement map, turning to greet the newcomers.

"Good, you're both here," Anne said, tucking a stray lock of hair behind her ear, her eyes flitting between Austin and Henry, "I've asked my dad to meet us here. He should be arriving any moment."

"What's the matter?" Henry asked, his instinctual leadership surfacing as he straightened up.

"The new arrivals," Anne started, "a few were sick when they got here. It seemed minor at first. Just some cold symptoms, but the numbers have been climbing since yesterday." She let out a sigh, her voice laced with worry.

"How many are we talking about?" Henry furrowed his brow, the weight of every new problem adding to his already heavy shoulders.

"Eighteen yesterday," Val interjected, her voice steady but her hands betraying her anxiety as she fidgeted with the hem of her sleeve, "and five more showed up at the clinic this morning." Austin rubbed his chin thoughtfully, considering the implications.

"Could it be the flu?"

"Doesn't quite seem like it." Anne shook her head, her lips pressed into a thin line. Before more could be said, Phillip made his entrance. He walked with a brisk gait that spoke volumes of his urgency, yet his expression remained composed - a collected front amidst growing concern.

"We haven't had the best variety in diet the last few years," Phillip began without preamble, addressing the room with a clinical detachment that belied the gravity of his words, "malnutrition weakens the immune system, making us more susceptible to diseases."

"Tell me about it." Austin crossed his arms, nodding as he listened. His gaze hardened at the mention of food scarcity, a threat far too familiar.

"Food supplies are getting scarce, and what we have could be contaminated. This can lead to widespread malnutrition and increase the risk of illness," Phillip paused to allow the grim reality to settle among them before continuing, "plus, access to clean water and proper sanitation has been limited, which increases the risk of waterborne diseases such as cholera, dysentery, and typhoid fever spreading rapidly among a large group." A heavy silence descended upon the room as the implications of Phillip's words sank in.

"What about the town's water filtration system?" Henry's brow furrowed as he leaned forward on the makeshift table that served as the town hall's strategic centre, his fingers drumming a staccato rhythm.

"It's not perfect," Anne admitted, looking at her father, "especially after years without proper maintenance."

"Phillip, how bad are the most serious cases?" The room felt heavy with Henry's question, every cough and fever now a harbinger of something potentially catastrophic. Phillip exhaled slowly, his eyes reflecting the weight of his medical responsibilities.

"There's one case that's particularly severe," he admitted, his voice steady despite the grim news, "the patient may need oxygen support soon, but our supplies are distressingly finite." A murmur of unease rippled through the room, and Austin caught Henry's gaze.

They couldn't afford to lose anyone else, not when every pair of hands was vital for their survival.

"Contagious?" Henry's question cut through the low whispers, his role as de facto leader demanding answers they might not be ready to hear. Anne, her usually bright demeanour dimmed by the gravity of the situation, nodded cautiously.

"If we're dealing with cholera, dysentery, or typhoid, it's spread by contaminated food or water. We can manage that. Sanitising supplies, boiling water—"

"However," Phillip interjected before anxiety could seed further, "if this turns out to be influenza or tuberculosis, or even a resurgence of whatever destroyed the world a few years ago, then we're looking at airborne transmission. Highly contagious. It could sweep through Fort Irwin like wildfire." Austin's jaw clenched as he observed the faces around him, each person suddenly a potential tinderbox of disease, any semblance of control precariously balanced on the edge of Phillip's next words. Austin's mind wandered to Beth, now silently praying that she was actively avoiding him and not actually ill.

"And what do we think it is?" Henry's voice pulled them back to the present matter. Phillip glanced down at the reports in his hand, each page a testament to their plight.

"Coughing, fever, diarrhoea," he listed, "symptoms shared across the board. That doesn't really rule out anything yet." His mouth tightened as he considered their options, all paths fraught with uncertainty.

"Great." Austin muttered under his breath, the sarcasm bitter on his tongue. It seemed the list of things that could go wrong in their tiny corner of a broken world had just lengthened, and the margin for error was thinner than ever. Henry's hand hovered over the worn surface of the table, fingers drumming a silent rhythm as he collected his thoughts.

"Listen," he began, locking eyes with each person in turn, "we need to manage this situation without causing a panic. Anne, Phillip, Val, you keep monitoring your patients. Any changes, no matter how small, I want to be informed immediately, and as soon as you have an inkling of what this is I want to know." Anne, her face drawn from worry and fatigue, gave a nod that seemed to draw on the last of her reserves.

"I'll go check on the ones we saw yesterday," she said, her voice steady despite the tension around them, "then I'll see the new cases from this morning." As she turned to leave, her gaze caught Austin's. For a brief moment their eyes locked, sharing an unspoken understanding of all that was at stake. The look was fleeting, but it spoke volumes of their shared history and the uncharted waters they were navigating together. She offered him a reassuring smile, which he met with a reproachable expression before looking back at the group. Once Anne had left the room, Austin turned back to Phillip, his brow furrowed with concern.

"What's our biggest worry?" He asked, his voice hushed but urgent. Phillip sighed, the lines of his face etched with the reality of their predicament.

"Oxygen," he admitted grimly, "we're already running low, and if this illness hits hard we won't have enough for everyone who might need it." He paused, glancing towards the door Anne had disappeared through. Austin felt a chill run down his spine. They were teetering on the brink, one outbreak away from disaster. With resources stretched thin and an invisible enemy threatening to strike, they were in a race against time, a race they couldn't afford to lose. Henry's steely gaze fixed upon Phillip, the weight of leadership etching deeper lines on his weathered face.

"We need to be smart about our supplies," he said, his voice a low rumble that carried the gravity of the situation, "assess everyone, but use what we have sparingly. We can't afford to waste anything." Phillip nodded, though the grim set of his mouth spoke of the internal struggle he faced. As a healer, rationing care ran counter to every instinct he had.

"And if it comes down to it?" His voice was hesitant, seeking some semblance of reassurance in an untenable situation.

"Focus on the children, then the able-bodied adults," Henry replied, his words slow and deliberate as the hesitation in his voice betrayed the reluctance of the decision, "if it comes to oxygen, we need to prioritise the young and the people who can help rebuild."

"God help us," Phillip murmured, running a hand through his thinning hair, the gesture conveying the burden of his role, "I hate it, but you're right." With a heavy heart he turned away, his steps echoing in the silence as he departed to check on the afflicted. Once Phillip had left, Henry shifted his attention to Austin, who stood with his arms crossed, his eyes reflecting the turmoil that roiled within him.

"Keep this under wraps for now." Henry instructed, knowing full well the challenge he presented. Austin's jaw clenched, the muscles working beneath his stubble.

"In a place like this words spread faster than wildfire," he countered, "people are going to notice the absences and start asking questions."

"I know," Henry nodded, a stern general preparing for the battles ahead, "but we can't spark a panic. Do what you can to maintain calm. We'll address the town when we have a better handle on things." They both knew that in the fragile balance of their post-apocalyptic society, fear could prove just as deadly as any disease. Austin rubbed the back of his neck, a tension-filled habit he'd developed over the last few years. He turned to Henry who was absentmindedly shuffling papers on the desk.

"What did Barnett say about Beth's sickness?" Austin asked, keeping his voice steady despite the rising concern. Henry looked up, his hands pausing mid-shuffle.

"He didn't give details. Just said she needed to take a day off." His voice held an edge of frustration, not unusual for the man in charge of holding together what remained of their community.

"Then I'll go see how she's doing." Val interjected decisively, already moving towards the door with purpose. Her medical training wasn't extensive, but in their situation anyone with even a hint of healthcare knowledge was invaluable. Once Val had left, the room fell into a tense silence. Austin met Henry's gaze, both men weighed down by the gravity of their responsibilities.

"We need a plan," Austin said, breaking the quiet, "if this sickness is spreading, we can't just sit on our hands."

"Our first step is containment. We need to figure out if this thing is contagious before it possibly wipes us all out." Henry leaned back against the wall, folding his arms as he considered their options.

"Right," Austin nodded, "I'll get a team together and start discreet patrols. We'll make sure no one's showing symptoms and wandering around and potentially infecting others."

"Good. And keep an eye out for any unusual gatherings or chatter," Henry added, his tactical mind always seeking to preempt problems, "if people start piecing things together—"

"They'll panic," Austin finished for him, "I'll do my best to keep things quiet. Redirect conversations if I have to." He knew all too well the delicate balance of order and chaos.

"Let's hope it's enough," Henry said, pushing away from the wall with a grim set to his mouth, "we've survived a lot, but an outbreak could be something else entirely."

"Survival's what we do." Austin responded with a determined glint in his eye. It was that unspoken bond between them, their shared determination to protect their people that kept them standing, even when the ground beneath them felt like it was crumbling away.

"Keep me updated." Henry instructed, returning to his papers now with a sharpened focus, each movement precise and measured.

"Will do," Austin confirmed, "but I need something."

"Anything if it helps." Henry looked up at Austin and stopped rifling through the papers, drawing all attention to him.

"I need you to speak to George and find out where Ben is," Austin stood firm, aware that Henry and George had agreed to keep their responsibilities separate from one another, "if we're gonna try to keep things calm around here, I need my right hand man back. Besides, he should've been back by now if it was just a simple supply run."

"I'll see what I can do," Henry nodded and turned his attention back to his desk, "you know, I didn't ask for your help with all this. But somehow, being on medical leave, you've been a true asset to the civilian side of things. I want you to know that." With a firm nod which was filled with gratitude at the sentiment, he turned on his heel and walked out of the room, already mentally preparing for the rounds he would have to make. The weight of the community's safety rested on his shoulders, but he wouldn't let it crush him - not while there was still breath in his lungs to fight back the tide of uncertainty threatening to engulf them all.

CHAPTER 14

Val hesitated for a moment before she knocked twice on the worn surface of Beth's front door. Her fingers tapped nervously against her palm as she stood there, the cool autumn air biting at her uncovered skin.

"Who is it?" Beth called from the other side of the door, feigning a cough that was clearly for the benefit of others.

"It's Val," the door opened suddenly and slowly, revealing Beth's bright features and relaxed demeanour, "are you actually sick? You look fine." Her eyes scanned Beth's face for any signs of illness as she removed her face mask.

"I'm fine," Beth's voice was calm, a stark contrast to the worry that had creased Val's brow on the walk over, "I just needed to step back from everything for a day."

"Good, because we've got enough of that going around." Relief flooded through Val, loosening the tightness in her chest. Beth's expression turned quizzical, prompting Val to elaborate on the wave of sickness sweeping through their friends and neighbours.

"Come in." Beth said, stepping aside to allow Val entry into the warmth of her home. The smell of fresh coffee hung in the air, comforting and rich.

"Thanks." Val's soft voice was laced with an odd mix of alleviation and concern. Beth walked into the kitchen and poured Val a cup of fresh coffee, setting it down silently on the island bench. Val wrapped her hands around the mug gratefully, the heat seeping into her stiff fingers.

"Is everything okay?" Beth broke the awkward silence, sipping her own drink before setting it down beside her and folding her arms across her chest.

"I came to check on you," Val stared at the mug, the steam dancing in the air as it escaped from the top, "there's an illness spreading around and you were sick today, so I wanted to make sure you were okay."

"Like I said," Beth shrugged casually, "I needed a day to myself."

"I'm glad you're not actually sick," Val let out a light laugh, almost mixed with a sigh of relief, "when we heard you weren't well we we're all concerned you'd caught what was going around."

"We?"

"Phillip, Anne and I were at the town hall with Austin and Henry discussing the bug that's going around. I offered to check in on you." Val offered a warm smile, noticing Beth's shift in demeanour at the mention of Austin's name but choosing to ignore it.

"Unlucky coincidence I guess," Beth smiled, "I didn't mean to worry you."

"You didn't. It would probably take a lot more than an infectious disease to kill you off." Val smirked, but just as rapidly as her amusement surfaced her expression shifted to one of concern. Beth smiled at the idea of being indestructible, and quickly shook the notion from her mind. She might be tough, but she wouldn't be arrogant enough to let her guard down at the thought of being invincible.

"So what's this bug then?" Beth cocked her head to the side inquisitively while Val recounted the recent events, the sickness that seemed to have clenched the town in an unyielding grip. Beth listened intently, her forehead creasing with concern.

"It's been less than a full day and cases are already climbing and climbing." Val concluded with a heavy sigh.

"What do you think it is?" Beth asked after a pause, her mug rested halfway to her lips. Val shook her head slowly, staring into the swirling depths of her coffee.

"I don't know," she admitted, "but I've got this sinking feeling, It's like the calm before the storm. Like everyone's going to get hit with this before it gets any better."

"They're a funny thing, gut feelings." Beth set down her mug, a thoughtful look painting her features as she considered Val's words. There was a gravity to the silence that followed, both women lost in contemplation of what lay ahead. The quietness lingered between them, heavy and laden with the unspoken anxiety of the town's plight. Val's gaze drifted off towards the window where a sparrow perched on the sill, momentarily distracting her from their grim conversation.

"Did you hear about Sabrina? She had the baby," Val broke the stillness, turning back to Beth with an incredulous shake of her head, "named her Victoria."

"Victoria," Beth's eyebrows arched in surprise as she repeated the name, "how do you know?"

"Phillip told me." Val replied, her lips curving into a wry smile.

"Victoria," Beth's eyebrows arched in surprise as she repeated the name, "that's interesting." Beth leaned back against her chair, pondering the loosely patronymic namesake. "Hardly a coincidence. She's deranged. Honestly, I wouldn't put anything past her at this point." Val scoffed, the sound sharp in the quiet kitchen.

"Probably not." A nod from Beth acknowledged the sentiment. It was no secret that Sabrina's actions often strayed far from rationality. They both knew there was more to the story than just a baby's name.

"Speaking of which, have you and Austin heard anything new from the investigation? About Sabrina and," Val shifted in her seat as if bracing for uncomfortable territory, "Chantelle's death, I mean." Beth's features tightened, a shadow crossing her face.

"If Austin's found anything, he hasn't told me." Her voice held a tinge of frustration, betraying the concern that gnawed at her over the unresolved case.

"Maybe he's keeping it close to his chest." Val suggested, though her tone implied she found the idea unsettling. Beth's eyes remained troubled, reflecting the myriad of uncertainties that haunted them all. The ceramic mug in Beth's hands trembled slightly, the black liquid within mirroring her own turbulent thoughts. She set it down with a clink against the granite countertop of the kitchen island and exhaled a shaky breath.

"Val—" She started, fingers interlacing and then parting nervously. The room felt suddenly smaller, the walls closing in as if to eavesdrop on the confession that loomed in the air between them. Beth felt the weight of her words before they even left her lips.

"What's on your mind?" Val's eyes softened, a quiet nod granting the permission Beth sought.

"Too much," Beth confessed, her eyes filling with tears at the thought of all the inner turmoil she held within, "sometimes I just want it to stop. I need to stop thinking, but I can't."

"You can talk to me, you know." Val pressed, her hand reaching out across the island bench in an attempt to bridge the gap between them. Beth took a tentative step closer, reaching out and grasping Val's hand in hers.

"I really tried, Val," Beth swallowed hard as tears escaped her eyes, rolling down her cheeks and tickling her skin, "I know you're mad at me, but you're about the closest thing I have to a female friend around here and I need you to know that I *really* tried to help her."

"I know," Val whispered, smiling and staring at their hands gripped tightly together, "but if I'm the closest thing you have to a female friend then you've got bigger problems." Their shared laughter filled the void as Beth wiped away her tears with her free hand. Val pulled her hand away slowly, handing Beth a box of tissues from the counter behind her.

"Thanks," Beth laughed awkwardly, dabbing at her pink cheeks and glistening eyes, "I know you're mad that I came back and she didn't, but—"

"I wouldn't say that," Val shook her head, "I'm sorry if I gave you the impression that I was." Beth looked up into Val's attentive gaze, seeking solace there. Her heart was a stormy sea, waves of doubt and anxiety crashing against her fragile hope. Each swell carried whispers of past failures and fears of future disappointments. She desperately wanted to believe in the comfort that Val's eyes promised, but shadows of uncertainty loomed large. Her mind was a tumult, thoughts swirling like leaves caught in a whirlwind, pulling her deeper into the abyss of her own self-doubt. Yet, amidst the chaos, she clung to the flicker of warmth in Val's gaze. It was a beacon in her tempestuous world, hoping it could anchor her to a fleeting sense of peace.

"Abraham," she said at last, her brow creasing with worry, "there's something off about him. Something I can't ignore." Val stood abruptly at the mention of Abraham, her chair scraping against the floor tiles. She had little patience for what she perceived as paranoia.

"Beth, we've got enough real problems without looking for ghosts in every shadow," she chided gently, "we need to focus on what's tangible. On getting through this crisis together." Beth knew Val was right, but there were dots connecting in her mind, forming a picture she couldn't yet understand.

"Val," desperation tinged her voice as she reached out, grasping for Val's arm before she could walk away, "do you remember that day near Mountain Gate? The voice on the radio?" Val's expression hardened for a moment, the memory obviously still a raw wound. She turned back, her resolve softening as she met Beth's pleading eyes.

"The day Chantelle was almost shot? How could I forget?" She murmured, the ghost of that day's fear momentarily passing over her features.

"Exactly," Beth pressed on, her conviction growing stronger, "that voice distorted through the static." Val's hand hovered in the air, her departure halted by the gravity in Beth's tone. Her eyes narrowed slightly, a silent question as to where this unexpected conversation was leading.

"Of course," Val said, shaking her head as a frown creased her forehead while she recalled the terror that had gripped them all, "that chilling voice. I can still hear it."

"Yes," Beth's voice trembled with urgency, "it was Abraham. There's something about him that doesn't sit right with me."

"Abraham," Val repeated, skepticism etching her features, "you're sure?"

"Without a doubt," Beth replied as she clasped her hands together on the kitchen island, as if trying to physically hold her thoughts in place, "but it's not just a hunch. He said something the other day, and it struck a chord. A dark, resonating chord that I recognised."

"What did he say?" Suspicion flickered in Val's eyes as she asked.

"Sinners," Beth whispered, the word falling like the tolling of a distant bell, "he used that exact word, *sinners*. And when he said it, it brought back that exact feeling. The fear, the confusion. It brought me back to that day near Mountain Gate." Val absorbed the information, weighing each word as if they were pieces of evidence to be scrutinised. The simple utterance of a single word had unearthed a haunting association for Beth, one that now cast a shadow over their present distress. Val's hand paused mid-air, her fingers forming a loose cage over the steaming mug.

"You need to stop," she said, her voice firm in an attempt to tether Beth back to reality, "this, this conspiracy you're spinning, it's insane." Beth met Val's gaze, her own eyes turbulent pools of conviction.

"It's not," she countered, the words edged with steel, "Austin was there. He heard Abraham say it too, and he agrees. He thinks it's Abraham's voice we heard on the radio, tormenting us that day." A frown tugged at the corners of Val's mouth, her skepticism unshaken.

"But why? Why would Abraham be out there killing people and scrawling the word all over the place?" The question hung between them, heavy with the burden of unspoken fear.

"Look at everything we know," Beth urged, leaning closer across the kitchen island, her fingers now tightly clasped around her own mug, her knuckles blanched with the pressure, "we can't ignore the facts. Abraham was the one Victor made the trade deal with. For children, Val. And every time Abraham speaks, it's scripture this and God's will that. It's like he's fixated. The people from Prescott, *his* people. They brought this sickness, didn't they? It's all too coincidental. And now, with everyone falling ill—" The room seemed to close in as Beth continued, her voice dropping to barely more than a whisper. Val's breath hitched, the implications clawing at the edges of her professional composure. The idea that someone within their midst could harbour such darkness was unsettling. Yet Beth's passion was infectious, her logic unnervingly sound. With each revelation, the shadows grew longer, the sinister puzzle inching towards completion.

"No, it can't—"

"Think about it, Val," Beth pressed on, her plea wrapped in the gravity of their dire situation, "we have to consider the possibility that Abraham is at the centre of all this. That somehow, he's linked to the chaos enveloping us." The silence that followed was punctuated only by the faint ticking of the wall clock, marking the passage of time and the weight of decisions yet to be made. Val's head gave a small, weary tilt as she absorbed the heavy cascade of Beth's convictions.

"That's, umm," she murmured, her voice threading through the tension like a needle pulling at seams, "it's a lot to take in." The notion of Abraham's guilt was immense, an unwieldy truth that strained against the fabric of their community.

"It's a lot of speculation," Beth sighed, "but the pieces fit."

"Maybe we should all sit down and talk this through." Val suggested tentatively. Her eyes searched Beth's, seeking a foothold in the stormy sea of implications. Beth's response came with a fervour borne of a past riddled with helplessness.

"On Catalina, I couldn't save everyone. The resources weren't there," her hands clenched into fists on the cool surface of the kitchen island, knuckles white, "but here we can actually do something. We have the power to change things." A shadow passed over Val's face, a flicker of pain or perhaps the onset of something more troubling.

"I want to believe that, Beth. I really do," she said softly, "but right now I've got this killer headache, and patients who need me. They're counting on me." Her gaze held Beth's for a moment longer, a silent thank you for the trust shared between them.

"Take care of yourself, okay?" Beth urged, watching as Val rose from her seat. Something akin to concern etched itself into the lines around her eyes. Val offered her a forced half-smile, making her way to the door. She paused, reaching for the handle, her silhouette framed by the threshold.

"Thanks for trusting me with this, whatever it is." With a quiet click, the door closed behind Val, leaving Beth alone amidst the echo of revelations. For a moment she stood motionless, her mind a whirling vortex of suspicion and strategy. Then, as if compelled by an invisible force, she started towards the stairs. Halfway up a gnawing doubt seized her, rooting her to the spot. The enormity of what lay ahead cast an ominous shadow across her thoughts. With a sudden resolution, Beth pivoted, her resolve hardening like steel. She strode back through the house, her steps quick and determined. Exiting the door, Beth emerged into the late afternoon light, the sun's rays casting long shadows that stretched before her like paths to be chosen. There was no turning back now - the pieces were moving, and she had a role to play. The air carried a chill promise of the coming night, and somewhere within it, the faintest whisper of destiny calling.

The thud of gloves against flesh punctuated the gym's heavy air as Reece and Chase danced around each other, their sparring an intricate ballet of jabs and feints. Sweat glistened on their focused faces, muscles coiling and releasing with practiced precision. That was until the door swung open with a determined push, drawing their attention to the figure striding purposefully towards them. Austin's presence was like a sudden drop in barometric pressure, his usual easygoing demeanour replaced by a grim set to his jaw that cut through the gym's atmosphere like a cold front. The smiles that had begun to form on Reece and Chase's lips faltered, morphing into expressions of concern as they read the urgency written all over Austin's face.

"Guys," Austin began without preamble, his voice carrying the weight of unspoken troubles, "I need your help."

"What's going on?" Chase lowered his hands, the protective gear suddenly feeling extraneous, and eyed Austin with a crease forming between his brows.

"Something big." Austin replied, his hands clenching and unclenching at his sides, a physical manifestation of his inner turmoil. He paused, glancing between the two men who had become more than just fellow survivors, they were comrades in the truest sense. Reece let out a light sigh before circling Chase, gesturing for them to resume their training.

"You worried about the bug going around?"

"Abraham," he said, the name hanging heavily between them, "Beth and I think he's the one from those radio broadcasts. The guy who's been marking his victims with *sinners* across their chests, or writing it on their homes." The revelation hit Reece with the force of a gut punch, the implications of Austin's words sinking in like lead through water. They knew the stakes had risen beyond their worst imaginings, and the game had changed. Now, it was no longer just about surviving, it was about confronting the darkness that threatened to engulf everything they'd fought to protect. Reece's fists froze mid-air, the padded gloves now an afterthought.

"That business with *sinners*," his voice trailed off, disbelief etching lines on his otherwise composed face, "wasn't that almost two years back?" Chase, still catching his breath from the sparring session, darted his eyes, his gaze flicking between Reece and Austin.

"What happened two years ago? Before you ran into us at the ranch?" He prodded, a hint of impatience colouring his tone as the weight of Austin's grave demeanour pressed upon them. Before Austin could elaborate, the heavy thud of boots echoed across the gym's polished floor. A group of soldiers, their faces set in concentration, made their way towards the training mats, oblivious to the tension that charged the air around Austin and his companions.

"Not here." Austin's voice cut through the room, authoritative and final. He motioned briskly towards the exit, leaving no room for discussion. The soldiers, sensing the urgency without understanding its source, hesitated only momentarily before retreating, their presence fading like shadows at dawn. The gravity of the situation bound Reece and Chase to Austin's side, ready for whatever came next.

Val pushed open the door to the clinic, her entrance stirring the quiet space like a gust of wind. Anne looked up sharply from the ultrasound monitor, her hand pausing over Julia's exposed belly. The gel on the wand glistened, forgotten. Val leaned against the frame, her stance betraying a weariness that seemed too heavy for her shoulders alone.

"I was just coming in for some supplies," she said, her voice less steady than usual, "but I've been feeling off."

"Are you okay? You don't look well." Anne's attention shifted fully to Val now, concern creasing her brow. She knew Val, always the one tending to others, rarely the one needing care. Julia, lying on the examination table, turned her head towards Val, dark eyes wide with surprise. She had known Val to be indefatigable, a pillar in the midst of chaos.

"I thought it was just the stress getting to me," Val continued, pressing a hand to her forehead as if trying to smooth away the discomfort, "but this headache has been drilling into my skull all morning, and it's only gotten worse on my walk here." Anne exchanged a glance with Julia, a silent communication passing between them. They both understood the significance of Val admitting to any kind of weakness - it spoke volumes about the severity of her condition.

"Sit down," Anne gestured to a nearby chair, her professional calmness coating her words, "let's take a look at you."

"Thanks." With a nod that conveyed gratitude mixed with reluctance, Val shuffled closer and sank into the chair, the lines of pain etched deep on her face. It was clear that whatever was spreading among them had claimed another victim. And this time, it was one of their own. Anne's expression softened with concern as she handed Val a surgical mask.

"Put this on, please," she instructed gently, her voice betraying the gravity of the situation, "I need you to head to the back room. I'll be with you shortly." Julia hovered uncertainly, her gaze flitting between Anne and Val.

"What's going on?" She asked, a tinge of fear lacing her words.

"Julia, you should go home now." Anne replied, her tone firm yet still kind, hoping to veil the anxiety that threatened to seep through. The statement hung in the air for a moment before Julia responded, her voice steady but her eyes revealing the depth of their shared history.

"I've known you far too long. I can tell something's not right." She took a step closer, a gesture of solidarity.

"Really, it's best if you head home," Anne insisted, her hands gesturing towards the door, "please, don't stop to talk to anyone. Just go straight home and wait for me. I'll come by later to check on you." Understanding the unspoken urgency, Julia nodded sombrely.

"Okay. If you say so." She quickly gathered her belongings, a sense of haste propelling her movements. With one last look filled with silent questions and concerns, she exited the clinic, the door closing behind her with a soft click that echoed ominously in the suddenly quiet space. The instant Anne crossed the threshold into the back room, she caught sight of Val swaying slightly as she rummaged through the medical supplies.

"Val?" Anne called out, her voice laced with concern.

"Anne." Val murmured, her hand reaching out to steady herself against the countertop. Her fingers brushed against a box of N95 masks and a bottle of Tylenol, but her coordination betrayed her and she missed the grip, sending a few masks fluttering to the floor. Anne rushed forward as Val's knees buckled. She wrapped an arm around Val's waist just in time, guiding her gently onto the nearest examination bed.

"You're burning up." Anne noted, her professional demeanour taking over as she retrieved the thermometer from the nearby cart. The beep of the thermometer confirmed her suspicions - 102 degrees Fahrenheit.

"I have it, don't I." Val's question was less of an inquiry and more of a resigned acknowledgment of her dire situation.

"You need to be at home resting," Anne instructed, her tone both comforting and authoritative, "you've got to keep yourself hydrated." Val nodded, her eyes reflecting the weight of her discomfort. She made an attempt to rise, a grimace passing over her features.

"I think I'll just—"

"Stay," Anne cut her off, placing a gentle hand on Val's shoulder to ease her back down, "you're not going anywhere like this." Her gaze locked with Val's, conveying a silent promise to take care of her.

"Reece," Val whispered, her voice barely above a breath, "could he—"

"Of course," Anne reassured her quickly, "I'll find him now, and he'll help you get home safely." She brushed a strand of hair from Val's clammy forehead, her expression softening. With that, Anne turned on her heel and headed for the door, ready to seek out Reece and bring him back to the clinic as quickly as she could.

The door to Reece's house creaked open, the familiar scent of aged wood and leather greeting them as Austin, Reece and Chase stepped inside. The room was cast in the dim light of the fading sun, shadows creeping across the walls like silent spectators to their grim conversation.

"Okay, spill it," Chase demanded, tossing his jacket onto the back of a chair, "what's this paranoia about voices and sinners?" Austin leaned against the sturdy oak table that dominated the room, his hands bracing the edge as if trying to ground himself from the weight of his own story. Reece stood by the fireplace, arms folded, his gaze distant but focused - a man revisiting a memory he'd rather forget.

"Couple years back," Austin began, his voice steady despite the undercurrent of unease, "we were headed along the coast when something weird came through the radio. Some whack job talking about sinners. Creepy as hell."

"Sinners?" Chase echoed, tilting his head slightly, encouraging the details.

"Sinners," confirmed Reece, stepping forward into the conversation, "we found some bodies. They were hanged from a roof rafter with *sinners* painted right there on the weatherboards." His jaw tightened as he recalled the scene, the word etching itself deep into their collective memories.

"God." Chase muttered, rubbing the back of his neck in discomfort.

"Wasn't just them," Reece added, his voice dropping lower, "days later, we were on our way to Redding and we found another body with the same word carved into his chest." Silence hung heavily between them until Austin broke it, the urgency in his voice cutting through the stillness.

"Last night, Beth and I met Abraham and he started calling people sinners too. The way he said it," he paused, searching for the words, "it was like hearing that voice come back to life."

"You just ran into him on the street?" Reece inquired, one eyebrow arching with an unspoken skepticism. Austin met Reece's wary look with a solemn nod.

"We were at her house," Austin replied, "talking more about Abraham when he just showed up like he'd been summoned."

"Right." Reece's expression shifted, the raised brow now furrowing into a line of concern. They all knew what this might imply, yet none wanted to speak it aloud. The past was resurfacing, and with it a chilling sense of foreboding that clung to the very air they breathed. Austin shuffled his feet, the weight of urgency in his stance.

"Beth's certain Abraham's up to something." He said with a conviction that was hardened by the brief encounter they had with the man. Reece shot him a skeptical glance, but Austin didn't waver. He understood Reece's doubts - it was no small accusation to make, but Beth's intuition had proven right too many times before, and her certainty was enough for him.

"Okay, so what's our next move?" Chase's voice cut through the tension. His hands were balled into fists at his sides, a physical manifestation of his readiness to act.

"We need Ben and Tyler here," Austin replied, running a hand through his hair, "we have to put a plan together." Chase nodded, but there was an edge to his voice when he spoke again.

"Sure, but we can't just sit on our hands waiting for them. People are getting sick, and if this thing with Abraham is as twisted as you think—" He trailed off, letting the implication hang between them.

"Tomorrow," Austin announced with sudden resolve, "I'll speak to Henry about organising a quarantine."

"If we lock down the town, keep everyone inside, maybe then we can keep a closer eye on Abraham." He met Chase's gaze squarely, reinforcing the seriousness of their predicament.

"Quarantine?" Reece's brow furrowed deeper, contemplating the logistics and implications. Yet, even as his mind raced through scenarios, he knew Austin's idea held water. It would be easier to monitor one man's movements in a stilled town than amidst the daily chaos that was now amplified by sickness and fear.

"Right," Chase muttered, acceptance in his tone, "containment might give us the control we need right now." They stood in silence for a moment, each man lost in his thoughts. The air in Reece's living room felt thick, charged with the gravity of decisions yet to be made, actions yet to be taken. They were at a precipice, and the steps they chose now could very well determine their fates.

Beth's heart thudded against her ribs as she pushed open the heavy doors of the town hall, her breath forming misty clouds in the chilly air. She had barely crossed the threshold when Barnett materialised beside her, his brow creased with concern.

"What's wrong?" He inquired, his voice low and steady, a rock amidst the swirling uncertainty that enveloped them both.

"Nothing." Beth replied curtly, her eyes darting around as if she could spot the answer to the troubles plaguing her town in the shadows of the foyer. But Barnett, ever the silent guardian, seemed unconvinced by her terse denial and fell into step behind her. They navigated the corridor until the muffled sounds of a heated discussion filtered through a set of imposing office doors. Without waiting for an invitation, Beth nudged the door open and slipped inside, with Barnett a silent shadow at her back. The room fell into a momentary hush as all eyes turned towards the newcomers. Henry, seated at the head of a long table, gestured for Beth to join them with a nod that betrayed neither surprise nor irritation at the interruption.

"Come in, Beth." He said, his voice carrying the weight of leadership and the weariness of a man burdened with too many crises.

She obliged, choosing a chair on the opposite side of the room, trying to make herself small and unobtrusive. Barnett leaned against
the wall near the doorway, arms folded, his presence both protective and inquisitive. George, whose back was to the window and
casting his face in sharp relief against the afternoon light, resumed
the conversation without preamble.

"As I was saying, we cannot recall the group from their mission as
food and other resources are scarce." He insisted, his hands spread
on the table as though to anchor his argument in reality. Henry
straightened in his chair, his fingers steepled in front of him, eyes
locked with George's in a silent battle of wills.

"I'm not stupid, George," he said calmly but firmly, "I know they all
have radios to communicate." The tension in the room ratcheted
up a notch, the stakes of their debate underscored by the quiet intensity of Henry's challenge. Beth watched the exchange, a sense
of dread coiling in her gut. The decisions made here could alter
the fate of everyone she cared about - everyone in this fragile community they had built from the ashes of the old world. George's
voice, laden with a weary resignation, broke through the charged
atmosphere.

"Even if that were true, Henry, we can't just break radio silence on
a whim," he said, the lines of his face hardening like drying clay,
"until we understand the full scope of this illness, the military must
maintain its course. Those radios, if they indeed had them, would
be for emergency use only." Henry's jaw tightened, a vein throbbing subtly at his temple.

"Would you not consider this an emergency? Damn it, George,"
he implored, leaning forward, his hands gripping the edge of the
table, "we need to think about our people out there, exposed and
unaware."

"Is her presence here necessary?" George cut in abruptly, nodding towards Beth with a dismissive flick of his wrist. Beth felt a surge of indignation as she pushed back her chair and stood, her pulse quickening.

"I came because I want to help," she stated, her voice steady despite the fluttering in her chest, "Val informed me of an outbreak. Something is happening, and I—"

"What exactly qualifies you to assist in this matter?" He challenged, skepticism etched in the furrows of his brow. George's gaze swept over her from head to toe, an inscrutable expression settling over his features. Meeting his gaze unflinchingly, Beth drew a deep breath.

"I have studied the profiles of every single person in this town," she replied, her words imbued with a quiet confidence, "as Henry's assistant, it's not just my job, but my responsibility to offer aid where I can." Her fingers curled into fists at her sides, ready to fight for her place in this room, for her right to stand alongside these men shaping the fate of their community. Henry's smile was a brief flash of warmth in the austere room, acknowledging Beth's resolve before he redirected his attention to George.

"You know as well as I do George," Henry began, his voice firm and resolute, "that our first duty is to protect this town and its inhabitants. That includes every single soul, military or not." The air between the brothers crackled with tension, a silent battle of wills that had clearly been fought many times before. George's jaw flexed, but after a moment he relented with a curt nod.

"If they're not back within the week, I'll use the radio. We can't leave them blind out there."

"But it's Monday—" Beth interjected, before being interrupted by Henry.

"Thank you, George." Henry said, the gratitude in his tone tempered with concern. With a wave of dismissal, he watched George stride out of the room, his military bearing never faltering. As the door closed with a decisive click, Henry's eyes landed on Beth.

"Henry—"

"Beth," he interrupted, the sound of her name in his authoritative tone demanding her full attention, "what really brings you here?" Barnett, who had lingered by the doorway, caught Beth's eye, his posture tense as if ready to leave the privy conversation. She gave a subtle shake of her head, signalling him to stay put. The trust between them was unspoken but understood - Barnett was an ally, and right now she needed all the allies she could get.

"I have concerns," Beth confessed, her gaze unwavering, her voice steady though her heart hammered against her ribcage, "there are things happening, patterns emerging that we can't afford to ignore." Her fingers grazed the brand on her arm once more - a telling alert that gave away her anxieties and hesitance. She took a deep breath, steadying herself for the revelations that could alter the course of their fragile existence. Beth's fingers paused over the brand, her eyes darting between Henry and Barnett.

"Go on." Henry implored. The air felt charged, heavy with unspoken tension. She squared her shoulders and met Henry's expectant gaze head-on, the weight of her responsibility settling firm upon her.

"Abraham," she began, her voice a low thrum of urgency that filled the small space between them, "I'm worried about him, about his role in recent events." Her conviction was a palpable thing, almost visible in the air between them. Henry's expression remained unreadable, but the lines around his eyes tightened just perceptibly.

"What recent events?" He encouraged, his voice betraying none of his thoughts.

"Abraham has been talking in ways that," Beth hesitated, searching for the right words, "that echo a darker time. Phrases that are resurfacing with an alarming frequency." She spoke slowly, her hands clasped before her like a fortress against the storm of doubts threatening to break her resolve.

"Are you suggesting my son is involved in something untoward?" Henry's tone was calm, but Beth could see the protective fire kindling behind his stoic facade. Beth desperately wanted to tell Henry about the radio calls, and the voice, and all the rest of her suspicions. But it was a delicate topic, to tell a man that his son might have been murdering people, branding people, and leaving their bodies to rot. Instead, she decided to approach the situation with a more pressing and obvious matter.

"Involved? I'm not sure," she admitted, "but this sickness coming here just as the others arrived from Prescott. It's way too coincidental—" She trailed off, allowing the gravity of the situation to seep into the silence.

"If what you're saying has merit, it needs to be explored. But you understand the delicacy of such an accusation? Against my own flesh and blood." Henry leaned back in his chair, the creak of the wood underlining the moment.

"Of course," Beth said quickly, "which is why I came to you directly. This isn't about casting blame, it's about preventing further harm." Her plea hung between them, earnest and raw.

"We'll look into this discreetly," he stood up, his movements deliberate, "you have my word."

"Thank you, Henry." Relief washed over Beth, though she knew this was just the beginning. There were more conversations ahead, more secrets to uncover. But for now, she had set the wheels in motion - a step towards unraveling the truth.

CHAPTER 15

Anne's steps were measured as she approached the modest house shared by Reece and Val, her hands clenched into fists at her sides, each one a small testament to her worry. The morning air was brisk, tousling her hair with an indifferent breeze. She didn't bother knocking when she arrived, pushing the door open with an urgency that felt like it echoed in her chest.

"Reece!" Her voice cut through the quiet of the house like a blade. Reece emerged from the kitchen, his face immediately registering concern at the sight of her taut expression.

"Anne? Is everything—"

"Val's sick," Anne said without preamble, each word laced with tension, "she needs you. She's at the clinic." Without a word, Reece grabbed his jacket from the hook by the door and raced out, his long strides quickly carrying him away from the house, away from the sudden and palpable void his departure left behind. Austin, who had been sitting at the kitchen table nursing a cup of coffee, looked up at her, his eyes searching. There was a shadow there, something unspoken that seemed to hang between them. Chase, leaning against the door frame with arms folded, clocked the silent exchange and decided this was his cue to exit.

"Guess I'll head out too." He remarked a little too casually, and slipped out after Reece, leaving Anne alone with Austin in the uncomfortable silence.

"Why weren't you home last night?" Anne turned towards Austin, her gaze softening slightly. Austin shifted in his chair, the wood creaking under his weight. He set down his mug, his fingers drumming on the table before he met her eyes.

"I had a lot on my mind," he confessed, the words heavy, almost reluctant, "came home late, figured it'd be best not to wake you. Then I left early for the town hall. Work's piling up." His explanation hung in the air between them, and for a moment Anne simply watched him, trying to read the subtext woven into his tired features. It was unlike him not to come to bed, to seek the comfort of their shared warmth. But she nodded, accepting his words while tucking away her concern. There would be time to unravel the true depth of what weighed on him later, once the immediate crisis with Val was resolved. Anne lingered in the silence that followed her question, her eyes searching Austin's face for clues. She could almost see the cogs turning behind his furrowed brow, the internal struggle as he weighed his words.

"Is everything okay?" She probed gently, leaning against the kitchen counter, a frown creasing her forehead. The air between them felt charged, heavy with unspoken thoughts.

"What do you mean?" Austin glanced up at her, his eyes clouded with an unreadable emotion.

"You've been," she hesitated, choosing her words with care, "you've been distant. Since your fight with Ben." Anne watched him carefully, noting the tension in his jaw, the way his hands clasped and unclasped on the tabletop. He sighed, a sound that seemed to carry the weight of the world.

"It's everything, Anne. The sickness spreading through town, not knowing where Ben's disappeared to after—" His voice trailed off, and he shook his head as if to clear it of troubling images.

"And?" Anne pressed, sensing there was more he wasn't saying.

Austin ran a hand through his hair, looking troubled.

"There's something else going on," he paused, as if considering whether to continue before adding, "I'll tell you more when I have something concrete." Anne noted the omission in his confession, the shadow that passed over his face as he avoided certain truths. But now wasn't the time to pry. Instead, she pushed away from the counter, her own worries surfacing.

"I need to check on Julia," she said, her voice edged with concern, "she's pregnant, and with this illness going around I want to make sure she's safe and quarantined at home."

"Of course," Austin nodded, understanding the gravity of the situation, "you should go to her."

"I'm sorry. I shouldn't have said that. That's her business."

"I'm sure you were just telling me as a friend, and not as a doctor," Austin stared into his half-empty cup, his expression stoic, "I won't tell anyone." He rose, his movements stiff as if carrying a burden only he could sense.

"Will you be okay here alone?" Anne paused at the doorway, torn between her duty to her friend and the man she loved before her. He offered a tight smile, one that didn't quite reach his eyes.

"I'll manage," Austin replied, "just take care of Julia." With a final, lingering glance filled with worry and unasked questions, Anne turned and stepped out into the brisk morning air. The walk was quick, the benefit of living in such a close community. Anne knocked softly on the door of Julia's home, a small assembly of concern knitting her brow. When she entered, the cozy living room was bathed in the warm glow of midday light filtering through semi-drawn curtains. Julia was ensconced on the couch, a worn paperback splayed open across her lap, its pages untouched as she stared into space.

"Hey," Anne greeted gently, closing the door behind her, "how are you feeling?"

"Morning sickness is kicking my ass," Julia looked up, offering a weak but genuine smile, "other than that I'm okay." Anne approached and took a seat on the edge of the coffee table, reaching out to place a comforting hand over Julia's. She could feel the subtle warmth radiating from her skin - a touch of fever.

"You're a little warm," Anne observed with a furrowed brow, "I think you should stay inside for a while, just to be safe."

"Safe? From what?" Julia's voice was laced with confusion.

"There's an illness going around," Anne explained, her tone carrying an undercurrent of urgency, "we don't know much about it yet, but until we do it's best if you keep yourself and the baby away from any potential risk." Julia's expression shifted from confusion to concern, her maternal instincts already on high alert.

"If you say so." She nodded slowly, acquiescing to the precaution. The air between them grew heavy, laden with unspoken thoughts.

"Does Ben know," Anne hesitated before continuing the question that hung in the silence, "about the baby?" Julia's eyes dropped to her hands, which now twisted the hem of her shirt in a nervous rhythm. She nodded again, this time a shadow crossing her features.

"He knows." She confirmed, her voice barely above a whisper.

"And how did he take it?" Anne probed gently, sensing the delicate nature of the conversation.

"It wasn't what I hoped for." Julia's voice broke slightly, her eyes brimming with unshed tears. She bit her lip, struggling to maintain composure.

"You need to understand something," Anne reached out, squeezing Julia's hand reassuringly, "Ben is in love with Beth. It's harsh, but it's the truth. You deserve someone who chooses you first, not as a second choice, and not as a default choice."

"It's not that easy." Julia's eyes met Anne's, vulnerability etched deeply within their depths. Anne's heart ached for her friend, caught in the turmoil of unreciprocated love and the complexities of an uncertain future.

"Moving on is not supposed to be easy," Anne continued softly, "but it's necessary, for you and your child. You can't live in the shadow of what might have been." A single tear escaped Julia's defences, tracing a silent path down her cheek. Anne's words, though kind, were the mirror reflecting a reality Julia had been reluctant to face. With a deep breath Julia nodded once more, accepting the bitter pill of truth Anne had dispensed with compassion.

"I thought that if I was carrying his child, he'd find a reason to stay with me," she confessed, her voice a fractured whisper, "but when I told him, he said he was coming back from his mission for *her*." Julia's fingers, trembling and unsure, brushed the small swell of her abdomen.

"Ben was already struggling with his own demons when he arrived. Maybe it wasn't fair of you to think you could piece him back together." Anne reached across the space between them, her hand resting gently on Julia's shoulder. Julia lifted her eyes, a storm of hurt swirling within their blue depths.

"I know," she admitted, her lips quivering, "but I wanted to believe that I could heal him."

"Sometimes," Anne said softly, "the heart sees what it wants. But healing comes from within. Ben has to find that path for himself, and it seems like Beth is the one he believes can guide him there."

Her words were delicate but laced with an unyielding truth. A sob broke free from Julia's chest, raw and revealing, as the dam of her composure crumbled. She leaned into Anne, seeking solace in the warmth of her embrace.

"I just wanted to be enough." Julia murmured, her tears soaking into the fabric of Anne's shirt.

"Julia, you are enough," Anne assured her, her arms tightening around her friend, "but Ben's journey isn't about your worth. It's about his need to mend what's broken in him, and sometimes that's a road someone has to walk alone or with the person they've chosen." In the shelter of Anne's hold, Julia allowed herself to grieve not just for the relationship she had hoped for but also for the future that had slipped through her fingers.

"Thank you," Julia managed to say, her voice steadier than she felt, "I just, I need some time to figure things out."

"Of course," Anne agreed, standing to leave but pausing at the doorway, "and remember, you're not alone in this. We're all here for you." With a final empathetic smile, Anne stepped out into the cool afternoon air, leaving Julia to navigate the tangled web of her thoughts, the book on her lap forgotten amidst the chaos of her heart.

Henry's gaze remained fixed on the desk as Beth watched him closely, noting the stoic set of his jaw, the way his hands rested calmly on the weathered wood. She cleared her throat, steeling herself for what she was about to reveal.

"I need to tell you something else about Abraham." Her voice was steady despite the churn in her stomach. The clawing need to explain, to unload her suspicions, became too much in the hours that had passed since the omission from their previous conversation.

"Do you have further proof of your prior accusations?" Henry turned his head ever so slightly but his expression remained unreadable. Beth sighed heavily, sensing the resentment in his tone yet her need to feel heard overcame her willpower to stop talking.

"I'm telling you this as the mayor of this town, as the sworn protector of these people. Not as Abraham's father."

"Alright," Henry leaned back in his chair, "go on."

"I think he was along the coast a few years back. Near Mountain Gate, there was an incident. A voice on the radio," she continued, her fingers tracing the grain of the wood as if to draw strength from it, "and there's more, about Victor and a deal with someone on the mainland. For children." The words hung heavy in the air, each one laden with implication and danger. Still, Henry's face betrayed nothing of the turmoil that must surely be brewing within.

"What would my son want with children?" He seemed carved from stone, a sentinel unmoved by the storm of accusations engulfing his own child.

"I don't know," Beth confessed softly, "but there were bodies along the coast. They had been strung up and—"

"My son was in Prescott, not on the coast." Henry's sharp words interrupted her, a sour warning to cease the recounting of her memories.

"Were you with him the whole time?"

"Abraham was in Prescott." Henry repeated, louder this time with anger lacing his tone. It was the first time Beth had ever heard him even mildly indignant. She inhaled sharply, about to delve deeper into her suspicions when Barnett's hand closed gently over her arm. She looked at him, finding concern etched into his furrowed brow.

"Beth, you need to calm down," Barnett said softly but with an underlying firmness that commanded her attention, "you've just laid out a lot of heavy stuff here, all about his son. Give him a moment to process it all." She faltered, her resolve waning under Barnett's earnest gaze. Maybe she had pushed too hard, too fast. Her eyes flitted back to Henry, searching for some sign of emotion, some hint of the inner workings behind that impenetrable facade.

"Sorry." She murmured, though her apology was more reflex than regret. The fire that spurred her on still burned fiercely, but she understood Barnett's point. This was not just information - it was a wound delivered to a father's heart. Henry finally shifted, turning to face them fully. In the dimming light, his eyes seemed to carry the weight of the world. Beth held her breath, waiting for him to speak, to deny, to rage - anything that would betray the thoughts swirling behind those guarded eyes. But all he gave them was a nod, a silent acknowledgment of the gravity of her words, and the unspoken promise that the conversation was far from over. Beth's hand trembled slightly as she lowered it, the apology lingering in the air between them like the last note of a sombre tune. She watched Henry, his face marked by the years and the wear of recent revelations, searching for a sign of forgiveness or further condemnation.

"Abraham has always been difficult to understand," Henry finally said, his voice low and gruff as he paused, looking past Beth as if gazing into a distant memory, "he's my son, and he's always held himself to this righteous standard. But a murderer?" The words seemed to stick in his throat, disbelief and pain warring within him.

"Look, I know," Beth started, her voice steadier now, "I wasn't exactly a saint before everything fell apart. But the world ending, it changes you. It might have changed Abraham too."

"Changed, yes," Henry murmured, almost to himself, "but how much?"

"Sometimes people do insane things when they think they're saving the world," Beth offered, her thoughts drifting momentarily to all the chaos and desperation they'd witnessed, "maybe the end of the world was just a catalyst for him." Henry nodded slowly, his expression still unreadable as he considered her words. Finally, he met her gaze again, a quiet intensity in his eyes.

"Alright," he conceded, his voice barely above a whisper, "but don't do anything rash, Beth. We can't afford more chaos, not now." Beth felt a flicker of resolve ignite within her. Henry's cautious agreement was all she needed to keep pushing forward, but her methods would need to be calculated and deliberate.

"Understood." She replied, her determination clear. Henry paced the length of the dim room, his heavy boots thumping against the wooden floorboards. The air was thick with tension, a silent witness to the gravity of their conversation. Beth watched him, her eyes tracing the lines of worry that seemed to have etched themselves deeper into his face.

"We need to be cautious about who we bring into this," Henry finally said, stopping short and turning to face them, "only those we can absolutely trust."

"Agreed," Beth replied, her mind racing through potential allies, "Austin, Reece, Chase, Val, Phillip—" She hesitated, the list in her head growing thin.

"Anne." Henry interjected firmly, as if the name should never have been in doubt.

"Of course, Anne." Beth nodded, though a slight crease formed between her brows at the oversight. Their gazes shifted to Barnett, who stood with his arms folded across his chest, an unreadable expression on his face. He met their scrutiny with a level stare.

"You can trust me." He said, the weight of his promise hanging in the air. Beth let out a slow breath she didn't realise she'd been holding. Trust wasn't easily given these days, but Barnett's assurance had a steadying effect.

"Is there anyone else?" Henry asked, looking between them both for confirmation.

"No one we should trust with this." Beth shook her head affirmingly, cementing her allegiance with the names already mentioned.

"Then it's settled," Henry said, his voice softening for a moment before he straightened up, resolve hardening his features once again, "we'll meet tonight, quietly, and figure out exactly what we know to be true." It was a small circle they trusted, but it would have to be enough. With a shared determination, they prepared to face whatever darkness lay ahead, united by a fragile thread of trust in a world that often seemed to have none left to spare. Beth pushed herself up from the weathered wooden chair, its legs scraping against the floorboards with a sound that seemed too loud in the tense atmosphere of the town hall. The air was thick with the promise of an impending storm, both outside and within their tight-knit circle of trust.

"I'll make sure everyone knows." She stated, her voice steady despite the turmoil churning inside her. Henry gave a curt nod, his eyes reflecting a depth of concern that mirrored her own. As she turned towards the doorway, she felt the weight of the meeting they were about to have - their very survival could hinge on the decisions made tonight. The door creaked open and Beth stepped out into the fading light, inhaling the cool air as if it could cleanse the unease from her lungs. She hadn't gone more than a few paces when Barnett's footsteps hastened behind her.

"Beth, wait up," he called out, soft-spoken yet insistent as he closed the distance between them, "why do you think Abraham is so bad? I mean, I just want to understand." She paused mid-stride, her back still to him. Beth wasn't one to shy away from confrontation, but fatigue was beginning to set in, fraying the edges of her resolve.

"I don't have the energy to be second guessed right now, Barnett." Her words carried a weariness that was hard to disguise.

"Hey," he said softly, coming to stand beside her, his expression earnest, "I'm not doubting you. I believe you. It's just, everything's a mess. I want to help. I'm trying to make sense of it." Beth turned, looking straight into Barnett's eyes. They were the eyes of someone who sought truth amidst the chaos, someone who needed to find clarity in the shadows that threatened to engulf them all.

"You don't know me well enough to understand," she began, her gaze unwavering, "but my gut, it's screaming that there's something dark about him. Evil, even." Barnett's Adam's apple bobbed as he swallowed, the gravity of her words sinking in. He was new to this dance of suspicion and betrayal, but he was learning the steps quickly.

"Okay," he said after a moment, his voice low, "I'll follow your lead on this." With a subtle nod, Beth resumed walking, her thoughts racing ahead to the gathering night and the meeting that awaited them. There was much to prepare, and little time for doubt. In these times, a gut feeling might be all they had to go on, and hers told her that evil lurked closer than any of them wanted to admit.

Beth's stride was purposeful as she navigated the road which led to the town's main thoroughfare. Barnett kept pace, a silent sentinel whose presence she felt rather than saw.

"Abraham thinks he's some sort of messiah," Beth said abruptly, her voice edged with frustration, "that his path is righteous, saving

the world by defining roles for women. It's archaic and it's dangerous."

"What do you mean *roles for women*?" Barnett frowned, the lines
on his forehead deepening.

"Exactly what you think," she replied tersely, "subservient, quiet.
I've seen men like him before. The apocalypse hasn't changed their
nature, only given them permission to act on it. I refuse to be a
pawn in whatever game he's playing." She declared as Barnett nodded, his jaw tightening.

"You won't be. Not while I'm around," he assured her, "you can
trust me, Beth. I won't let him mess with what we've built here."
Beth stopped in her tracks, turning to face him. She studied Barnett's determined gaze, searching for any hint of duplicity. Finding
none, she exhaled slowly.

"Trust is earned, Barnett. Not just handed over. I don't know you
well enough yet. But for now, I guess we want the same thing."

"Fair enough," Barnett conceded, "so what now?"

"We need to get the others and inform them about the meeting
tonight." Her eyes darted around the main area of the town, noting
the absence of people out and about, mostly due to the illness.

"Lead the way." Barnett said. With a subtle nod, Beth resumed
walking, the weight of impending decisions heavy on her shoulders but lighter by a fraction with Barnett at her side. The sterile
scent of disinfectant greeted Beth as she pushed through the clinic doors, her gaze sweeping the sparsely furnished waiting area for
familiar faces. Instead of the familiar presence of Val or Anne, she
found Phillip at the reception desk, his face drawn with concern
beneath the harsh fluorescent lights.

"Phillip," Beth called out, her voice low and urgent as she approached, "where is everyone? I thought I'd find Val and Anne

here." He looked up from his paperwork, the lines on his forehead deepening.

"Val's sick. She's at home now, and Anne," he paused, a hesitant flicker in his eyes, "I believe Anne is with Julia." Beth's heart clenched at the mention of Julia, knowing the tangled web of emotions that surrounded her situation.

"Listen, there's a meeting tonight at the town hall. It's important. Can you make sure Anne knows?"

"Actually Beth," Phillip started, glancing back towards the corridor where patients awaited him, "I've got my hands full here. Could you—"

"Of course." Beth cut in, her reluctance masked by a brisk nod. She had no desire to confront the woman who she had thought Ben loved more than her, but the urgency of the gathering left no room for hesitation. Stepping back into the daylight, she hesitated only a moment before making her way towards Julia's house. Barnett caught up to her, his stride purposeful.

"Beth, wait," he said, his voice carrying a note of understanding that stopped her in her tracks, "let me go to Julia's. You don't need to walk into that minefield."

"Why would you offer that?" She eyed him warily, sensing the unspoken knowledge in his gaze. Barnett's mouth twitched with a resigned half-smile.

"I'm not blind, Beth. I see the way things are," his voice was gentle, yet it bore the weight of truth she tried to avoid, "it must be hard for you." Hard was an understatement. The very thought of facing Anne at Julia's house, where the echoes of Ben's indecision hung like stifling air made her stomach churn. But Barnett offering to shoulder this burden surprised her.

"Thank you." She murmured, feeling an unexpected kinship in the shared acknowledgment of the mess they were all entangled in.

"Besides," he offered her a soft smile, "I'm trying to do something nice for you. Maybe start earning some of that trust."

"It's a start." Beth let out a soft laugh which surprised them both. With a final nod, she watched Barnett turn towards Julia's home before she set off to find the others, her resolve firming with every step. Today, there were bigger demons to face than the ones lurking in the shadows of broken hearts. Beth's heart pounded with a sense of urgency as she dashed through the settlement, her boots kicking up dust in her wake. The late afternoon sun stretched long shadows across the ground, mirroring the growing unease within her. She arrived at Reece's house, breathless, the news of the meeting pressing against her lips like a sealed envelope. Austin and Reece looked up from where they stood on the porch, their conversation halting as Beth approached. Concern etched Reece's features, his eyes flickering with the kind of distress that only came with loved ones in peril.

"Val's too sick," he blurted out before she could speak, "I can't leave her side." Beth's gaze softened, understanding the weight of his words.

"She needs you," she acknowledged before turning to Austin, her voice finding strength again, "but we need you both at this meeting. You know it's important."

"She'll be okay for a little while, Reece." Austin's jaw set, determination lighting his eyes. Reece hesitated, torn between his heart and his duty. After a tense moment he nodded, relenting to the gravity of the situation that loomed over them all.

"Okay," Reece agreed, though the reluctance in his voice was palpable, "I'll come. But if anything happens—"

"Nothing will happen." Beth assured him, though the promise

tasted like ash on her tongue. They both knew the fragility of such assurances in their current world.

"Nothing will happen." Beth assured him, though the promise tasted like ash on her tongue. They both knew the fragility of such assurances in their current world.

"Anything else?" Reece's tone was impatient, the air around them growing thin.

"I haven't been able to find Chase yet," she said, shifting the focus, "can you grab him on the way? I need to prepare what I'm going to say tonight. Just get things in order so we can talk it through more clearly."

"Sure." Reece sighed while Austin nodded, his gaze lingering on Beth a moment longer than necessary. Beth spun on her heel and strode away, her mind awash with the information that had to be shared, the alliances that needed to be forged. As the distance between her and Reece's house grew, so did the tension in her shoulders, a physical manifestation of the mental burden she carried. Unseen, Austin excused himself and followed her path, propelled by an invisible force that seemed to draw him ever closer to Beth. His steps quickened until he was walking beside her, matching her brisk pace.

"Wait up, can we talk?" There was an urgency in his voice that made her stop and turn towards him, her expression guarded.

"About what?" She asked, although she already felt the undercurrent of unspoken words between them.

"About everything." Austin said, the breadth of that single word encompassing more than just the impending crisis.

"Later," Beth insisted, knowing that any personal discussion now would only serve to distract her from the imminent meeting, "right now I need space to think." Without waiting for a response, she continued on her way, but Austin fell into step beside her once again. When they reached her place, he didn't ask permission before crossing the threshold into her home, a silent assertion that some conversations couldn't wait. Beth's movements were mechanical as she reached for the amber bottle on the kitchen counter, the smooth surface cool under her fingertips. She poured the liquid with a practiced tilt, watching it splash into the glass with a satisfying ripple. Turning, she offered the second glass to Austin, who was leaning against the doorframe, his posture betraying a tension that matched her own.

"Is that really a good idea before the meeting?" Austin's voice was casual, but his eyes were searching, fixed on her. She let out a laugh, brittle and short-lived.

"I just need something to take the edge off." Beth said, meeting his gaze defiantly. Her fingers curled around the glass, seeking solace in the burn that would follow. Austin crossed the room slowly, stopping within arm's reach.

"I came here because we need to talk about what happened." He said, his voice carrying an unfamiliar gravity. Beth shook her head, a strand of hair falling across her face.

"I don't want to talk about it." She replied, her voice steady even as her heart raced. There was too much at stake, too many pieces in play for them to indulge in personal drama. Austin's jaw clenched, and he took in a deep breath before speaking again.

"I have to tell Anne. I feel horrible, Beth."

"Can it wait until we've sorted through this mess with Abraham and the sickness going around?" She asked, her tone softening despite herself. There was a pause, the space between them charged with unspoken words and shared guilt.

"There are other things I need to consider now," Austin finally said, his eyes never leaving hers, "our relationship, it's not just about us anymore." Beth felt the weight of his words settle over her like a shroud. The future was uncertain, their paths intertwined in ways neither of them could have predicted. But there was no time for hesitation, not when every moment counted.

"Understand this, Austin," she said, her voice low, "whatever this is or isn't, it can't be our focus right now. We have a town to protect, lives at stake. That's what matters." Austin nodded, the lines of his face etched with conflict. He understood the gravity of their situation, even if it pained him to set aside their personal turmoil.

"Sure Beth." With a weary acceptance, he pushed away from her and made his way to the other side of the kitchen to lean against the wall, leaving Beth alone with her thoughts and the untouched drink in her hand. Beth's hand trembled slightly as she set the glass down on the counter. Her gaze was steady when her eyes met Austin's, holding a sharp clarity that belied the drink she'd poured.

"You should've thought about Anne before it happened." She said, her voice carrying an edge of steel. The light from the kitchen window cast a stark contrast over Austin's features, accentuating the stubble along his jaw and the furrow between his brows. He shifted uncomfortably, leaning back against the wall with his arms folded across his chest.

"I remember you asking me to make you feel something other than anger." He replied, his tone defensive yet tinged with regret. Beth let out a mirthless groan, shaking her head.

"Are you serious? I'm no saint but Jesus fucking Christ Austin, it's not my job to stop you from cheating on your girlfriend. It was wrong. I shouldn't have said that, but I wanted you in that moment. I needed something, and you wanted me too. But it wasn't on me to say no. You kissed me. You threw me on the table. I'm not the one in a committed relationship—"

"What about Ben?" Austin's anger flared, his voice rising, his hands unfolding and slamming down to his sides.

"What *about* Ben? He isn't here, Austin," Beth let out a dry, empty snort as she laughed, "and even if he were, it doesn't change the fact that we are *not* together." She took a step closer to him, her own anger surfacing.

"Fuck you Beth. Do you even have any guilt?" Austin shouted back, his voice breaking the charged air as it grew louder, penetrating the silence with the force of a fist. She moved toward him with swift, determined steps, closing the distance between them in just a few strides. The air between them crackled with a volatile mix of anger and unspoken pain.

"Guilt? I have plenty of guilt," her words were fierce, her tone laced with a bitter mix of aggression and heartache as she shoved his chest in raw frustration, "more than you know. You think I wanted *this*? You think any choices I've made have been easy for me?"

"Right, It's always about you," he retorted, his voice dripping with sarcasm, "any excuse to justify doing whatever the fuck you want." They were locked in a battle of words that did nothing to resolve the chasm between them. His accusation hung in the air, a blunt instrument wielded in desperation. Beth's eyes flashed with defiance, refusing to back down. Anguish intertwined with anger as she struggled to articulate the conflict within her, the emotional maelstrom none of them seemed able to escape.

"You're the one making this about me," Beth's voice rose, a tremor betraying the deeper hurt beneath her defiant words, "you're putting all your anger and guilt and regret onto me and it's not fair." Her heart thundered in her chest, the enormity of their situation closing in, the pressure of the looming meeting adding weight to her words. Austin's voice cracked with the weight of his accusation.

"Are you fucking kidding me? You're the one who—"

"You sure didn't stop me though," Beth cut in sharply, unwilling to let him dictate the narrative, "and now you want to turn this on me, like *I'm* the one who made promises I couldn't keep." Austin's jaw clenched, and he turned his back on her, raking his hands through his hair in exasperation. When he faced her again, his eyes were hard, a challenge in them that was impossible to ignore.

"My heart broke that night," his voice was tense, but quieter, as if resigning himself to the impossibility of their situation, "I told you I loved you, and then I never thought I'd see you again." There was a flicker of vulnerability in her eyes, a quiet plea for him to understand the complexity, the impossibility, of the choices that lay before her. The silence between them was a living thing, stretched thin and ready to snap.

"We don't have to talk about this again—"

"But then you came back, Beth. What was I supposed to do? Watch the woman I love fall in love with someone else all over again?" Austin's accusation was pointed, an arrow loosed from a taut bowstring, aimed squarely at her heart. Beth stood her ground, though his words struck her with precision, each landing its targeted blow. She took a deep breath, steadying herself, the frayed edges of her composure barely holding, the enormity of their entangled past collapsing in like a tidal wave.

"Austin—"

"Are you just waiting for him? Hoping he'll come back to you and using me in the meantime until he makes up his mind?" Austin's words were probing, searching for some truth that might alleviate his guilt. Beth sighed, her anger dissipating as quickly as it had arrived. She looked away, finding a spot on the floor to focus on.

"I'm not using you. I don't know what I'm waiting for," she admitted, her voice softer now, almost vulnerable, "right now I just need to get through whatever's going on with Abraham and this illness, plus we still have Sabrina and Josh to figure out. There's a lot of shit going on, and once it's done I can sort out my feelings about Ben, and what I feel about you." Austin's expression softened at her words, his posture relaxing as he took in her resolve. There was something formidable in her determination to put the welfare of others first, even above her own tangled emotions. He nodded slowly, recognising the magnitude of the task they faced together. His jaw clenched as he watched Beth take another slow, deliberate sip from her glass. The amber liquid sloshed slightly as she set it down with a clink on the counter, her gaze steady and unreadable.

"Julia's pregnant," he said, the words heavy between them, "Ben might come back to town just to tell you that he needs to be there for Julia and their baby." Beth's expression didn't waver, but something flickered behind her eyes - a flash of pain or resignation, quickly masked. He watched her fingers dance along the rim of her glass, as if contemplating another drink, a way to drown the complexity of her feelings. But she refrained, placing her palm flat against the countertop as though grounding herself.

"If you're not here to help me get ready for tonight's meeting, there's the door." Beth's nod towards the exit was dismissive, yet there was an undercurrent of plea in her tone, a silent call for support she was too proud to voice outright.

"Fine," Austin hesitated, the muscles in his neck tightening, "I'll see you later." He took a step towards the door, feeling the weight of their unresolved tension like a physical barrier. His hand hovered over the doorknob, the cool metal an anchor to the moment.

But then he stopped, the silence in the room pulsating with all the words they hadn't said. Slowly, he turned back to face her, his eyes searching hers for some kind of sign. Beth straightened, her arms crossing defensively as she met his gaze.

"What is it, Austin? What do you want?" Her question was sharp, cutting through the quiet with an edge that spoke of vulnerability and strength intertwined. For a moment, neither of them moved, the air thick with the gravity of what had passed between them and what loomed ahead. Austin's resolve crumbled as he took in her defiant stance, the air between them charged with an electric current of unspoken desires. With a few strides he closed the distance, his voice low and steady, betraying the storm of emotions brewing inside him.

"I want to finish what we started last night." He declared, the words falling like a dare. Beth barely had time to register his intent before his hands found her, his touch igniting a fire that raged through her veins. She gasped, startled by the sudden intensity, but her body betrayed her surprise as her arms instinctively curled around his neck. Her fingers tangled into his hair, pulling him closer, her earlier defences dissolving into the heat of their embrace. With a swift movement born of urgency, Austin lifted Beth, her legs instinctively wrapping around his waist as if they belonged there, once again ignoring the pain in his shoulder. Their breaths mingled, quick and ragged, as he carried her to the couch. The world outside this room, the meeting, the looming threats, they all faded into obscurity against the immediacy of their need for each other. He placed her down with a haste that spoke volumes, the sound of fabric tearing at seams echoing in the quiet room as they fumbled with buttons and belts. Austin lifted his shirt over his head, revealing the tense lines of his torso, muscles honed from a life shaped by survival and determination. Beth matched his urgency, discarding her top and exposing skin flushed with a mixture of desire and something deeper, a vulnerability she rarely allowed herself to show. Their eyes locked for a fleeting second, a silent acknowledgment of the precipice they teetered on. They came together in a kiss that was both a collision and a merging, a passionate dance that spoke of longing, regret, and an insatiable hunger. It was a moment suspended in time, where past hurts and future uncertainties were consumed by the blaze of the present. And then, with a motion that was both tender and fierce, Austin bridged the final gap between them, joining them in a way that felt both like a beginning and a reckoning. The connection was elemental, raw, as if in this act they could both find solace and escape from the chaos of their fractured world. Beth's moan was a mingling of need and release, the sound muffled against Austin's shoulder. Her teeth grazed his skin, a primal act that seemed to draw him even closer into her. With a fierce grip her hand found purchase on the muscle of his thigh, urging him deeper, her nails pressing crescent moons into his flesh. Their bodies moved together in perfect rhythm, each push and pull erasing the lines between them. The world beyond the four walls of the room fell away - there were no secrets here, no looming threats, just the raw and undeniable truth of their connection. The heat of their union filled the small space, the air charged with the electricity of their combined energy. Beth felt the weight of loneliness and anger lift from her chest, replaced by the heavy beat of Austin's heart against her own. She clung to the moment, to the feeling of being anchored to another soul amidst the tumultuous tide of their reality.

CHAPTER 16

The door to the town hall creaked open as Austin and Beth slipped through the gap, their shadows stretching long across the floor from the setting sun behind them. They were greeted by a hush that blanketed the room, punctuated only by the faint rustle of protective masks shifting over anxious faces. Austin's gaze skittered across the assembly, deliberately bypassing Anne's corner where she sat with Phillip, their faces obscured by the clinical white of N95 masks. Anne's eyes locked onto them for an uncomfortable heartbeat before Austin could look away, her stare sharp enough to slice through the tension thickening in the air. Henry, seated at the head of the table with a weariness that seemed to pull his shoulders towards the ground, managed a nod in their direction. The lines etched into his face spoke volumes of sleepless nights, and it was clear that the weight of leadership pressed heavily on him now more than ever.

"Sorry we're late." Beth murmured, her voice barely above a whisper, but loud enough to draw the attention of every wary eye in the room. Henry didn't stand, but his presence filled the room as if he had. With a sigh that seemed to carry all their collective fears, Henry leaned forward, resting his forearms on the cool surface of the wood before him, his fingers interlaced tightly as if to brace himself.

"You're here now," he said, his voice carrying the gravelly tone of exhaustion, "there's a few things on tonight's agenda, so let's get started. We can't beat around the bush any longer. This sickness, it's spreading too fast. We need to take serious measures." Beth felt a chill snake up her spine - she knew what was coming. The unspoken dread that had been hanging in the air was about to be voiced, and it felt like the final nail in the coffin of their normalcy.

"What kind of measures?" Anne asked hesitantly, feeling Austin's gaze on her but not meeting his eyes. Out of the corner of her eye, she saw him look away as quickly as he had looked at her.

"We have to quarantine the town," Henry declared, a definitive edge to his voice that brokered no argument, "complete lockdown, effective immediately. It's the only way to contain this until we know who's sick, who isn't, and what we can do about it." There were nods around the room, a silent consensus among the fearful glances exchanged. Beth felt Austin's hand brush against hers, a fleeting touch that spoke of solidarity in uncertain times. As the reality set in, the enormity of the task at hand loomed over them, a dark cloud threatening to burst at any moment.

"How many are sick?" Austin's gaze finally drifted across the room, settling on Anne and Phillip who looked like pale ghosts behind their masks. His voice was steady, but the undercurrent of concern was palpable. Anne's eyes flitted from face to face, her usual stoicism faltering as she spoke with a meekness that was alien to her.

"It might be easier to list who's well. Besides us here, there's another thirty or so who are asymptomatic for now," she swallowed hard, her eyes darkening, "but by morning, we'll know more. This thing takes hold fast."

"Do we even know what it is yet?" Reece interjected, his words laced with worry. Phillip's response came after a heavy silence, his voice clinical yet tinged with a dread that mirrored their own. "Likely cholera, dysentery, typhoid, maybe tuberculosis. All possible with the state of sanitation, plus everyone is weakened from malnutrition. And they're highly contagious." Beth looked towards Austin before setting her eyes to the floor, contemplating her earlier suspicions of whether or not Abraham had introduced the sickness into their community. Her urge to speak out was quickly crushed by her need to keep the peace with Henry until she had more concrete evidence - whatever the sickness was, whether it was naturally caused or brought in intentionally, there was no way for them to provide the proper healthcare.

"So how do we treat it?" Chase leaned in, his brows furrowed in concentration, seeking some sliver of hope.

"Without antibiotics and modern medicine," Phillip started, pressing the bridge of his nose in a vain attempt to fend off the headache brewing, "our best path is hydration and oxygen. But if our water supply is contaminated, which is highly likely, hydration becomes a critical issue. And oxygen is scarce." He sighed heavily. The room fell silent, each person grappling with the grim reality - the tools they needed to fight this were far beyond reach. Austin clenched his fists, feeling helplessness rise like bile in his throat. The battle ahead was not only against an unseen enemy, but also against the limitations of their new world.

"It could just be the flu," Anne offered, her muffled voice behind her mask cut through the tense air, though her eyes betrayed the optimism her words tried to convey, "but even if it is, our immune systems aren't what they used to be."

"What's the likely outcome for everyone then?" Beth, her hands knotted together, leaned forward with a question that seemed to hang heavy on everyone's heart. Phillip adjusted his glasses, which had begun to fog slightly from his breath against the mask.

"It depends," he said solemnly, "if it's something like TB, survival without modern medicine is possible but challenging. There's a high risk of death and long-term complications. The success of survival relies heavily on the individual's health, living conditions, and their body's ability to mount an effective immune response." Phillip concluded, looking around the room.

"And if it's the flu?" Henry's lips thinned, the gravity of their situation settling in.

"Even the flu isn't simple anymore," Phillip continued, his gaze steady despite the grim prognosis, "most healthy people might survive influenza without modern medicine, but we're facing severe illness and complications, especially for the vulnerable among us. And without medical care, antivirals, or supportive treatments, mortality rates are likely to climb well beyond what we've known before." A silence took hold, punctuated by the distant sound of a cough from outside - a stark reminder of the invisible threat surrounding them. Henry stood up, a weariness in his stance that echoed the collective exhaustion of the room.

"People shouldn't be walking around, especially if they're sick. So we implement a quarantine," he declared, his voice resolute despite his evident fatigue, "everyone must stay in their homes. Food rations will be distributed by military personnel." He looked at Austin, seeing the same determination in the younger man's eyes that he felt within himself.

"I might not be in fighting condition but this is something I can help with." Austin nodded slowly.

"I need you to go back to work and lead the charge," Henry's tired gaze landed on Beth, "and you'll coordinate a census of the sick, working with Anne and Phillip. You'll take Barnett with you on your rounds." Beth nodded, her mind already racing with logistics and plans. She knew there was no time to waste - every moment mattered now.

"I can do that." Beth offered a half smile, looking towards Anne who looked away suddenly, staring at nothing in particular.

"I'll speak with George about getting more military personnel around town," Henry added, as if reading the concern in her eyes, "we need all hands on deck." As the meeting began to disperse, each person was acutely aware that the world outside the town hall had changed irrevocably. They were stepping into a new reality, one where their resilience would be tested like never before. Beth's eyes met Anne's across the room, and for a moment, there was a silent exchange that spoke volumes. The air between them felt charged, thick with unsaid words and unasked questions. But as quickly as it came, the connection broke, Beth's gaze dropping to her scuffed boots, a sense of unease twisting in her stomach. Anne rose from her seat with a clinical efficiency, the rustling of her protective gear punctuating the silence.

"Is there anything else?" Anne's voice cut through the heavy atmosphere, her hand on the back of the chair, poised to leave. She took a deliberate step towards the door, her movements suggesting an urgency to return to her duties.

"Wait." Henry interjected firmly, halting Anne's exit. His hands rested on the table before him, and despite his evident weariness he commanded the room with an authority that had become second nature. Beth felt Henry's gaze settle on her, and she let out a small sigh, glancing once more at the door and finding Austin's steady presence. In his eyes, she found a quiet encouragement, a silent nod that urged her to talk.

"Something strange is going on," Beth began, her voice steady but low, almost reluctant as her hands clenched into fists beside her, betraying her nervous energy, "I can't shake this feeling, it's too much of a coincidence that this sickness has erupted right after—" She trailed off, not wanting to point fingers, yet unable to ignore the nagging suspicion clawing at the back of her mind.

"Go on, Beth." Henry urged, leaning forward slightly. Beth swallowed hard, steeling herself against the weight of her next words.

"It feels like it might have been planned." She confessed, the last word hanging in the air like a dark cloud. Silence enveloped the room as the gravity of her statement settled upon each person present. Anne's scoff cut through the tension, a sharp sound that seemed to ricochet off the town hall's aged walls.

"Planned? A mass sickness? That's absurd," disbelief was etched into every syllable, her eyes narrowing beneath the plastic shield of her mask, "there's no way."

"Are you telling me there's *no* way someone could have broken into a lab and stolen something?" Beth met Anne's skepticism with an inscrutable gaze.

"I mean, when I was at UCLA I did some work in the Infectious Disease Division—"

"And what did you work on?" Beth's voice was tinged with a weariness that matched the bags under Anne's eyes. Anne thought back to her work in the laboratory, her days handling and studying various types of influenza, hepatitis, malaria, ebola, just to name a few. But just as quick as the memories had flooded her mind, she pushed them aside, unwilling to accept Beth's speculation.

"Look, I don't have time for conspiracy theories," Anne's tone was terse, her patience frayed at the edges like the hem of her well-worn coat, "I need to check on the sickest. We can indulge in wild speculations after if we must." Without waiting for a response, she turned on her heel, her movements brisk as she headed towards the door. Phillip watched his daughter leave, a soft sigh escaping him as he pushed his glasses up the bridge of his nose.

"She hasn't slept much," he confided to the group before setting his gaze upon Beth, the lines of concern visible even behind his mask, "with Val out we're both stretched thin. I'll see you in the morning. We'll go over the census and patients together." He gave a reassuring nod towards Beth, a fleeting gesture of solidarity, before nodding to the others and taking his leave, the door closing quietly behind him. In the ensuing silence, Austin glanced at Beth, a frown tugging at his lips.

"He's right, they're exhausted," he acknowledged, before his voice lowered to a grave timbre, "but Beth and I, we've been talking. Putting the pieces together." His brown eyes flickered with the same suspicion that had taken root in Beth's thoughts, a shared unease that neither could fully shake off. The others exchanged glances, the seed of doubt now firmly planted among them. The notion of a sinister plot lurking beneath the chaos of illness was chilling - a possibility that none of them wanted to entertain, yet could no longer ignore. Henry's hands trembled faintly as he massaged his temples, his gaze unfocused. Beth, sensing a shift in the room's dynamic, moved towards him slowly.

"Henry, are you alright?" She inquired softly, her voice laced with concern. He looked up, and even in the dim light of the town hall his pallor was evident.

"I'm just, I'm not feeling great," Henry confessed, his voice barely above a whisper, "stress, probably." But his attempt at nonchalance fell flat. Beth reached out, her fingers brushing his forehead. The heat that radiated from his skin was undeniable.

"You're burning up." She said, her tone edged with worry.

"Sorry everyone, I just need to sleep this off. Big day tomorrow." Henry muttered, pushing himself to stand. His apology was quick, almost rushed as he avoided their gazes, unwilling to see the concern mirrored in their eyes.

"Henry—"

"Make sure to lock up Beth." He requested as he steadied himself on the back of a chair before shuffling towards the exit. The moment the door clicked shut behind Henry, a heavy silence settled over the group. They exchanged uneasy glances, each aware of the implications but hesitant to voice them aloud. Reece broke the silence, his voice sharpening with emotion.

"He's sick." He stated flatly, glaring at the closed door.

"We don't know that," Beth countered, "it could just be exhaustion." Her response came swiftly, a reflexive defence, but Reece was having none of it.

"He's sick Beth," he snapped, his frustration boiling over, "don't be so fucking naive." The accusation hung in the air, thick and unchallengeable. Beth's lips pressed into a thin line, her retort dying before it could take form. Her silence was a reluctant concession to Reece's blunt assessment. The tension in the room seemed to grow heavier with each passing second, as if the air itself was thickening with uncertainty. Barnett's gaze swept over the group before landing on Beth.

"So," he began, his voice cutting through the silence like a knife, "who takes charge if Henry is down?" Beth felt every pair of eyes fix on her as if she held all the answers. But she didn't, she never had.

"We've never talked about it," she admitted, her voice tinged with a helplessness that made her stomach twist, "there's no plan for if he were to get sick, or worse. I'm just a glorified secretary, really. There's no hierarchy here." She shook her head, a strand of hair falling across her face. Barnett's eyebrow arched, a silent challenge to her words. But it wasn't a challenge she could rise to, not now, not when their makeshift society seemed to be fraying at the edges. Chase shifted in his seat, the scrape of his chair against the floor punctuating the quiet.

"What about George," he asked, turning to Austin, "could he step in?" Austin leaned back, his gaze distant as if picturing the ramifications of such a shift.

"Henry and George agreed to keep things separate. Town and military, church and state," he finally said, dragging his eyes back to meet Chase's, "they support each other, sure. The military does supply runs, we provide them with housing and keep track of resources. But they're not supposed to take over. It's about balance, not control." Beth wondered how much balance they could maintain in a world that seemed determined to topple everything they tried to rebuild, as she noted Austin's inclusion of himself as part of the town instead of the military. Her fingers drummed a nervous rhythm on the wooden table, her gaze flitting from one face to another. Tension knotted the air thick as rope.

"I don't know," she said, her voice steady despite the uncertainty clawing at her insides, "George might not be what we need if he takes over. I just, I've got a bad feeling about him."

"Since when do you get a good vibe from anyone?" Reece's voice cut through the room, sharp and edged with frustration. He stood with arms crossed, his stance rigid. Beth bristled, heat rising to her cheeks as she met his glare.

"In my experience," she shot back, her words slicing the tense atmosphere, "pissed off men with corrupt agendas tend to have misguided intentions. It's not about *vibes*, it's about surviving." Reece's eyes held hers for a charged moment, then he looked away, the fire in his gaze dimming. His shoulders slumped slightly, and when he spoke again, his voice was quieter, almost strained.

"I'm sorry Beth," he said, rubbing the back of his neck, "your theories, they've got Val all worked up, and with her being sick—" He trailed off, the weight of unspoken worries evident in his hollow tone.

"Is she okay?" Beth's anger dissipated as quickly as it had flared, replaced by concern. She knew all too well the toll that fear could take on a person, especially in times like these. Reece nodded slowly, but his eyes didn't meet hers.

"Yes, she is. For now." The last two words hung between them, heavy and ominous.

"That's good—"

"I'm sorry for snapping at you. I'm just stressed, that's all. I should go check on her," Reece glanced once at the door before turning back to the group, the crease between his brows deepening, "sorry again." He mumbled and then made his way out, his departure leaving a silence that seemed to echo off the walls of the town hall. Austin stepped closer to Reece, his voice low and steady.

"Make sure you wear a mask around Val." He said, the concern etched into the lines of his face. Reece simply nodded, the heated exchange from moments ago already fading into the background of more pressing worries. He turned on his heel without another word, his silhouette disappearing through the threshold of the door that groaned softly behind him. Beth let out a weary sigh as she scanned the remaining faces - Austin, Chase, and Barnett. Their eyes were shadows of uncertainty in the dimly lit room. The clock on the wall ticked on, indifferent to the tension that thickened the air.

"We should probably all go to bed." She murmured, her gaze lingering on the hands of the clock, willing them to stop and grant them respite from the relentless march of time.

"Wait," Barnett interjected, his voice cutting through the haze of exhaustion, "what's the story with Abraham?" His eyes were fixed on Beth, searching for answers she wasn't sure she was ready to give. Before Austin could speak, Beth turned towards Barnett, a decision forming amidst the chaos of her thoughts.

"Walk me home," her voice was a blend of command and vulnerability, "I'll fill you in." Austin caught her eye and gave a curt nod, understanding the unspoken message between them. He then turned to Chase, motioning with his head towards the door. Together, they made their way down the road, their footsteps synchronising in the still night. As they departed, Austin cast a final glance back, his silhouette framed by the darkness before being swallowed whole by it. Beth secured the town hall doors with a click that sounded far too loud in the quiet. She turned to find Barnett at her side, his presence a solid assurance against the whispering doubts that danced at the edge of her mind. They walked side by side, the gravel beneath their feet crunching like a metronome counting down the seconds until the world would change again.

"So tell me," he pressed slowly, "tell me everything you think you know."

"Abraham," Beth began, her voice barely above a whisper, "he's a puzzle with missing pieces, but I know enough to be wary." Her words floated between them, a tentative offering to the trust she hoped to build.

"What do you know?"

"Back near Mountain Gate," she started, pausing as if to steady herself against the recollection, "there was this voice on the radio." Her eyes flicked to Barnett, gauging his reaction. The air was crisp and the moon a slender crescent, barely casting enough light to pave their path. Beth and Barnett moved with purposeful strides, the silence around them a canvas for her revelations.

"Radio?"

"We got separated, and Austin had to break radio silence to contact us. They were these shortwave radios so we know this other voice had to be close, or at least that's what Ben told me. It was chilling. The man, he kept calling us *sinners* over and over in this menacing tone." She continued as Barnett's brows drew together, a silent prompt for her to continue. She swallowed, feeling the memory claw its way up her throat.

"It's okay," Barnett smiled softly, sensing her hesitation to relive the memory, "you don't have to talk about it—"

"Ben and I were headed to this campsite and Austin and the others, they found some people," the words tumbled out, stark and heavy in the night, "all of them hanged in front of their home like puppets with *sinners* scrawled on the wall in what we hope was red paint." A shudder coursed through Beth, visible in the quiver of her shoulders. Barnett's jaw clenched, his eyes a mirror of the horror that the story painted.

"You hope?"

"Austin said no one went close enough to see what it was, but Luis said it was probably blood."

"Who's Luis?"

"Val's brother," Beth said quickly, pushing the memory of him from her mind and answering his question before he could even ask it, "we don't know where he is. Austin kicked him out after he did some shady shit."

"So, what happened next?"

"Well, then there was another body," she pressed on, her voice now soft and desolate, "Ben, Reece, and Val found him strung up on a fence with the same word carved into his chest." For a moment, they walked in shared silence, the echoes of the past reverberating between them.

"Where was this?"

"Near Redding. They went on a supply run and found him on the way. From then on we were cautious, always looking over our shoulders," Beth confessed, her hands clenching at her sides, "but after we got stuck at that ranch over winter, nothing else happened. We thought maybe the group behind it had moved on. When Abraham first arrived he was quoting scripture left and right. He kept saying children are the future. That women should know their place." The shadows seemed to lean in closer as she spoke, and Barnett's presence felt like the only solid thing in a world tilting towards madness.

"What for?"

"No idea. Back at Catalina," she continued, her eyes reflecting the flicker of moonlight, "the man who had us, he was dealing with someone over here on the mainland. There was apparently this trade for children." She faltered for a breath, her face etched with troubled lines.

"Kids? What kind of trade involves *kids*?" Barnett's steps faltered beside her, his brow furrowing. Beth shook her head, the chill of the night not accounting for the tremor in her limbs.

"I don't know what they wanted them for," she whispered, her gaze lost to the darkness between the buildings, "but I've seen the way Abraham looks at the kids here, heard the fervour in his voice. It's like he believes he's some kind of prophet or messiah."

"Believes?" Barnett's tone sharpened with skepticism.

"More than believes," Beth corrected herself, her voice growing firmer despite the fear, "he acts like he's been chosen to save us all. Like it's his divine mission to guide the children, or something. To lead us through this evangelical apocalypse in his mind." As they approached her front door, Beth felt the weight of the day's revelations and the secrets yet to share. But there was something else too, a flicker of solidarity in Barnett's gaze that told her she wasn't alone in this fight, and in that moment, the heavy burden she carried felt just a hair lighter. They had stopped walking, standing now before the dimly lit entrance to Beth's home. The weight of her conviction pressed into the silence that followed.

"A messiah," Barnett's face contorted in confusion, "that's a pretty heavy accusation, Beth."

"He thinks he's a saviour." She concluded, her declaration a quiet thunder in the stillness of the looming crisis. Barnett's hand rose slowly, the gesture heavy as though it dragged through the thick tension hanging in the night air. He rubbed his eyes, weariness and disbelief warring on his features, yet his gaze upon Beth held a steadiness that spoke of an unwavering resolve.

"I believe you," he said, the words resonating with sincerity, "it's a lot to take in, but I trust what you're saying. Why tell me all of this?" Beth regarded him, her breath forming ephemeral clouds in the chilly night. In the dim glow from the moonlight, her eyes shimmered with a vulnerability she seldom allowed others to see.

"I don't know," she admitted, "but I do know that for whatever reason, I trust you." It was a simple truth, unadorned and raw.

"Thank you," Barnett replied, a note of gratitude softening his voice, "can I ask you something?" His eyes had held hers for a moment longer before he ventured further into the delicate territory between them. A smile touched the corners of Beth's mouth, a faint curve that scarcely hinted at mirth, yet it softened the hard lines of recent days.

"You can ask," she said, her tone laced with both caution and a trace of camaraderie, "no guarantees I'll answer." He nodded, accepting the terms of engagement. Then, his attention shifted subtly, drawn to her arm.

"What's with the brand?" The question, though softly spoken, seemed to cut through the stillness. Beth's reaction was instinctual, her hand moving to cover the spot on her arm even though the fabric of her shirt already concealed it. Her eyes darted down briefly, then back up to meet Barnett's inquisitive look. She didn't speak, letting the unspoken hang heavily between them - a secret sealed beneath her skin, one that told stories she wasn't ready to voice.

"Marcus," she began, her voice barely above a whisper, "he was the one who did this." Her fingers trembled as she reached up, rolling back the sleeve of her shirt to reveal the crude brand etched into her skin - a symbol of ownership, a physical representation of her pain. Barnett's gaze shifted to the mark, his brow furrowing as he took in the stark evidence of her torment.

"Why?" His question hung in the air, heavy with implications Beth knew all too well.

"Women, we were nothing to him but cattle," she said, her voice laced with a bitterness that tasted like bile, "objects to be used at his discretion, discarded when no longer needed." Her eyes darkened with memories she wished could be erased.

"So he labelled you?"

"He *branded* me and me alone," she spat out the word as if it were poison, "his to claim, untouchable by others."

"He was the worst, you said?" Barnett's jaw tightened, anger flashing in his eyes on her behalf. Beth gave a hollow laugh devoid of humour.

"One night with Marcus was close to a lifetime of horror compressed into hours." She looked away, her gaze distant as though peering into a past that still held her in its vice-like grip before continuing, gesturing vaguely to her body, "these scars, they're the roadmap of his cruelty, and Victor's." Beneath the moonlight, Barnett saw not just the physical marks but the deeper wounds carved into her soul - the resilience borne from suffering, the strength forged in the fires of hell itself - and in that moment he understood the magnitude of trust she had placed in him by sharing her darkest truths. The chill of the evening crept up Beth's spine as she and Barnett stood just outside her front door. The quiet of the night was a stark contrast to the turmoil that roiled within her, spilling over in her words.

"Is that why Abraham's words about women unsettle you so much?" Barnett's voice was gentle, probing not just for understanding but for the deeper currents beneath her fierce exterior. Beth nodded, her gaze fixed on her front door.

"I can't accept a world where we regress because of chaos," she said firmly, her voice steady despite the shiver that ran through her, "the apocalypse isn't an excuse to treat half the population like livestock. Death is preferable to that brand of oppression." Barnett's brow furrowed, recognising the conviction that burned in her eyes. She had been through trials that would have broken many, yet here she stood, unyielding.

"Isn't that stance a bit extreme?" He asked cautiously, his own experiences grappling with the notion.

"Extreme," Beth echoed, a wry smile touching her lips as she wrapped her arms around herself in an attempt to ward off more than just the cold, "I've lived the extreme, Barnett. I've felt the weight of chains, both literal and metaphorical. I won't endure that again." Her eyes met his, unflinching. She could see the concern etch deeper lines into his face, but she hoped he understood. She had survived Marcus, she had survived Victor, she could survive anything - but survival wasn't enough if it meant sacrificing who she was at the core. Barnett offered a gentle nod, the moonlight casting shadows across his solemn expression.

"Thank you Beth," he said quietly, his voice carrying a weight of gratitude that matched the gravity in his eyes, "for trusting me with all this. I'll help however I can."

"Even though we're practically strangers to you?" Beth found herself asking, her curiosity piqued by his readiness to stand beside them amidst turmoil.

"Strangers," Barnett echoed, and there was a brief flicker of something like amusement in his tone before it sobered, "in a place like this, after everything we've all been through, no one's really a stranger anymore." He paused, looking up at the sky as if searching for the right words among the stars.

"I guess—"

"I lost my family, my parents and my sister to the pandemic. There's no one left for me to help but people like you." He met her gaze as Beth felt the honesty of his grief mingle with her own, a silent acknowledgment of shared loss. She took a deep breath, the cool night air filling her lungs, and released it slowly.

"It's a sad truth, isn't it," she mused aloud, wrapping her arms around herself, "the one thing binding us together is loss. We've all walked through hell to get here, and—" She trailed off, her gaze dropping to the ground, to the shadows that played at their feet.

"And?"

"I doubt it's over yet."

"Probably not." Barnett agreed, his voice a soft baritone that carried a note of solidarity. They stood there for a moment, two silhouettes under an indifferent sky bound by the invisible threads of shared hardship and the unspoken understanding that the road ahead was still uncertain.

"Thank you," Beth whispered softly, "for walking me home."

"Of course," Barnett smiled, a warm genuine smile that radiated hope and confidence within her, "any time." Beth's hand lingered on the door handle, feeling the cool metal against her palm. With a final nod to Barnett, she stepped inside and clicked the lock into place. The silence of the house greeted her, a stark contrast to the chaos of the world outside. She drifted through the living room, her fingers grazing over the back of the plush sofa, the fabric still soft and unmarred by the harshness of their new reality. Shadows clung to the corners of the room, where an old armchair sat facing the cold fireplace, its hearth devoid of warmth. Moving towards the kitchen, Beth pulled open the refrigerator. The light from within cast a sterile glow over rows of provisions - cans and boxes neatly arranged, all labels facing forward. Yet despite the orderliness, there was an emptiness to it, a hollow promise of sustenance in a time when every meal felt like a countdown. Her reflection stared back at her from the glossy surface of the microwave - a woman who had somehow kept the vestiges of civilization intact amidst the decay. She closed the fridge with a soft thud and leaned back against the counter. Beth's gaze roamed over the remnants of what could have been - a dining table set for a family that might never gather, picture frames that would remain unfilled. They had come here seeking refuge, a chance to rebuild something resembling a life. Now, each carefully chosen decoration, each piece of cutlery, seemed like a relic from a dream that was slipping further away.

"Damn it." She whispered into the quiet, her voice carrying the weight of their collective grief, the frustration of their thwarted hopes. It was supposed to be different, they were supposed to be safe here, to flourish even. But the spectre of disease, of an unknown adversary loomed over them, tarnishing the very idea of sanctuary. With a weary exhale, Beth pushed herself off the counter and made her way through the darkened living space. She reached out, her fingertips brushing the wall switch, and the house plunged into darkness. Only the faint moonlight filtering through the blinds guided her now. Ascending the stairs, each step creaked under the burden of realities too heavy to bear alone. At the top, she paused, looking back at the shapes of furniture below shrouded in shadows. A pang of longing for normalcy, for a future snatched away settled in her chest. Shaking off the melancholy, Beth continued down the hallway. The carpet muffled her footsteps, a silent companion in the solitude of the night. Reaching her bedroom, she pushed the door open and stepped over the threshold. She walked directly to the bathroom, undressing and standing before the mirror to examine her naked body. Her scars confronted her boldly, their raised texture demanding her attention. She gently traced them with her fingers, as if she were drawing a line through the unmarked areas of her skin, connecting the dots to form a continuous path. She focused on the brand on her arm, one that had healed with time but never fully allowed her to forget her past. Yet, her past was the source of her strength, linking the innocence she had in Eatonville with the resilience she found on Catalina. Each scar was a testament to a new milestone she had reached in becoming the person she needed to be to confidently face her future. Shutting off the lights suddenly, as if to extinguish the memories that had crept into her mind, she walked over to the bed. With a practiced motion, she drew the covers back and slipped beneath them, welcoming the cool embrace of sheets that promised a few hours of respite. As she lay there, staring at the ceiling, the contours of her life before the fall of society played like a silent movie behind her eyelids. She clung to those images - a testament to the strength that had carried her this far. With one final curse uttered into the void for good measure, she closed her eyes, surrendering to sleep's uncertain sanctuary.

CHAPTER 17

Beth traced the raised lines of her scars with a tender touch, a silent homage to the battles etched into her skin, as she thought about her conversation with Barnett the night before. Her reflection in the bathroom mirror revealed more than she wished to see. Her eyes once vibrant, now carried the weight of sleepless nights, and her once unblemished complexion bore the stains of relentless hardship. With measured movements she covered her lean frame, the fabric of her shirt grazing the scars as if acknowledging their presence. The pants followed, methodically fastened to shield her from the world that had demanded so much of her flesh and spirit. The rhythmic knock at the door did little to hasten her steps. She descended the staircase with measured resolve, each footfall a muted drumbeat against the wooden planks. At the threshold stood Barnett, his tall frame a pillar in the dimly lit corridor. His hand extended an N95 mask, a barrier against the invisible enemy that continued to plague their fragile existence.

"Ready?" His voice was steady, a rock amidst the swirling chaos outside.

"Not really," she replied, her tone betraying none of the reluctance that clenched her heart like a fist, "I'm not a doctor. I'm not a nurse. I did a first aid course once when I was like, sixteen. How am I expected to check on every single person and figure out how sick they are?"

"Well," he spoke in a steady voice, trying to soothe her anxiety, "Anne and Phillip are taking care of the people who are really sick, so someone needs to go and check on everyone else." Barnett reached out with his hand, offering her a mask.

"I don't know if I can—"

"Go back inside then," Barnett's voice shifted slightly, clearly showing his frustration, "while everyone else is doing their part to help you can sit inside and—"

"No, you're right," Beth accepted the mask hastily, her fingers brushing his for a fraction longer than necessary, "I'm sorry. I'm ready."

"Good," he swallowed hard, taking in a deep breath before turning on his heel, "let's go then." Beth trailed Barnett through the desolate streets, the once vibrant heart of Fort Irwin now pulsing with a muted rhythm. They reached the town hall, its robust doors standing ajar in silent invitation. Inside, the familiar scent of old paper and dust greeted them, mingling with the faint hint of antiseptic that clung to everything these days. She navigated the rows of filing cabinets with practiced ease, pulling open the drawer which contained the files for each citizen at Fort Irwin. The metal groaned, yielding to her touch as she withdrew her clipboard and several thick files.

"This should be a good place to start." Beth murmured, flipping through the pages to scan the names of those they needed to check on first, her voice low and ambivalent.

"Are you sure you're good?" Barnett's question was matter-of-fact, his gaze lingering between the list in Beth's hands and the hesitation written all over her face.

"Yes," her nod was firm, her voice tinged with resolve in stark contrast to her expression, "I had a moment. I doubted myself. But you're right, I need to do my part too."

"If it makes you feel any better, no one's doubting that you can do this," Barnett's face softened as he reached out and touched her arm lightly, "no one except you."

"The extent of my medical knowledge comes from binge watching Grey's Anatomy and House and ER," Beth glanced up from the list, locking eyes with Barnett as her expression turned serious and impassive, "I know I'm not expected to perform surgery or provide treatment but I'm sure there are more qualified people here who can do this."

"If there are, they're probably all sick anyway," he removed his hand from her arm, dropping it idly by his side, "do you always do that?"

"Do what?"

"You're scared Beth," Barnett raised an inquisitive eyebrow, "I can see it. Not to go and check on people or because of the position you've been put in, but you're definitely scared."

"Your point?"

"I've seen you angry, and I've seen you a little happy I think. But you seem to go cold and distant when you're scared."

"I don't need you psychoanalysing me, thanks," she spat bitterly, grabbing a clipboard from the table and attaching the sheet to it, "I get enough of that from Henry and Austin and the rest of them."

"Beth, I—"

"Come on," she slammed the filing cabinet drawer shut suddenly, "we don't have time for this. We need to identify who's sick, who isn't, and keep the healthy ones confined at home if we can. And when this is over, I'll have Phillip write me a referral to a psychologist." Her tone was laced with resentment and sarcasm as she marched through the doors of the town hall, wanting to remove herself from the conversation as quickly as she could. The clinic was not far, a beacon of fragile hope amidst the desert's expanse. As they entered, the sound of their boots echoed off the sterile walls, marking their passage through the deserted corridors.

"Good morning." Phillip stood by a window, his eyes tracing the horizon before settling on Beth and Barnett as they approached. His posture, though weary, remained unyielded by the weight of his responsibilities.

"Who's sick? Anyone I can cross off this list?" Beth asked without preamble, her fingers tightening around the clipboard.

"Better to assume nothing," Phillip replied, his voice even, "too many have fallen ill. Start from scratch, visit everyone. Note who is sick, how severely, then report back. Give these to anyone who might still be well but living with someone infected. It's the best we can do for now." He handed them a box filled with the new currency of survival - masks and latex gloves. Beth accepted the offering, her hand brushing against the cool plastic as she shared a sombre look with Barnett. They were the barrier between hope and despair, armed with little more than fabric and determination. With a final nod to Phillip, they stepped back into the unforgiving world, ready to tally the cost of a new plague upon their dwindling community. The sun was beginning to rise above the horizon, casting a golden hue that belied the grim task at hand. Beth and Barnett, their faces obscured by masks, walked with purpose towards the first address on the list.

"Chris Adams and his father, John." Barnett read aloud, his voice muffled but determined as they stopped before a house that mirrored the desolation of the world around them. Beth's fist rapped against the weathered wood of the door, the sound hollow in the quiet street. A cough answered from within, more of a signal than a greeting, followed by a raspy invitation to enter. Pushing the door open, Beth stepped inside, her eyes adjusting to the dim light. Chris was sprawled on the couch, a pale shadow of health, but alive.

"Chris Adams? I'm Beth and this is Barnett. We're from the town hall," Beth took a cautious step towards him, "how are you feeling?"

"Fine." The man uttered softly.

"And your father?" Barnett asked, his tone gentle, almost cautious.

"Back bedroom." Chris muttered between laboured breaths, waving a shaky hand towards a narrow hallway.

"Can I check on him?" Beth interjected, her gaze softening with concern. The nod she received was weak but sufficient permission. They navigated the hall, the silence oppressive, broken only by the distant sound of ragged breathing behind them. In the back room, the air was still, carrying the unmistakable scent of death. Under a quilt that had seen better days lay John Adams, lifeless.

"I was hoping we'd start on a better note." Barnett sighed. Beth's previous resentment and anger towards him had faded, replaced by a need for his support.

"I don't know what to say to him," she turned away from the bed, her eyes seeking Barnett's in a silent plea for guidance, "I've never done this before."

"I have," Barnett confessed solemnly, his face unreadable behind the mask, "I had to tell my best friends' mother that her son had died in combat."

"What's the right way to say it?" She pleaded, furrowing her brow as she searched his face for his charge.

"Kindly, but don't dance around it." Barnett met her gaze before looking back down the hall. Beth exhaled softly, a mix of dread and resolve mingling in the sigh.

"I've never done this before." She repeated, her voice barely more than a whisper.

"Be kind, and tell him the truth. That's all you can do." Barnett replied, placing a reassuring hand on her shoulder before they returned to face Chris and the new void in his world. Beth approached the couch, her shadow stretching across the tattered carpet as the afternoon sun filtered through the grimy window. The words she had rehearsed faltered on her lips, but the gravity of the situation left no room for hesitation.

"Chris," she said, her voice steady despite the tightness in her throat, "I'm sorry to tell you this, but your father, he's passed away." Chris blinked up at her, his eyes glassy and unfocused. Confusion flickered across his gaunt face before it smoothed back into a mask of exhaustion.

"No, you're wrong," he murmured, his voice barely above a whisper, "please, just let me sleep now. Come back later." Before Beth could respond, his breaths evened out, slumped against the threadbare cushions as he faded into unconsciousness. She exchanged a look with Barnett, the air between them heavy with unspoken words. Without another word, they stepped outside into the harsh clarity of the desert sun. Beth took the clipboard from Barnett, the paper slightly damp from her gloved hands, and made two marks - one for John, deceased, and another beside Chris' name, sick. Her movements were mechanical, the pen scratching coldly against the list before she handed it back to Barnett.

"Let's keep going." She said, her voice devoid of its usual warmth as she picked up their box of medical supplies and turned towards the next dwelling on their sombre pilgrimage. Barnett nodded, squinting against the light as he read the next names aloud.

"Melissa Baker and her aunt, Alice." He said as they approached the modest house. Beth rapped on the door, her knuckles making a hollow sound against the wood. A muffled voice called out from within, cautious yet clear.

"Who is it?"

"Beth Taylor. I work with Henry. I'm here to check on everyone." Beth announced, her words practiced and precise. There was a shuffling sound, and then the door cracked open. Melissa's wary eyes peeked out, framed by a bandana that covered her nose and mouth.

"Hi." Melissa greeted her cautiously, the tension in her voice betraying her attempt at normalcy. The door opened just enough to allow a sliver of life from inside to spill out onto the porch where Beth and Barnett stood waiting, the world around them holding its breath.

"How are the two of you holding up?" Beth's voice held a steady calm as she peered through the narrow opening of the door.

"My aunt is sick. I'm fine though, been taking care of her." Melissa responded, her eyes darting between the visitors, the bandana muffling her words. The strain in her posture spoke volumes about the nights spent awake, the days filled with worry.

"Take these," Beth said, extending some masks and gloves towards her, "it's better protection." Melissa's hand shot out, snatching the supplies with an urgency that belied her earlier claim of wellness. She offered a quick nod of thanks before shutting the door, the click of the latch sounding final. Barnett's pen paused for a fraction of a second over the clipboard before he marked Alice's name with a stark 'S' for sick and beside Melissa's, a circumspect 'W' for well, making notes that she was at risk. They turned away from the door, heading to the next house on their grim tour. The sun bore down mercilessly as they traversed the desolate streets, the heat doing little to dispel the chill that clung to Beth's spine - even with winter approaching, the sun was still warm, and an unwelcome presence. Barnett walked ahead, his tall frame casting long shadows on the cracked pavement.

"Megan Coleman and her niece, Isabella." Barnett announced, his voice breaking the heavy silence that seemed to envelop the neighbourhood. Beth approached the door, her knuckles wrapping against the unyielding wood. No sound came from within. She shared a glance with Barnett, a silent exchange of concern passing between them. Barnett stepped forward and knocked again, louder this time, his fist making the door shudder in its frame. Silence hung in the air like a thick fog, only the distant cawing of a bird punctuating the stillness. Beth's breath formed a cloud of vapour in her mask, her heart pounding against the fabric. There was something unnerving in the quiet, something that gnawed at the edges of her resolve.

"Could they have gone somewhere?" Beth's question was more to break the silence than a search for an answer.

"Maybe." Barnett replied, although the pit in his stomach suggested otherwise. Beth reached for the door handle, her gloved hand pausing as she found it unyielding, locked. A silent signal passed between her and Barnett before they stepped off the porch, their boots crunching on the path that led to the side of the house. The air was heavy with the scent of neglect, the once vibrant neighbourhood now a mausoleum of memories. The sun hung low, casting an orange hue over the desolation as they navigated around discarded toys and garden tools. At the back of the house, Beth's hand met the doorknob, turning it with ease this time. The door creaked open, revealing a darkness that seemed to swallow them as they entered. Inside, the musty odour of stale air assaulted their senses, mingling with the faintest hint of decay. It was a smell Beth had come to know too well - one that spoke of life's impermanence. They moved through the quiet hall, their footsteps muffled by the dusty carpet as they approached the bedroom at the front of the house. The door stood ajar, inviting them into a scene that stilled Beth's breath. Megan and Isabella lay in bed, wrapped in each other's arms - an embrace that transcended mortality. Their faces were peaceful despite the blood that had dried on their noses and lips, untouched by the chaos that reigned outside the walls. Beth swallowed hard, the lump in her throat stubborn. She blinked away the sting of tears that threatened to fall, refusing to let grief take hold.

"How old was Isabella?" Her voice was barely audible, choked by the weight of what they had found.

"Six." Barnett whispered, his stoic demeanour faltering for a moment before he marked off two more names for the dead.

"Let's go." She said, her tone firm despite the sorrow that clawed at her insides. They exited the house, leaving behind the stillness of the room where Megan and Isabella lay. As they stepped back into the light, Beth quickened her pace, eager to escape the confines of death. She didn't look back, knowing that some images would be imprinted in her mind forever - haunting her in the quiet moments when the harsh reality of their existence allowed for reflection. House after house, room after room, the sun was dipping below the horizon and casting long shadows across the dusty ground as Beth and Barnett stepped outside from another home. The air carried the chill of evening, and a breeze stirred Beth's hair, sending wisps across her face. She brushed them aside with a grim determination that had become second nature in these trying times.

"We should take a break." Barnett admired her resolve, but recognised the wariness in Beth despite her attempts to persevere.

"Who's next?" Beth asked, her voice steady despite the fatigue that tugged at her muscles and clouded her mind.

"Beth, we've been at this for almost six hours straight," Barnett hesitated, his gaze lingering on the setting sun, "maybe it's time to call it a day and get some rest."

"Who's next?" She repeated, her tone unyielding. With a sigh Barnett consulted the clipboard, his finger tracing down the list until he found the next entry.

"Ryan Brooks, his wife Sharon, and two children they're caring for. Sarah Chapman and Emma Hudson."

"Children they're caring for?" Beth's brow furrowed slightly.

"Found the girls not long after the pandemic started," Barnett replied, his voice tinged with the sorrow that came from too many stories like theirs, "Ryan and Sharon lost their daughter in the first outbreak, so they were happy to take care of kids who'd lost their parents. Guess they needed each other." Beth nodded slowly, absorbing the information. A family patched together by loss.

"We can't leave them wondering if help will come tomorrow."

"Then where do we stop? We won't get through the whole list today." Barnett rubbed his head with his free hand, clutching the clipboard to his chest.

"One more," Beth insisted, "one more and we'll call it a day." Without another word, they moved towards the Brooks' residence, their footsteps kicking up small clouds of dust that danced away into the fading light. Beth's footsteps slowed as they neared the house, her mind replaying Barnett's words. *Guess they needed each other*, she thought with a softness in her eyes belied the hard set of her jaw. She reached the door first, rapping her knuckles against the wood in a rhythmic pattern that seemed too loud in the quiet of the dying day. The silence that followed felt heavy, oppressive, and Beth exchanged a glance with Barnett, her green eyes clouded with concern.

"Maybe they're resting," Barnett suggested, a hint of hope in his tone that he didn't feel, "we can check on them first thing in the morning." Beth shook her head, resolute, betraying no sign of the fatigue that tugged at her limbs. Understanding the futility of arguing, Barnett stepped forward and gave the door a louder, more insistent knock. Moments passed before the sound of shuffling feet approached from within and the door creaked open. Before them stood a teenager, pale and drawn, her eyes dimmed by sickness. Beth offered her a weary smile, the corners of her mouth lifting in a facsimile of warmth.

"Hi, I'm Beth. What's your name?"

"Sarah." Came the hoarse reply, the girl's voice barely above a whisper.

"Sarah," Beth repeated, "how are you feeling?"

"I'm sick." The girl whispered, covering her mouth with the blanket wrapped around her shoulders.

"And how are Ryan, Sharon, and Emma?" Beth asked gently, peering past Sarah into the shadows of the house for any sign of movement. Sarah's gaze never wavered, her expression unreadable as she delivered the words like a death knell.

"They're dead." The air seemed to grow colder, heavier, as if the gravity of those words pulled everything downward. Beth's heart clenched, the weight of another loss settling on her shoulders like a familiar burden. She met Barnett's eye, finding the same sorrow reflected back at her, and nodded silently.

"May we come in?" Beth's voice was steady despite the shock, her eyes never leaving Sarah's hollow face. The teenager gave a slight nod and stepped back, her arm listlessly gesturing towards the staircase. Beth glanced at Barnett who nodded grimly, and they crossed the threshold. As they ascended the stairs, an acrid scent grew stronger, seeping through the fibres of their N95 masks and clawing at their senses. They exchanged a glance, each steeling themselves for what lay ahead. At the top, Beth's hand trembled on the doorknob of the side bedroom before she turned it with resolve. The door swung open to reveal a tableau of tragedy - a young girl lay still in bed, flanked by the figures of the two adults. Beth's gaze lingered on the peaceful expression of the child, a stark contrast to the violence that had unfolded beside her. Ryan's chest was static, his features frozen mid-sigh. Beside him, Sharon's arms bore the evidence of her final, desperate act - dark ribbons stained the sheets beneath her wrists. Beth's throat tightened, and she surreptitiously reached up to adjust her mask, disguising the urge to retch. Sarah's voice cut through the silence, causing both Beth and Barnett to startle as they hadn't heard her follow them upstairs "Emma died in her sleep and Sharon, she said she couldn't bear losing another daughter. She was out of her mind and killed herself in the bed, right next to her. Ryan found them like this after he woke up, then just lay down beside them. He didn't get up again." Her eyes flickered with a distant memory. In the dim light of the room, shadows clung to the corners and the air felt thick with unspoken words. Barnett's jaw clenched as he looked away, unable to hold the scene before him any longer.

"How long?" Beth swallowed hard, reaching out to close the eyes of the child in the bed before her, the silence of the room pressing against her skin.

"Few days," Sarah's gaze was hollow as she stared past them, "after he died, I fell asleep on the couch downstairs. Only woke up this morning." There was an unsettling resilience in Sarah's tone, something that spoke of a young life already too acquainted with loss. As if emerging from a long night, her eyes held a clarity that suggested she'd weathered the worst of the illness.

"Come on." Beth said gently as she motioned towards the door. She turned away from Emma, Ryan, and Sharon's silent forms lingering in the periphery of her vision, a tableau of tragedy seared into her memory. They descended the stairs, the creaks underfoot punctuating the stillness. In the living room, Sarah sank into the couch. Her body was there, but her spirit seemed distant, fixed on some unseen point as she absorbed the reality of her solitude. Beth exchanged a glance with Barnett, the weight of their task etched into the lines of his face.

"We can't leave her here alone." He stated firmly, more to himself than to her as his hand reached out, offering a new N95 mask to Sarah.

"You're coming to the clinic with us." Beth said, her tone leaning to more of a command than a suggestion.

"Thank you." Sarah didn't protest, accepting the mask with a mechanical nod. It was a fragile lifeline, a thin barrier between her and the world that had crumbled around her. Barnett's eyes met Beth's, a silent acknowledgment of the unspoken bond forming in this shared moment of humanity. With a gentle prod, they coaxed Sarah to her feet, ready to escort her away from the house that was no longer a home. The clinic's doors swung open with a sense of urgency, admitting Beth, Barnett, and the shell-shocked Sarah into its antiseptic embrace. The fluorescent lights hummed overhead, casting stark shadows on their faces as they navigated through the narrow corridors. They found Phillip in his office, his eyes tired but otherwise alert, poring over medical charts that seemed to multiply with each passing hour.

"Phillip, Sarah needs a place to stay for tonight," Beth announced, her voice steady despite the gravity of the news she bore, "or for a while." She hesitated, the weight of the words settling like lead in her stomach.

"Ryan, Sharon," he looked up from his desk, searching Beth's face for an answer he already knew, "Emma?" Beth shook her head slowly as his expression shifted from concentration to concern, absorbing the sombre update.

"Sarah will need a place to stay until she's feeling better," Barnett stepped forward, attempting to alleviate some of the weight from Beth's shoulders, "and then a new home." Phillip rose from his cluttered desk, his movements deliberate, a man accustomed to crisis.

"Of course," he agreed without hesitation, "she can stay here tonight. Anne and I have been rotating shifts to keep this place running." As they spoke, an elderly figure emerged from the back room, her posture unbowed by age. She introduced herself with a firm handshake, her grip strong and reassuring.

"Betty," she said, her voice carrying the rasp of experience, "I'll take care of Sarah." Without waiting for instruction, Betty guided the young girl through the maze of the clinic to a makeshift recovery area, the cot beds lined up with military precision. Phillip watched them go, admiration flickering briefly in his eyes before he turned back to Beth and Barnett.

"Betty won't take no for an answer," he smiled, his voice tinged with respect as a look of pride swept over his features, "she's been invaluable since last night. Walked right up to the clinic doors with a thermos full of tea and demanded I take a break. She's a retired army nurse. Probably seen more than most, and she's still standing." Beth nodded, acknowledging the unspoken truth that survival hinged on the strength of people like Betty. She glanced at Barnett, noting the grim set of his jaw, the way his eyes lingered on the hall where Sarah had disappeared. They were all bound by the same purpose - to endure, to care, to soldier on despite the odds stacked against them. Beth lingered for a moment, her gaze fixed on the stooped figure of Betty as she fluttered in and out of the depths of the clinic.

"Thank you Phillip," she said quietly, the simplicity of her words belying the depth of her gratitude, "she sounds pretty remarkable." Beth murmured, more to herself than to Phillip. The admiration in her tone was clear, even as fatigue etched lines into her face.

"She is," Phillip nodded, his eyes shadowed with the weight of their shared burdens, "how did you go today?"

"Sixteen dead," Beth continued, her voice steady despite the gravity of the news, "and pretty much everyone else is sick, or living with someone who is."

"Only about a quarter through." Barnett chimed in, his hands clenched at his sides, knuckles whitening.

"Then there's more work to be done. You'll need to inform Aaron and Mary at the town hall. They'll coordinate the," Phillip's voice held the undertone of an order, though his expression softened slightly at the edges as he paused, "the removals. Go home after that." As they left the sanctuary of the clinic behind, the evening air greeted them with a cool caress, whispering promises of rest and respite before the dawn called them back to duty. The walk back to the town hall was shrouded in silence, broken only by the crunch of their boots against the gravel. Beth felt each step reverberating through her, a relentless march that mirrored the pounding ache behind her eyes. They found Aaron and Mary in the back room, an island of stillness amidst the chaos. Mary's posture was rigid against the wall, her eyes fixed on something unseen beyond the windowpane. Aaron stood too close, his hand resting possessively on her arm, the authority he wielded palpable in the confined space. Beth cleared her throat, drawing their attention.

"We have addresses," she said, her voice devoid of emotion yet as commanding as Henry's would have been in the same situation, "sixteen dead across thirty-six homes. They'll need to be dealt with before nightfall." Aaron's response was a curt nod, his eyes never leaving Beth's - assessing, calculating. Mary remained silent, her presence diminished under her brother's looming figure. Despite not formally meeting Aaron prior to the encounter, Beth was in the wrong frame of mind for introductions. He held out his hand for the clipboard, its surface marred by a day's grim tally. Aaron's hand met Beth's as she passed it to him, his fingers brushing hers with unintentional intimacy. Beth withdrew swiftly, a silent tension coiling within her, every scar hidden beneath her clothes screaming a stark reminder of vulnerability. She kept her gaze trained on the siblings, watching the dynamics that played subtly between them. Mary's stance was a frozen image of endurance, her jaw clenched tight enough to whiten the skin at the corners of her lips. Aaron perused the list with a clinical detachment, his reaction meticulously measured, revealing nothing of his thoughts.

"Much appreciated." Aaron murmured, the words laced with a finality that suggested their presence was no longer required, nor desired. Beth felt the dismissal like a cold draft, an unspoken command to vanish from his sight. With a last glance at Mary, whose stoic expression wavered for a mere second, Beth turned on her heel before pausing and turning back to face the siblings, a dark expression on her features.

"Mary, I—"

"We're busy," Aaron's interruption was as authoritative as his cousin's, leaving a bitter taste in Beth's mouth, "any business you have with Mary can wait until the morning." Beth looked past him, recognising the fear and loathing in Mary's features. It was the same look Beth had seen in herself every time she had faced a mirror on Catalina, and if there were any mirrors on Alcatraz she was sure she would have seen it there too.

"Mary—"

"Just go, Beth," although her voice was gentle, her tone was resolute and aimed to convey strength, "I'm fine." Beth nodded to her before turning to leave. The exchange with Aaron was brief and businesslike, but it left an unsettling chill lingering in the air long after Beth and Barnett walked through the doors of the town hall. The walk back to Beth's house unfolded in silence, a quiet procession through streets that once hummed with life. Doors closed, windows shuttered, the world outside seemed to hold its breath as they passed. They entered her home, a sanctuary amidst chaos, closing the door on a day that had left its indelible mark. Beth found herself at one end of the couch with Barnett at the other, both lost in their own thoughts as they stared at the wall. It was an off-white canvas, marred by shadows that played across it in the waning light. Time stretched between them, filled only with the subtle sounds of the house settling into dusk.

"How old was Emma?" Beth's voice broke the stillness, a whisper barely louder than the sigh of wind outside.

"Twelve I think," Barnett replied, his tone bearing the weight of certainty and sorrow mingled together, "are you okay?" His question hung in the air, tentative, reaching out across the gulf of shared experience. She nodded, her motion mechanical, eyes fixed on her hands. The gloves were now a second skin, clinging to her fingers and stained with the residue of the day's grim work. She hadn't noticed she was still donning them until now, yet there they were

- a barrier she had forgotten to remove. Barnett's mouth opened, perhaps to offer comfort or further inquiry, but Beth cut him off.

"I'm going to change," she said, her voice steady despite the tremor she felt inside, "there might be something on my clothes." Her gaze lifted to meet his, a silent plea for understanding.

"We should be careful with what we track with us throughout the day." He said grimly, still staring at the wall.

"You should go too. Change, shower, rest. We have to do this again tomorrow." Beth remained at the end of the couch, her words suggesting action while her actions reflected her exhaustion. He acknowledged her words with a nod, a silent agreement sealed between them. Tomorrow would come, relentless and unforgiving, and they would face it as they had today - side by side, carrying the burden of survival. Barnett heaved himself up, every muscle protesting the day's toll. He shuffled towards the door, a lone figure etched against the dimming light of the quiet room. Beth remained seated, her gaze lingering on the wall in front of her. He paused at the threshold with hand resting on the doorknob, his back a solid line of weariness.

"Beth," he began, turning just enough to catch her eye, "you can't let this eat at you. For some reason I know you'll find some logic to blame yourself for this but none of this, *none of it* is your fault. We're doing what we have to, given the hand we've been dealt." The words hung between them, an offering of solace meant to bridge the distance their ordeal had carved into the evening air. Beth's response was a simple nod, her acknowledgment as silent as the dread they both knew would come with the dawn. With a sigh that seemed to carry the weight of the world, Barnett opened the door and stepped out into the encroaching night. The soft click of the closing door punctuated his departure, leaving Beth alone with the ghosts of the day. As the echo of Barnett's footsteps faded, Beth turned her attention downward. She stared at her hands, still encased in the latex barriers that had shielded her from the contagion but not from the sorrow. She flexed her fingers, the material bunching and stretching with each movement. The gloves whispered against her skin, a tactile reminder of the reality they faced, a reality that clung to her as stubbornly as the sweat upon her brow. With deliberate slowness, she uncurled her fists, watching as the creases in the gloves smoothed out, only to crease again as she clenched them tight, the sweat underneath swirling in and out of the folds as she moved them. It was a quiet battle, waged in the space between breaths, in the sanctuary of her solitude. Beth rose, the weariness in her limbs a stark contrast to the urgency in her mind. The house was quiet, save for the faint creaking of the floorboards beneath her feet as she made her way to the staircase. Her movements were mechanical, each step an effort to shed the day's grim tableau. The gloves came off first, peeled from her skin with a sound like whispers, and dropped to the floor - a litter of latex that trailed behind her like a breadcrumb path of sorrow. Next her shirt followed, the fabric heavy with the day's sweat and despair. It fluttered to the ground, joining the gloves in silent testimony to the trials endured. As she ascended the stairs, each rise brought her closer to the solace she sought. The zipper of her pants gave way, the metal teeth yielding without protest. She stepped out of them, leaving them crumpled on a stair, an unwanted companion to her ascent. Finally, in the privacy of her own space she stood for a moment, her skin bared to the air that seemed to carry remnants of desolation. With a deep breath that filled her lungs with the stagnant air of the still house, she pushed open the bathroom door. The shower beckoned, a promise of cleansing not just the grime but perhaps a layer of the day's harsh reality. She turned the tap and the water cascaded down, steam rising to fog the mirror where her reflection should have been. But she was past reflections now, past seeing the scars and the bags that had become her new visage. Beth stepped into the spray, the water hot enough to redden skin and burn away thoughts. Droplets pattered against the tile, a rhythm that slowly drowned out the echoes of the day's ghosts. She closed her eyes, letting the water course over her, washing away the invisible weight that clung to her, ready to face tomorrow and do it all over again.

CHAPTER 18

Beth's boots crunched over the gravel as she walked beside Barnett, the frigid morning air nipping at her body. They had been at this grim task for a week now, trekking from one family home to another as they marked off names of the sick and the dead. Once they had finished visiting each home, they started the process all over again. The tally in her notebook was tilting ominously - more lines crossed out in black than those left untouched, more dead than alive, more sick than not.

"Looks like the Miller house is next." Barnett muttered, his voice barely breaking through the silence that had become their companion. Beth nodded, her throat tight. She had stopped trying to fill the void with conversation days ago - the bleakness of their duty swallowed her words whole. At each door, Beth braced for the worst. But as they neared the end of their second round, the unexpected happened - hope, fragile and tentative, began to emerge. Some of the sick were rallying, their fevers breaking and their breaths drawing deeper and steadier. Those who turned the corner seemed to keep on the path to recuperation. Still, the relief was a drop in an ocean of grief.

"I'm glad Megan and Jason pulled through," Beth gazed over the list in Barnett's hand, watching him mark their names off for recovery, "they're handling their parents' deaths well."

"Seems like we might be coming out the other end." Barnett said as they left the Miller house, the siblings thankfully coming out the other side of the illness, albeit weakly.

"Miracles amidst the mayhem." Beth murmured, watching the sun breach the horizon, casting long shadows over the makeshift graves that dotted the yards. As they approached the heart of the community, the church's stained glass windows glinted, catching the first light of day. Voices rose in unison, a hymn swelling into the air. Beth's steps faltered for a moment. She knew inside sat the recovering and the hopeful, clinging to Abraham's every word.

"Are you going in?" Barnett asked, pausing by the entrance.

"No," Beth shook her head forcefully, her avoidance of the place had become a ritual in itself, "we have work to do." She couldn't bring herself to listen to Abraham's sermons about divine judgment and salvation. His rhetoric of a second coming and the purification and refinement of the world through sickness - it didn't sit right with her.

"It's Sunday, Beth. We deserve a day off." Barnett shrugged, his face unreadable, and stepped inside the church without her. Left alone outside, Beth leaned against the cool stone wall, closing her eyes against the warmth of the rising sun. The sound of fervent prayers and proclamations sifted through the walls. She could almost feel the weight of Abraham's words, painting vivid images of repentance and a promised salvation that felt so distant from the reality beyond the church doors.

"Empty promises," she whispered to herself, "the sick don't get a *day off*." Beth knew the power of hope, but she also knew the danger of false prophets. Abraham's influence was growing, and she couldn't help but wonder if people were surrendering to the allure of easy answers in their desperation. Pushing away from the wall,

Beth decided it was time to move on. The list of families awaiting their visit was short enough for her to continue without Barnett, and daylight wouldn't wait for anyone - not even for a reluctant saviour offering solace in a world coming undone. She pushed on alone, thankful for the peace of continuing the task in solitude. Finally, the day had been long and the list of homes to visit had grown short. Beth's fingers were numb as she folded the paper, the list that had become her constant companion over the past week. The clinic around her hummed with a cautious optimism as Anne and Phillip tended to the few who were showing signs of recovery. Sarah, whose stamina seemed inexhaustible, moved between beds with a gentle efficiency, offering water and words of encouragement.

"Is there anyone we've missed?" Anne's voice was weary but hopeful, cutting through the low murmur of the clinic. Beth shook her head as her gaze lingering on the names that blurred together, each one a person, a life touched by the relentless disease.

"No. We've seen everyone twice now. Just a few more rounds to make sure." She said, tucking the worn paper into her pocket. Her voice was steady, but inside the dread of what those final rounds might reveal gnawed at her.

"Then give us the count, Beth. What's the tally now?" Phillip's question came gently, but it landed heavily in the quiet space.

"167." The number felt heavy on Beth's tongue, like a stone sinking into the depths of her stomach. It was the kind of number that would be etched into her memory, stark against the backdrop of the community they had all fought so hard to keep alive.

"167." Phillip repeated, his searching gaze met Beth's eyes as she nodded solemnly, the lines around her mouth deepening with the weight of their shared loss. In the silence that followed, the flicker of hope from the improving patients seemed like the faintest glimmer in an otherwise darkened room. Phillip and Anne exchanged a silent glance, steeped in the unspoken understanding that fell between those who had witnessed too much loss. Beth's throat tightened as she added to their burden with her next words.

"That leaves us with 143 alive," she said, the number stark against the greater loss, "including Sabrina's newborn baby."

"Out of curiosity," Phillip's voice was low, nearly a murmur, "how many from the original Fort Irwin community?"

"113," Beth responded, each digit a sombre drumbeat in the clinic's hushed air, "including five from the group that was rescued on Catalina." She watched as Phillip absorbed the information, his jaw setting with a determination that couldn't quite mask the sorrow in his eyes.

"You're confident in your numbers?" Anne's question was more accusatory than she had intended, her tone doubtful of Beth's diligence.

"I've been at this for a week," Beth responded dryly, glancing at Anne before looking back towards Phillip, "and before that I was in charge of the town census. I don't need to check my lists to know those numbers are accurate." Anne straightened up, a briskness returning to her demeanour as if the action could somehow ward off the gravity of their reality.

"We should call for a meeting. Everyone needs to hear this together. The town hall—"

"No," Beth cut her off sharply, "that's a terrible idea. Aaron and Mary have pretty much commandeered the place. It's like they've set up their own little domain there."

"My house then," Phillip suggested, an edge of urgency to his voice, "we can meet there discreetly. Give me about an hour." Beth opened her mouth, a retort ready on her lips about the risks of such gatherings when a call from beyond the clinic's partition sliced through the tension.

"Phillip!" Betty's voice was taut with need.

"Better make that two." There was an apologetic tilt to Phillip's brow as he turned, stepping quickly towards the sound, leaving behind a room charged with unspoken fears and the brittle veneer of control. Beth found herself alone with Anne, the air between them thickening into an uncomfortable silence. She stared at the clean linoleum floor, the pale walls, anything to avoid Anne's scrutinising gaze. They were allies in grief but strangers in coping - where Beth felt drowned by the tide of death, Anne seemed to seek refuge in the structure of routine, the illusion of normalcy amidst chaos.

"I'm glad you've managed to avoid getting sick." Anne finally said, though it did nothing to ease the stifling atmosphere. She sounded sincere enough, though her statement was more of a courtesy than a genuine comment for Beth's wellbeing. She offered Anne an obligatory smile.

"Likewise."

"My time at UCLA," Anne tilted her head in contemplation, "the rotation in the lab, it taught me a lot about precaution I guess." Beth nodded, her mind racing ahead to the meeting, to the hard truths that would soon spill into the open. She knew the numbers by heart, but speaking them out loud was a different kind of reckoning - one that would make the losses real in a way that statistics on paper never could. Beth shifted in place, her gaze lingering on the rows of empty beds. The silence clung to them like a shroud. She cleared her throat, searching for something, anything, to pierce the uncomfortable quiet.

"How's Austin doing?" Her voice sounded foreign in the stillness, having not spoken to him for almost the entire week.

"Austin is fine." Anne's tone was brisk and efficient as she glanced up from the clipboard she was holding, giving Beth a measured look. She nodded, though her thoughts were already elsewhere, tumbling towards the meeting and the statistics and the inexorable count of lives lost. The clinic's air seemed to thicken with every passing second, the walls closing in.

"I should go." Beth said abruptly, the words tumbling out. Anne's mouth opened, perhaps to offer some platitude or another task. But before the sound could form, Beth had spun on her heel and fled through the door, the slam echoing behind her like a gunshot. The outside world greeted her with a dusky sky, painting the horizon in shades of bruised purple and orange. She took deep gulfs of the fresh air, trying to expel the clinic's sterility from her lungs.

"Beth." Austin's voice cut through her escape, his footsteps quickening to catch up with her retreating form. She stopped but didn't turn to face him, her body language as closed off as her mind felt.

"I'm going home to rest," she stated flatly, her eyes fixed on the road ahead, "before the meeting tonight."

"Meeting? What meeting?" Austin asked, falling into step beside her despite the clear signals to back off.

"It was just decided," she said, more out of obligation than any desire to converse, "haven't had a chance to tell anyone yet. Phillip's house in about two hours." She said without looking at him, her pace quickening as she tried to leave him behind, the weight of their losses growing heavier with each step towards solitude. The gravel crunched under Beth's boots as she strode down the dimly lit path, Austin keeping pace beside her. The sky had deepened to a dark indigo, and the first stars of the evening were beginning to prick the velvet night. Her shoulders hunched against the growing chill, a physical manifestation of the burden she carried within.

"Hey," Austin's voice was gentle and probing through the wall she'd erected around herself, "how're you holding up?"

"You don't need to do this Austin," Beth's steps faltered before she forced them onward, her voice coming out as a hollow echo of itself, "spare me the pleasantries." He stopped, causing her to halt and face him.

"I'm not trying to make small talk Beth," his eyes searched hers in the failing light, earnest and tinged with concern, "this last week I've seen it eating at you from afar. Tell me, really, how are you?" She met his gaze, the pain and exhaustion etched in her features.

"It's been hell," she confessed, her voice barely above a whisper, "every house is a new horror. So many dead. I feel like I'm drowning in it." Austin stepped closer, his presence a steady anchor.

"I can only imagine—"

"Can you?" She bit back, an edge of bitterness seeping through.

"Hey," he spoke sharply, moving a little closer and lightly resting his hand on her arm, "don't snap at me. I'm not a punching bag."

"I'm sorry," she whispered, "after everything you all did to build something normal again, this place has just fallen apart. It's not fair." She gestured vaguely towards the town, her hand trembling slightly.

"None of it is." He agreed softly, removing his hand from her arm and taking a step back.

"I was so angry at you," Beth looked up to meet his gaze, her eyelids fluttering, "when I got here I was so mad at how you'd all carried on as if nothing was going on out there, and I thought this place was so untouched—" She paused, searching for the right words.

"You were angry at us for living while you were just surviving," he interjected softly, swallowing hard as he stared at her, "and now

Fort Irwin's suffering and you feel guilty for being mad at us for having what you didn't."

"Yes," she conceded without argument, "surviving isn't the same as living, and right now I'm not sure which one I'm doing." They stood there for a moment longer, two silhouettes against the encroaching darkness, grappling with the weight of a world turned upside down.

"You're feeling defeated," he said after a pause, his voice gentle but firm, "it's okay. Just don't let defeat sink its hooks in too deep." The soft crunch of gravel underfoot was the only sound as Beth trudged forward, her shadow stretching long and thin in the fading light. Beside her, Austin's footsteps kept a respectful distance, his figure blurred at the edges by the growing dusk. Beth halted, her gaze fixed on the horizon where the sun bled its last hues into the sky.

"I've been through worse," she replied, her voice carrying a quiet strength that belied her worn appearance, "I'll survive this too." Austin nodded, though she didn't turn to see it.

"The list, is it long?"

"167," she said, the number rolling off her tongue with a heaviness that felt like lead, "some of them were from Catalina. The ones you managed to save."

"Anyone I know?" His voice held a hint of trepidation.

"Josh," her eyes finally met his, sharing a moment of silent grief, "and a few of the other girls."

"Josh," Austin's surprise was palpable, and he ran a hand through his hair, a gesture of disbelief, "well at least we're spared the trouble of confronting him about Chantelle." Beth felt a grim smile tug at the corner of her mouth, but it didn't quite reach her eyes.

"In all the chaos, I'd almost forgotten about that. It seems like forever ago we were trying to figure out what happened." They stood there for another beat, the world around them dimming further into twilight, sharing the weight of a reality that had shifted beneath their feet, irrevocably changed yet again.

"It's been a long week." Austin sighed as Beth's gaze lingered on the fading light of the day, her mind a whirlpool of loss and resilience. "How's Val doing?"

"Much better," Austin said, his face softening at the mention of their friend's name, "she's pretty determined to start helping out at the clinic as soon as she feels up to it." A genuine smile cracked through Beth's sombre facade. Val, the once indomitable force before the sickness, was clawing her way back to strength. It was a beacon of hope amidst the wreckage.

"Have you spoken to Jennifer?" Beth's voice held a thread of concern as she asked about another of their small community. Austin's eyes clouded over.

"Yeah, she's hanging in there. But it's been tough. She's lost a lot of the kids she was helping teach at the school." His voice trailed off into the encroaching darkness.

"News spreads so quickly here." Beth mused, thinking of all the information that seemed to circulate with unnerving speed.

"In a small town, news travels at the speed of boredom." Austin remarked with a wry twist of his lips.

"Where did you get that from?" Beth asked, a spark of curiosity lighting her tired eyes despite the heaviness that hung between them.

"Read it somewhere," he shrugged lightly, "some author, I think." They shared a moment of silence, the quote settling around them like an unspoken truth, filling the space with its poignant accuracy. Breaking the silence, Beth rubbed her temples, feeling the exhaustion seep into her bones.

"I need to rest before tonight's meeting," she said, her voice barely above a whisper, "make sure to ask the others if they can come, will you?"

"Of course." Austin replied, but he hesitated as she started to turn away. He wanted to say more, to offer some comfort, but the words wouldn't come. Instead he simply watched her retreat, her shoulders squared against the weight of the world she carried as she gathered the shards of her resolve, a silent sentinel as she navigated the path home.

"Is the worst of it over?" Chase looked around at the group, his eyes settling on Phillip. Looking older than the days that had passed, Phillip nodded slowly. The evening light faded to a sombre twilight, casting long shadows across his living room where they all sat, encircled by the weight of shared grief.

"We're pulling through, but we've lost so many." His eyes met Beth's, seeking confirmation.

"167." Beth said, her voice steady despite the hollow feeling behind her ribs. She kept her gaze fixed on an old photograph on the wall, unable to look anyone in the eye.

"168," Anne corrected quietly from the corner of the room before she turned to pour herself a drink, "Henry died an hour ago." The clink of ice against glass seemed disproportionately loud in the hushed atmosphere. Beth clenched her jaw, feeling the sting of tears she refused to shed. Henry, the gentle soul who always had a kind word for everyone, was gone just like that. It was a blow, another name added to the haunting litany she recited in her mind every night. Barnett's voice cut through her thoughts, brusque and pragmatic as ever.

"What happens now?" He asked, looking around at the faces clouded with uncertainty.

"What do you mean?" Austin's brows furrowed, his arms crossed defensively over his chest as if warding off the next wave of bad news.

"Who's in charge?" Barnett pressed, his gaze sharp and assessing. He looked at each of them in turn, as though trying to read their thoughts. For a moment, the room fell quiet again, save for the ticking of the clock and Anne's soft exhalations as she sipped her drink. The question hung heavily in the air, unanswered, yet demanding attention. Beth exhaled slowly, trying to dispel the weight of despair that seemed to press down on her from all sides.

"There's no plan," she said quietly, her voice steady despite the tremors she felt within, "Aaron and Mary are holding the reins at town hall, and their father—" She paused, her lips pressing into a thin line as she considered the militaristic overtones of their governance.

"George couldn't handle both the military and the town," Reece took in a slow, deep breath, "and he wouldn't want to."

"There's a reason Henry wanted to keep everything separate," Beth continued, a hint of disbelief colouring her tone, "and Abraham's preaching, gathering believers. They're latching onto his narrative. That this is the second coming, that the sickness is some divine instrument of purification." Her eyes flicked to each of the faces in the room, noting the concerned expressions and mouths set in grim lines.

"Purification." Austin shifted uncomfortably, his hands clenched into fists at his sides. Reece's face was a mask of skepticism, his arms crossed over his chest defensively. Chase stared at the floor, the shadows of defeat playing across his features.

"Refinement, purification. Abraham says that all this, this death and suffering are meant to prepare us for renewal," the last word tasted bitter on Beth's tongue, "you can ask Barnett. He's been attending some of the sermons." All eyes fell to the man standing casually against the wall as he straightened, staring at each of them evenly.

"I was a devout man myself, before the world ended," he said slowly, staring at each of them before settling his gaze on Beth, "you can't judge me for trying to maintain a connection to my faith. It's been a rough week. I was trying to find some peace." Beth nodded before turning and pacing slowly back and forth, as the group settled in their satisfaction with Barnett's response.

"*Peace.*" Anne scoffed from where she stood, glass in hand, her tone dripping with scorn. Phillip looked up at Beth as she stopped pacing.

"Do you have the list?"

"Yes," she said, pulling out a folded sheet of paper from her pocket and handing it over to Phillip, "Henry's name needs to be crossed off." Phillip took the list from Beth, unfolding it with hands that were surprisingly steady. His eyes quickly scanned the names, his brow creasing with each line he read. He stopped suddenly, his breath catching audibly before he whispered two names aloud.

"Sarah Jenkins. Lee Jenkins," the room went still, every eye turning to Phillip as he swallowed hard, the reality hitting him like a physical force, "I delivered Lee not long ago." He muttered, his voice barely carrying across the sombre gathering. Beth nodded solemnly, the weight of their collective grief anchoring her to the spot. She knew the toll each name etched onto that list took on Phillip - he was more than their medic, he was a friend and confidant to many who no longer had a voice.

"Who?" Chase chimed in, his curiosity piqued more than his resolve to stay quiet.

"I took over for Sarah at the town hall," Beth replied softly, "when she went on maternity leave." The silence following Phillip's stricken revelation was palpable, hanging like a shroud over the room.

"And what about the ages? What's the spectrum look like?" Anne, seeking to break the tension or perhaps merely curious, turned towards her father. Beth didn't wait for Phillip to find his voice again - she had the numbers etched into her mind like the names on a gravestone.

"Twenty-four children under the age of eighteen," she said, her voice steady despite the weight of the information, "thirty-four were aged fifty and above. It's rare to find a house that hasn't been touched by loss."

"Oh, and you remember all that off the top of your head?" Anne asked with an edge in her voice that bordered on anger and spitefulness. Beth's response was quick, her calm belying the storm of emotions she fought to keep at bay.

"Because I've spent the last week doing nothing but visit these families, Anne. I've seen their faces, marked off the living and the dead, and it's all up here," she tapped her temple, "like reading and re-reading the same tragic two-page novel, eight hours every day for a week straight." Anne's response was a pursed-lipped glare before she spun on her heel to refresh her drink, her back to the group as if shutting out the reality of Beth's words.

"Alright, let's focus on what to do next," Reece interjected, his voice firm, redirecting their attention, "about Abraham, Adam, Aaron, Mary—" A sudden sharp knock cut through the strained atmosphere, causing everyone to startle. Phillip rose from his seat, moving towards the door to answer it. But before he could reach the handle, the door swung open abruptly, inviting another gust of uncertainty into the already tense room. The door's creak careened through the silence, slicing the tension as Abraham and Aaron stepped confidently into the flickering lamplight of Phillip's living room as if Reece had somehow summoned them by name. Their shadows stretched long and ominous across the floor, merging with the darkness that seemed to follow them.

"Leaving your doors unlocked at night," Abraham tutted disapprovingly, a wry smile playing on his lips as he surveyed the gathered faces, "that's a safety hazard." Austin rose to meet their uninvited gaze, his posture rigid with unease.

"What're you doing here?" His voice, although steady, bore an undeniable edge. Abraham's eyes gleamed with a knowing look as they flicked towards Barnett, who stood a shade apart from the rest.

"There is nothing concealed that will not be disclosed, or hidden that will not be made known," he said smoothly, reciting his passage with ease as his tone was laced with a gratitude that didn't quite reach his cold eyes, "a little bird informed me. No matter how hidden something may seem, the truth will eventually come to light." Barnett offered nothing but a subtle nod, aligning himself physically, and symbolically, behind Abraham and Aaron. Beth's heart lurched at the betrayal, her eyes locking onto Barnett's in a silent plea for an explanation.

"No." Confusion mingled with the dull ache of hurt that settled in her chest - she felt the sting as if it were a physical wound. Clearing his throat, Abraham shifted the focus away from the silent exchange.

"A lot has happened in the past week," he began, his voice solemn yet underlined with a strange vibrancy, "it is with a heavy heart that I acknowledge my father's passing. In light of recent discussions, the consensus is clear. Fort Irwin holds too much sorrow, too many ghosts with our loved ones gone and our resources dwindling, the decision was made. Staying is no longer viable." A collective breath seemed to be held among those gathered, as if bracing against the tide of what Abraham might say next. The very walls appeared to lean in, absorbing the gravity of his announcement, while the silence thickened, laden with unspoken questions and fears.

"No." Beth whispered softly, her fists clenched as Abraham continued, his voice assuming the cadence of a preacher at the pulpit.

"In one week's time," he proclaimed, "we will embark on a journey to the Biltmore Estate in North Carolina. A place I've been preparing for us. A sanctuary where we can all begin anew, far from the shadows that have fallen over Fort Irwin." A silence befell the room, broken only by Reece's incredulous chuckle.

"You're joking right," his eyebrows arched in mockery, "we don't even have the fuel to think about a trip like that."

"Nor the sanity," Anne added sharply, her words slicing through the tension, "a month on foot? To a haven that might be just as ravaged as here?" Her arms folded across her chest, skepticism etched onto her features.

"Our engineer has been busy retrofitting vehicles with solar panels for months," Aaron stepped forward, the faint glimmer of pride in his eyes, "fuel won't be an issue. We've tested them, and they work perfectly. How do you think we've been getting around?"

"Not only do they work, but we've also ensured that Biltmore is more than ready to welcome us," a smug tilt appeared on Abraham's lips while he spread his hands wide as if to embrace the vision he painted, "imagine fields ripe with produce, gardens blooming. A true Eden for all of us to plant our roots and grow." Beth felt her stomach churn. It was all too perfect, too convenient. The calculated assurance behind Abraham's eyes didn't sit right with her, nor did the sudden emergence of this well-laid plan while they had all been fighting for survival. She remained silent, yet her mind raced, unease coiling tighter with each passing second. Beth's realisation cut through the silence that had settled in the room, each word edged with a mix of anger and confusion.

"The men who weren't with you when you arrived—"

"I did mention they were on a private mission." Abraham's smile was thin, a mere curve of his lips that didn't reach the coldness in his eyes. He spoke with a nonchalance that irked her.

"Private mission," Beth echoed, her tone sharp as she took a step closer, "you mean to say they've been out collecting supplies while we've been here, struggling to keep people alive?"

"Fort Irwin was a lost cause from the start," Abraham replied smoothly, his voice betraying no hint of remorse, "especially with my father's weak leadership." The disdain dripped from his words like poison, and Beth felt it seep into the already heavy air of the room. Austin shifted uncomfortably beside her, his gaze fixed on Abraham.

"And this move, is it optional?" He asked, the question hanging between them like a noose. Abraham gave a light shrug, as if the fate of everyone in the room meant little more than an afterthought.

"If you want to survive, you'd best come with us," he said casually as his eyes locked onto Beth's, a glint of something sinister flashing within, "besides, Ben and Tyler are eagerly awaiting your arrival at Biltmore." Beth caught the mocking undertone, the cruel twist of his mouth as he savoured their unease. It was clear Abraham relished dangling hope just out of reach - playing God in a world that had lost its bearings. Despite Austin's steady presence beside her, Beth felt the ground shift beneath her feet, the familiar sensation of control slipping away once more. Chase's chair scraped against the floorboards as he lurched to his feet, every muscle in his body taut with barely restrained fury. Reece reacted swiftly, his hands clamping around Chase's waist like a vice, holding him back from closing the distance to where Abraham stood, exuding a calm that only stoked the anger in the room. Abraham stood unwavering, unflinching.

"Let me go!" Chase protested, his struggle against Reece's grip was strong yet the older man maintained his grasp, his stance like a tree trunk rooted firm in its place.

"Tell us what you've done!" Beth's voice cut through the tension like a shard of ice. She surged forward, propelled by a mix of desperation and rage. But Austin was quicker, intercepting her path and wrapping his arms around her, pulling her back against his chest.

"Easy." He murmured close to her ear, even as she thrashed in his hold, her eyes never leaving Abraham's unperturbed face. Abraham's gaze flickered to Beth, then back to the others, his smile thin and unyielding.

"My men have been out gathering supplies." He replied, the simplicity of his statement belying its weight.

"Supplies," Beth spat out the word like venom as her chest heaved against Austin's grip, her heart pounding in her ears, "did those *supplies* include Ben and Tyler? Did you take them to force us to come with you?" She continued to struggle against Austin's unyielding control, knowing she could never break free of his grasp but continuing to fight regardless.

"You all needed convincing," the smile that curled Abraham's lips was cold and calculating, "I knew you would not come of your own volition, so I needed something to convince you." Anne stood motionless except for the slightest tremor of her hand. She watched as Beth's defiance crumbled into despair, her cries echoing off the walls while her legs kicked futilely at the space between herself and Abraham as Austin held his arms around her. She watched as he pressed his face against hers, attempting to soothe her anger.

"Fuck you," Beth screamed, her voice breaking under the strain of grief and betrayal, "Austin, let go of me!" Austin held firm, his own emotions carefully concealed behind a mask of stoicism, even as Beth's tears streamed down her face. Abraham's shadow receded with his departure, the finality in his voice casting a chill over the room. Phillip glanced around the room, at the pained faces of Beth and Chase, at the expressions of Austin and Reece struggling to soothe their friends.

"Why Biltmore?"

"It seemed far enough away that we could all escape the memories of such a sinful place. We leave in one week." He announced, the decree hanging like a guillotine above their heads. Aaron followed in his wake, the two silhouettes merging with the darkness beyond the threshold. The moment the door clicked shut, Austin's arms loosened and Beth's fury found a new target. Her gaze locked onto Barnett, betrayal etched into every line of her face.

"Why?" She demanded, the single word laden with an agony of confusion and hurt. Barnett, stoic as ever, met her eyes but offered no explanation, no justification that could mollify the sense of treachery. Silence stretched between them, charged and dense. Beth's fist shot out, driven by a tumult of emotions, connecting with Barnett's jaw with a force that reverberated up her arm. He stood unflinching, a statue amidst the storm of her wrath as pain exploded in her knuckles and through her wrist. A strangled scream escaped her lips, her hand throbbing in time with her racing pulse.

"Jesus Beth." Austin barked, concern flashing in his eyes as he moved to examine her, waving Phillip over with an urgent gesture. Phillip approached, his medical instincts kicking in as he reached out for Beth's injured hand with gentle, practiced movements. Across the room, Anne's patience snapped - her tolerance for the night's dramatics had frayed to its end. She rolled her eyes at the scene before her, her voice slicing through the tension, cold and detached

"Enough of this. I need to sleep," she turned on her heel and ascended the stairs, each step a punctuation mark to her dismissal of the chaos below, "I'll be sleeping here tonight. I'm too tired to walk home." Beth stood, cradling her hand close to her chest, the weight of the evening's revelations pressing down upon her. In the midst of loss and deception, even the solace of retribution seemed to slip through her fingers like grains of sand. Barnett silently left the house, closing the door softly behind him. Phillip's fingers were deft and deliberate as they cradled Beth's swelling hand, the skin already purpling with the onset of a bruise.

"Try not to move." He murmured, examining the extent of the damage beneath the dim light. Beth winced but remained silent, her eyes fixed on the pattern of the rug beneath her feet - a feeble attempt to distract herself from the throbbing pain and the turmoil that had overtaken the room. The air was thick with unspoken questions and the residue of betrayal that hung stubbornly like the aftermath of a storm. Austin stood close by, his posture rigid with tension, the lines around his mouth drawn tight. His gaze occasionally flickered to Beth, a mixture of worry and frustration etching itself onto his features. He knew better than to offer empty reassurances, understanding that some wounds went deeper than flesh.

"What the fuck just happened?" Reece leaned against the wall with his arms crossed over his chest. The usual calm collectedness that he carried like armour seemed to waver, revealing a hint of doubt. Reece was accustomed to control, to strategy, but the evening's events had unraveled even the best laid plans. Chase paced like a caged animal seeking an escape. Each step echoed his rising agitation, a physical manifestation of the group's collective anxiety. He shot occasional glares towards the door through which Abraham, Aaron and Barnett had all exited, as if willing it to reveal answers or retribution.

"Keep it elevated," Phillip instructed, reaching for a bandage to secure a makeshift splint, "and ice. We need to minimise the swelling." She glanced up, catching the concern in Austin's eyes and the shared confusion between Reece and Chase. Their faces were mirrors of her own inner chaos - reflections of a reality none of them had been prepared to face.

"He has them," Beth looked up at Austin, defeated, "Ben and Tyler, and anyone else who was with them." Tears of frustration and concern filled her eyes as she looked down at the floor in a feeble attempt to subdue them.

"What do we do?" Reece looked around the room at the strewn furniture which had been shuffled during the commotion.

"What *can* we do? We have to go with them." Chase threw his arms into the air, frustration and anger evident in his tone.

"We should have questioned it," Reece observed, tension etching into his brow, "they were gone for too long. We should have pushed them for answers."

"I wonder what happened to them," Beth said softly, ignoring Reece's statement, "how they got caught up by Abraham's men."

"I'm sure we'll find out eventually." Reece offered, moving over to the chair Chase had displaced and pushing it back.

"Let's just get through tonight," Austin finally said, breaking the discussion, "and tomorrow we'll make plans." His words were a lifeline thrown into uncertain waters, a reminder that despite everything, they still had each other. For now, that would have to be enough.

CHAPTER 19

Ben lay motionless, the sheets of the hotel bed tangled around his legs from his earlier tossing and turning. Each breath seemed to echo in the dark room of the *Four Jacks Hotel and Casino*, a stark contrast to the silence he yearned for. His eyes were wide open, fixated on a crack in the ceiling that meandered like a dried-up riverbed. He was aware of Neil's measured breathing from the other bed, Dustin's occasional mumble in his sleep, and Shauna's faint silhouette against the window - moonlight casting her as a guardian statue. Eddie lay sprawled on the floor, snoring softly. The stillness was a facade. Inside, Ben's mind raced laps through his mind. Julia's pregnancy was an unexpected curveball which juggled with thoughts of Beth, the woman who held his heart hostage. Decision weighed heavy, dragging him into an abyss where sleep became the enemy, elusive and taunting. With a weary sigh, he swung his legs over the side of the bed, feet finding cold solace on the carpet. The others needed rest for the journey ahead to Twin Falls, then on to Pocatello, but restlessness had claimed him entirely. A decision made, he reached for his BDU pants crumpled at the foot of the bed, pulling them on with quiet resignation. The casino floor greeted him with its stale air of desperation and faded glory. Slot machines glistened lazily in the dim light, their lack of electronic chimes a ghostly chorus to lost hopes. The once vibrant carpets now dulled and worn, led him through the labyrinth of tables and machines. Each step was a reminder of the stillness of the hour. At the far end a solitary figure sat hunched over a slot machine, a beacon of shared insomnia. Tyler's fingers drummed a mindless rhythm, pressing buttons without intent, the darkness from the screen reflecting the moonlight outside and painting his face in shades of melancholy blue. A half-empty bottle of scotch rested beside him, a silent testament to attempts at numbing reality.

"Could've sworn you were all about hitting the sack early." Ben remarked, his voice barely above a whisper as he approached Tyler's island of solitude. Tyler glanced up, the corners of his mouth twitching into a semblance of a smile.

"Just keeping the ghosts at bay." He muttered, nudging the bottle towards Ben with the back of his hand. The clink of glass against the metal machine seemed to fill the space between them, a bridge across the silence.

"Haunting memories or spirits from the bottle?" Ben quipped, though the heaviness in his chest diluted the jest. He settled beside Tyler, the faux leather of the chair sticking to his skin, a subtle reminder of the dissonance between this place and the world outside. Ben slouched into the chair, the cushion exhaling under his weight.

"Both." Tyler laughed lightly, shifting sideways to face Ben.

"Hitting it big tonight?" He cast a sidelong glance at the screen's unchanging display of darkness before turning to his friend with a wry grin. Tyler's laugh was a dry rasp as he handed over the scotch.

"Oh yeah, I've hit the jackpot," he jerked his head towards the bar where the stocked shelves displayed an endless selection of alcohol, "see that? All mine if I just keep at it." Ben smirked, accepting the bottle. The liquid burned a trail down his throat, carrying with it a fleeting warmth.

"Fuck that's strong," Ben passed the bottle back to Tyler, "easy on that. Dawn's not as far off as we'd like." The light from the moon outside flickered across Tyler's face, casting shadows that seemed to accentuate a knowing look in his eyes.

"You're not here for the ambiance," Tyler's tone shifted, "what's got you pacing the floor at this hour?" Ben hesitated, the words thick on his tongue.

"Julia's pregnant." He confessed, the admission seeming to carve out a space in the silence of the casino.

"Damn," Tyler's response was quiet but not surprised, "and Beth?"

"Not pregnant, I hope." Ben quipped, tracing a pattern on the armrest.

"That's not quite what I meant." Tyler offered his friend a half smile before turning to face him properly, abandoning his pretend play at the slot machine.

"She's still there," Ben placed a tentative hand over his chest, clutching softly at his shirt, "she's always there."

"Anyone with two eyes and half a brain could see that," Tyler said bluntly, fixing Ben with a steady gaze, "you're in love with Beth. How could you not be?" Ben's jaw tightened, the truth of Tyler's words settling like sediment within him. He nodded slowly, unable to dispute what even a casual observer could discern. The bottle sat between them, now a simple afterthought, a silent witness to confessions and crossroads. Ben's fingers drummed a restless cadence on his thigh, the turmoil within him far louder than the soft clink of the bottle every time he took a drink and set it down. He glanced sideways at Tyler, whose silhouette was intermittently illuminated. "I don't know," Ben finally exhaled, the words shuddering out of him like a building about to collapse, "I don't know what to do."

Tyler took a slow draw from the bottle, eyes never leaving Ben's face.

"Protection's a rare commodity these days," he remarked with a tinge of resignation, "what did you expect would happen?"

"Nothing. I wasn't thinking," Ben admitted, rubbing his face in frustration as a weary sigh slipped through his fingers, "I just, I was grieving. I needed something, *anything* to fill that void while being apart from her."

"Jesus Ben," Tyler muttered, setting the bottle down with deliberate care, "fucking Julia wasn't going to be your magic cure." His voice held an edge, sharp and unyielding as the broken world outside. Ben flinched, the truth slicing through him. He felt hollow, an echo chamber for his own mistakes.

"I feel like shit, Tyler," he said quietly, "I'm not here looking to justify anything. I just wanted to talk. You're my friend." Tyler's snicker was dry as the deserts that surrounded Fort Irwin.

"If you want validation, you won't find that here," he picked up the scotch again, holding it out towards Ben either as a lifeline or a further descent, it was hard to tell, "but if you need something to numb the pain tonight, well—" His hand wavered with the offer. The bottle dangled there between them, the amber liquid catching the light, casting fleeting golden hues onto their faces. It promised oblivion, a respite from the relentless churn of regret and longing. Ben stared at it, the weight of his choices pressing down on him, the pull of temporary forgetfulness against the stark silhouette of dawn's obligations. Ben swirled the remnants of scotch in the bottle, the clink of the glass a sharp counterpoint to the distant, mechanical hum of something he couldn't quite make out, letting his mind wonder if there was a generator at the hotel. Tyler's gaze was fixed somewhere beyond the dim light, lost in thought or memory.

"Remember when an apocalypse was just a plot for a bad movie?" Ben half-grinned, trying to nudge the heaviness from his chest with a bit of levity.

"Bad movie," Tyler raised an eyebrow, "I used to think it'd be kinda cool, you know? Like, living off the land. No rules, no work, no taxes. Chase and I could find a place to just exist without all the hate and judgement. Turns out, not so much."

"No, not so much," Ben agreed, his words slurring slightly around the edges, "it just means watching everything you've ever cared about either die or disappear."

"Or burn," Tyler gestured vaguely with the bottle, encompassing the unseen devastation beyond the walls of the casino, "everything burns eventually." Ben sighed, tossing back some of the last of the drink before setting the bottle between them with more care than he felt. The room felt too small, reality pressing in, suffocating.

"Time to call it," Ben said finally, pushing himself up from the leather chair, "we've got an early start."

"I guess so." Tyler nodded, taking one last pull from the bottle before standing unsteadily. They trudged through the dimly lit maze of the casino, their steps echoing hollowly against the silence as they made their way back to the room. As dawn crept over the horizon with a reluctant grey light, they loaded their gear into the Humvee. Shauna's hands moved deftly, checking each strap and buckle. Eddie double-checked their supplies, his face drawn tight with unspoken thoughts. Dustin's eyes were shadowed beneath the brim of his cap, the weight of responsibility settling upon his young shoulders. Neil leaned against the vehicle, his gaze distant, perhaps seeing landscapes that no longer existed outside the confines of their journey. Each movement was mechanical, a mimicry of life before the world had changed. Ben lifted a heavy pack, the straps biting into his palm. His head throbbed in time with his heartbeat, a dull reminder of the night's failed escape. But the mild hangover was a mere whisper compared to the cacophony of his thoughts - Julia, Beth, the life growing inside someone he didn't love, and the life he could have had with someone he did. The silence among them was a tangible thing, filled with the unsaid. They all bore scars, some visible, others buried deep. Today was another step forward in a world that only knew how to spiral into chaos.

"Let's move out." Ben's voice was rough, gravelly with the remains of sleep and alcohol. He glanced at his companions, their faces etched with the same resolve that kept them moving, kept them alive. One by one they climbed into the Humvee, the engine rumbling to life beneath Dustin's steady hands. The silence carried them forward, a shared burden among the remnants of humanity, searching for a fragment of hope in the ash-grey morning sky. The first light of dawn streaked across the horizon, painting the scenery with hues of pink and orange as the Humvee rumbled northward on the US-93. Fields lay stretched out on either side, vast and empty, a stark reminder of the world that once was. In the growing light, an anomaly appeared - a bright glow that seemed out of place amidst the desolation. Dustin squinted into the distance, his hands involuntarily squeezing the steering wheel tighter.

"What the—"

"Slow it down, Dustin." Ben said, his voice cutting through the hum of the engine. Dustin eased off the gas, the vehicle coasting as they all peered ahead, trying to make sense of the unusual sight. The light intensified, flickering like a beacon in the distance. Shauna lifted her binoculars up, her brow furrowing as she focused on the source of the light.

"Looks like a car fire, about a click up the road."

"Should we turn back? Might be trouble." Tyler shifted uncomfortably in his seat. Ben sighed, running a hand over his stubbled chin. He had pored over those maps countless nights, memorising routes and landmarks.

"No roads to Twin Falls except if we backtrack to Wells, then it's another six hours through Cedar Creek or Snowville. We can't afford that detour."

"Got it, sir." Dustin's grip tightened on the steering wheel, his knuckles white against the worn leather.

"Proceed with caution." Ben instructed firmly, his eyes never leaving the fiery glow that now cast long shadows across the asphalt. As they neared, the details emerged through the murky light of pre-dawn. The car was indeed ablaze, its flames licking hungrily at the air, crackling and popping as if fuelled by the very despair that had swallowed the world. The fire illuminated the skeletal remains of a petrol station to their left, its pumps standing like silent sentinels to a time long passed. To their right, a forest green house loomed, its colour almost unnatural against the drab surroundings.

"I'd suggest it could've been an accident," Shauna scanned the scene cautiously, "but that's probably wishful thinking."

"Keep your eyes peeled." Ben murmured, his gaze shifting from the inferno to the structures flanking it. They were all too familiar with how quickly a situation could turn, how danger lurked in the most innocuous of places.

"Always do." Came Tyler's reply, his hand instinctively resting on the butt of his pistol. The heat from the burning car washed over them as they passed, the smell of scorched metal and gasoline filling their nostrils. Ben's mind raced, considering every possible scenario - it was a trap, or an accident, or a sign of other survivors. But there was no time to ponder. The world waited for no one, and they had a destination to reach come hell or high water. The carcass of the car engulfed in flames sprawled across the road like a fallen behemoth, its fiery breath a barrier they could not pass.

"Dustin, take a left here." Ben directed tersely, pointing towards the deserted petrol station. With precision borne of necessity, Dustin swung the Humvee to the side, tires crunching over debris. Before they could find reprieve, a shadow darted across their path - a car blanketed with solar panels skidded into view, cutting off their escape. Its sleek form was a stark contrast to the desolation that surrounded them.

"Shit!" Dustin braked hard, his hands gripping the wheel with white-knuckled intensity. Almost simultaneously, another vehicle roared up from behind, boxing them in between calculated hostility.

"Out! Now!" Ben's command cut through the tension as he reached for his own weapon, a sense of urgency propelling him. The first light of dawn cast an eerie glow, rendering the scene ghostly and ethereal - faces were mere smudges, details obscured by the dimness.

"Fall back!" Tyler was already in motion, instinct and survival melding into one fluid movement. He vaulted from the back of the Humvee, boots hitting the ground with purpose. A green VW Beetle sat innocently by the curb which had now become his shield, a bastion amidst the chaos. Gunfire shattered the morning's fragile calm, splitting the air with deadly intent. Bullets ricocheted off asphalt and metal, each report a thunderclap against the quiet beginnings of day. Ben's heart hammered in his chest, a drumbeat urging him forward, even as every sense screamed danger.

"Move!" He barked at the others, his eyes scanning for threats, mind racing with tactics and trajectories. The world had shrunk to the space between breaths, the gap between life and death measured in the span of a heartbeat. Neil's silhouette flickered through the gun-smoke, a shadow dancing precariously on the edge of fate. A sudden crack split the air, a sound all too familiar, and Neil stumbled, his leg giving way beneath him as if the bullet had severed the strings of a marionette. His instincts kicking in, Tyler lunged towards Neil, dragging him behind the relative safety of the green Beetle. The car's windows, once reflecting the tranquility of dawn, now shattered under the barrage of gunfire.

"Stay down!" Tyler barked, his voice a harsh whisper lost amidst the cacophony of battle. His fingers found Neil's wound, pressing hard to stem the flow of blood that sought to claim the earth. Above them, bullets sang their deadly lullaby, each one a potential end. With grim determination, Tyler raised his weapon, sighting through the fractured glass, returning fire to unseen ghosts that hunted them in the morning light. Ben's gaze locked onto the house - a beacon of hope, a fortress in the storm. With a predator's grace, he dashed across the open ground, each step laden with peril. Reaching the porch, he didn't hesitate - his boot connected with the door, the force of his resolve shattering the serene blue and white frame. The glass yielded before him, splintering into a thousand shards that danced like ice crystals in the burgeoning sunlight. "Inside, go!" He commanded as Shauna and Eddie surged past him, their own weapons at the ready. Together, they dove into the chaos of the home, turning domesticity into a battlefield.

"In here." Shauna's breaths were ragged but focused as she reached the side room, her arms swinging a chair with practiced desperation through the window to clear their line of sight. Glass rained down like a broken chandelier, the remnants of peace scattered by survival.

"Where's Dustin?" Ben demanded, a sharp edge of concern slicing through his tactical tone. He scanned the room, the void where Dustin should have been gnawing at him. Shauna's eyes darted back the way they had come.

"I thought he was right behind us." She answered, her voice tight with the strain of uncertainty. Her words hung heavy, an unspoken fear that clung to the stale air of the house now baptised by gunfire. Together, they turned their attention outward, laying down a protective veil of cover fire for their besieged comrades outside. The rhythm of their shots punctuated the symphony of survival, a desperate plea for the morning to spare them just a little longer. Ben's gaze darted through the fractured window, past the sparks and smoke that snarled into the dawn. His eyes locked onto the Humvee where Dustin lay motionless slumped over the steering wheel, a silhouette of stillness against the chaos.

"Dustin!" He roared over the cacophony of gunfire, but his cry was just another echo in the ballet of bullets. He dropped to one knee, rhythmically squeezing the trigger of his rifle, sending rounds towards the unseen assailants to cover Tyler and Neil's vulnerable position. Casings tumbled across the wooden floorboards, clinking like morbid chimes.

"Neil, move your ass!" Eddie's voice shredded through the gunfire, desperate and raw. The anguish of command that came with seeing a brother at arms wounded and exposed. But Neil was lost in a haze of pain and shock, hand clasping his thigh, dark blood oozing between his fingers. Ben's heart hammered against his ribcage, a drumbeat urging him to act.

"Tyler! Get inside, now!" Ben bellowed, but the words dissolved into the bedlam. Pinned behind the VW Beetle, Tyler couldn't discern the urgency, the plea for survival from his friend. With no time for hesitation, Ben crawled low and fast, dodging debris and death, reaching the side door. He eased it open, just enough to squeeze through, the cool air kissing his sweat-drenched skin. Shauna and Eddie continued their suppressive fire, a relentless storm to shield their own. Amidst the threshold clutter, Ben's hand found an abandoned shoe - mundane amidst madness. With a flick of his wrist, he hurled it towards Tyler. It arced through the air, a silent siren in the gunfire. The shoe struck the side of the Beetle with a thud next to Tyler who snapped his head around, instinctively searching for the source. His eyes met Ben's, a silent communication more potent than any shout. The message was clear, and Tyler nodded, a brief dip of his head amidst the thunderous noise. A mutual understanding forged in the crucible of conflict. With one last glance at Neil's defiant form, Tyler began his perilous journey, every muscle tensed for the crawl to salvation.

"Neil, damn it, move!" Tyler's voice was a serrated edge cutting through the cacophony as he shook Neil's shoulders, desperate to drag him from the line of fire. But Neil was a man possessed, his leg painting a macabre trail, his finger hammering the trigger with reckless abandon.

"No, you go," Neil barked between shots, shoving Tyler away with an unexpected vigor, "I'll cover you!" Tyler hesitated, his loyalty warring with survival, then the reality of their dire situation sank its teeth in. With a ragged breath, he lunged towards the house, each movement a clash against his instincts to stay with his comrade. Bullets churned the air, but Ben's beacon pulled him forward. He dove, rolling over the shattered threshold and colliding with Ben. Dust and splinters filled the air as they hit the ground, a tangle of limbs and laboured breaths, their hearts pounding against the wooden floorboards.

"Are you hurt?" Ben panted, his eyes speaking volumes of gratitude and fear. Before Tyler could reply, the other door burst open with a violence that jolted them from their brief respite. Eddie stood in the doorway, a silhouette framed by chaos, his weapon an extension of his will. There was a flash, a crack that split the air like thunder, and the assailant's life ended before his body hit the ground. Tyler's gaze locked onto the lifeless figure, the finality of it stark and sobering. Then his eyes snapped up to meet Eddie's. Nods were exchanged between them, a silent acknowledgment of the necessary brutality.

"Got your back." Eddie said, his tone steel wrapped in velvet, and he pivoted back to the fray, his gun barking death as he guarded the door. Tyler rose to his knees beside Ben, the weight of survival heavy on his shoulders, but there was no time to mourn, no time for regret. They were still in the eye of the storm, and every second counted. Ben's boots connected with the floor, a solid thud echoing in the modest room as he surged to his feet. Adrenaline coursed through him, his survival instincts taking over. He reached for Tyler with haste, who was still regaining his bearings on the floor, and hauled him up. Together they stumbled into the adjacent space where Shauna had made her stand, the echo of gunfire resonating off the walls.

"Shauna!" Ben shouted, a warning lost amidst the cacophony of bullets and shattered glass. Shauna, caught in the momentary distraction, swivelled just as a bullet found its mark. Her body jerked violently from the impact, a spray of crimson blooming across her shoulder, and she staggered backward before collapsing with an ominous thud. The air sucked out of the room, replaced by a palpable dread that clung to every surface like grime.

"Shauna!" Tyler's voice sliced through the turmoil, tinged with raw panic. He darted to her side, pressing his hand against the wound in a futile attempt to stem the tide of blood. Responding to the urgency, Eddie backpedaled into the room, his weapon never lowering as he kept his focus on the potential threats lurking in the hallway. He was the anchor in their storm, unwavering even as chaos swirled around them. Ben anchored himself at the window, rifle braced against the sill. His fingers worked mechanically, finding targets, squeezing the trigger, the recoil a familiar jolt against his shoulder. Each shot chipped away at the enemy's resolve, buying precious seconds for his team. The smell of gunpowder stung his nostrils, a bitter reminder of the reality they faced.

"Keep pressure on it." Ben barked over his shoulder, sparing a glance at Tyler's desperate ministrations. Shauna's face was etched with pain, but she clenched her jaw, refusing to succumb to the darkness threatening to claim her consciousness.

"Stay with us, Shauna." Tyler implored, his hands slick with her blood, his eyes burning with determination. He would not let despair take root - there was no room for it here, not when their lives hung by such a tenuous thread. Eddie shifted, a silent sentinel between them and the unknown, his gaze scanning the dim corridor for signs of movement. The tension in his posture spoke volumes - they were far from safe, but he would stand guard until his last breath if necessary. The battle raged on, the sound of gunfire a terrible symphony that played for an audience of warriors, each note a harbinger of life or death. In the cramped room, amidst the debris of their shattered sanctuary, they fought not just for survival, but for each other. Shauna's agony sliced through the brief lull, her scream a raw edge against the drone of spent gunfire.

"We're boxed in!" Eddie's voice boomed next, urgent and ragged. Ceasing fire, Ben crouched lower, his eyes sweeping the desolate street from behind the shattered window frame. Dust swirled where bullets had danced, yet now an eerie stillness held sway.

"Anything?" Ben leaned towards Eddie, his voice barely above a whisper.

"It's quiet," poised like a statue save for the slow turn of his head, Eddie met Ben's gaze, "too quiet."

"Shauna," Tyler's hushed tone was firm, commanding even in chaos, "you need to keep it down." Her teeth found the fabric of her sleeve, biting down to stifle her cries. With practiced hands, Tyler unfurled a cloth from his pack, wrapping it snugly around her wounded arm and shoulder, securing it with a tight knot. Her breaths came out in muffled gasps, eyes shut tight, trusting his makeshift tourniquet to stem the tide of red.

"I'll check the perimeter." Eddie murmured through gritted teeth, determination etched on his face. He was always the one willing to step into the fray, a testament to his unwavering loyalty. Ben's jaw clenched. Every fibre of his being wanted to be the one out there, in control of their fate, but he knew Eddie was right. Reluctance flickered in his eyes before he gave a curt nod.

"Be careful." He said, his voice barely above a whisper, carrying the weight of unspoken fears. Eddie nodded, his grim expression unchanging as he turned on his heel and moved towards the hallway. Each step was measured, the crunch of glass under his heavy boots punctuating the silence that had descended upon the house like a suffocating blanket. The sound seemed thunderous amidst the hush, a reminder of how fragile their safety was. He reached the door, pausing only for a heartbeat to survey the street beyond. It was a desolate tableau, bathed in the faint glow of pre-dawn light, deceptively peaceful apart from the car ablaze in the middle of the road. With a deep breath that did little to steady his nerves,

Eddie slipped outside. The cool air hit him sharply, carrying with it the acrid scent of gunpowder mixed with burning rubber and metal. Eyes narrowed, he scanned the surroundings, every shadow a potential threat, every silence a prelude to chaos. Keeping low, he advanced towards the VW Beetle that offered the nearest cover. Reaching the car, Eddie crouched beside it, his gaze fixed on the lifeless figure of Neil lying a few feet away. With a surge of adrenaline fuelling his movements, Eddie closed the distance between them, his hand reaching out to feel for the pulse he prayed he'd find. But there was nothing. Just the cold, undeniable truth that Neil had bled out, leaving behind a dark pool that glistened ominously under the first light of dawn. Eddie's throat tightened, a mix of sorrow and anger bubbling within.

"Damn it." Eddie whispered, the words lost to the void. His hand lingered for a moment on Neil's shoulder, a final gesture of camaraderie, before he steeled himself once more. There was no time for grief in this situation - survival demanded they move forward, always forward, even when the way was stained with the blood of friends. Eddie pivoted on his heel, the sharp sting of a bullet grazing his leg cutting through the chaos. He stumbled, gravity claiming him as he fell to the ground with a grunt. His hand clamped over the wound, feeling the warm flow of blood between his fingers. Inside, Ben was a flurry of motion at the window, his rifle barking out retorts to the invisible threats outside. He squinted across the dimness towards the petrol station, seeking targets in the shadows.

"Ben!" Tyler's voice sliced through the air, urgent and alarmed. In a swift, practiced manoeuvre, Tyler lunged forward, his body colliding with Ben's just as a red dot danced over where Ben's chest had been a heartbeat before. They hit the ground with a thud, dust motes swirling around them as they struggled to reorient themselves. The sniper's missed shot echoed in their ears, a reminder of how close death hovered.

"Jesus—" Ben's words were cut short by the gruff shout from beyond the shattered windows.

"We need them alive, you idiot! Ben and Tyler!" The two men exchanged a look of bewilderment, eyes wide with the sudden realisation that they were valuable to someone outside. The voice carried authority, its command halting the sniper's finger.

"They know our names." Tyler whispered softly, confusion and shock etched the lines of his face as he squinted at Ben.

"Come out now," the voice boomed again, "or we'll finish off your man on the ground!" Ben gritted his teeth, a surge of protective fury coursing through him. The sniper's hesitation bought them moments - precious seconds where decisions meant the difference between life and death. They couldn't leave Eddie or Shauna, but neither could they let this unseen enemy dictate their fate.

"Tyler—" Ben began, but the rest of his strategy went unsaid, their next move unclear even to him.

"Don't move!" Eddie's voice was strained from pain and urgency as it pierced through the haze of gunfire and confusion, attempting to anchor Ben and Tyler to safety with his words alone. No sooner had the command left his lips than a heavy boot connected sharply with his midsection, forcing a gasp from him as the air heaved out of his lungs.

"Out, now! Or he gets another round!" The disembodied voice demanded, cold and devoid of mercy. Ben's protective instinct flared, a fierce need to shield his friends overriding the pounding fear in his chest. He locked eyes with Tyler, finding unspoken agreement there. They moved together, a unit forged in crisis, reaching down to haul Shauna upright. Her breaths came in short and painful gasps, her injured shoulder a testament to the chaos they'd endured.

"Easy, Shauna." Tyler murmured, though his eyes never left the shattered threshold before them. Together, the trio shuffled down the debris-littered hallway, their movements deliberate, bracing for whatever hell awaited them beyond the broken door. The cool morning air hit them like a slap as they emerged, the transition from the house's shadowed interior to the dawning light disorienting. Before they could adjust, before they could even contemplate their next move, a blunt force struck each of them from behind. Stars exploded behind Ben's eyelids, a grunt escaping him as he crumpled to the ground, the taste of dirt and blood mingling in his mouth. Hands, rough and impersonal, yanked at his wrists and bound them tightly with coarse rope that bit into his skin. His feet were next, secured just as mercilessly. Through the ringing in his ears, he heard Shauna's stifled cry, and Tyler's low growl of defiance. They were dragged like rag dolls across the uneven road, their bodies jostling against the asphalt. A van loomed ahead, a spectre of uncertainty - their next cage, another chapter in this waking nightmare. Ben's mind raced, every tactical thought he'd ever learned surfacing and sinking in the tumultuous sea of his consciousness. But strategy meant little when his hands were tied and their fate rested in the hands of their captors. Dazed and disoriented, Ben's attempt to rise was a feeble struggle against the ropes binding his limbs. A sudden sharp impact at the back of his head sent him sprawling once more, face up to the pale sky, its light mocking his vulnerability. The throbbing in his skull resonated with every heartbeat, blurring the edges of reality. Through the haze, a figure loomed over him - a silhouette etched against the dawn sky. Squinting, Ben's focus sharpened on a face that tugged at the threads of his memory. Recognition flickered like a dying ember as the man's features came into his distorted and blurry view, carved from Ben's past with an unsettling familiarity.

"Rocky!" Another voice called out, jarring Ben from his stupor. The familiar man turned on his heel, issuing orders with a cold efficiency that chilled Ben's blood despite the warmth of the rising sun.

"Strip 'em," he barked to his subordinates, "weapons, armour, anything that's not scorched or shot to hell."

"Rocky." Ben whispered, watching through slitted eyes as another man nodded curtly, making for their abandoned Humvee with purpose.

"Take it back to Fort Irwin," the familiar man instructed, "and tell him it's done." A heavy silence fell upon them as the familiar man approached once again, his gaze sweeping over the prone figures of Ben, Tyler, Shauna, and Eddie. With a gesture, he commanded one of his men to tend to the wounds of the fallen. The man knelt beside Shauna first, his hands surprisingly gentle as he examined her shoulder, then moved to Eddie, assessing the extent of his injuries. Lying there, bound and helpless, Ben tried to piece together the fragments of his situation - the identity of the familiar man, and what fate awaited them beyond the grim certainty of the present. But his head throbbed and his mind raced. He could only watch through his blurred vision as their captors rifled through the pockets of the dead, harvesting the spoils of battle with detached efficiency. The air was thick with the scent of smoke and iron, and somewhere beneath it all the faintest trace of betrayal lingered, unspoken but palpable. Rough hands gripped Ben's arms, hoisting him from the cold ground. He stumbled forward, his feet dragging as he was hauled towards the van. The metal surface of the vehicle felt biting against his skin as they pushed him inside, the confined space amplifying every grunt and shuffle.

"Watch your head." A mocking voice said as Tyler was thrust in beside him. Shauna followed, wincing audibly. Eddie was next, grunting from the effort it took to move with his injured leg.

"Where are you taking us?" Ben's voice was rough, strained from the dust and the lingering taste of blood in his mouth. Laughter echoed from the front seat, deep and knowing.

"Get comfortable." The driver called back, a hint of southern drawl colouring his words. The engine rumbled to life, sending vibrations through the floor of the van.

"We've got ourselves a long drive ahead," another man entered the passenger side, "North Carolina ain't just around the corner." In the dim light that filtered through the small windows, Ben could make out the outline of Tyler's jaw set in determination. Shauna leaned back against the wall, her breaths shallow and controlled despite the pain that was coursing through her shoulder. Eddie's eyes were closed, his forehead creased in concentration or prayer, Ben couldn't tell which. The familiar voice belonged to someone he knew, but in his confusion he couldn't quite figure it out. It hung in the air around him, an unasked question that he wasn't sure he wanted answered. Instead they all settled into the uneasy silence, each lost in their thoughts as the van pulled away, leaving behind the acrid scent of smoke and the warmth of the rising sun.

CHAPTER 20

"I have to go and see Beth." Austin insisted, his voice low but firm. The tension in the air was palpable, charged like the static before a storm. His fingers were curled into fists at his sides as he stood resolute against Anne's questioning gaze.

"You're out of your mind," Anne's voice rose with incredulity, her hands thrown up in exasperation, "you're that determined to get yourself caught? With soldiers posted at every corner?" Austin's jaw clenched, the muscles working under his skin as he met her stare.

"I haven't seen her since the meeting," he said, a note of desperation underlying his words, "I'm worried about her."

"Worried," Anne's eyes narrowed, searching his face for something, anything that might make sense of his recklessness, "why does it matter so much?"

"Because she's my friend, Anne." Austin replied, a hint of pleading creeping into his tone. He took a step towards the door, ready to leave.

"Did you fuck her?" The question sliced through the tension like a blade, stopping Austin dead in his tracks. He turned slowly, his expression a mix of shock and disbelief.

"Are you seriously asking me that now? With everything that's going on?" His voice was barely above a whisper, yet it filled the room, bouncing off the walls and underscoring the gravity of the accusation. Austin's hand lingered on the doorknob, his resolve faltering as Anne's voice cut through the silence that had settled between them. Her eyes were red-rimmed, her posture rigid with the burden of unspoken fears.

"It's all I can think about, Austin. Ever since that town hall meeting, ever since Abraham messed with everything and you," she hesitated, her voice low and trembling, "you changed. You've been distant, evasive. It keeps replaying in my mind over and over." He let go of the doorknob, his shoulders sagging under the weight of her words. His gaze fell to the floor, unable to meet hers. The room felt stifling, the air thick with accusation and doubt.

"Anne—"

"You don't touch me anymore. You don't look at me, not the way you look at her." Her voice was soft and quiet, similar to how a child might talk to their mother after being reprimanded.

"Anne, you're being irrational." Austin muttered, though his voice lacked conviction. He turned away from her, his footsteps heavy as he attempted to escape the conversation, to escape the look of betrayal that marred her usually gentle features. But her next words halted him once more, echoing down the hallway like a verdict.

"Maybe I am crazy Austin, but not about this," Anne's voice was sharp, insistent, "if there's nothing to hide, then just say no. Did you sleep with Beth? It's not complicated. If it didn't happen, then it should be easy to say no." Austin paused at the end of the hallway, his back still to her.

"Fucking hell, Anne." A war raged within him, truth wrestling with fear, loyalty clashing with guilt. Slowly, he turned around to face her, the distance between them charged with unspoken confessions. The dim light from the bedroom cast shadows across his face, hiding his eyes.

"Do you love her?"

"Anne—"

"They're simple questions, Austin. If the answer is no, then it should be a simple answer." Anne's voice cracked, her plea almost a whisper now as her chest heaved with the effort to keep herself composed. Austin opened his mouth, yet no sound emerged, his internal struggle rendering him mute before the woman he had vowed to always be honest with. Silence stretched between them, a gulf widening with every second he remained wordless. His throat felt dry, words lodged deep within, unyielding. The moment held, fragile and tense, a single thread of trust threatening to snap under the weight of unsaid truths. The air was thick with the unspoken as Austin finally broke the silence, his voice low and strained.

"It's not a simple answer," he murmured, the words tumbling out like stones, "to either question." Without another glance at Anne, he turned his back on her once more, his footsteps heavy with the weight of their fractured trust as he descended the staircase. Anne remained motionless for a heartbeat before folding inward, her slender form collapsing onto the edge of the bed they had shared. Shadows from the moonlight outside danced across her as she buried her face in her trembling hands, her body racked by silent sobs that spoke volumes of betrayal and heartache. Austin slipped through the back door into the night's embrace. Clad in black, he became a shadow among shadows, moving stealthily towards the fence. With practiced ease he vaulted over it, landing softly on the other side in the dusty sand field that stretched behind their home. The world around him was eerily quiet, save for the distant footsteps which echoed through the quiet streets, military patrols enforcing the curfew. He paused a moment to catch his breath, his chest rising and falling beneath the dark fabric of his shirt.

His mind raced with images of Anne's tear-streaked face, but he pushed them aside. There was no turning back now. With a swift glance around Austin set off again, crossing the field diagonally. Grains of sand kicked up behind him, whispering of his hurried passage. He reached Blackhawk Drive and crouched low, his eyes scanning for any sign of movement. Two soldiers emerged, their silhouettes stark against the dimly lit street. They patrolled with a casual indifference that belied the tension hanging in the air. Austin held his breath, waiting for the right moment. As soon as the soldiers passed he darted forward, slipping down the alley that ran behind Beth's house. Every step he took felt like a further betrayal, yet he moved with a determination that was fuelled by worry for his friend and the chaos that lay beyond the safety of familiar walls. Beth's fingers trailed along the cool metal shelves inside her fridge, the hollow echo of emptiness mirroring the pit in her stomach. The meagre offerings seemed to mock her with their insufficiency. With a deep sigh, she calculated whether consuming it all would offer some semblance of comfort or just remind her of the trouble that lay ahead. As she leaned in, contemplating the remnants of her life as represented by the dwindling food supplies, an unexpected knock at the back door jolted her upright. Her heart leapt into her throat. Only after a fleeting spike of panic did logic seep back in - any unwelcome visitor would have made their presence known at the front entrance, with authority and likely under orders. Composing herself, Beth shut the fridge door with more force than necessary and approached the sliding glass that separated her from the outside world. She peeked through the curtain, spotting Austin's shadowy figure waiting with an air of urgency. She slid the door open just enough for him to slip inside.

"Jesus Austin, what're you doing here?" Beth hissed, her voice low but laced with alarm as she glanced over her shoulder before yanking the curtains closed once more.

"I needed to talk to you." He replied tersely, his eyes scanning the dimly lit kitchen as if expecting to find answers hidden in the corners. Beth folded her arms across her chest.

"Now? We've been locked down tighter than Fort Knox. You know that."

"I know, but I had to see you." Austin's gaze settled on her, dark and intense.

"We're walking on a razor's edge here," Beth's shoulders dropped slightly, wariness giving way to a flicker of concern, "you shouldn't have risked it."

"Sometimes risks are worth taking." His voice was steady, but Beth saw the muscle ticking in his jaw, betraying the storm beneath his calm exterior.

"Just keep your voice down," she let out a breath she hadn't realised she had been holding, "I've had patrols past my door every half hour." Forcing a tight smile, she motioned towards the bar stools at the kitchen island. The silence between them charged with words unspoken and fears unvoiced, each aware that the town's curfew was the least of the dangers lurking outside the fragile sanctuary of Beth's home. Austin leaned against the countertop as he sat, watching as Beth rummaged through drawers for something. Her movements were brisk, her focus elsewhere, as if the act of leaving required no more thought than discarding an old pair of shoes.

"Are you ready to go tomorrow?" He asked, his voice cutting through the silence that had settled between them. Beth paused, a wry smile playing on her lips as she turned to face him, a dishtowel clutched in one hand.

"Ready? I didn't bring anything here with me," she said, her tone

light but tinged with a certain resignation, "not much to pack."
Austin tilted his head slightly.

"I didn't mean belongings, Beth."

"I know what you meant," her response was sharp and impassive, "it must be harder for Anne and Julia though, leaving their homes behind." She glanced around the sparse kitchen, its once familiar edges now sharpened by the reality of impending departure. The mention of Anne stiffened Austin's posture subtly, a reaction he hoped Beth wouldn't notice. He pushed himself off the counter and leaned back in the chair.

"What about your plan?" He asked, skirting around the reference to Anne. Beth's laugh was hollow as she shook her head, abandoning her search in the drawer.

"My plan," she echoed as she moved past him towards the refrigerator, "you think I have some sort of master plan to get us out of this mess?" She pulled open the door, revealing the barren shelves inside.

"Figured you might," Austin admitted, following her with his gaze, "after all, you're always one step ahead."

"Maybe once," Beth conceded, reaching for a half-empty bottle tucked away at the back of the fridge, "but not this time. This time we're just playing the hand we've been dealt." She unscrewed the cap and took a measured swig, her eyes meeting his over the rim of the bottle. Austin watched as Beth's fingers gripped it tightly, the casual ease of her clutch belying the tension that seemed to radiate from her. He wanted to believe there was a way out, that Beth had an ace up her sleeve, but the stark truth was laid bare in her candid admission. There was no plan, only the hope that somehow, they would make it through what came next. Beth extended the bottle towards Austin, a wry smile twisting her lips.

"No thanks."

"Go on. We might as well empty this," she said, her voice laced with a fatalistic edge, "it's not like we can pack it for the trip." Austin slowly took the bottle from her hands, the glass cool and slightly damp against his palm. He tipped it to his lips, feeling the liquid burn its way down his throat, the warmth spreading through his chest. He set the bottle on the counter with a soft thump, his eyes never leaving Beth's face.

"I don't believe for a second that you haven't spent the last week locked away in here," he gestured to her vast, empty living room, "coming up with some way to get us out of this."

"What do you want from me, Austin?" Beth asked, leaning back against the fridge, her arms folded across her chest. He hesitated, his mind racing. The question wasn't just about the moment, about the drink or the late-night intrusion - it was about everything that had led them here.

"I want your mind. I want that girl," he started, then paused as he took a deep breath, "I want that resilient woman, that version of you who never gave up on Alcatraz or Catalina. " Beth's gaze dropped to the floor, a bitter laugh escaping her. When she looked up again, her eyes were hard, her jaw set.

"My mind," she echoed hollowly, "you think I've got some grand scheme tucked away? That I'm holding onto some brilliant escape route?"

"Isn't that what you do?" His words were almost a plea, searching for the strength in her he had always admired.

"Used to," she corrected, a strand of hair falling across her face as she shook her head, "but no one listened when it mattered. Abraham has Ben and Tyler now, and what choice do we have? We go with him, and make sure they're safe." Her voice cracked slightly on their names - an admission of defeat that Austin had never heard from her before.

"Then that's what we'll do," Austin said firmly, his resolve steeling at the sight of her distress, "we stick together, keep them safe, and figure out our next move from there." Beth's expression softened, a weary sense of camaraderie passing between them. They were in this together, bound by circumstance and the need to protect those they cared about, and in that moment Austin knew that even without a plan, they would face whatever came next side by side. Austin's fingers traced the empty bottle's label, his gaze never leaving Beth's face.

"I'm just along for the ride now," she whispered, wiping away a single tear that had fallen down her cheek, "I'm done trying to make people listen."

"I'm sorry," he said, his voice a low thrum of sincerity in the dimly lit kitchen, "for not listening to you when it could've changed things." Beth's laughter was a sharp crack in the otherwise muted room, her shoulders shaking with cynicism rather than amusement. She tilted her head, regarding him with a mix of pity and disbelief.

"And what do you think *this* is?" She challenged, leaning back against the counter with a deliberate casualness. Her eyes filled with tears from her frustration but she refused to let them fall. The silence hung between them, heavy and expectant. Austin's throat tightened, words lodged like stones.

"Beth—"

"You don't even know," Beth continued, pushing off from the fridge to pace the small space between the sink and the refrigerator, "you want to know what I think? I think Abraham's been playing us all along." Her steps were measured - each one seemed to draw the air tighter around them. Austin's eyes snapped up, catching the glint of conviction in Beth's gaze.

"Playing us?"

"Abraham, he's been planning something big. Not just some temporary shelter or a safe zone," she paused, running a hand through her hair, her face set in grim determination, "he's moving us to a fortress. A large estate that he's been prepping, probably for months now. Maybe even a year. Somewhere he can keep an eye on everyone through a handful of exits while playing God as he *rebuilds* the earth or whatever grand delusion he's harbouring."

"An estate—" The word felt foreign on Austin's tongue. But as he spoke it, images began to coalesce - high walls, surveillance cameras, gates guarded by those loyal to Abraham's cause. It made a chilling kind of sense, and it explained the meticulous control, the orchestrated movements of their lives that had become increasingly suffocating.

"Exactly," Beth confirmed, her voice dropping to a whisper that carried a weight of its own, "a controlled environment where he can monitor every single breath we take, and we're all just pawns in whatever twisted game he's playing." Austin watched her, the woman who always had a plan now seemingly without one, and yet her insight cut through the fog of confusion and fear. Abraham's endgame was coming into focus, and it was far more sinister than any of them had anticipated.

"Well, shit." Austin's fingers traced the patterns on the stone countertop as he watched Beth pace back and forth, her silhouette intermittently illuminated by the dim light spilling from the kitchen. The bottle in her hand was half-empty, but her words were razor-sharp, slicing through the haze of alcohol with unsettling clarity.

"Think about it Austin," she spat bitterly, swigging from the bottle, "a church, a congregation mourning their dead. It's perfect for manipulation. Everyone looking for answers, for comfort. And then there are the women and children. Pawns, every single one of us." Her voice dripped with cynicism. Austin's brow furrowed, trying to keep up with her rapid connections.

"What?"

"Messengers for his so-called divine mission," she sneered bitterly, "he preaches about the second coming like some baby Messiah will pop out any minute and save us all. The women? Breeding machines awaiting to deliver the chosen one who'll lead his holy army. It's sick." Austin swallowed the knot forming in his throat.

"To what end, though?" He needed to grasp the full scope of Abraham's plan, if only to combat the dread rising within him. Beth's laugh was hollow, devoid of humour.

"Fucked if I know. I just," she trailed off, staring at the remnants of liquor swirling in the bottle, "some people aren't looking for anything logical. They can't be bought, bullied, reasoned, or negotiated with."

"I always thought you had everything figured out, Beth." Austin managed a weak laugh, trying to lighten the mood despite the gravity of their discussion. She tipped back her head, taking another defiant gulp.

"Some men just want to watch the world burn." There was a bitter edge to her smirk as she met his gaze, handing the bottle to him.

"Which famous philosopher said that?" Austin asked, offering her a half-smile as he took a drink and handed it back to her.

"Michael Caine, The Dark Knight." She raised the bottle in a mock salute, her eyes glinting with dark humour. Austin closed the gap between them, his steps measured as he navigated the tight space in the kitchen. The room felt smaller somehow, the walls closing in with the weight of their conversation.

"What's your move then?" His voice was steady, but his eyes betrayed the concern that shadowed his thoughts.

"I don't have a move to play." Beth's hand trembled ever so slightly as she brought the bottle to her lips again, the liquid catching the dim moonlight that filtered through the curtains drawn tight across the windows. She took a long pull, the sharp scent of alcohol permeating the tense air between them.

"Sure you do." He met her stance, unblinking, looking down at her and studying her face. Lowering the bottle, she met Austin's gaze with a fire that belied the calm facade she projected.

"First, I'm going to make sure Ben and Tyler are safe," she declared, her voice laced with a steely resolve, "then I'm going to torch the ground under Abraham's feet. With me on it too if I have to."

"Isn't that a bit drastic?" Austin asked, the furrow of his brow deepening. He understood the stakes, but the thought of Beth sacrificing herself was something he couldn't stomach. A scoff escaped her, and she waved the bottle as though it were an extension of her arm. He didn't respond but instead reached for the bottle, his fingers brushing against hers as he took it from her grasp. Without a word, he tipped the container back, feeling the burn as he swallowed the last of its contents. The finality of the empty bottle echoed in the silence that followed. Beth watched him, her expression unreadable for a moment before she broke the stillness.

"You're not staying here tonight." She said abruptly, her tone leaving no room for argument.

"Where did that come from?" Austin's brows knitted together in confusion, his thoughts momentarily diverted from the chaos that awaited them at dawn.

"Because you need to be sober enough to get back home without getting caught," her words were firm, but there was an undercurrent of concern that softened the edges of her command, "it's dangerous enough without adding drunken stumbling into the mix." Austin knew she was right, the reality of their situation settling over him like a heavy cloak. With a resigned nod, he placed the empty bottle on the counter, the hollow sound a stark reminder of the sobriety he needed to face. The room was charged with tension, the silence broken only by the clinking of glass as Beth retrieved another almost-empty bottle from the cupboard. Austin watched her with a hollow feeling in his chest, the weight of his confession hanging between them like a suffocating fog.

"I don't think Anne wants me there anymore." Austin muttered, his voice betraying the hurt he tried to conceal. Beth turned, bottle in hand, her eyes meeting his with a mixture of surprise and concern.

"Why?" She probed, her fingers idly twisting the cap off the bottle. Austin exhaled slowly, a bitter laugh escaping him before he could stop it.

"I told her." He said simply, leaving the magnitude of those words to hang heavily in the air. Beth's lips parted slightly, a pause in her movement as she processed his admission. She took a slow drink, letting the liquid fortify her before she spoke again.

"What *exactly* did you tell her?" Her voice was steady, but Austin could see the curiosity burning behind her gaze.

"Not much," he lied, his eyes dropping to watch the play of light on the bottle in Beth's hand, "but she knows." Beth nodded slowly, taking another sip before addressing him again.

"Was this really the right time for that kind of honesty?" The question was pointed, carrying an edge that made Austin wince.

"Anne was insistent," he replied, his voice a mixture of defence and defeat, "she wouldn't let it go." Raising an eyebrow, Beth set the bottle down on the counter with deliberate care.

"Well, at least she won't have to worry about anything at Biltmore." She mused, her tone edged with a dark humour that didn't quite reach her eyes as confusion furrowed Austin's brow.

"What do you mean?"

"Anne will be *necessary*," Beth explained, her expression growing distant as she considered the implications, "and he, he won't *touch* her. Not if he wants to keep her healthy, not if he wants to keep her sane." She spat the words as if they were poison. Understanding dawned on Austin, and he felt a cold shiver run down his spine. He knew the stakes had just risen, the game they were all unwilling players in had shifted into something far more sinister. With a heavy heart, he watched Beth take another drink, wondering how much more they'd have to endure before this nightmare ended. The silence stretched between them, taut as a wire.

"But what does that mean?" Austin's perplexed voice filled the gap. Beth's gaze on him was incredulous, her eyes wide with disbelief at his naivety.

"Really? You haven't pieced it together," she shook her head in exasperation, "Abraham believes the second coming of Christ is upon us."

"I know," Austin said, irritation lacing his words, "you said that already." He clenched his jaw, fighting the frustration boiling inside him.

"Right, but you don't get it," Beth leaned forward, her voice low and urgent, "Abraham sees himself as a messenger. A herald for this supposed messiah. And this *second coming*? It's not just an event, it's a message. One he intends to spread." Head tilted down, her dark green eyes looked up at him, somehow a balanced and contradictory mix of emptiness and ferocity. Confusion clouded Austin's face as he tried to follow her train of thought. He was a man of action, not one for deciphering cryptic prophecies or unraveling religious zealotry. But he needed to understand, to grasp whatever twisted logic was driving Abraham if they were going to survive this.

"Go on." He pressed, his focus sharpening on her words.

"Think about it," Beth acquiesced, her tone insistent, "he'll want doctors close by, medical professionals like Anne, to ensure that his *message* is born healthy, free of any complications."

"Born," Austin echoed, a cold realisation creeping into his heart, "you mean—"

"Exactly," Beth cut in, her lips curling into a bitter smile, "the women are nothing more than vessels to him, envelopes for his grand message. All part of his deluded vision to repopulate the earth under his divine guidance, led by his second coming of Jesus Christ." The revelation hit Austin like a physical blow, his mind reeling from the implications. The pieces fell into place, forming a picture so grotesque he could scarcely believe it. Abraham's plan was more than just control, it was manipulation of life itself, with Beth and countless others reduced to mere carriers for his fanaticism.

"Jesus." He muttered, a curse and a prayer all at once.

"Literally." Beth quipped, raising the bottle in a mock toast once more before taking another drink.

"You should go easy on that." Austin's voice was a strained echo in the sparse kitchen, his mind grappling with the grotesque notion.

"You want to know what I've been doing this last week? Cooped up here all alone," Beth slurred, her words weaving through the thick air of intoxication, "I've been going over and over what's going to happen. All the scenarios in my head. I've played out every single one. I've thought about every word he's said, every bible passage he's spat at me, and every possible scenario comes to the same conclusion." With unsteady arms, she hoisted the nearly empty bottle to her mouth, its contents sloshing before she tipped it back, finishing it off. Austin watched her sink into that hollow cheer, the liquid courage fuelling her bitter bravado. The bottle clinked against the countertop as she set it down with more force than necessary, her eyes glinting with a rebellion that was both fiery and tragic.

"But after what happened on Alcatraz and Catalina—" His attempt to reason through history's warning signs was abruptly cut off.

"Yes, and we get to experience it all over again," Beth's voice dripped with sarcasm as she swayed unsteadily on her feet, "welcome to the apocalypse, enjoy your stay." With a swaying step, she reached out for another half-empty bottle, her determination clear in the tight set of her jaw. But Austin was quicker, his reflexes honed by necessity. He snatched the bottle from her grasp, the glass cool and firm in his hand, a stark contrast to the warmth of her skin.

"You don't want to be hungover for the long drive," he said firmly, though his heart hammered with concern for her well-being., "it's going to be a rough couple of days. You should take it easy." Beth fixed him with a hard look, her eyes narrowing as she weighed his words.

"I'll need a clear head when we get there," she responded, her voice steely, "so I'd rather be drunk now and get it out of my system." There was a resolve in her stance, a desperation to cling to control in a world that offered none. Austin recognised the impulse, knew it all too well himself - the need to feel something, anything, other than the dread of the unknown that awaited them at dawn.

"Fine." Austin's hand trembled slightly as he relinquished the bottle, the weight of it leaving his grasp like the fading remnants of hope. Beth didn't hesitate - she tipped the bottle back, a sharp gulp punctuating the silence between them. Lowering it, she met Austin's gaze with an unspoken finality that tightened around his chest.

"You should go." She said softly, her voice carrying the weight of unshed tears and unsaid goodbyes.

"Are you in love with Ben?" The question caught in his throat, but Austin forced it out, his need for truth greater than his fear of its answer. Her nod was small, almost imperceptible. But to Austin, it was a seismic shift in their reality.

"I shouldn't have slept with you." Beth admitted, her confession slicing through the already charged air.

"Hey," Austin's breath hitched in his throat, his own heart aching, "we were both there. It's a mistake we made together." As he spoke, he fought to keep his voice even, to mask the torrent of emotions threatening to break through his carefully constructed facade. Beth's eyes held his for a moment longer, a silent conversation passing between them before she looked away, signalling the end of their shared confession.

"You should leave now," she insisted more firmly this time, "you're right, it'll be a long couple of days. You need rest." He understood the dismissal, the need to be alone with her thoughts, and her regrets.

"Sure." As Austin turned towards the back door, the soft rustle of Beth's voice stopped him mid-step.

"Make things right with Anne," she called after him, her tone laced with a sobering clarity, "tell her it was a mistake, one that will never happen again." Without looking back, Austin moved towards the door, each step heavy with the burden of his unrequited love and the daunting task of seeking forgiveness from a woman who had every right to turn him away. Sleeping with Beth he might have been able to come back from in time, but Anne knowing his love for her was another thing entirely. He stepped into the cool night, the door closing behind him with a soft click that echoed like a period at the end of a sentence - a chapter of their lives concluding in the quiet darkness.

Dawn had barely broken when the base sprung to life, its occupants herded towards a fleet of military vehicles and minivans all clad with solar panels, some loaded with supplies looted from Fort Irwin's meagre stockpiles. Beth watched through a veil of fatigue as families and individuals were sorted like chess pieces across a board of steel and rubber. Her eyes darted from face to face, but it was the void where George and other familiar soldiers should have been that caught her attention. Left behind, she surmised, to erase the last traces of their occupancy.

"Reece, Val, Chase—" She muttered under her breath, ticking off each name as though trying to find reason in their scattered arrangement. She could see Anne's knuckles white against the metal frame of one van, Phillip's stoic expression as he climbed into another. Austin avoided her gaze, his silhouette framed by the rising sun as he stepped into a truck further down the line.

"Ma'am?" A soldier gestured impatiently towards an open van. It was Beth's turn to be moved, another pawn in this grand scheme that was slowly coming into focus. With her head still buzzing from the night before, she approached the vehicle, her movements automatic as the weight of impending change hung heavy on her shoulders.

"Actually," came a calm voice, "there's been a slight modification." Beth turned sharply at the touch on her shoulder, finding Abraham there with a benign smile that didn't quite meet his eyes. His fingers rested lightly, yet unmistakably possessive.

"Sir?" The soldier's eyes darted between Abraham and Beth.

"She'll be accompanying me." He announced, addressing the soldier beside her before she could respond.

"Perfectly fine where I am, thanks." Beth shot back, attempting to keep her voice even. Abraham's hand tightened ever so slightly.

"Nonsense." He insisted softly, ushering her away from the van and towards a sleeker, more menacing Humvee. Reluctance dragged at her feet, but she complied, her mind reeling with questions she dared not voice. As she slid into the plush seat, she caught Barnett's eye in the rearview mirror. The quick, guilty shift of his gaze confirmed her suspicions - whatever game Abraham was playing, Barnett was equally a part of it. She held back a sigh, settling into the silence that hung between them like a curtain, knowing that beyond it lay a stage set for a drama none of them truly understood. The Humvee growled, a low rumble that seemed to echo the restless turmoil in Beth's chest as they drove away from the only semblance of stability she had known in recent times. Her gaze lingered on the receding town, its structures shrinking into nothingness against the sprawling vastness of the desert. Dust billowed behind them, a sandy shroud veiling her past as Fort Irwin Road stretched out ahead, an asphalt ribbon cutting through the arid wilderness. Beth's eyes followed the interplay of light and shadow on the ground, the morning sun casting elongated silhouettes that danced with the undulating terrain. The world outside was transforming, and with it a chapter of her life was closing, the finality of it settling in her stomach like a stone. The unfortunate beginning of the next chapter, however, played heavily on her mind. She turned her attention inside the vehicle, her eyes resting on Abraham. He was absorbed in a book, his expression one of serene concentration that belied the tension thrumming through the air. The title eluded her, obscured by the angle at which he held the paperback. Curiosity gnawed at her, but she suppressed the urge to lean closer - there was no benefit in giving him the impression that she was interested in anything about him. Time ticked by, marked by the steady crunch of tires over gravel whenever they veered off the main road. After what felt like hours trapped in a silent bubble, punctuated only by the occasional static crackle of the radio or Barnett's terse responses to unseen voices, Beth broke the silence with a question that had been clawing at the back of her mind.

"Is there a reason you wanted me in the car with you?" Her voice was casual, but the undercurrent of suspicion was impossible to mask. Abraham lowered his book, his fingers marking the page as he met her gaze.

"Simply to keep an eye on you. I've been informed you can be quite the troublemaker." He replied, clearing his throat. His tone was matter-of-fact, almost bored.

"Really," Beth's brows arched, feigning surprise, "I wonder who could've given you that impression." She let her eyes drift pointedly towards Barnett, who focused intently on the road ahead, his knuckles white on the steering wheel. She tilted her head back slightly and swallowed hard, attempting to subdue her breathing that had increased along with her heart rate. Barnett's jaw tightened but he said nothing, leaving the accusation hanging in the air like the dust that trailed behind them. The silence stretched, taut as a wire, as Abraham resumed his reading, the soft rustle of turning pages occasionally breaking through the hum of the vehicle. Beth, her gaze fixed on the endless expanse of desert beyond the window, felt each mile unfurl like a ribbon of dread. The landscape was barren, the harsh sunlight throwing sharp shadows that seemed to mock her with their clarity. She shifted in her seat, trying to find some comfort in the leather that stuck to her skin, her mind churning with thoughts she couldn't silence. North Carolina was a whisper away, yet the distance felt insurmountable - a gulf filled with uncertainty and the heavy weight of Abraham's watchful eye. The Humvee's interior was claustrophobic, the air thick with tension that clung to her like the dust coating the vehicle's exterior. She pulled her gaze away from the window, resisting the urge to fidget, to give away the storm of emotions brewing inside her. Beth could feel Abraham's presence like an imposing threat - it was oppressive, filling up the space with something dark and unreadable. She wondered if he sensed her anxiety, if he derived some twisted satisfaction from her discomfort. But she wouldn't grant him the satisfaction of seeing her squirm, she had weathered worse storms than the one brewing within the confines of the vehicle. As the hours drew on, the sun began its slow descent, painting the sky in shades of orange and pink. Beth watched the colours change, taking a strange solace in the beauty of it all, even as it served as a stark reminder of the passage of time - the relentless march towards an unknown fate at Biltmore.

CHAPTER 21

Beth's eyelids fluttered open, a reluctant gesture that admitted the intrusion of daylight. She lay motionless for several moments, savouring the remnants of deep sleep that clung to her consciousness like cobwebs. Her body felt heavy and disconnected, a testament to the exhaustion that had claimed her for nearly two full cycles of day and night. The Hoppner Room, with its high ceilings and ornate furnishings, was shrouded in a soft morning glow that filtered through the heavy drapes. The room whispered of a bygone era, a far cry from the modern accommodation she had grown accustomed to at Fort Irwin. Beth's gaze lingered on the intricate patterns carved into the dark wood of the fireplace mantle before she pushed the plush covers aside and swung her legs over the edge of the bed. With leaden limbs, she rose and dressed herself in silence. Her movements were mechanical, driven by the necessity of blending in rather than any genuine desire to greet the world. As she stepped out of her room, the quiet hush of the third floor enveloped her. The thick carpet muted her footsteps as she made her descent, tracing the path to the main hall that had been etched into her memory upon arrival. The banquet hall loomed before her, grandeur and excess evident in every arch and column. Long tables stretched across the room, laden with an array of breakfast foods that seemed almost vulgar in their abundance. The residents, a mixture of weary travellers and wary survivors, sat shoulder to shoulder, their eyes rarely meeting as they focused on the task of eating. Beth paused at the threshold, her senses assaulted by the cacophony of clinking utensils and muffled conversations. Despite the vastness of the hall, the air was thick with the smell of freshly baked bread, sizzling bacon, and rich coffee - a stark contrast to the rationed meals and shared hardships that had marked their recent past. The voracity with which the people ate spoke volumes of their collective hunger, not just for food but for normalcy and stability. It was a scene of silent desperation masquerading as a feast, each person silently grappling with the reality of their situation while greedily scooping mouthfuls of scrambled eggs or tearing strips off flaky bread rolls. For a moment, Beth stood rooted to the spot, observing the tableau with a detached curiosity that bordered on surreal. Then, with a steadying breath, she stepped forward and allowed herself to be drawn into the fray. Her fingers grazed the back of an empty chair, but she did not sit, instead scanning the room for familiar faces and taking the measure of her surroundings. The absence of guards at the entrances and exits did not escape her notice, nor did the undercurrent of tension that seemed to hum beneath the surface of this civilised setting. Beth tucked these observations away, a puzzle to piece together later as she moved closer into the hall. Jennifer's sudden appearance was like a whirlwind, her grip firm as she latched onto Beth's hand and pulled her towards an already crowded table.

"You need to eat." She urged with a bright enthusiasm that seemed out of place in the sombre atmosphere of the banquet hall.

"Sure, Jennifer." Beth allowed herself to be guided, though her eyes remained vigilant, darting to each doorway, each potential exit. The absence of military oversight was jarring, the open doorways gaping like silent questions. She pondered if she could have been wrong, but the thought was fleeting - her trust in their precarious safety had long been eroded.

"Look at this," Jennifer said, waving her hand over the spread before them, a bounty that belied the desolation that lay just beyond the walls, "I haven't seen food like this in, well, I can't even remember." She was practically beaming as she presented Beth with a plate, piled with scrambled eggs so fluffy they seemed to mock gravity, and toast that promised a comforting crunch.

"Thanks." Beth's fingers grazed the edge of the plate, her gaze never quite leaving the yawning entrances. Her responses were automatic, almost detached, as if she were saying words for the sake of conversation and maintaining a facade of attempting to fit in.

"There's loads of food, and gardens and crops, and fresh bread and milk," Jennifer beamed between mouthfuls as she raised her glass of fresh orange juice to her lips, "I can't remember the last time I had fresh juice."

"How do you know all that?" Beth asked, her voice tinged with suspicion. It was unlike her to be caught unawares, to miss vital information.

"Orientation yesterday," Jennifer replied, her voice dropping to a conspiratorial whisper, "I guess you must've slept through it."

"Orientation." Beth echoed softly, the word tasting like ash on her tongue.

"Yes," Jennifer smiled, "I suppose you'll get your own personal tour at some point." She had been asleep while the world moved on without her, while plans and rules and alliances were being forged. She took a mouthful of the eggs, the rich flavour a stark contrast to the blandness of rationed meals she'd grown accustomed to. This opulence was a double-edged sword - comforting yet alienating - and Beth knew better than to let down her guard, even as the warmth of the breakfast tempted her to do just that. Taking the smallest of bites, Beth allowed herself a moment to relish the flavours that had become distant memories. She chewed slowly, her eyes scanning the banquet hall with an attention that betrayed nothing of her inner turmoil. The room was bustling with life, a stark contrast to the silence of her solitude in recent days. As she took another bite, she searched through the sea of faces for any sign of Ben or Austin, but they were nowhere to be found. Her heart sank with their absence, a silent alarm that whispered warnings she couldn't ignore. She caught Val's eye from across the room, a silent exchange that carried the weight of unspoken fears. Without hesitation, Beth pushed back her chair and stood, leaving behind the plate of barely-touched food as she made her way towards her friend.

"Val," she greeted softly, her voice steady despite the concern knitting her brow, "how are you?" Val's reply was terse, her focus never wavering from her meal.

"Fine." It was a simple word, but it hung heavily between them, laden with meaning that only those who had survived the unspeakable could understand. Beth's gaze flitted to Anne, whose eyes remained fixed on some distant point, and then to Julia, who seemed lost in the gloom of her thoughts, staring despondently at her untouched plate. Something was amiss, but before Beth could voice her concern, the clink of heavy boots and the measured steps of a soldier interrupted the moment.

"Miss Taylor," the soldier addressed her formally, his tone brooking no argument, "you missed orientation yesterday, would you please follow me." Beth turned to face him, her expression carefully neutral.

"If I have to." She replied slowly, the practiced calm in her voice hiding the flicker of resistance that danced in her eyes. Beth offered a nod, an acknowledgment of the command more than a gesture of understanding.

"This way." He motioned for her to turn and leave the banquet hall. Following the soldier, her mind raced with questions, each step taking her further from answers and deeper into uncertainty. She risked a glance backward, seeking some semblance of solidarity from Val, but received only a cool and unsympathetic stare in return. The soldier's presence was a firm reminder that time for comforting friends had passed.

"Where are we going?" Beth's voice broke the uncomfortable silence as she followed him through the halls. The soldier remained as stoic as the statues adorning the hallways, offering no reply. His silence conjured in Beth a chilling memory - she could almost feel the cold grip of a guard at Alcatraz, leading her through labyrinthine corridors, each step uncertain and fraught with dread. A shiver raced down her spine, and she forced the flashback to recede into the recesses of her mind. They traversed the expansive main floor, footsteps echoing off the wooden floors and the soft rustle of the soldier's uniform punctuating the stillness. Eventually they arrived at the imposing doors of the library where Abraham sat ensconced by the hearth, the fire casting dancing shadows upon his features. Without a word, the soldier took his place by the door before receiving a curt nod from Abraham and promptly excusing himself.

"Beth." Abraham intoned, his voice resonant in the hallowed space as he gestured to the chair opposite him.

"Abraham." Beth hesitated, her feet rooted to the spot. Her eyes roamed over the grandeur of the room - the rows upon rows of leather-bound spines, the heavy drapes framing tall windows, and the rich tapestries that whispered tales of a bygone era. It was beautiful, intimidating, and somehow imprisoning.

"Very well." Abraham said, his voice laced with feigned patience. He stood, the leather of the chair sighing under his weight, and crossed the room to place his book on an ornate mahogany desk. The tome made a soft thud as it joined a neatly stacked pile of similar volumes.

"What am I doing here?" Her voice was soft and calm, a triumphant attempt to hide the confusion and fear that swirled within her.

"You missed orientation." He continued, turning back towards her with a measured gaze.

"Apparently I needed two days of sleep more than a guided tour," Beth replied dryly, rubbing at her eyes which still felt gritty from slumber, "but I'm sure I'll catch the next one. Do you have a daily schedule?"

"Nor should there be obscenity, foolish talk or coarse joking, which are out of place, but rather thanksgiving," Abraham cited before gesturing towards the soldier who had escorted her, standing now like a sentry by the library's entrance, "Jacob will show you around."

"Thanks for the offer, but I don't need a babysitter." Beth retorted with sarcasm dripping from each syllable. Her remark was met with a low laugh from Abraham, a sound that seemed to reverberate against the countless spines of the books surrounding them.

"Humour that is vulgar, disrespectful, or mocking is considered inappropriate, Beth. Mockery, especially about serious things, is portrayed as the behavior of a fool. It's not for your protection that he'll be accompanying you." He said, the amusement clear in his tone. Beth let out a small, humourless scoff and took a deliberate step deeper into the library. She glanced over her shoulder at Abraham, catching the flicker of the fireplace reflected in his calculating eyes. Despite the warmth of the room, a chill traced the length of her spine.

"Then whose protection is it for?" She asked, though she suspected she wouldn't like the answer.

"Let's just say, Jacob's presence is as much for us as it is for you." Abraham replied cryptically.

"Right." Beth turned away to hide her unease, pretending to be engrossed in the sheer magnitude of literature that surrounded her. She trailed her fingers along the polished wood of a nearby shelf, the leather-bound volumes standing sentinel-like in their ranks. The musty scent of aged paper teased her nostrils, a reminder of a simpler time when her greatest concern had been finding the perfect reading spot, not navigating a world brimming with veiled threats and watchful guards. Beth's fingers grazed the leather spines arrayed before her, a tactile history of thoughts and dreams pressed into pages. She felt the weight of countless stories, each holding its breath and waiting to be opened. The library was a sanctuary, a place where time seemed to stand still, except for the steady tick of the grandfather clock in the corner.

"Enjoy reading, do you?" Abraham's voice cut through the hush of the room, pulling her from her reverie. She turned slightly, nodding without meeting his gaze.

"I do."

"Good," he said, a hint of satisfaction in his voice, "you may read any book that catches your fancy." Beth's eyes widened a fraction, a flicker of surprise she couldn't quite suppress.

"I *may*?" Her fears had culminated into a single moment, where Abraham's words confirmed that they were merely prisoners in his imposing confinement, one where they were granted permission to exist.

"Provided it is approved by me first." He concluded, his voice devoid of any tone - humourless and lacklustre.

"Ah, and there it is," her surprise morphed into skepticism, responding with a layer of sarcasm thick enough to rival the dust settling on the untouched volumes, "the beginning of your control." She resumed her perusal of titles, but her mind worked furiously behind the facade of casual interest. From the corner of her eye she noticed Abraham observing her. His scrutiny was unapologetic, as if trying to decipher her thoughts.

"You're quite perceptive." He remarked, almost admiringly. Beth faced him fully then, her expression neutral.

"And what gave you that impression?"

"Your persistence, your pushiness," he listed plainly, "traits that can be both annoying, and strangely enough enticing."

"*Enticing*," her eyebrow lifted, the word hanging between them like an unsolved riddle, "well, I'll do my best to be neither annoying nor enticing." She assured him, her voice even though her heart hammered against her ribcage. Abraham turned away to gaze at the flames dancing in the fireplace. The subtle light played across his features, casting shadows that seemed to momentarily conceal his true intentions.

"I doubt that you can help it. For the lips of the adulterous woman drip honey, and her speech is smoother than oil. But in the end she is bitter as gall, sharp as a double-edged sword." Abraham's grunt perforated the silence, a clear signal that shifted the atmosphere from contemplative to commanding. Beth clenched her fists at her sides, digging her nails into the palms of her hands.

"Excuse me?"

"Jacob." He called out, his voice reverberating against the mahogany-laden walls of the library. Beth watched as the obedient soldier appeared almost instantly, materialising from the shadowed corridor like a phantom summoned at will.

"Do they just wait around all day for orders?" She couldn't help but question the dynamic aloud, her gaze flickering briefly to Jacob before settling back onto Abraham.

"Soldiers follow commands," Abraham replied curtly, his tone brooking no argument, "it's what they're trained to do."

"Trained," Beth pursed her lips, "or forced?"

"Give her the same orientation as the others." He gestured towards Jacob with a dismissive flick of his wrist, ignoring her dubiousness. Beth bristled at the thought, feeling like just another pawn in Abraham's meticulously controlled game.

"I'm not going anywhere until I see Ben." She stated firmly, locking eyes with Abraham in a silent challenge.

"You'll see him, in good time," his response was immediate, his smile thin and unamused, "he's a little tied up right now." The phrase lingered ominously in the air, a cold whisper that seemed to wrap around Beth's spine and squeeze. Her face contorted with tension as she clenched her fists and dug her nails into her palms, her knuckles turning white. She could feel the pressure building, her nails digging deeper into her skin. Visions of ropes and chains and dark places flashed in her mind, igniting a spark of fear for Ben's predicament. Her skin felt hot and prickly as she squeezed her hands tighter, trying to relieve the tension building inside her. The pain from her nails digging into her skin made her wince. Without another word, Jacob motioned towards the door, his presence an unspoken command. With a final glance at Abraham, whose eyes held a smug assurance that unnerved her, Beth walked ahead. Her light footsteps were silent on the plush carpet as she exited the warmth of the library into the unknown expanse of Biltmore. Beth's thoughts churned with unease as she followed Jacob's measured steps, the ornate details of the gallery blurring past her. They paused at the threshold of the main hall, where he gestured broadly.

"All meals will be served in the banquet hall." He remarked, his voice flat and devoid of the warmth that food and companionship usually promised.

"Sure." She nodded, a terse movement, barely registering the information as her mind still grappled with the implications of Abraham's words about Ben. As they ascended the grand staircase to the second floor, the plush carpet hushed their footsteps, the opulence of Biltmore a stark contrast to the turmoil within her.

"Every bedroom here is occupied," Jacob explained, leading her down a corridor lined with portraits that watched their passage with silent scrutiny, "and this is the children's area."

They stopped briefly by an open door, revealing the Oak Sitting room. Its walls echoed the distant laughter of children, a sound that seemed alien in the tense atmosphere of the estate. Beth lingered on the threshold absorbing the scene - a temporary shelter for innocence in a world turned uncertain. Yet her heart ached to find her friends, to confirm they were safe. They moved on, reaching a void that opened to the vaulted ceiling of the banquet hall below. She leaned cautiously over the balustrade, scanning the emptying space for familiar faces. The room, however, offered no solace, no sign of them amongst the few stragglers. Beth looked up slightly at Jacob, her eyes searching for a hint of empathy in the man's otherwise stoic facade.

"Where are my friends?"

"Come." Jacob urged, drawing her away from the overlook. As they spiralled up another staircase, the silence felt heavier, more charged. At the top Beth caught sight of a soldier ascending further, towards the fourth floor.

"What's up there?" She asked, her curiosity piqued.

"Off limits." Was all Jacob offered, his expression unreadable. The words hung in the air like a challenge, solidifying the boundaries of her confinement. With a final glance upward, Beth followed Jacob's lead, the echoes of her own footsteps a reminder of the many questions left unanswered. Jacob's steady pace never faltered as they left the echoes of the children's area behind. Beth followed, her eyes scanning every detail, memorising turns and doorways. They traversed down another long corridor, the walls adorned with paintings that seemed to watch them pass, silent witnesses to their procession. As they entered the third floor living hall, a group of women encircled the fireplace. Their heads were bowed in fervent prayer, hands clasped tightly. Among them, Sabrina's profile was distinct, her lips moving in silent supplication.

"Of course." Beth glanced at the scene and felt a snort of derision rise within her. She stifled it into an eye roll, her patience for theatrics threadbare.

"Faith remains for some." Jacob remarked dryly, noting Beth's reaction without glancing her way.

"Seems like wasted breath to me." Beth retorted under her breath, her gaze lingering for a moment longer before moving on. They circled back towards the staircase hall, Jacob's gait measured and unhurried, threading through another maze-like hallway that nearly looped them back to Beth's room.

"Every room on this floor is also occupied." He said, his voice devoid of inflection, stating a simple fact.

"Occupied," Beth mused aloud, thinking of the vastness of the estate, "yet there still aren't enough rooms for everyone."

"Indeed," Jacob conceded with a slight nod, "some families have been relocated elsewhere."

"Elsewhere," Beth echoed, frustration sharpening her tone, "and where exactly is *elsewhere*?" All these vague answers were chipping away at her patience. Jacob remained quiet, the silence hanging between them like a curtain veiling a secret. Beth gritted her teeth at the lack of information but decided not to press further. She had recently learned the art of picking battles, and this wasn't one she would win. They descended the staircase to the bowels of the grand estate. The basement was a contrast to the floors above, practical and unadorned. Here, the air was tinged with the scent of soap and warmth from the laundry room. Rows of linens hung neatly, swaying slightly as they passed by. In the kitchens, the clatter of pots and the sizzle of something cooking filled the space, while the kitchen courtyard lay quiet and empty, save for a few scurrying workers attending to their tasks.

"Through here are the services essential to the estate." Jacob explained, gesturing broadly to encompass the laundry, the bustling kitchen, and beyond.

"Essential, yet hidden beneath the surface." Beth murmured, taking in the sight. It was another piece of the puzzle, another layer of the estate's secrets revealed, yet so much remained out of reach, shrouded in mystery and silence.

"And where would you suggest we move the kitchen and laundry to," Jacob's patience was wearing thin, his tone laced with frustration and sarcasm, "we could call a contractor to have them renovate the place if the layout isn't suited to your standards." Beth's gaze followed the line of soldiers stationed like statues at each staircase leading to the darkness of the sub-basement. A flicker of curiosity crossed her features, but it was swiftly replaced by a smirk tinged with cynicism.

"Let me guess, off limits?" She quipped, unamused, eyes still locked on the guarded stairwell. Without a hint of irony Jacob nodded his confirmation, his face an unreadable mask. Beth's smirk faltered as the reality of her confinement sank in.

"There are gardens and crops on the estate. Some animals too for fresh eggs and milk and meat. Abraham has provided a sustainable and bountiful life for us here," Jacob concluded, motioning up the staircase, "you may return to your room."

"That's it then? That's the grand tour?" Her voice echoed slightly in the cavernous space, a note of incredulity threading through her words.

"Correct." He replied curtly, his nod just as terse as before.

"Can I go outside for some air?" She asked, though the tightening around her chest suggested she already knew the answer.

"Also off limits."

"Fine," she exhaled sharply, betraying her frustration, "back to my room then." She turned on her heel, feeling Jacob fall into step behind her, his presence as stifling as the heavy air that pressed down upon them. Ascending the stairs between the second and third floors, the silence of the estate seemed to resonate with every step until a sudden grasp on her arm shattered it. Beth recoiled instinctively, yanking her limb free with a jerk that sent Jacob lunging forward out of reflex.

"Easy Jacob." Came a familiar voice, its owner raising a hand to halt the guard's advance. Beth's eyes narrowed at Barnett who had appeared seemingly from nowhere. His grasp may have loosened, but the assertiveness in his posture spoke volumes of his newfound authority.

"Look at you, climbing up the ranks." Beth spat, her voice dripping with disdain. She assessed him with a glare that could have curdled milk, noting the smug tilt of his head and the subtle lift of his chin, the telltale signs of power gone to someone's head. Barnett met her gaze unflinchingly, a shadow of something undefinable flickering across his features before he composed himself. The air between them crackled with tension, a silent standoff that left no room for pleasantries. Sensing the shift in dynamics, Jacob took a cautious step back, eyes darting between the two as if anticipating a storm about to break. Barnett extended his hand, an offer dangling in the air between them.

"Beth, please. I need to explain—"

"No," Beth's voice was a cold blade, her sarcasm as biting as the chill that crept into the grand hall, "I respectfully decline your enlightenments." She turned away, but Barnett caught Jacob's attention with a swift gesture.

"Miss Taylor seems a bit uneasy," Barnett said, his eyes never leaving Beth's defiant stance, "some fresh air might do her good. I'll escort her around the grounds." Jacob hesitated, ever the watchful sentinel, his gaze flitting to the open windows where the sun teased the horizon.

"But sir, the grounds are—"

"Off limits. Yes, I'm aware," Barnett cut in smoothly, "but it's just a short walk, and she won't be alone." There was a command in his tone that brooked no argument.

"Yes, sir." After a brief moment of scrutiny Jacob nodded once and retreated back down the stairs, his steps fading to silence. Outside, the morning was crisp, the sprawling lawns dew-kissed and glistening. Beth followed Barnett in reluctant tandem, her footsteps measured and wary. They descended the grand staircase to the road, their shadows stretching long and distorted on the gravel pathway. The south terrace beckoned, its expanse offering no solace from the tension that hung between them like a shroud.

"Look at all this." Barnett began, gesturing expansively towards the Rose Garden, his voice a strained attempt at casual conversation. He barely managed a single syllable before Beth whipped around, her hand striking his cheek with a resounding crack. The slap echoed through the foliage, a sharp punctuation to the silent fury that had been building within her. Barnett recoiled, hand flying to his reddened skin as shock painted his features. Beth stood rigid, chest heaving, her eyes alight with a fire that burned hotter than the morning sun cresting the distant hills. Beth's hand throbbed with a mixture of pain and satisfaction as Barnett, holding his cheek, stared at her in disbelief.

"Fuck you." Her voice was filled with a blend of anger and venom and betrayal that had been building up inside her for over a week, ever since he had stood firm behind Abraham and Aaron at Phillip's house that night.

"Beth—" He barely managed to speak before she delivered another slap, her hand darting through the air like a viper targeting its prey. As she lifted her hand for a third strike he intercepted her motion by grabbing her wrist before it could reach his face.

"How could you? You told him about our meetings, about everything we tried to keep private!" Her voice trembled with suppressed rage as she berated him.

"I'm sorry Beth," Barnett stammered, the red imprint of her hand stark against his skin, "I did tell him about the meetings, but believe me when I say I didn't tell him anything he didn't already know about you." Beth's confusion mingled with her anger, her brows knitting together as she ripped her hand away from his grasp.

"Didn't already know? What do you mean?"

"There's someone on the inside, someone who knows you very well." He sighed, his eyes averting before meeting hers again.

"Ben?" The name escaped her lips before she could stop it, her heart racing at the thought.

"No, not Ben," Barnett shook his head, his gaze earnest, "it's a soldier in Abraham's ranks. Someone much higher up than me." Beth's mind raced as she processed this new information, but she found no foothold for belief.

"That's impossible." She said, her voice laced with denial. Beth's thoughts churned like a violent sea, each wave crashing with the name of a potential traitor. But before she could anchor to any one suspect, Barnett's voice cut through the tumult, laced with remorse.

"I'm sorry Beth," he began, his gaze clouded with regret, "I truly am. There was no clear path out, not for any of us."

"Sorry doesn't change anything," Beth snapped, her voice sharp and unforgiving, "you could've warned us. Given us something to go on against Abraham's plans."

"His plans are like a fortress," Barnett said, shaking his head with a bitter scoff, "layer upon layer. You couldn't just smash through. You had to creep in, play your part. I sat through his sermons, nodded at his madness, pretended to believe. He talked about this estate, stocked with supplies, a place where we'd all be taken care of. I saw the way people looked at him, like a prophet. So I played along, but I had no idea about Ben and Tyler." Beth eyed him warily, her trust as fragmented as a shattered mirror.

"And why should I believe a word you say now? How do I know this isn't another performance?"

"Ask me anything," he urged, stepping closer as his hands opened in a gesture of sincerity, "anything at all." Her lips pressed into a thin line, Beth considered her next words carefully.

"Where is everyone? The estate is not nearly big enough for everyone from Fort Irwin. Where are they being kept?"

"Families, the elderly, they're at The Inn on the opposite side of the grounds," Barnett replied without hesitation, "it's a short drive, maybe ten minutes. On foot though, it'd take you about an hour and a half." His voice held a steadiness that seemed to invite belief. Beth processed the information, a faint glimmer of hope piercing the fog of betrayal. Here was a detail, a tangible place she could picture, and with it a sliver of trust for Barnett. She steeled herself against the emotion, knowing full well that hope was a dangerous thing to hold onto.

"And where are my friends? I've seen Val and Jennifer, but the rest—"

"Come with me," he insisted suddenly, clasping her upper-arm with his hand and dragging her back towards the main structure, "maybe this will regain your trust." Beth's skepticism clung to her like a second skin, the shadows of deceit playing across Barnett's features doing nothing to ease her wariness. Yet, despite her reservations she found herself trailing behind him as they navigated the estate's perimeter. The kitchen courtyard lay ahead, a maze of shadow and stone that promised secrecy or entrapment.

"Where are we going?"

"Keep quiet," he hissed, "and stay out of sight." Barnett whispered, his gaze locking with hers. It was an echo of their past conspiracies, a time when trust hadn't been so scarce. With a nod he turned away to engage the watchful soldier stationed at the stairwell leading downward. Beth crouched beside a stack of crates, her heart hammering against her ribcage. She watched as Barnett's animated gestures drew the soldier's attention, his authoritative tone masking the treachery of their ploy. In the brief moments their backs were turned, Barnett flicked his wrist towards the stairs, a silent signal. Taking a deep breath, Beth darted from her hiding spot, slipping through the archway and into the belly of the estate. The dimly lit corridor stretched before her, its walls lined with cobwebs and secrets. She paused, allowing her eyes to adjust to the darkness that swallowed every corner, every crevice. With each step, Beth willed her presence to become invisible, her footsteps mere whispers on the cold, concrete floor. Left turn taken, she entered a narrow passage, the air thick with dust and disuse. Her gaze flitted from one store room to the next, the doors slightly ajar revealing nothing but the remnants of a world put on hold. The last room awaited, its entrance shrouded in an almost tangible darkness. Beth hesitated, the outline of the doorway taunting her with the unknown. Her pulse quickened, each beat a drum of anticipation and dread. As her eyes penetrated the void, she leaned forward, straining to discern what lay beyond the threshold of shadow. She took an involuntary step back, a chill crawling up her spine - not from the coolness of the subterranean chamber, but from the realisation that some truths are found only in the dark. It was eerily quiet, almost as if she had descended layer upon layer, unable to hear the muffled sounds from the busy banquet hall above - the thick walls had rendered the sub-basement soundproof, hidden from the bustling convention upstairs. Beth's eyes traced the outlines of the storeroom, her senses heightened in the dim light. Shadows clung to the edges, but there in the far end a shape took form - human, bound to a chair. Her heart clenched tightly as she recognised him.

"Ben." Her voice was a whisper, a breath suspended in the musty air of the sub-basement. His head lifted, and his eyes, adjusting to the sudden intrusion of another presence, found hers. Confusion etched his features, giving way to a dawning realisation as he met her gaze. The corners of his mouth turned upward in a weary smile, a beacon of warmth in the cold room.

"Thank God." He murmured, the relief in his voice weaving through the darkness and wrapping around her. A tear betrayed Beth, slipping down her cheek, reflecting the scarce light. She moved towards him, every muscle tensed with the urge to close the distance, to free him from his bonds.

"Did you find anything, Rocky?" The stillness shattered like glass as a voice echoed from down the corridor.

"I knew you'd make your way down here eventually." A voice appeared directly behind her, the familiar timbre of a voice which froze her in place, horror washing over her. She knew that voice, its cadence, its power. It haunted her, an omen of danger she had hoped to never hear again. The words caressed her spine, each syllable a chilling touch. Beth drew in a sharp breath, the sound of her own heartbeat thunderous in her ears. She didn't need to turn to confirm the owner of the voice - it was imprinted in her memory, a spectre from a past she could not escape. Her resolve solidified, the fear mingling with a defiant spark. She wouldn't let this voice command her fate, not now, not when Ben needed her. But as she stood there, caught between a friend in need and the ghostly echo of her adversary, she realised that no matter how carefully she tread, some traps were set just beneath the surface waiting for a single misstep. Beth pivoted on her heel, the sudden motion causing a wave of dizziness as she came face to face with the owner of that familiar voice. He stood ominously close, his presence an oppressive force that made the air around her seem to thicken and still.

"You," a nauseating cocktail of fear and revulsion surged through her veins, her stomach churning as if ready to expel the dread that had taken residence there, "how are you here?"

"Hello Beth." Luis said, his voice deceptively soft - a serpent's hiss wrapped in velvet. Her legs wobbled, betraying her as she stumbled forward, the world tilting precariously. His hand shot out, grasping her arm with a vice-like grip, steadying her only to assert control. The warmth of his touch burned against her skin, igniting a primal urge to recoil, to escape. But it was too late, she was caught in his snare. Dragging her away from the storeroom's gloomy confines, Luis's grip never wavered. In the dim light Beth's eyes locked onto Ben's, his expression a silent scream of protest. His lips moved, mouthing words she couldn't hear over the pounding of her own heart. Her cries were laced with desperation, yet there was no stopping Luis as he hauled her farther from Ben's helpless form. With each step, the storeroom receded into the shadows, retreating into a darkness that seemed to swallow all hope. The last glimpse she had was of his eyes, wide and filled with a fear that mirrored her own, before the door swung shut with an ominous thud, severing their connection.

"Let go of me!" Beth gasped, finding a flicker of defiance amidst the despair. Her voice was frail against Luis's looming figure as he dragged her deeper into the labyrinth of Biltmore's hidden veins, away from prying eyes and into the unknown. The realisation had dawned on her, between her kicking and struggling to break free from his hold, that it was Luis who had been the one to tell Abraham of their group. It was Luis who had told Abraham how to control them. It was Luis who had taken Ben and Tyler in a successful effort to ensure they would follow Abraham to Biltmore. Luis slammed Beth against a stone wall, pinning her arms at either side of her as she struggled against his grasp.

"Just as fiery as I remember." He smirked, his dark eyes filled with menace. Her lips sneered before spitting at him, her saliva hitting just below his eye and trailing down his cheek. He responded with a harsh punch to her jaw as she stumbled to the floor before he pulled her up and dragged her further along the corridor. Her muffled cries were stifled by her exhaustion, every fibre of her being struggled to protest against his pull, leading to the culmination of mental, physical and emotional defeat.

DYSTOPIA SERIES

In a world decimated by plague and fractured by power, a group of survivors clings to hope in the face of unrelenting darkness. What begins as a desperate search for safety becomes a relentless battle against tyranny, fanaticism, and the ghosts of their own pasts.

Led by fierce loyalty and fragile trust, they navigate captivity, betrayal, and shifting alliances in a brutal landscape where freedom is a fleeting illusion and survival demands impossible choices. As one woman is thrust into the heart of rising regimes and twisted ideologies, her strength becomes the spark of resistance - and the key to reshaping what remains of humanity.

In this emotionally charged, post-apocalyptic epic, resilience is forged in the fire of adversity, and the greatest battles are waged within.

DEADWEIGHT
BOOK ONE

In a world silenced by plague and ruled by violence, a chance encounter sparks a fragile alliance among those who refuse to give up. As a small band of survivors journeys south in search of sanctuary, their hope is shattered by a brutal regime that thrives on fear and control.

Trapped within a fortress of despair, they face a chilling test of endurance, loyalty, and the will to resist. When escape feels impossible and choices come at devastating cost, each step becomes a fight not just for survival - but for the soul of what's left of humanity.

In this haunting beginning to a gripping post-apocalyptic saga, courage is forged in captivity, and the seeds of rebellion take root in the unlikeliest of places.

DOMINION
BOOK TWO

After a narrow escape from unthinkable captivity, the search for peace leads Beth and her allies to a fragile stronghold deep in the wastelands. But even in a place that promises safety, danger wears many faces - and some threats come not from outside, but from within.

As a deadly force spreads and power shifts into the hands of a rising zealot, tensions boil over into chaos. Bound by loyalty but torn by doubt, Beth must confront the price of survival in a world where faith can become a weapon, and no sanctuary lasts forever.

In this tense continuation of the series, strength is tested, trust is shattered, and the fight for freedom is more treacherous than ever.

DEFEAT
BOOK THREE

In a world ruled by fear and fanaticism, one woman's captivity becomes the crucible of a quiet rebellion. Trapped behind gilded walls, Beth faces a cunning tyrant whose vision for humanity is as seductive as it is brutal. To survive, she must become both a weapon and a whisper of resistance.

As secrets fester beneath a crumbling empire and the line between faith and control blurs, Beth risks everything to reclaim her voice - and her future. But freedom, like truth, comes at a cost.

This harrowing chapter in their journey explores the price of defiance in a world where breaking free is only the beginning.

STILL TO COME

More information can be found at
www.ceshorland.com

www.ingramcontent.com/pod-product-compliance
Lightning Source LLC
Chambersburg PA
CBHW031736180726
48283CB00005B/1533